# THE CONSEQUENCE OF SKATING

**BOOKS by STEVEN GILLIS**

Walter Falls

The Weight of Nothing

Giraffes

Temporary People

# The CONSEQUENCE of SKATING

A novel by **Steven Gillis**

Black Lawrence Press
New York

Black Lawrence Press
www.blacklawrence.com

Executive Editor: Diane Goettel
Book Design: Steven Seighman

Copyright © 2010 Steven Gillis

Excerpts from *Moonlight* copyright © 1993 by Harold Pinter. Used by permission of Grove/Atlantic, Inc.

All rights reserved. Except for brief quotations in critical articles or reviews, no part of this book may be reproduced in any manner without prior written permission from the publisher:

Black Lawrence Press
115 Center Avenue
Pittsburgh, PA 15215
U.S.A.

Published 2010 by Black Lawrence Press, an imprint of Dzanc Books

First edition September, 2010
ISBN-13: 978-0-9826228-7-2
Printed in the United States

The Consequence of Skating *is a work of fiction. Real places and events have been changed and fictionalized. All characters are products of the author's imagination and any resemblance to actual persons, living or dead, is entirely coincidental.*

*For Mary*

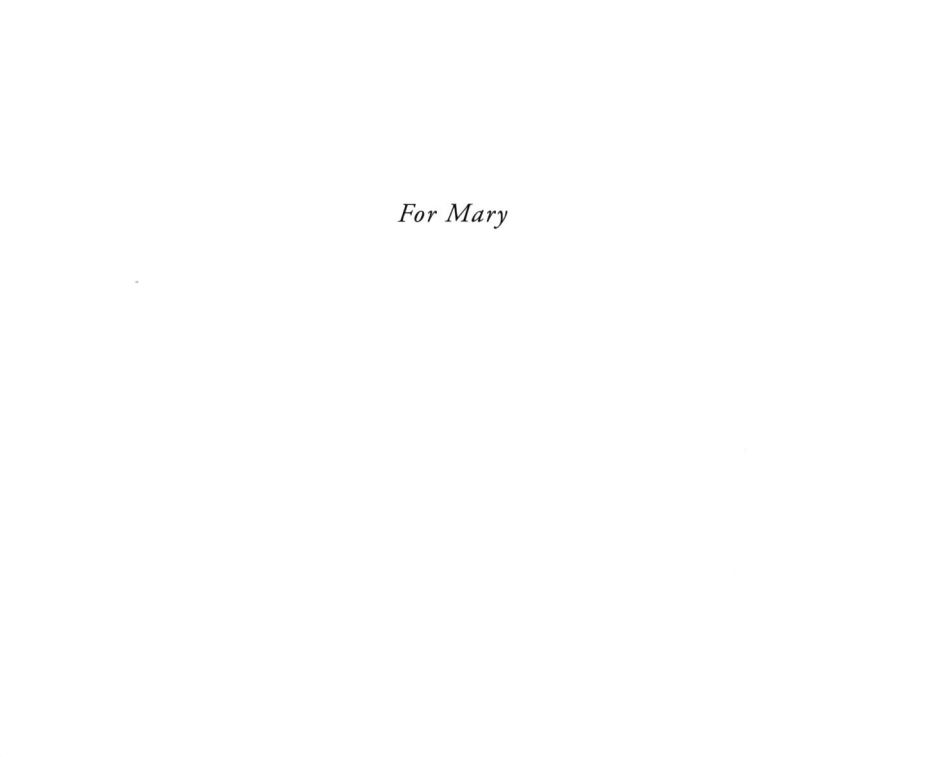

"Though I have no productive worth, I have a certain value as an indestructible quantity."
—**Alice Adams**

"If I love you, what business is it of yours?"
—**Goethe**

"Call it self-defense/You can obfuscate/And manipulate/But it's only at your own expense."
—**Barenaked Ladies**

# THE CONSEQUENCE OF SKATING

# 1

HERE IS WHAT I know: The world is round, not flat, though at every turn there are crack sharp edges. I know Ethan Hawke but not Jeff Bridges, know history has its Hannibals, its Hank Aarons, Henry Millers, Hitlers and Horatio Algers, and that human nature is constant, will keep producing each. I know my current affairs, both public and private, know Norah Jones can sing and Gwen Stefani wishes, know Gabriel Orozco is a whale of an artist, that Sonny Liston took a dive and Elin Nordegren took one on the chin. I know Brando was for a short while our greatest actor, and Ludovic, not John or Ted or Bobby, our greatest Kennedy. I know water boils at 212 degrees Fahrenheit, and at 211 degrees you have nothing but steam. I know beans are a nut and tomatoes a fruit, but have no idea about the cumquat or rutabaga. I know Peter O'Toole has received eight Oscar nominations without a win, that George W. stole the 2000 election, that in Russia it's considered impolite to leave an open vodka bottle unfinished, and that in China there are 1.4 billion people who have never seen a single Mickey Greene performance.

 I know the heart pumps almost 2,000 gallons of blood every 24 hours, that smell triggers memory more than any other sense, that praxeology is the science of human action, and that my own recent acts are vulgar and vaudevillian. I know the speed of light is 983,571,057 feet per second, and that a flashlight shined into space will still take 100,000 years to cross the Milky Way. I know eggs are designed so they can't be crushed from the sides but can be easily cracked in the center. I know Jim Mora coaches football and that Don Sebastian de Morra was a midget. I know sex at times is life-affirming, from foreplay to climax to the deep sweet slumber, and still there are days when nothing feels better than a good shit. I know Harold Pinter was the best playwright of the twentieth century, that he and Beckett were good friends, that the final play Pinter performed in was Beckett's 'Krapp's Last Tape,' and that 'The Homecoming' had no less than 224 Pinter pauses.

 I know heroin works through our opioid receptors, that rehab is an execrable purging, and when I sleep at night my dreams try to heal me. I know how to skate and dance, though I can't ride a horse or draw a decent picture. I know about the Urumqi riots in Xinjiang, know Navanethem Pillay is the United Nations' High Commissioner for Human Rights, that Brangelina is legit and Jessica Biel isn't, that Mike D'Antoni and Kiki Vandeweghe coach the Knicks and Nets respectively. I know some Spanish but not Chinese, know my mother loved my father though she admitted this only after he was dead.

I know I loved Darcie, and that she loved me, and that here is proof again the world is round, how things turn and catch the slope, gather speed, so that despite all efforts to hold on, things churn and roll away.

———

    Tonight I'm watching the Corkscrew snake in cold metal turns. The orange rails wind, the train of cars tarped and chained together, the carousel wheel making pin-spoke shadows through the center of the park. My job, as part of my probation, is to guard the grounds. It's one in the morning, in the dead of winter, the temperature cold enough to reach beneath the layers of shirt, jacket and sweater I'm wearing and freeze my skin.

    Ten months ago, I did Pinter on hard candy, was Stanley in 'The Birthday Party,' high on Aunt Hazel, doped and nodding on stage at the Galaxy Theater. My timing off, unable to manage the gaps and pauses, I uttered the scripted, "Uh-gug... uh-gug... eee-gag..." before losing the thread, my body shaking from too much kabayo, I fell from my chair, Goldberg and McCann staring and waiting, Meg and Petey wondering what to do.

    I was 32 then, am 33 now, a one-time working actor with a solid resume and decent reputation. That night the cops came and carried me off the stage, the paramedics in latex gloves assessing the damage. Following my arrest I spent a month in rehab. My brother Jay arranged everything, hired an attorney who petitioned the court for probation. At Marimin, I was given methadone and naltrexone, left to shiver and puke in my room. Toward the middle of my third week, I began feeling better, re-read Pinter's 'Moonlight,' and parts of Mises' five-volume treatise on human action.

    Mises is Ludwig Von (1881-1973) the one-time

leader of the Austrian School of Economics, and father to the modern application of praxeology. Mises contends that every conscious act has its root in self-satisfaction, that people act in order to improve their situation, and must have a specific dissatisfaction—or *uneasiness*—to resolve otherwise they can't act. Assuming this is true, I should be perpetually kinetic, as I have enough dissatisfaction to keep the hamster wheel going forever. Darcie left me while I was in rehab, moved all her shit out of our apartment. My agent dropped me. No one will hire me now. I'm tested three times a week for every sort of drug, stimulant and depressant, pharmaceutical and organic, weed, heroin and blow. I have to pee into a cup, am ordered to see a therapist, expected to talk about my *condition*, discuss my dreams, ambitions and disappointments. I'm asked about mom and dad, Jay and Ted, my career before and after. I'm questioned about Darcie and my addiction, which I see as one and the same and blur as I talk about either.

My counselors at Marimin were sympathetic, encouraged me to maintain a sense of forward thinking, presented me with short poems and passages from 'I Ching.' *I intend* is the mantra they had me repeat. *I intend* to perform again, *I intend* to produce a version of Pinter's 'Moonlight,' *intend* to remain sober—my few sips of whiskey here at Birch Bow Adventure being medicinal and no big deal. *I intend* to make amends to Darcie, *intend* to convince her to love me again, *intend* to show her that I understand all about love and don't excuse what I did because of our problems. This is a lie, of course. I blame love for everything and don't understand a single thing about it.

―――

The ceiling of my booth is tin. The metal traps the cold, floor open to the dirt beneath. My shift runs from 9:00 p.m. until 5:00 a.m. five nights a week. As an actor, there was talk of turning my time at the Bow into a documentary, or a reality show with scenes sketched out and other actors brought in. A contract was drawn up, but the court would not sign off, refused to let my punishment morph into a spectacle. I get it. That's cool. There's a definite protocol which needs to be followed, a lesson I'm supposed to learn. I appreciate this, want to prove that I'm repentant and accepting of all forms of retribution.

Working the night shift keeps me from performing in plays or movies, even if someone did want to give me a part. Isolated, the owners of the Bow expect me to walk the grounds once an hour, but there's no point really. After October the park's abandoned, all the rides chained and the wind chill down around three below zero. Only the ice rink and the aquarium remain open for a few hours during the afternoon. I bring my skates, visit the fish, walk the grounds between these two points mostly, though once a night I do a full loop and stare out at the lights from the city beyond the fences. Aldwich is a city of actors. Shakespearian and avant-garde, dramatic and comedic, creative, imitative and method, trained by Adler, Stanislavski, Strasberg and Katselas, disciples of Meisner, Ouspenskaya and Berghof, Michael Chekhov and Uta Hagen, at work in movies, plays and tv, adherents to the metaphysical method, the identity and substitution schema, sense memory and muscle memory. A stick can't be shaken in Aldwich without hitting at least three performers.

Forty years ago we were a different town, dependant on industry, relying on our metal works factories for commerce, plants owned by Ford, by Kenmore and Whirlpool and others producing steel for cars, refrigerators, washers and dryers, furnace ducts and vents. When the recession hit and markets across the board imploded, Aldwich's economy went with it.

Within two years, every third job was lost, plants were closed and labor moved overseas. Looking to silk purse a sow's ear, a group of investors decided to buy the old Raviery steel mill from Ford. The property was rezoned and converted into a co-op, with a theater on the ground floor and artists' studios above.

A crazy plan, a risk for sure, expanding the arts at a time when people had no money. Somehow though, the Raviery Theater did brisk business. Tickets were priced to sell and people out of work came looking for diversion. Soon another theater opened, and a bar with live music, a cinema-plex specializing in independent and art house films. Businessmen took notice, politicians and investors. The state stepped in, offered tax breaks for movies and plays produced in Aldwich. Filmmakers scouted locations. Writers and actors came hoping to land new projects. More theaters opened, writers and producers making their own plays and films, until steadily all the old industry gave way, the shops and services reinvented, the factories gutted and replaced.

Today Aldwich thrives. Television shows, studio and indie films, plays and musicals are in constant production, our Aldwich Arts Festival a huge success each summer. Sundance and Tribeca, Toronto, London, Edinburgh, Boston and New York now keep an eye on us. Our music, film and theater departments at the University rank in the top ten nationally. We're a community devoted to the particulars of making money through a good show, our approach one of self-preservation and artistic integrity, both practical and prescient. Recently however, investors have begun backing less high-end theater and artistic films, complaining of the narrow draw, anxious to offset the latest economic downturn. More commercial shows are brought in, tourist-friendly plays and other accessible programs meant to appease a larger audience; 'Mary Poppins' and 'Rock of Ages.' While Aldwich still takes pride in her artistic aesthetic, a third of our stages are now filled with mercantile productions of 'Dr. Seuss,' 'The Blue Man Group,' and 'The Lion King.'

A sign of the times. Twice before I crashed and burned at the Galaxy my agent called with offers for me to play a dancing troll in 'The Hobbit: The Musical' and Gaston in 'Beauty and the Beast.' I refused, my sights higher. I was more arrogant then. And now? I realize how much things have changed, how need creates a different perspective, an altered sense of the choices that are really out there. Short on cash, if I was somehow offered a part in this winter's 'Shrek on Ice' it would serve me right, I think, to climb inside the costume and play the donkey's ass.

―――――

Outside, I zip my jacket, pull my grey cap over my ears, tug on my gloves and kick through the snow. The air's frigid, cuts under my collar, stings my nose and threatens my chin. As I walk, I think about my friends, all finished with their rehearsals and performances for the night, while I'm here walking the grounds with carnival ghosts. "Whose fault, Mick?" I say this to be clear and not feel sorry for myself. There's a reason for what I did, though I can't in any rational way explain it. I think: Here's the thing—the thing, yes, that is what it is—there are reasons for all that happens, but all that happens isn't reasonable. Despite what Mises wrote, human action defies logic. Our moral compass is more primitive, as Stephen Toulmin explained. Shit comes and goes because we make it so, but we rarely make it so because we know what we're doing. Mistakes occur as we cause them, mishaps and misfortunes, our errors and successes individually ordained. We act, yes, but half the time we're clueless. That I did duji up on stage as Darcie prepared to leave me was all part of a perfect storm, the product of a long list of earlier conditions I failed to manage.

For guarding the Bow, I'm paid three bucks an hour, a prison wage, toothpaste and candy-bar money. I've already blown through my earlier savings, am pretty much broke and rely on occasional loans from Ted and the work I do for Jay to sustain me. Jay owns properties in and around Aldwich, buys and sells houses and buildings for profit. I do odd jobs each afternoon, painting and drywall, putting in new toilets, windows and floors. I'm good with my hands, a skill I seem to have accidently acquired. The work suits me. Jay is generous, keeps me on his payroll even though the latest downturn in the housing market has cut a huge hole in the center of his business. He tells me not to worry, insists I'm still a bargain. "Cheap labor. Don't sweat my problems." He slips me cash under the table.

---

I walk counter-clockwise, which seems right, past the Corkscrew, the Gyro Jump and the Tilt-A-Whirl. The path from my booth through the grounds is narrow, carved by my boots, the snow crushed to ice. Being at the Bow is purgatorial, a terrestrial isolation, like walking across Reykjavik, as foreign as the moon. I think of love and loss, remember how mom grieved when dad died, though she used to break his heart routinely. I picture Darcie on stage, the way she channels Gabrielle Drake, Mary Anderson and Stephanie Beacham, is small framed, a sinuous shape, handsome like Geraldine Chaplin in 'Dr. Zhivago,' her look also slightly off center, like Amanda Plummer. There's a ferocity in her eyes, both sexy and vulgar. She commands the stage and screen in ways unexpected, the audience following her without knowing why.

The tarp on Shivering Timbers has come loose, the

train of orange cars for the roller coaster supposed to be covered with a plastic blanket, the draw ropes are frozen in place, the cold causing one strap to snap. I go over and jerry rig the tie back down. The effort is simple enough yet makes me feel as if I've accomplished something ingenious. I think of Darcie again, how I miss her too much, how I don't want to miss her at all. I wonder what she's doing now, if her rehearsals are going well and whether she misses me while performing. Love is a battlefield, to quote Pat Benatar. The first time I fell, I was seventeen and dating a girl named Geena. A Connecticut transplant, Geena had ropey threads of strawberry hair, her features feline, her nose flat and nearly pink, her eyes large and olive, her upper lip with a trace of downy whiskers. I was head over heels and wanted to sleep with her, though I wasn't completely sure about the protocol. There seemed some need on my part to love Geena completely before we had sex. I don't know why, I was young and uninitiated, had no clue what I was doing.

Eventually we got down to it, would slip off in the late afternoons and evenings and improvise scenes. Lying or kneeling, I'd concentrate on the moist muff and fleshy puff spaces, the nipples and nether deep hollows. Geena came like a jellyfish. Still, when I went to sweep back her hair and nibble the lobes of her ears, she'd stop me, gently at first and then more insistently. Not all things, Geena said, were made for public consumption. Her ears, she said, were not for display. This part she chose to save. I told her I understood, though really I didn't. Curious to see what I was missing, I began looking for ways, would roll down the windows while driving, hoping the breeze would catch her hair. I bought her earrings, a brush, an iPod with headphones I couldn't afford. None of this worked. Geena started wearing hats. She brought a swim cap to bed, swam against the current. I'd be in her mouth, pressed full atop her tongue, and all I'd want to do was touch the sides of her head. When I did, she'd slap my hands, sit up, her lips moist and fresh with me, demand to know why I wasn't satisfied with what she was willing to offer.

My answer was shameless. I said it was never a question of being dissatisfied with what she gave me, but that with our love we should be able to share everything. Geena didn't bite. She pushed me down, showed me her foot, gave me the soft inseam of her thigh, told me to be happy. "Love is this," she said. "It's more than what you want, it's what I agree to give you."

Maybe so, but shouldn't lovers agree to give what is asked for? I spent hours on my own, fantasizing about the shape of her ears, the flap and lobe and auricle. I read books, learned about the semicircular canals and auditory nerve, the cochlea and vestibule and Eustachian tube, how the ear worked on a series of vibrations, the brain interpreting the movement of the anvil and stirrup bones. I stared at other girls' ears for the first time, at the cup of flesh on the sides of their heads, and found myself aroused. Days passed when I was convinced there must be something terribly wrong with Geena's ears, that they were malformed or damaged somehow. I became uncomfortable, and then sympathetic, wanted her to know whatever the reason, I was there for her and could be trusted. Thinking myself clever, in this way I hoped to wear her down.

When she did, at last, give in, we were sitting on my bed. I remember the moon through the window, and the surrounding shadows cast. Geena was quiet as she used two fingers to move her hair back, her head tipped away from me and then brought closer. My heart was racing. I stared for several seconds at her right ear and then her left. Both were perfectly normal, each altogether ordinary ears, handsome in size and design, unadorned and unspectacular. Their convention came as a relief. These were ears I was sure I'd enjoy kissing and whispering into. Geena's gesture moved me, her willingness to show me. We embraced tenderly before undressing to consummate the intimacy of the moment.

Still, love's a funny thing. Even when we make ourselves completely naked, there's a want and need for more. The mystery over, the titillation terminated, Geena and I broke up the following week.

———

Back in my booth, I stomp the chill from my boots, beat my gloved hands together. Cold air passes through the wood walls. I have a portable heater, a series of metal coils set in a silver box. I run an extension cord from my heater to the nearest outside socket and turn the switch to high. My thermos is a red Donald Duck I've had for years. I remove the cup, sip small amounts of whiskey, find my cell phone at the bottom of my backpack. Another gift from Jay, the phone is a company cell with all the bells and whistles. I touch the screen and access the internet. Headlines appear. I get an update on the news, click on the links and squint at the screen to read from what's offered.

While much of my focus is damaged of late, my interest in news remains constant, dates back to dad. A classically trained guitarist, Charlie Greene advocated kettle stirring from the stage, confident about using his platform to incite social reform. Much as his contemporaries—CSN&Y, Joni Mitchell, Jackson Browne, Richie Havens, Country Joe, Joan Baez, Bob Dylan and Hendrix—tied their music to political dissent, dad taught me the importance of being educated, said knowledge was the key to challenging authority, encouraged me to maintain a political voice, to read with a critical eye, trust no single source, and accept only his love as gospel. From dad I acquired a sense of history, the effect of movements, the consequence of protest and resistance, SDS, the Weathermen and Black Panthers, the

Bay of Pigs and Vietnam, Kennedy and Khrushchev, El Salvador and Chile, Russia and China, Reagan and Nixon, Martin Luther King and Malcolm X. In college, and after, I studied Bosnia, Lincoln and Cambodia, Lemkin and Rwanda, Carter, Kissinger and Johnson, civil rights and civil unrest, Israel and Palestine, Iraq and Iran, Huey Long and Huey Newton, Eugene McCarthy and Herbert Humphrey, Joseph McCarthy and the Tydings committee. If my own political involvement has lapsed, I remain still interested in the storyboard of each event, the characters involved and what makes their ducks waddle.

Ted feels the same, which is in part the reason why we remain friends after all these years, sharing a fascination with the personal side of the news, how at the heart of every conflict is just people dancing. Tucked in the back of Ms Keldaker's sixth grade homeroom, the view through the window a playground of grey stones and leafy fields, Ted and I met in 1988, two kids in black t-shirts and blue canvas Converse, Greene and Grevnik placed side by side in alphabetical seating. Our friendship evolved from there, remains after all this time a reliable thing, what we share substrata, our differences superficial. Where I have an actor's good looks, a kind of Viggo Mortensen meets Ed Burns mug, a raw sort of athletic build, tennis-player tall and leanly muscled, Ted is shorter, a thin pepper stalk, his metabolism that of a hummingbird, his basal metabolic rate generating energy at an accelerated pace, exposing him to episodes of heightened activity, acuity and creativity. Pale complexioned, with large round eyes and fine features, he is a brilliant assembly of hair and chin, knees and elbows.

As a journalist, Ted's essays have appeared in Slate, Mother Jones, the New Republic and dozens of other journals outside the political blog he runs online, The Harry Tick. His writing is delivered as wry commentary, the content served hot, a tea made of green leaves and battery acid. Much of my education now comes from Ted. I click over to the Tick, read what he's posted. Each day he reports the news as absurdist theater, the headlines as Ionesco might write them, with sanity and reality two old neighbors doing slapstick. Just last week Ted wrote about South Africa barring the Dali Lama from attending a peace conference, the authorities insisting the Dali Lama's presence would draw too much attention to ongoing conflicts, and to quote Thabo Masebe, "not be in South Africa's best interest." Ted mined the irony of Masebe's statement, wrote an essay titled, "A Part of the Tide," where he addressed the particulars with savage humor.

Tonight on the Tick, Ted's posted a piece on Biljana Plavsic, the former president of Bosnia, imprisoned in Sweden after being convicted on charges of crimes against humanity. During Plavsic's reign, more than 40,000 Muslims and Croats were slaughtered. Now, after just a few years in prison, Plavsic is about to be released early, an independent tribunal finding her to have "demonstrated substantial evidence of rehabilitation." Ted writes: "What does that mean exactly? *Substantial evidence of rehabilitation*? This is a woman who murdered 40,000 people! Did she dash off 40,000 letters of apology to 40,000 families? Or write 40,000 times on the blackboard, 'I will no longer advocate acts of genocide.' How is the Iron Lady of Bosnia even eligible for parole?" Ted wants to know, "Who makes these decisions? How is Plavsic any different from Hitler? From Idi Amin or Pol Pot? Are we that far removed from Nuremburg? What next? Will our apathy continue redefining celebrity until Plavsic lands a $5 million book deal, goes on tour and appears on Oprah?"

Ted is this, all energized, liberal in his politics, anti-war, anti-imperialism, anti-theocracy and fundamentalism. He believes in democracy, in humanity and secular reason. Assertive toward his commitments, his inclinations are romantic, his faith filled with an intelligent muscle. When we debate, I argue against logic, insist man is as he is, untamed at best and a bit crazed mostly, while Ted quotes Mises, knows the treatise better than me, was the one who turned me on to 'Human Action.' "Logic is everything," Ted says. "Logic distinguishes man from animals, as man relies on rational thought and doesn't react to stimuli solely by instinct."

Maybe. Sometimes. I don't know. Instinct's a funny thing, everyone responds differently. Most of the time, it seems to me, what people call logic is just a voice in their head screaming, "Do it!" Where I'm impulsive and chase after kite strings, Ted's motives are more refined, if no less indulgent. Once, in seventh grade, we made a mini-rocket launcher powered by potato gasses, and used the head of a Barbie doll as our projectile. My aim was off, and I accidently blew out the windshield of Karrie Marshal's Toyota Camry. Ted ran across the street before I could stop him, and confessed to Karrie that his invention had misfired. By the time I caught up and admitted my role, Ted had already convinced Karrie that my involvement was minor.

Little has changed. Still today, Ted's decisions are quick-wired. A classic overachiever, genetically predisposed, Ted is self taught on bass, plays stand-up and electric for the pop/jazz band the Harsh Puppies. With graduate degrees in both Political Theory and Computer Science, his skill set is unique and freaky. Back when we were in college and sharing an apartment on Chester Street, Ted wrote the software program for our V.F.C.—the Virtual Fornication Creation— on a whim, taking my idea and running with it, scribbling his first notes on the front of a Captain Crunch cereal box. Crazy for sure, the genesis was inadvertent, a comment I made after being dumped by a girl. Unlike with Darcie, losing Gayle was no big deal. I was not head over heels, was just 21, and when Gayle asked if I loved her, I could only shrug. She took offense to my indifference, did not appreciate my ambivalence, refused to find it funny when I told her I had mixed feelings about what she was saying. Storming off, she hooked up with another guy, forgot all about me within a month. Only then did I begin to miss her.

I told Ted that I'd started imagining Gayle having sex with this new guy, that I found the idea oddly erotic, and as a joke said how cool it would be to have a machine I could use to watch Gayle screwing someone else. Ted considered the possibility, said actually it wouldn't be that hard, that all he needed was a digital photo of *the Target*—he called Gayle *"the Target"*—and he could make a software replica, write a code that would allow Gayle's features to replace the face of some other girl participating in an existing porno flick. The process, Ted said, would be more than a cheap cut-and-paste, would totally supplant the original image, creating a third, virtually real film.

I assumed Ted was just riffing, but went ahead and pulled up a digital shot of Gayle and gave it to him. Four days later, Ted downloaded a clip for me to watch, said "It's just a prototype. I can make it better, for starters though," he pointed at the screen. There was Gayle, her head mounted to the shoulders of a naked girl, straddling one guy, bouncing like a hand puppet while a second guy made well timed advances toward her mouth. From what I could see, there was no way to tell the film was fake, no seam that showed the head interchanged, no dead giveaway even though I was intimately familiar with Gayle's body.

Amazed, I mentioned as much to friends, told them to come by and see what Ted had done. One by one they watched Gayle, then spoke with Ted, excited by the chance to have their own lovers perform as virtual whores, the strange arousal of seeing one's significant other commit artificial infidelity. They brought photos, wanted Ted to post headshots and make their girls dance. Ted was accommodating at first, and still the process took time. He was only then perfecting the program, working with the coding and such, was busy with school, with his music and the earliest incarnation of what would become The Harry Tick. He did a few more clips as favors, told everyone else sorry, but he was closing shop.

Too late. Word was out, requests came from all over. Complete strangers, having heard rumors, called to ask if it was true. The doorbell rang early and late, envelopes slipped into the mailbox and under the door. Ted explained to everyone the service was no longer available, and still the demands poured in, money now offered, were hard to ignore. Men came with photos of their wives, others brought shots of themselves, wanting their heads imposed into the action in order to watch their own virtual revelry. Women, too, requested the same, for these were modern times. Ted was asked about a database, a place where famous actors and actresses might have their faces stored and people could pay to watch Julia Roberts suck cock or Reese Witherspoon take it up the ass. The possibilities grew exponentially, limited only by our imagination and what Ted agreed to do.

The problem was not in the program, but in the association, as Ted worried his working with the V.F.C. would taint his credibility and limit his chance to become a serious journalist. As I had never intended any of this, we decided to sell the puppy off. The father of a friend gave us the name of an attorney—Evanston P. Church—who advised us to form an LLC and apply for a patent on the V.F.C. in our company name. A list was made of all the legal concerns our V.F.C. presented: matters of appropriation, copyright infringements, the need to purchase permission to use particular films, the risk of retaliatory charges from non-consenting *targets*. Church helped us understand the dos and don'ts of the V.F.C., the selling points and stipulations. We put out feelers, received offers from companies in the adult entertainment industry looking to make full use of the V.F.C.'s potential. Paramour,

Inc. presented the best deal. Ted insisted I take 50 percent of the cash for coming up with the original idea. I declined, said ideas were cheap, agreed to 15 percent and quickly ran through that.

In the years since, despite Ted's effort to disassociate himself from the V.F.C., computer geeks, filmmakers, professional programmers, producers and engineers all tracked him down. Ted ignored them at first, denied he was that guy, but when those who called swore their interest was in the fundament of his creation and that they didn't associate the V.F.C. with porn, he agreed to talk. A new network of friends sprang up, a group Ted speaks with often now about his newest ideas. His latest program, years in the making, is visionary—there is no other word—as it ties together Ted's political ideologies and computer skills, is a program intent on resolving factional statesmanship, patented under the name *Government Objectivity Design;* the great justiciar, the preset known as G.O.D.

———

Inside my booth, I have room to take two steps in any direction before I have to turn and start over again. Mostly I sit, or stand hunched beneath the low lean of the ceiling, and stare out the window. At some point during the evening, I take out my copy of Pinter's 'Moonlight' and read. I have compiled a binder full of notes as to how I see myself directing and producing the play, and every night I review these as well.

I put a Pop Tart on top of my heater, wait for the frosting to melt and the fruit to leak. Sitting now, I reach for my backpack, take out my notes and dog-eared copy of 'Moonlight,' read the scene where Fred says to his brother Jake: "You were writing poems when you were a mere child?" and Jake replies: "I was writing poems before I could read."

I think of this, what Pinter's saying about who we are and where things come from. I read another scene, the one where Fred says to Jake: "I've decided to eschew the path of purity and abstention and take up a proper theology." I smile here, always, the implication as it relates to my own addiction and current reform. Fred's right about abstention, it isn't the sobriety that's pure, it's the ability to maintain control. My problem was never in imbibing, but my inability to manage the dope. Freud did all right with his habit, Coleridge and Cocteau, Dickens and Marcus Aurelius, Picasso and Poe had their opium, Havelock Ellis peyote, Sarah Bernhardt, Tallulah Bankhead and Cole Porter cocaine, Disney and Ken Kesey, Cary Grant and George Washington, Thomas Jefferson and Lewis Carroll, all had their favorite dip and toke. Even Mohammed smoked hashish, and where did I go wrong then? Why couldn't I manage things better? Hell. I reach for my thermos, take another sip.

My plans for 'Moonlight' are reverential, are also, I admit, an attempt for resurrection, given how far I've fallen. Having failed at love, having failed for the most part with my career, having hit a mid-level rung of comfort without risk, I've turned to Pinter for revivification. In my mind, Pinter is the Kingfish, along with Beckett, and the best playwright of the last 70 years. (I could list others, but why bother?) I've read each of Pinter's plays, his novel and short stories, his interviews and biographies, essays and poems, his Nobel Prize lecture, 'Art, Truth and Politics,' which lays out everything he has to say on writing and war. A conscientious objector, beginning in 1947, Pinter spent the next sixty years, until his death in 2008, speaking out against imperialism, condemning America's involvement in Nicaragua and El Salvador, Vietnam and Chile, Cuba and Afghanistan, Panama, Grenada, Indonesia and Kosovo, Yugoslavia, the Persian Gulf, Iraq and Iran. Many of Pinter's best known plays are politically charged and deal with issues of power and abuse. Since college, I've taken seminars and taught classes, done workshops and appeared in four Pinter productions. I've dug through archives to find old BBC footage of Pinter as Stott in 'The Basement,' and Leo McKern and Vivien Merchant—Pinter's first wife—in 'Tea Party.'

'Moonlight' has been called a comedy of menace, inspired by Pinter's estrangement from his son, Daniel though Pinter denied any conscious intent. The play is elliptical, takes a sibyl's torch to love and loss, isolation and abandonment, memory and denial, the precariousness of reality and how memory blurs, confusing what is, was and can't be anymore. The writing's funny as hell and often leaves me weeping. I want to do the play because it deserves a new showing, because it is one of Pinter's last, and least understood, works, is brilliant and difficult, completely worth the journey, and quite possibly may save my life.

―――

Around 2:00 a.m., I walk the grounds again. This time I head north, toward the rink, which is halfway between my booth and the aquarium. I have the keys and bring my skates to the park, my gloved fingers squeezing the blades, hold firmly to the edge.

Once inside, I turn on the lights, sit and pull on my skates. The ice is rutted from the over-forty men's hockey league, guys who come twice a week and play their no-contact games, grind their blades as if to see how much of the rink they can turn into frosty shavings. I get the shovel and some water from the hose, smooth out what I can of the surface before I skate. The exercise allows me to stimulate my endorphins, provides the body with a natural high. When I'm warm enough, I peel off my coat and continue around the rink until my legs and lungs feel the exertion.

I estimate the distance I cover, compete against myself from one night to the next. When I was seven, dad brought Jay and me out to Parrot Lake for the first time. Novices, we learned to move around the ice on single blades, established a measure of balance, sampled the consequence of getting too full of ourselves and rushing along before we were ready. Tricks took time, and mostly failed, while even during a normal glide, if I wasn't focused, I fell suddenly on my elbows and knees. These tumbles provided their own lesson, taught me to concentrate on the moment and not lose sight of what I was trying to achieve.

Dad wore thick gloves, with wraps around his wrists to protect himself from a fall. A student of Parkening, disciple of Segovia and Pepe Romero, Clapton and Joe Satriani, Jonny Greenwood, Eddie Van Halen and Brian May, dad risked the ice for Jay and me, skated to us each time we went down. Mom stayed off the ice, was not a fan of the sport, was a dancer years ago, modern stuff, Erick Hawkins, Paul Taylor, Martha Graham. A professional performer, she remains lithe, a handsome woman, dark like Salma Hayek in 'Frida.' Filled with attitude and bluster, a hoarder of secrets, mom preached candor then clawed cat-like when caught in a lie. Dad was more forthcoming, reflective in his approach, a surveyor and assessor, passionate about politics and music. Less inured than mom to the minutia of each moment, his heart collected the detritus, accumulated too much residue, created a dangerous condition that grounded him in time.

At the recital where mom and dad first met, dad played Bach on his guitar, 'Five Refractions of a Prelude,' based on Bach's Lute Prelude. He spoke before and after performing about the politics of Bach's time, of August the Strong, King of Saxony, about the aristocracy in Bach's hometown of Leipzig and the economic discrepancies as the feudal system ran on.

With each comment, dad played a chord, drew parallels to America under Eisenhower and Kennedy. Mom liked dad's playing, invited him for a drink. They spent the weekend together. At some point mom said, "You will love me," and dad did. They married ten months later. Dad cut down on touring, arranged session work, recitals and club dates in and around Aldwich. Mom danced until Jay was born, returned to performing for a short while then retired when I came along. She began to write reviews and feature pieces, essays and exposés, critiques and commentaries on dance. Each year she went to the Vail International and Edinburgh Festivals, to San Francisco and New York City, Sadler's Wells and London's Royal, covered everything from tap to jazz, ballet to modern. The affairs she had, the flings and such I didn't learn about until later, were casual and insignificant, she claimed, leaving me to wonder now, if she never took them seriously, what did this say about dad?

In 'Moonlight,' Pinter wrote: "My father was a very thorough man.... He was a truly critical force ... adhered strictly to the rule of law... which is not a very long way from the rule of thumb." My dad had similar traits, was thorough by degrees, an analytical presence who managed to be generous and supporting. When I first began acting, dad sat me down and talked more about the significance of history, of linking past to present and knowing the how and why of greatness, of influence and emulation. He took me to plays, had me watch films I'd never heard of, with actors I'd never seen before. I was told to enjoy the journey, the highs and lows. Dad applauded my failures and successes. I miss him now, think often of the way he loved Jay and me, and mom, too, though he never quite understood why her feelings for him were inconsistent and detonated time and again like a rechargeable blast. If there is something I should have learned from their relationship, an example to take with me, I've dropped that ball, failed to absorb the lesson, tend rather to mimic dad too closely. My own love confused, I duplicate his effort to find happiness under rocks and stone.

———

I skate long enough for my body to get loose, then pull benches from in front of the bleachers onto the ice. I've become, in the last few months, a fan of barrel jumping, have seen clips on YouTube and googled the history, use the benches to set an approximate distance and try to make the leap. The adrenaline rush is different from skating, the aftereffect of missing a jump more severe. (Falling, as they say, is like flying for a time.) I know the first world record for barrel jumping was set in Saranac Lake, New York, in 1925, by Edmund Lamy, the distance 27 feet 8 inches. The current world record is 29 feet 5 inches—a total of 18 barrels—by Yvon Jolin of Canada. On my best nights I've gone 21 feet, though I crash more on my longer attempts, pop my shoulders and bruise my ass.

I start tonight with the benches placed at 10 feet, my style smooth, hands low and back bowed, I generate speed, then leap with legs and arms extended. The short jump alerts my brain to what I'm doing. I land without incident, go around again, move the benches further apart, circle the ice and make another pass. By my fifth attempt, I'm at 20 feet. This distance requires more concentration. I miss just the same, fall hard, skid into the boards, smash my tailbone and crush the cigarettes in my pocket. I get up slowly, check myself for serious harm, bend over and resume skating.

I finish with six swift laps, then head back outside where the cold air hits me first as a relief and then as something harsher. I think about Darcie, am tempted to call her, despite the late hour. A bad habit. Sometimes when I phone, I tell her, "I don't want to love you anymore." She laughs at this, at how hard I try to sound convincing. Other nights, I ask her to come see me. She groans and hangs up. A week will pass before I get the nerve to call again. Lately when I phone, she sets the ring to voicemail, forces me to leave a message.

    I take my flashlight from my jacket pocket and shine it at the moon. Love's a struggle, don't I know? A few years ago, I played Taylor in Sam Shepard's 'Curse of the Starving Class,' and watched while the two lead actors, playing Wesley and Emma, had an offstage affair that crested and exploded like a melon dropped from a rooftop. (Emma: "That was my chicken and you fucking boiled it! You boiled my chicken! I raised that chicken from the incubator to the grave and you boiled it like it was any old frozen hunk of flesh!") The end of their relationship was not pretty. Carol—the actress playing Emma—baked ex-lax into brownies and left them in Gary/Wesley's dressing room before the final show. Gary on his toes, squirmed through the last scene, shit running down his legs as he delivered his lines about the eagle that swooped up a cat, how the cat and eagle fought in mid air, the cat tearing at the eagle's chest and the eagle trying to get free. "But the cat wouldn't let go," knowing if the eagle dumped her she'd die.

    Love is this, I think. My love for Darcie clings like cat claws. Dad's love, too, clung tight to mom right through his final five-night stay at the Regency Palace Hotel. Love is the china bowl knocked from the table's edge, the glass I watch shatter, helpless. I kneel and try to put the pieces back together, but how can I? Seriously, *fuck*. I leave my phone in my pocket, think of my month at Marimin, how I haven't done Nixon, black tar, red chicken, brick gum, any dirt or gato since my release, and assure those who ask that my channel swimming days are over. When I say this to Darcie, swear I'm off the junk for good and that everything can go back now to how it was before, she tells me it doesn't work that way, that our problem was never the dope, "you dope." She actually says this, insists I need to let go of the past and look forward. "Buck up, Mick," she says this too, sounds just like my counselors at Marimin.

Buck up, sure. "Look forward to what?" I ask, am desperate to know, but she won't tell me. The day I was released from rehab, I came home to find Darcie gone, our apartment empty, a note pinned to our bedroom door. "Baby steps," she wants me now to "take care of the cat."

———

# 2

I LEAVE THE Bow and drive home, fall into bed just after 5:30 a.m., kick off my shoes but keep my socks. My alarm goes off at 11:00 and I immediately pull the blanket over my head and howl. The howling is necessary, part of my morning routine, the exertion meant to wake me, forces me to rise from bed rather than drift back to sleep. I shout twice more, just to be sure, roll and toss the blanket off, stand until the chill from the floor passes through my feet.

Everything is recovery. Think. Act. Redo. Everything is… The cause and effect causes cause and effect, the link inexorable. Try to imagine otherwise. I try to imagine the before and after without one or the other. It's impossible. No chicken or the egg, but the egg rolling while the chicken crosses the road. What set them in motion? Will they survive? It's the inhale and exhale, one to the next, the constant connect and disconnect, the catalyst craving more. Simply put, B must follow A, and C then B, something with something, action with reaction, the pitch with the swing and the hit with the field. There is no way around it. I take one step and then another, until I am across the floor and in my kitchen. In my kitchen, I turn on the machine for coffee. Once I have turned on the coffee, I go and rinse my cup.

The radio I use as my alarm is still playing as I come out of the bathroom, a voice o/n the FAN rattling off sports scores, the late morning talk jocks—Rock and Red Bone—delivering their shtick *baadum-baadum*. The target demographic for the FAN is men between the ages of 18 and 60. Aware of their audience, sponsors run commercials for penile enhancers—pills and salves to enlarge the average dick, cure erectile dysfunction and thicken a narrow rod. There are ads for strip clubs and dating services, hair restoration products, gambling sites and divorce attorneys. Once every 90 minutes or so, the FAN also plays commercials for the V.F.C. as owned now by Paramour. The commercials are meant to entice, are read by a girl who puts air beneath every word, says things like, "Guys, ever wonder what the wife would look like getting down and dirty with Mr. Big?" and "Hey fellas, want to see your head where it's never been before?" It's all at this point amusing to me, the money I made and spent from our invention, my contribution to society a spicy debit, the connection here too, how Ted went from the V.F.C. to G.O.D. all pretty wild.

Unorthodox in its heterodoxy, Ted's G.O.D. is designed as a political rapture, rational and utilitarian, he hopes to provide governments with a program that achieves a *sustainable rightfulness,* a correct way of governing for the betterment of the whole. A grand plan, to be sure. Ted relies on history, praxeology and ethics to present an objective methodological synthesis—a synthetic *a priori*—dependent on all things that came before. The intent is to filter out subjective factors and resolve conflicts by making sure ill-advised histories do not repeat. *G.O.D. Knows*, I can see the bumper stickers. Ted smiles when I say this. His program consists of an enormous database covering eight thousand years' worth of cultural evolution: Rome, Egypt and Greece, Mesopotamia, the Indus and Aegean periods, Victorian and Renaissance England, China and Spain, Germany and America, monarchies, oligarchies, democracies, republics, dictators and sovereigns, presidents and popes all added to the mix. A hundred libraries' worth of text have been digested, the whole of Will and Ariel Durant's 'Story of Civilization,' Volumes 1-20, de Tocqueville on the development of democracy, Machiavelli and Nietzsche, Hegel on civility and consensus, Calvin and Hooker, Luther and Knox. From this Petri dish of information, G.O.D. digests, weighs and matches, applies and draws out applicable facts, answers questions concerning the troubles in Kenya, in Chechnya and Myanmar, Iraq and Iran, Cleveland and Palau, Detroit and Dubai, Sri Lanka and Korea, China, Venezuela and the Czech Republic. *What is* addressed through *what was*, everything examined with an eye toward serviceable solutions.

    The idea is noble, is quixotic, is both brilliant and wishful. I'd like to have faith, but all of this is beyond me. The idea of a totally logical, detached and dispassionate arbitrator reconciling problems that have repeated and repeated and repeated themselves for tens of thousands of years seems tenuous. From what I've seen, dictators want nothing to do with logic, prefer subjective rants to objective calculations. People, too, are skeptical, prone to trust a Bernie Madoff before a Mahatma Gandhi. Over the last two years, Ted has found this true, has tested the waters with mixed results, his theory complicated by partnerships and political side deals that skewed initial expectations. Early application proved problematic, residual circumstances unforeseen. Throughout, Ted has been resilient, setbacks met with adjustments. He revisits and revises, remains dedicated and determined, all as I continue to play with 'Moonlight,' pitch about the Bow and dream of Darcie.

―――

My laptop is by the coffee maker, in the center of the kitchen counter. The headlines come up on my computer in a neat blue font. I scan down, do a quick search for the stories I've been following. Since Monday, I've been tracking the climbers on K2, groups from America, France and Denmark, Italy and China planning to scale the mountain. Currently on their way to a base camp at 16,000 feet, the summit for K2 is 28,000 feet, the second highest mountain in the world. The pictures I've seen show a harsh series of jutties, all stone and ice, jagged buttes, peaks and crags, more dangerous to climb than Everest. Near the summit, the temperatures fall to thirty below zero, the air already thin, requires special tanks to breathe. The mountain is a blistered bump, as stark as an unloved heart. The entire undertaking amazes me, I wonder what the climbers are thinking. All the extreme involved, exactly what point is there in scaling a mountain just to get to the top? Yesterday, I said this to Ted and he laughed.

I read a few more headlines, check my emails—nothing from Darcie—then click over to The Harry Tick and see what Ted is up to. I read reports from Iran and the growing unrest with Mahmoud Ahmadinejad and Ayatollah Ali Khamenei. After this, I pour my coffee and take it with me into the bathroom, shower quickly and dress. My bathroom is small and the mirror steams. When I wipe it down my face appears as if out of nowhere, surprising me. Naked, I picture Darcie, stroke myself twice then stop. The sadness that comes over me, in the mornings mostly, when I'm acutely alone, is disturbing, even after ten months. *You would think...*, I think, but then I stop.

Jay has me doing drywall patches in West Aldwich. The drive takes ten minutes. The heater in my truck is uncooperative as always—no matter where I set the dial, it delivers arbitrary bursts. Right now it's blasting chilled air up the legs of my jeans. I've switched the fluids, checked the vents and the fan and everything seems fine, but there's obviously still a problem. "Crazy," I turn on the radio, listen to Dave Matthews sing. Most of Aldwich is built out from its center. I pass Parrot Lake, glance at the ice. Today's house is a saltbox, white wood framed, brick fireplace and chimney in the kitchen. I spend the afternoon replacing panels. By the time I leave, I'm covered in dust. Before my shift at the Bow, I usually run errands, shop for groceries, gas up my truck, do my laundry and grab a bite to eat. Each night I'm tempted to track down Darcie, though mostly I resist. My life these last ten months has all the elasticity of a fence post, the need for deviation constant, my want to resume the life I had before but with no chance yet. After nine months at the Bow, I've learned to address my isolation in stages, one hour at a time. One hundred eighty days in, 1,440 hours down and more to come. At some point the austerity is its own form of addiction, the challenge to make it through each day.

At 5:30 p.m. all is dusk. I drive back toward home. The light across from Parrot Lake turns red. The moon sits high, reflects white off the ice. The color of the lake is silver, the ice thick from weeks of cold, the wind leaves pressure points buried like white veins frozen along the surface. In the distance, I see someone skating laps near the center of the lake. I watch for a moment, follow him cutting wide circles, hands held in, with shoulders rolled, knees bent to settle into the turns, smooth as quicksilver. When the light changes, I switch lanes, cut over, turn and slide onto the gravel, close to the shoreline. I watch for another minute, check the time, then get out. The wind off the lake catches my skin with the coldest sort of hunger, the air hitting my face burns my nose. I sit on the bumper of my truck and pull on my skates.

The kid on the ice has his gray knit cap yanked down over his ears, his brown coat zipped high, his metal blades making a long ssssuuusshh-ssssuuusshh-ssssuuusshhing sound. His gloves are slight, his jeans stuffed into the tops of his skates. The moon is brighter here, a hundred yards from shore. I time my approach so I can fall in behind when the kid passes, but he's skating too fast for me to keep up. I go with him once around, lose distance, my chest pounding while my head drops, I imagine how comical I must look, my stride a struggle, the speed beyond anything I achieve at the Bow. Halfway through our third lap, my legs turn heavy, give way to a smoker's puff and grind.

The kid in contrast is unflagging, as efficient as spur gears, his blades set along the ice are radial teeth greased and churning parallel to the axle. I want to see his face, decide to coast, allow him to circle and come past me again. I shift to the right, out of his skating lane, stop and turn so I'm facing him as he glides around. Ten yards away he looks up, sees me there. His face puzzled, he cuts quickly left, back through the heart of the lake, away from me, shoots around to the far shore where he stands and waits until it's clear I won't follow. I head back to my truck and am gone.

At the Bow, I take a Pop Tart out and warm it on my heater. The smell is sweet yet artificial. I sip from my thermos, sit inside my booth, my legs stretched, am judicious with my intake, don't try to get drunk, but show responsibility by monitoring my consumption. "Constructive convalescence," this is what my counselors at Marimin called the course of recovery. Each day an inch made, though I doubt auditing whiskey shots brought into the Bow is what they had in mind.

Outside, the wind wraps itself around the frame of the Terror Twist and Mammoth Falls, freezing the face of the metal. The only footprints in the snow are mine or Terrance's from the shift before. I take a second sip of whiskey, lean over and find my 'Moonlight' notes in my backpack. Around 11:00 p.m., I walk to the aquarium. Inside, I pull off my gloves. The air presents a jungle warmth that settles over my skin like a fever. My face thaws. The floors are slick, the sounds of water moving through the pumps and the occasional fish splashing. I shine my flashlight down the first hall, keep the main light off. The sharks notice me just the same, swim to the front of their tank. I go to the freezer and bring up fresh chow, give the big boys a bit of something extra. I like that I'm able to do this, the sharks in their tanks and me close enough to almost touch them.

When I head outside again, the wind catches me as if it's been lying in wait. I think of Darcie, warm in bed, though which bed now I can't be sure. The bed we used to sleep in at my apartment is a mattress of feathers, soft and covered with flannel sheets. While I was at Marimin, Darcie came with friends and a truck, took all the other furniture, the dresser, bookshelf, table and chairs. The only thing she didn't take was our bed, the old mattress not what she wanted, she told me later, "The fluff has gone flat."

Since Darcie left me, I've not been to her new place, have not been invited, do not know where she lives, have only her cell phone to call. When I stop at the Mecca and ask her to take me home, she refuses and says, "What you're wearing, Mick, will clash with the drapes." There it is then. There's Darcie in high form. Who couldn't love her? Who wouldn't be crazy mad? Four years ago, Darcie was playing Ophelia at the Briklen Theater. ("Life and love are hell. But the heart's misery only the heart can tell.") I didn't know her then, had read a few reviews, heard from friends that she was the real deal and I should check her out. I went to see her Ophelia, realized fairly quickly she had scary talent, was the sort of actor you couldn't stop watching, even when the focus on stage was somewhere else.

After the show, I asked around, went to Kooper's for a drink. When Darcie came in, I introduced myself, congratulated her performance. She asked me to repeat my name. I ran through a short list of credits, told her I was about to open as the Orator in Ionesco's 'The Chairs,' and invited her to come see me. She said thanks but, "Sorry, I can't."

Two weeks later, Darcie called. "Come audition," she said. The part was for Jim in a touring production of 'The Glass Menagerie.' Darcie was already set to play Laura, the shy shut-in at the heart of the play. I went and read, was called back the next day. Darcie was there and did the dance scene with me, stopped halfway through. I went outside for a smoke. The director came and found me and gave me the part. The tour started that summer and lasted ten weeks. Darcie's performance was the key to our production. On stage, I followed her lead, how she morphed into Laura, took on her physical damage. As Jim, I strutted and briefly kissed Laura before abandoning her early in the final act. Darcie found this funny, teased me after our show in Richmond, Virginia, sitting in the hotel bar doing shots of tequila. "You'd never leave me really, would you, Jim?"

I stuttered in reply. Darcie laughed, touched my wrist, told me to take her upstairs and fuck her like Laura.

I did as asked. My Jim was tender and patient, Darcie's Laura timid and trusting, surrendering in phases. When I finished, sweetly petting, gently holding, Darcie rolled me over and said, "Ok Mick, now it's my turn."

We moved in together after the tour, settled on the south side with our books and clothes and Darcie's cat. As working actors, we took on different projects, plays and pilots, commercials and indie films, music videos, educational clips and serialized tv. During the day I taught theater at Carter High School, while Darcie ran student workshops at the Performance Mecca. Afternoons and evenings we had auditions, rehearsals and shows. Our relationship relied on synchronicity, our personalities in chorus, Darcie hit the high notes, managed to inject even the most mundane activities with jazz. Late at night, we'd wind down with a bit of weed, have a drink after performing, come home and do a line or two of blow. Our intake was casual, Darcie a healthy participant enjoyed kicking back with a bit of yay-yo. I loved her foolishly and completely, the way she stimulated and moved me exceeding affection, became quickly a need.

In the mornings, Darcie performed yoga exercises, impervious to any residual effect from our partying the night before. I usually woke hung over, my head a sandbag overstuffed. Darcie offered no sympathy, believed in responsibility, said I was expected to handle my own shit. I watched how hard she worked preparing for auditions, reading and reviewing scripts, rehearsing the parts she got, and inspired, I tried doing the same. I did not have Darcie's talent, but was equipped with certain skills, could do comedy and drama, stage and film, musicals and cabaret where I sang a little and played guitar. After 'The Glass Menagerie,' I worked steadily, did guest shots on tv, landed secondary roles in two films, then got the lead as Norman in Alan Ayckbourn's 'The Norman Conquests.' "All right. All right. I love you. I'm sorry."

A lucky streak. While I was Norman, Darcie was Sally in Brecht's 'The Threepenny Opera.' My reviews were solid, Darcie's off the charts. I was happy for her, proud when her show was extended, though mine was not. I did a walk-on for 'CSI: New York' as Policeman #2, auditioned but didn't get the role in a new Jerry Bruckheimer series, did a commercial on cable for Kettle Pop rice cakes, then missed out on the second lead in the new Bruce Willis flick. I tested for a CW comedy, 'Neighbors,' got the role, but the show was cancelled three episodes in. The commitment cost me a chance to play Gus in Pinter's 'The Dumb Waiter.' Darcie blew on her hand, pretended to roll dice, said choosing roles was like picking a lover, "If you're a whore too long, all you're doing is getting fucked."

She did Albee that fall. I did Thornton Wilder again, in dinner theater. Darcie wore costumes in our apartment, wore short skirts and no skirts, had me when she wanted and never when she did not. In our second year together, Darcie did a movie with Steven Soderbergh. She did Genet's 'The Maids' on stage and won two awards. I did an infomercial, hosted a game show for six weeks on cable, did Rosencrantz in a modernized version of the Stoppard play that did not go over well. (Guildenstern and I were store clerks in a mall.) Darcie took me to parties where we got high with Ethan Hawke, with Kristen Johnston and Shia LaBeouf. We held hands, though Darcie's no longer seemed as firmly set in mine. She wandered off at different social settings, let other guys circle around. Where I used to be amused and secretly aroused by Darcie's flirting, her gamesmanship all part of the tease, my confidence was not what it once was. Guys with clear agendas and better resumes now sized me up. I grew uncomfortable, imagined overtures and overtime adventures, a bit of betrayal, as in another Pinter play.

I did some blow on my own, to calm my nerves, started trying to discuss with Darcie the status of our affair. I was thinking about the future, wanted Darcie to define us and nail things down, but she wasn't game. "Define this," she'd say, and stand there breathing. "What's this?" she'd stare at me with a look of mock confusion, jabbing at the air. "What is it, Mick?" She'd extend her finger and poke at the space between. If her answer was meant to show she saw our relationship as organic, indivisible and with no further need of classification, I felt instead her avoidance. We began to quarrel over little things, our connection labored. I bought a bit more blow, did lines at lunchtime in the bathroom at Carter High, stared at my hands like an old jock whose prowess had always come naturally, and falling into a slump lacked the resources to figure out what was wrong.

I auditioned for John Sayles, but didn't get the part. Before coming home, I stopped for a drink, snorted lines through a clipped plastic straw. Two nights later, I went out with friends and was offered dreck. As blind dates go, the introduction went well. My appetite was robust, my constitution consumptive, I got some cash and bought more shit. Darcie was doing Tony Kushner, was Harper Pitt in 'Angels in America.' Each night she performed to sold-out crowds at the Asbonne Theater, was working with the best people in Aldwich. I got a call-back to an audition I did for the latest Kelsey Grammer sitcom, then lost the part, drove to East Warren for H. I kept my baby bags of birdie powder in an old peanut butter jar, invited Darcie to join me, hid the shit when she said no. I was thinking about the temporariness of all things, the cycle I was in and hoped to quit, how I just needed some luck to fall my way. That spring, through a series of generous connections, I landed the part of Stanley in 'The Birthday Party.' To celebrate, I bought a new bindle, asked Darcie again if she wanted to try. Her no this time was weary, she warned me as Harper, "I feel... that something's going to give." She cautioned me about Aunt Hazel, said, "This is not a rabbit hole I'll pull you out of, Mick."

I answered as someone already in over his head, "Not to worry," then fired up the ack-ack gun, loaded my cigarette with shit, waited for the caballo to push through the blood-brain barrier, stick to the opioid receptors and convert to morphine. The rush was transcendent, like getting hugged by warm fleshy pearls. I was careful at first, made it almost a week into 'The Birthday Party,' modifying my modifier, until Darcie was invited to read for Pedro Almodóvar's new film and my minor inroads seemed just that. I bought more horse, made flamethrowers with blow and ferry dust, overdid my trip. A rough ride, my feet in the stirrups, I was drawn into high waters, taken by the undertow, the current leading toward rapids that swelled and swept me away.

---

A checklist here of things to do: Get over the hump. Get a handle. Get a clue. Get down to it. Get my shit together. Get backing for 'Moonlight.' Get actors to work with. Get my staging set. Get my life in order. Get my resume redone. Get ready for when my probation is over. Get a foothold, a leg up, get organized. Make plans that are concrete. Clean the kitchen. Change my sheets. Tune my truck. Make only constructive calls to Darcie. Make calls that let her know I haven't given up. Make restitution. Make advances. Make amends. Make nice when nice is called for. Become proactive. Become relevant. Become political again.

Become inspired. Become informed. Find the right course of action. Find happiness. Find love. Find sense in the daily madness, the humor in all that is obviously insane. Initiate improvements. I want to find Darcie and tell her this. I want to laugh and say what is undone can always be fixed. I want to read her my list. I want to show her what I have, repeat as needed, for as long as it takes.

---

    I work Wednesday for Jay in East Glenn, replacing old windows with Pella energy savers. I pry the old frames loose, scrape away the spent caulk, sand and then prepare the space with a fresh bead of latex caulk, set the new Pella in place with shims and a level, nail the window down and use more wooden shims to keep the window from shifting. The job is easy enough, requires a bit of concentration in order not to chip or crack the glass. When I finish, I drive back uptown for a burger before my night at the Bow. With what time I have, I plan to hit Target, stock up on supplies, tuna and coffee, cat food, cigarettes and soap. Maybe, if I hurry, I can toss a load of laundry in at home, make some phone calls and change the sheets on my bed. All of this is the highlight of my routine, the period between 5:30 and 9:00 p.m., where everything feels dodgy, the open waters testing my resistance. My temptation to do something different is like bugs in the breadbox, the way they scurry and crawl up my arms, into my hair and nose and mouth when left unsupervised.

    I think of Darcie and have to tell myself not to call or go see her. I think of calling Feldman and scoring some scag. I've no real interest in doing so, no craving or desire to do dope, but the thought occurs to me just the same, as nothing more than that, a symptom of my frustration with how things otherwise are, these moments feeding a certain irrational need. If I'm not constructively occupied, I'm susceptible to diversions. I strike a bargain, dismiss all notions of getting high, promise that if I wait now I can still call Darcie later, when she's done with rehearsal and I'm at the Bow. The compromise is temporarily effective, works like duct tape patching up a broken wing. My heater clicks and hisses, makes the sound of someone saying "Yeah but, yeah but, yeah but," over and over and over again.

    The traffic's heavy on Welton Avenue. Both Burger Barn and Target are a few miles up. The snow from earlier in the day leaves icy patches on the road, people coming home from work shoot through yellow lights, change in and out of lanes. I imagine what plans everyone is rushing to for the night, have no such hurry of my own. The light across from Parrot Lake turns red, I stop and look out on the ice, see the kid from the other day is back skating. I watch him glide through the center of the lake, set his blades where the depth of the freeze is deepest. The evening is gray-bare, the sun down, what leaves remain on the trees this late in winter appear in the distance sparse and clutching. The kid bends and gives his pace speed, cuts across twigs trapped frozen in the surface of the ice. His movements are fluid, each part of him, his head and arms, legs and back, perfectly in sync. The shadows give chase. As he comes around, he chases in turn.

    I leave the road, drive to where I parked the other day, stay in the truck this time, sit for a while and continue watching. My window steams, I roll it down, feel the cold. The moon sits over the lake, white and distant. After a minute, I reach for my skates, get out of the truck. The kid notices, and unlike before, abandons his laps and skates toward me. I think he's changed his mind and wants me to join him now, but as I set my skates by the bumper of my truck and take a step toward the ice, the kid stops at the shoreline, picks up a rock and throws it at my head.

"What the fuck?" The rock misses and lands on the roof of my truck. I look for cover as the kid finds another rock and launches it. He has his cap pulled down nearly to his eyes, his thin gloves moist, carry frost from the lake. I bring my hands up for protection as the second rock sails past. "Quit following me!" The kid's voice is angry and hardline, though there's a fatigue set in the center that anchors the sound. I lower my hands only enough to peek over my fingertips, tell the kid, "I'm not following you. I just came to skate."

Unconvinced, he has his arm cocked, is ready to throw again. He argues against my claim, presents evidence, empirical data, Wittgenstein's logical positivism set on skates. "You saw me and you came down."

"To skate is all."

The third rock lands a few feet to my right. I duck my head, think to charge, then say, "All right. Fuck it." I turn and walk back to my truck. My hands are cold as I grab my skates and toss them inside. I reach for my gloves, there on the dash, big and fat compared to the thin bit of nothing the kid has on. I'm ready to go, don't plan on anything else, but am uncomfortable in retreat, the confluence of everything that's been forced on me these last ten months, culminating now with a twelve-year-old kid running me off. My reaction is more defiance than charity, I spin back and storm down to the ice, shove my gloves into the kid's chest. "Here," I say. "Dumb shit. Don't you know it's fucking cold out?"

---

I miss the turn for Burger Barn, drive to Target where I buy tuna and bread and juice, coffee and cereal, Pop Tarts and food for the cat. I also buy a new pair of gloves, black Marmots on sale. The incident at the lake distracts me from thinking about Darcie, a good thing, I think, even though I'm not completely clear about what just happened. Why did the kid attack me? Not trusting strangers is one thing, the caution required, the world not as it once was and all that, but if he was worried about me stalking him, why not split? Why not just take off like he did the other night? Why come toward me? Why skate close enough to pitch rocks, where if I wanted I could have rushed him from the shore?

Hubris, don't I know. People are nothing if not a mystery. Even when you think you have them figured out, you can never be sure what to expect. It's almost 7:30 when I finish at Target and get back in my truck. I head east on Welton, stop at Burger Barn where the girl at the drive-through window hands me my order with green fingernails. The kid's still skating when I pass Parrot Lake. I park again on the slope, parallel this time, closer to the ice, narrowing the distance between the shoreline and the passenger side door. My headlights are on, the truck still running, I'm not quite sure what I'm doing, think maybe I've spent one too many nights alone, the isolation starting to get to me, making me soft and sentimental. Maybe I just want the kid to know I'm not really a menace, that too many people think differently these days. I check to see if he's wearing the gloves, find them large and sticking out the ends of his sleeves like jumbo paws. I honk, wait until he comes to the shore again, lean over and hold the bag with burgers and fries out the side window, ask if he's hungry.

He stands half on the ice, near the passenger side, pulls off the gloves and tries tossing them to me, but I say, "Keep them. I got a new pair."

His hair hangs down in front from beneath his knit cap. He hesitates, seems less hostile toward me now, unsure what to do, he doesn't skate off. The gloves were a good idea, I think, the food tempting. I wonder if I shouldn't just give him the bag and go, that anything more is too much. I take out my wallet, show him my ID from Carter High, the card I still have from before they fired me. I tell him I teach, or used to, hand him my keys, make clear I'm not some crazy out trolling for kids. "I'm just into skating." I say he can eat in the truck or I can leave the bag. "It's up to you."

He considers this, holds my keys, looks at my ID, at the burger bag and then back at me before climbing in, careful with his skates. Next to me, he seems smaller now, caged and tamed, different than before. I tell him, "I'm Mick," hand him the bag, let him dig in. He stuffs the gloves and my keys in his pocket, takes out a burger, says "Cam."

The wind outside moves the branches of underbrush near the shore, the snow on the ice sent into a swirl. I reach for my burger, talk about skating, tell Cam about Jay and dad, and how I used to skate on Parrot Lake when I was a kid. The front seat of my truck is a cracked black vinyl, the padding below long gone flat, I've covered the seat with a large beach towel. The towel is blue, attached to the vinyl with duct tape. Both the towel and tape are also worn past the point of usefulness, the chill creeping through the surface. Cam grabs fries, eats steadily, one mouthful after the next. He takes another bite of burger, mentions a brother, Bob, a skater, too, nine years older, in the army, stationed in Basrah since June.

The blades on Cam's skates scrape against my rubber mat, the condensation on the steel dripping off into a minor puddle. I ask about his shoes and he points across the lake, gives me back my keys so we can drive and get them. It takes a few minutes to reach the north side of the lake, and by then Cam has finished his second burger, the fries and coke. He adjusts the switch to the heater, flicks it back and forth, gets warm air to blow through the vents, I don't know how.

In profile, Cam's cheek and jaw have the fine edge of

an India ink drawing, his frame, even inside his winter jacket, seems wiry and wound like a spring. I pull up on the opposite shore. As Cam still has his skates on, I climb out, collect his shoes, hand them to him as he removes his skates, wipes the blades with the end of his shirt, then stuffs his feet into white high tops, not exactly suitable for snow. I ask where he lives and if he wants me to drop him.

He deals with his laces, doesn't answer.

I say, "Did you walk or did your folks bring you?"

"I walked."

"When are you supposed to be home?"

"No time," he tells me.

"There's no such thing as no time."

Cam shrugs, keeps to his story. "I don't have a time."

"No? And how's that?"

"I just don't. I can go when I want."

"All right," I try this. "When you want, where do you go?"

Cam holds his hands in front of the heater. I take out a cigarette, roll down my window, wait for Cam to answer. When he doesn't, I try again, say, "So you can stay out all night, at your age and no one cares?" The comment is meant to point out the flaws, but registers in ways I didn't intend. Cam's mouth is small, a thinness to his lips, which part and quiver then close down quickly, the back teeth set. I look at his eyes, a dark brown unguarded. I tell him I'm not trying to pry, that I don't want to get in his business. "It's just that I need to make sure you're ok. Skating alone on the lake man, at night, is not a great idea."

"I'm fine," he shakes everything off, is back as he was before when tossing stones, looks at me across the seat, holds his stare while preparing to leave if I continue to press.

"Ok," I have no more argument. "If your folks are fine with it."

"My mom," he corrects me when I reference his parents

again, tips his head back, his chin up, pauses half a beat, like Darcie when she offers less than the whole story, making me uneasy. I ask about his mom then, direct my questions this way, wonder what she thinks about his skating alone at night, and here he finally tells me.

———

Terrance is waiting in the parking lot at the Bow. Wearing an oversized trench coat, the collar turned up, his head covered by a New York Yankees baseball cap, the blue faded, white tube socks stuck in at the sides to cover his ears, he looks like an oversized beagle. I pull into the Bow just before 9:00 p.m., get out and sign Terrance's card. The signatures are meant to confirm our coming and going, but if we were looking to conspire, we could easily sign the cards off site and at any time we wanted. Terrance burns a blunt while waiting, blows smoke as I take his card, then gives me his fist to hit. The Bow does not allow guests at the park while we're working, but Terrance is cool, says only, "You babysitting now, brother?"

I have Cam carry his skates back to my booth, show him how to set the heater. On high, the frost melts from the window. We stay inside and toast a Pop Tart, then bundle back up and take a tour of the grounds. The Corkscrew iced, catches the glow of the moon. Cam walks with me past the rides, climbs ladders and sits in cars. I watch him in an effort to make sense of the moment, how he's here with me and the way things happen. I think about what he told me, why he was out on the ice and not at home, consider the forces at play that set us in one another's orbits.

We go to the aquarium, where the smarter fish notice I'm not alone. Sharks and muskellunge swim closer to the glass. I cut pieces of beef heart stored in the fridge and let

Cam feed the piranhas. The red bellies swarm, made crazy by the snack. Outside again, we check the rear gates, then walk to the rink. Cam pulls on his skates, takes off his coat, circles the ice while I finish smoking. The bleacher lights cast everything in yellow. The sweatshirt Cam wears is gray, the sleeves too long. Without a jacket, his narrow shoulders and chest are exposed, his arms and hips like watch gears turning. I step onto the ice and do a few laps. When I feel ready, I pull three benches from the side, don't explain anything before I take a half turn around the rink, launch and land an easy ten-foot jump. Cam stops and studies my effort. I reset the benches and make a wider pass, stretch my legs out in front, my hands reaching for the ends of my skates. I touch down with a wobble, then skid and slide on my ass.

 Cam waits until I get up, comes from the right, glides off around the rink. His laps are smooth, his concentration clear, he rolls his shoulders, shoots past me, his eyes wide as he races toward the benches, sets his sights and makes the leap. I watch him land, see the way he keeps himself together, holds the ice steady beneath his skates, his effort stellar. I think again how crazy things are, all the hard slaps and permanent wounds, the way we fall back then marshal on, while the gods in need of amusement find ways to fuck us. The world is this, indiscriminate in its fortunes, does nothing to intervene when a twelve-year-old kid is separated three times from mom, dad and brother. What else is there then for Cam to do but skate in the chill of the icy curves he carves?

 I watch some more, offer instructions the best I can, what I know but can't do myself. Cam listens, is smart this way, he goes again, leaps and soars even further. I skate by, laughing. Who knows why anything happens? "All right, man," I say. All right, and leave him the benches.

# 3

ON THE FRONT wall of my apartment, unframed, in the space where Darcie's Rothko print once hung, is a photograph of Pinter in the revival of 'Krapp's Last Tape,' Beckett's one-character requiem about a life revisited through memories lost and recorded. The photo was taken in 2006, at the Royal Court's Jerwood Theater, after Pinter's surgery for esophageal cancer and two years before his death. At 76, Pinter's features in the photograph are exhausted yet unbowed. In costume, he's staring out from behind an ancient desk, his arms folded, not so much relaxed but settled in, his left hand pinning his right arm down. When asked about his health at the time, and the focus of his days, Pinter said: "I think the main bearing on my life at the moment is simply to survive. To remain here. That's been my main concern. And that comes down to very simple facts. How you use your energy, and as your energy grows, very gradually, how you actually dispose of it."

I think about this now, in the morning after dropping Cam at home, how important it is to use my energy wisely. In his Nobel Prize lecture, Pinter said: "I believe... as citizens, to define the real truth of our lives and our societies is a crucial obligation which devolves upon us all." No doubt. Truer words. I stand in the kitchen and switch on my computer, check my emails—again nothing from Darcie—scan the headlines for the latest news. The K2 climbers have reached their base camp and are waiting for the weather to clear so they can proceed to the summit. Students in Malaysia, Haiti and Pakistan mount political protests. Different energies, different forces. I click over to the Tick. This morning Ted has posted a piece about Leyla Zana, the Turkish activist sentenced to ten years in prison for what prosecutors described as "producing propaganda for a terrorist organization." The organization in question is the P.K.K.—the Kurdistan Workers' Party—the propaganda a statement Zana made suggesting "the P.K.K. is fighting for freedom and democracy."

Freedom and democracy. "There is your propaganda," Ted writes of Zana having already served nine years in a Turkish jail during the 1990s for a similar offense. The Turkish army supports the court's ruling. "This is the same army that has slaughtered Kurds, Afghans and Iraqis for much of the last century. What is terrorism?" Ted asks. "Is it somehow not terrorism if the carnage is authorized by the state? What is democracy? And freedom? What is propaganda and legitimate revolution? What's the authoritative definition and why is it always the guy with the biggest stick who gets to answer?"

I have no better response than "Because." The local

news is carried online at www.aldwich.net. I click over, check the Arts first, want to see who I know is performing where. Darcie's in rehearsal for a revival of Tracy Letts' 'Killer Joe.' I scan for updates, look for any additional references, a photograph or sites with new postings on Darcie. After another minute, I sign off, think about my own day ahead, how I'm to gather my energy and effectively dispose of it. I call Cam at the number he gave me, leave a message on his cell as he's supposed to be at school. I think of what I'm doing as I hang up the phone, how I'm directing energy at someone who, before yesterday, I didn't know at all. The thought gives me a vague sense of optimism, the possibility for what I'm not sure. I finish eating then feed the cat.

---

    This afternoon I put in the final window for Jay. The sun shines through the glass without quite warming the room. Each Thursday after work and before my shift at the Bow, I head back into the city for therapy. As part of my probation, I spend an hour with Dr. K. "Welcome to the Krazy hour," I try to make light. Tonight I stop at Wendy's first for a burger. The drive-thru runs around the rear of the blacktop lot. Cam calls and we make plans to meet tomorrow. I get my burgers then drive uptown, phone Ted along the way. The guard in Kyle's building makes me sign in. I've dealt with the same guard once a week for nine months, and each time he stares at me as if he might know me from somewhere else.

    Kyle's older, maybe sixty, not some young buck working for the court in order to augment his career, but successful enough in his practice to donate an evening a week. He wears fancy Italian shoes, expensive slacks and a lamb's wool handknit sweater, has dark hair and dull green eyes, his face no longer boyish is roughed over in the center, like a slightly battered fruit. A disciple of Albert Ellis, Kyle instructs me with imperatives, lectures me on Rational Emotive Behavior Therapy—R.E.B.T.—dismisses normal forms of therapy, says, "My job is not to make you feel good," then tries to do just that.

I sit in the chair across from Kyle, pull a burger from my Wendy's bag, am careful with the ketchup. Kyle's office is furnished in cinnamon cherry wood, the chairs and desk with curved overlay, very chic. Kyle crosses his legs, asks about my week. I answer as always, talk about my afternoons spent working for Jay and my nights at the Bow, making rounds, checking the rides and clearing the snow. My routine serves as both alibi and proof that I'm recovering to the point of conformity. I almost boast about being able to handle a bit of whiskey, but decide in favor of keeping certain things secret. I don't mention Cam, limit myself to what Kyle already knows. Every few minutes, Kyle writes on his pad. His pen is gold. Each time he finishes writing he clicks the top, moves us on to something else.

Tonight, he asks if I'm still skating and feeding the fish. I don't lie, tell him it's a perk of my probation. Kyle jots something down, finishes, clicks, then says, "And your job entitles you to these perquisites?"

I'm convinced of it, remind him that I haven't missed a night of work in nine months, that it's going to be ten degrees tonight and I'm eating Pop Tarts off a heater. "I have to do something."

"You mean something beyond the work you're assigned?"

"Right," I'm defensive now. It happens this fast, Kyle making it easy for me to put my foot in it. I tell him with less certainty, "I'm doing enough of what I'm supposed to."

"This you've decided?"

"Yes."

"There is a quota then? A place where you feel you are owed something, because doing what you're supposed to isn't enough?"

I shrug. Kyle writes again. I look at the wall behind his desk, at the Marca-Relli painting framed in gold with shapes inside made to look like a man writhing. Kyle moves us on, wants to discuss my impulses, my state of mind and what I think when I'm off skating.

"You mean what do I think when I'm thinking?"

"When you think, yes."

I tell him honestly, "When I think, I think about Darcie."

"And what do you think when you think about Darcie?"

Rather than answer, I say, "I also think about 'Moonlight.'"

"Your play?"

"Pinter's. And I think about getting high."

"You think about getting high?"

"Sure. I think."

"And what do you think when you think about getting high?"

"I think about what I miss, what it was like and what I liked."

"Like Darcie?"

"No." I reach for more fries, tell Kyle, "My thinking about the dope is passive. When I think, I only think about how I used to get high. I don't think about getting high. My thinking's no big deal. I think therefore I don't, get it?" I say this about the duji, wait for Kyle to finish writing in his notes, answer when he asks me then to explain the difference between thought and impulse. "When I think," I say again, "it's only that. It's me inside my head. I haven't gotten high in ten months, so there's no temptation."

"You mean intent?"

"Intent. Right. There's no intent," I give Kyle this, admit as they impressed on me at Marimin, "There's always temptation." I say more about my thinking, that "I'm working my way through everything the best I can. I'm concentrating on disposing of my energy efficiently. Still, it's reasonable to think about these things, don't you think?"

"It's normal to think." Kyle agrees with this, repeats the ethos of Albert Ellis, "Action is what matters," then cautions me again about thinking myself off the ledge. He holds his pen in his left hand, asks more about Darcie and if I've contacted her this week. I know what he's doing, his asking not arbitrary, he's trying to draw a link between my thoughts and action, between my calling Darcie and the dope, how my thinking of either tends to trigger impulses, blurring lines until I'm screwing up again. I disagree and let him know, "It's not the same. My thinking about the dope is a reflex that comes and goes. Darcie remains in my head always. Unfiltered," I say. "I have no safety switch on my intake valve."

"And yet you manage to deal with this how?" His method is Socratic, he expects me to perform all the heavy lifting. I finish my food, take out a cigarette, lean forward and tap Kyle's knee. The physical contact startles him though he doesn't move his leg. I answer his question with "I'm recovering in stages. The dope is something I'm glad to be done with."

"And Darcie?"

"I accept that she's gone."

"But you think of her actively?"

"I think, yes."

"Then what is it that you accept?"

I draw hard on my cigarette, tell Kyle, "I accept that I'm here now and Darcie isn't." This is true enough. I'm good with stating the obvious, am relieved Kyle lets me smoke, imagine all his other clients who rely on their Marlboros and Lucky Strikes. Without a cigarette, I'd probably blurt out the wrong thing, say about Darcie that I'm no better now than before. Instead, I try to present a coherent argument, organize what I'm saying, tell Kyle, "Here's what I mean."

I take another minute to explain the difference between my fixating on Darcie and the dope, how what I need to do with Darcie is accept our separation. "I love her, loved her," I say, "and that's a good thing. To love. It's what we're supposed to do, what we all aspire to, right? The effort then to undo these feelings is unnatural. How am I supposed to get over loving her and move on? There's no twelve-step program, no curative for me to ingest. The whole thing is counterintuitive, like trying to learn not to breathe. But I can acknowledge it, understand that things have changed and move on. As for the drugs," I insist my relationship is just the opposite, that what I'm trying to do is move away from something intrinsically unhealthy. "Thinking about dope doesn't make me want to get stoned again. Whatever thinking I do acts as a release, requires less energy than trying not to think, if that makes sense."

"And yet," Kyle doesn't miss a beat, follows everything back to its inception, "your need to think about Darcie and the drugs remains rooted in your tendencies toward addiction."

"Sure," I don't argue the point. It's true. "But that doesn't mean I will act on these thoughts because I think of them. If thinking always led to action, we'd all be screwed for sure, don't you think?"

Kyle writes, clicks, doesn't answer. He wants to dig further, explore the root, asks next about mom and dad. The subject comes up at every session, Kyle's interest in connecting the dots. I've already told him my family had nothing to do with what happened at the Galaxy, or before, but Kyle says I should humor him, believes on a fundamental level "all things are linked."

"Right," I say. "But not all things connect." I remind him that the court is only interested in keeping me off dope, and that's all I signed on for. Kyle notes my resistance, suspects there's more he should know, asks specifically about dad.

"Dad's dead," I answer with this simple truth. "He's gone." I give him nothing else, stall through the last few minutes of our session, get up at 8:00, toss my Wendy's bag in the trash, promise Kyle, "Next time, man," and beat a path to the door.

---

Outside, the chill catches me flush, causes me to shake. I pull on my hat and gloves, head to my truck. Despite the cold, people stand in lines in front of the theaters and clubs. Aldwich at night comes alive, is a city that understands the value of a good performance. Last winter, during a storm, people abandoned their cars when the streets became impossible to navigate and walked downtown, all to make the opening of Horton Foote's 'Dividing the Estate.' Plays on their way to London and New York come here first, are fine-tuned and tested, favorable reviews carry weight, while shows panned are reevaluated, restructured and often shut down. There is a production of Pinter's 'Betrayal' playing now that the critics gave five stars. I've caught the Sunday matinee, am jealous and impressed, wish I might have auditioned for Jerry, or Robert, imagine how I would have played the parts.

Jerry: "I must speak with you. It's important."
Robert: "Speak."
Jerry: "Yes."
Pause.

'Betrayal' is staged with an inverted chronology, the scenes moving from present to past, the device emphasizing

Pinter's view of language, the way our communications are flawed, lost in translation, filled with a fundamental disconnect, words wielded inefficiently and worse. As Pinter said: "The speech we hear is an indication of that which we don't hear. It is a necessary avoidance, a violent, sly and anguished or mocking smoke screen which keeps the other in its true place. When true silence falls we are left with echo but are nearer nakedness. One way of looking at speech is to say that it is a constant stratagem to cover our nakedness."

Nakedness, for sure. Everything's a cover. Coming from Kyle's, I think how hard it is to strip down and make clear exactly what I want to say. Last night, with Cam, I tried being honest when he asked about my working at the Bow. I explained what happened at the Galaxy, about my doing scag and what came of that. I mentioned but did not blame Darcie, offered examples of my recovery and pledged for better days to come. Cam listened while we walked, silent at first, and then wanting to know if I was ok, he answered before I could, said "You're ok now, right?"

I drive across town with the heater in my truck rattling, my radio tuned to WAUE. The local college station gives homegrown bands airplay, Ted's group, the Harsh Puppies, has a song called 'Front the Talk' in the current cycle. Thursdays and Saturdays the Pups appear downtown. A jam band, like Phish or Wilco on a smaller scale, Ted flatpicks bluesy riffs and runs, beats the struts like Tim Gaines, plays stand-up bass for acoustic sessions, all quick finger tugs and thumping. His body functions at ultimate velocity, he jumps about on stage, drinks power shakes before going on, siphons the nectar from fruits, devours burgers and fries and doughnuts dipped in chocolate frosting just to maintain his weight. With his music, Ted gives himself over and unwinds from his other work, tries briefly not to think about his writing and reporting, the Tick or G.O.D.

I get to the Bow just before 9:00 p.m., avoid the Thursday temptation to skip out and go hear Ted play. My shift drags, my concentration compromised, my sessions with Kyle always throwing me off. I spend my night reading 'Moonlight,' the chill in my booth resisting all effort to warm the space. I want to call Darcie but don't. I visit the fish, watch sand and lemon sharks lay low against the bottom while tigers and white tips and zebras circle the tank. Later, I go to the ice rink, set up benches and practice my jumps. My mechanics are faulty and I crash twice hard, thump and bounce on my back.

I think again of Cam, of what I told him last night and what he told me. His mom—Kate Mayhre—is at St. Mercy's, a guinea pig tested, the meds she's on to treat her CML—Chronic Myelogenous Leukemia—failing, the docs are looking for a better fit. Arrangements were made for Cam to stay with family friends for a week, but he didn't want the supervision, couldn't tolerate being watched over, so he created a deception, invented stories where everyone thought he was being looked after by someone else. It's a delicate ploy, clever enough over a short period but hard to keep going for more than a few days. I push the benches from the ice, compare Cam's situation to my own, the way we both want to control our own shit, even when the crap's already hit the fan.

As an adult, I need to understand circumstances don't always go the way we want. I'm not pleased by this, but have learned to take a philosophical view. In the last few months, Ted has encouraged me to read Hegel. To broaden my perspective, he's discussed with me the line: "What is rational is actual, what is actual is rational." Hegel believes everything rational presupposes mere existence, that what happens is weighted by actualities and their contingencies, with each event an unavoidable offshoot of something else. In other words, things occur not because of arbitrary forces in the universe but because people act, correctly and less so. Consequence sits at the center of Hegel's theorem. Ted wrote about this on the Tick, used the United States invading Iraq as an example: "What flows rationally from America's aggression is the resistance demonstrated by the Iraqi people. The contingency is the deaths and murder, the injustice and atrocities that came from that resistance, and what Hegel refers to as the *awful accidents*." These *accidents* are foreseeable, Ted insists, are the part of human action Hegel suggests man must take responsibility for and learn to resolve.

Easier said than done, even Ted admits, and turns to G.O.D. As I don't understand G.O.D. the same, I'm left to my own devices, wonder how, if the rational presupposes existence, are we to stop bad shit from happening? The only way seems by catching it before the initial act. But how do we do that? How could Iraq have stopped the United States from invading? How could we as a people have stopped George and Dick? How could Cam have stopped his mom from getting sick, his brother from enlisting, or his dad from taking off?

When I crashed at the Galaxy, the actual consequence was my arrest and probation, the contingency everything that's followed since; Darcie leaving and my inability to get real work. Here I am, a product of my own bad judgment, the rational becoming actual, which sucks for me. What I try to do now is make choices that won't get me in any more trouble, my goal to avoid becoming another *awful accident.* I take a counterintuitive approach, start with what not to do first. Once I achieve effective inaction, I feel safer, believe that I am better off. From there I try to decide what to do, but this is even harder, my actions filled with consequence, it scares me lately, putting one foot in front of the next.

———

I fall asleep after my shift, lie face down with my arms spread and my feet hanging off the bed. My alarm rings and I howl, roll over, lie on my back, listen to the sports scores on the radio, stand with my blanket over my shoulders. The door to my bedroom is open, and looking out, I can see down the hall, almost to the front room where Darcie did her yoga each morning, in a spaghetti-strapped t-shirt and bare legs, stretching on a thin rubber mat. The sounds she made during downward-facing-dog and flying-crow reminded me of sex. I'd lie in bed and listen, a sensual awakening, no matter how much I partied the night before, my sleepy cock still stirred.

I howl again, shake my head, instead of thinking about Darcie I tell myself to "stay in the moment." This is another one of the things my counselors at Marimin preached: *Productive deconstruction*, a tearing away of the past in order to rebuild the present. I repeat the words, and still I find it impossible to forget what came before. We are what was, this is true always. I picture Darcie in 'Twelfth Night,' in a remake of Kershner/Moore's 'The Luck of Ginger Coffey.' I see her with me at The Dive Inn, see us laughing and talking. The wind blows under the fire escape outside my window, rattles the bars.

I turn off the radio, go into the kitchen, dump the grounds from yesterday's coffee and start fresh. My 'Moonlight' notes are still in my backpack, dropped in the chair by the door as I came home last night. I think of another scene in the play, recall the lines: "Personally I don't believe (death's) going to be pitch black for ever because if it's pitch black for ever what would have been the point of going through all these enervating charades in the first place?" I like the line, "these enervating charades," how Pinter's mocking those who treat life as some stopover before the hereafter. Enjoy the moment, Pinter seems to be saying, for who knows what's to come? It's a nice sentiment, both a caution and a comfort, like a plump uncle patting your head with a heavy hand.

I shower while my coffee warms, wrap a towel and sit on my bed, strum a few chords on my guitar, the Martin flat top I inherited from dad. I think about Kyle and what he asked me last night, the whole story he wants to hear and suspects I'm keeping from him. I have for months now denied there's anything I'm hiding or am afraid to address, insist repression is not my problem and that my memory works just fine. It's the conveyance that's hard, how to make what happened clear with just words. The reason dad died, how he quit his music, quit the things he loved, this is what bothers me and I don't want to discuss.

I strum Clapton, have no great skill, can make a few notes sound familiar, am hardly even playing when compared to dad. By the time I was born, dad was working long hours at Hurbert & Steine to support the family, had all but given up guitar. A student of strings, dad sold high-end instruments to top-grade performers. Industrious, he created a network, contacted musicians, colleagues and friends, orchestras and bands, manufacturers and collectors in order to catalogue their needs. He studied the market, brought H&S a new list of clients, became expert in all things Martin and Yamaha, Ibenez and Washburn, Gibson and Fender and Guild, acquired and sold instruments by Tirvanas, Julian Britain and Johan Stott, landed first-rate pieces by the luthiers Guarneri, Testore and Forster.

Mom traveled more as Jay and I got older, covered festivals and recitals, did interviews and articles, worked on a book about Balanchine and a documentary on the choreographer Chris Elam. That she made no real money at her efforts, and indulged her practice just the same, while dad labored at H&S and played guitar only in stolen moments, was noted but not openly discussed. What dad knew of mom's affairs was kept quiet, too, remained a secret from us. In the course of his restraint, dad's heart suffered, the symptoms also initially hidden, and then too obvious to deny, became an open concern.

All things decline, some with grace and others under siege. Dad grew weary, his chest in spasms, a pasty gray to his skin, like cheap meat exposed too long to the sun. With mom away, dad fixed our dinner, went back to work. I watched him closer then, asked him to teach me chords on the guitar. He was patient despite my minor skills, let me play his 354CE Taylor and Martin flat top, introduced me to Johnny Winter, Adrian Legg, Jeff Beck and Santana, showed me Clapton and Muddy Waters. Time passed. The year I appeared in 'The Kentucky Cycle,' mom went to Europe for three weeks. Dad's health took a serious turn, declined to a point of crisis, genetic clots and a hardening of the walls, aortic stenosis the frosting on the cake. Mom seemed sincerely worried when she came home. As a concession to the severity of dad's sickness, without offering apology for past indiscretions, she arranged with Hurbert & Steine for dad to take a leave of absence. The offer was a kindness, an act of contrition, a chance for dad to concentrate exclusively on his music.

Adjustments were made, a reduction in dad's schedule, the means to manage a short list of clients from home. Mom cancelled trips, did not go out at night. The opportunity to have mom near and practice guitar all day improved dad's health. His fatigue declined, the graying in his gills and slip of his grip. His energy returned. He grew his hair out slightly, whistled more, joined two groups for local shows, mastered pieces by Joe Hymas and Ottmar Liebert, Ritchie Blackmore and Alison Stephens.

The arrangement was supposed to last through the end of the year. It went five weeks. Here, too, the way we plan, the gesture made, what remained was the erosion. Soon, both Steine and Hurbert began to call, asked dad to come into the office and meet new clients, deal with collectors and merchants if just for a few hours. Mom also backtracked, interrupted dad's practice, stuck her head into whichever room he was playing and got him to run to the market, do the laundry or take out the trash. In September, she took a trip to St. Louis to cover the opening of Paul Taylor's new dance, 'Beloved Renegade,' which was set—ironically enough—in the hour of the lead performer's death. She called to say she needed to stay an extra two days, returned out of sorts, complaining about the weather, and with a whisker rash on her cheek.

    What to make of this? What to make of anything? How often we try to reshape the course of history by plowing straight the curves in roads where nature has brought the weeds in close and altered the shoulders. But what chance of effecting permanent change when nature is relentless? What likelihood for us to repair tire tracks that have already driven the road and rutted the shoulders so deep that all the artificial filler is just that, a transitory replacement? After another week of interruptions, dad gave way, his heart once more in paroxysms. He strummed a requiem on his favorite guitar, lost his footing, stuttered during conversations, nodded off watching sports on tv. That Monday, he got up and showered, put on his suit and tie and spent the day at Hurbert & Steine. He went back the next day, and the next, and the day after that.

    The damage done, mom went to Massachusetts for the Jacob's Pillow Dance Festival, spent time with David Rousseve and Jason Samuels Smith, wrote intimately in her journal and posted laudatory reviews about the dance. Dad made light of his condition as his heart grew worse. Love is this, the heart invaded, the heart infected, the heart inflamed.

Jay and I took him to dinner, took him aside, took him to task. We tried to persuade him to retire, to go back on sabbatical, to work part-time and focus on his music. We suggested a cruise with mom, a trip they could take, but mom was in San Francisco, mom was in London, mom got a call late from a man who wouldn't leave his name. We spoke with mom, Jay more patiently and I less so, until dad intervened, said I didn't understand. He was right, of course. I asked dad to tell me, "What are you thinking?"

He played Tarrega's 'Estudio Brillante,' his fingers on the nylon strings curled and offering the sort of caress mom might have envied if she saw. He smiled, and closed his eyes, held his guitar like a child, gentle in his lap, then asked in turn while he played, "Do you hear that?"

In decline, unable to alter the prognosis, dad on his birthday booked a five-night stay in a suite on the 14$^{th}$ floor of the Regency Palace Hotel and threw a party for friends. He was 59. The event was catered with mom as hostess, Jay and I pouring drinks and hanging up coats. People ate moose milk cheese and jumbo shrimp, drank champagne and beer and sat by dad's side. Nothing was said about his heart. Off his meds, dad entertained, was irreverent and unreserved. Live music was played with dad strumming from his bed. In the middle of a tune by Pepe Romero, dad's heart expanded like fragile fairy wings, shuddered and broke. Dad's doctor later told us, in a statement so absurd I could only turn away, "There was no suffering."

After dad died, mom moved to New Mexico, sold the house, got rid of dad's car, most of his instruments, the furniture and books. I got one of his guitars, some of his favorite clothes, his watch and a bit of money Darcie and I ran through. Whenever I say to mom and Jay that dad died of an acute case of paradoxicality they get pissed and tell me to let it be. Still, that's what it was, an inability to connect with what he wanted. I think about this in terms of me, the things I want and don't have and the reason why. I sort through the detritus, the personal residue, the choices made and not made, the memory and manner in which love and dreams afflict me on either side. On our way to the Regency, dad snapped his fingers to show how fast time went, said "You see that, Mick?"

I reread 'Moonlight' in the months following dad's funeral, was moved in new ways by its obliqueness, how Pinter tapped into the disconnect, the complexity and ambiguity of all things that pass between us. I tried losing myself in the language, convinced I would come away with a greater understanding, but got caught in the middle instead, could not find my way out, lost dad and Darcie, too, took duji from the jar and wound up croaking, "Uh-gug," and "Eee-gag," in a totally different production than I had planned.

———

# 4

JAY HAS ME painting a house in West Glenn. My hair is still wet from the shower as I head to my truck, nearly freezes inside my cap. My windshield's frosted over, I have to scrape before I can drive. I repeat this: *I have to scrape before...* My heater's no help, tosses out cold air. If I turn the heater off, my windshield clouds, and if I turn her on I'm equally fucked. I feel I'm in some epic battle, the picking of my poison with no alternative. I shut off the heater and crack my window. The temperature outside is fifteen degrees, by the time I reach West Glenn the left side of my face is numb and my shoulder frosted.

The walls of the house are primed. I cover them with

a green latex semi-gloss hi-hiding paint, use a Wooster pro roller, get as much of the first coat done as I can. My radio's tuned to WRVR—the River. I listen to Ray Lamontagne and Ingrid Michaelson, switch to NPR in the middle of the afternoon, get Fresh Air with Terry Gross. Today's guest is Ronald C. Arkin, an artificial intelligence expert from Georgia Tech. Arkin designs robots to use in combat. "In the heat of battle," Arkin says, "the human mind clouds. Concerns turn to personal survival, to acts of cowardice, or heroism, or extreme savagery. With robots the human element is eliminated, the only decision made is the one which is best for achieving the ordered mission."

Is that right? *The ordered mission?* What the fuck? I try to make sense of what Arkin is saying. If *the ordered mission* is killing people, how exactly are humans removed from the equation? All of Arkin's doubletalk adds up to his creating a more efficient killing machine. What he wants to do is set metal monsters free to murder and maim with impunity and how is this intelligent? If robots are used, the carnage simply becomes easier and more extensive, like the drones Obama has hovering over Afghanistan and Iraq that wipe out entire villages with the push of a button. The sort of efficiency Arkin wants is bullshit packaged as progress. I think, if *the ordered mission* is to bring war to a close, why not do the opposite, why not make everyone fight naked, hand-to-hand, and force the issue until we all realize what war is and ultimately fails to deliver?

I make a note to tell Ted, stop painting by 5:00 p.m., clean up, wash the roller and fold the tarp, carry the ladder and remaining equipment into the garage. Cam has taken the bus to the hospital after school, is just getting back when I pull up. His house is a gablefront, white with black shutters. We go to skate. I ask about his mom and he answers in clipped assurances, says she's ok. We stay on the lake for an hour. At one with his blades, Cam moves with the fluidity of flight. Afterward, we eat at Falzo Deli, have sandwiches and dark potato slices. I wash my face in the bathroom. Cam puts his hat in his pocket. He wants to come with me to the Bow, reminds me it's Friday and he doesn't have school tomorrow. I appreciate his asking, but don't think it's a good idea.

Our booth is red plastic, the table between us pressed wood. I explain that I'm not supposed to have anyone with me at the Bow, that we shouldn't make a habit of his staying out all night, and how it's likely someone will come by the house to check on him. As I say this, Cam continues to eat his sandwich. He listens and doesn't argue, accepts that he has asked and I have answered. His cooperation is not what I expect. Unlike other kids he doesn't plead or offer unsound reasons why I should give in to what he wants. His reaction, I realize, is based on experience, life having given him an early peek behind the curtain, he knows now, sooner than most, how shit happens. Rather than interrupt, he just lets me keep talking.

I compare Cam's restraint to my own way of managing disappointment, how I'm less rational, continue to bitch and beg Darcie to take me back. I lack the same maturity Cam has at twelve, went to see Darcie not three weeks ago, after my shift at the Bow. I'd had a rough night, one where I was chased around the grounds by shadows. Driving downtown, I parked and walked, stopped twice for coffee, sat for awhile then walked some more. Darcie did morning workshops at the Mecca. I got there around 10:00 a.m., found her putting a group of students through a reading of Horton Foote's 'Trip to Bountiful.' The kids were on stage, Darcie in a chair down below, in a green sweatshirt, black jeans and purple converse sneakers. Her sunglasses were up on her head. I sat beside her, waited, then leaned over and whispered, "I don't know of anything prettier than a scissortail flyin' through the sky."

The line was the only one I remembered from 'Bountiful.' Darcie finally acknowledged me, turned and said, "You look like shit." I told her I hadn't been home since the Bow. She said I should go to bed and I invited her to come with me.

"I'd love to but I just washed my hair."

I tried to remember the next line but couldn't, went ahead and confessed, "I miss you."

Darcie groaned. The kids on stage watched. I didn't mind. I hadn't had an audience for months, and eager to make the most of the moment, I reached for Darcie's hand, leaned in again and kissed her. She let me at first, then bit my lip hard. I left bruised and with the kids laughing.

I should have known what would happen. Always in front of people Darcie's intractable. In private she's more impulsive, is apt to surprise, to indulge in ways she can still dismiss and deny in the morning. What I've learned about relationships—in hindsight, sure, but still I know—is that they fail mostly because we refuse to see the other person for who they really are. The key is understanding and not expecting lovers to act differently simply because we hope they might. Back in college, I worked as a lifeguard at the university pool, had the late afternoon shift when the club and college teams came to practice. The pool provided a white chair on stilts, some six feet off the deck, where I sat and watched the swimmers do their laps and the divers practice their pikes and flips and inwards.

I liked the girl divers especially, in their fitted suits, their hair free and flowing, their strong thighs and arms wetted as they bounced and soared, their three-step hurdle laying the tip of the springboard down and launching them bird-like. Knowing they couldn't fly indefinitely, in the brief time they were airborne they'd flaunt the full range of their abilities by twisting and spinning several feet above the pool.

When their maneuvers were complete, they'd straighten and enter the water, rip the surface with such precision that the splash was drawn down as if into a vacuum.

I watched, in particular, one girl who performed best off the platforms, launching herself from 5 and 7 and 10 meters, spinning and twirling and hitting the water with so much force that she'd shoot to the bottom of the pool and leave me holding my breath for several seconds until she emerged. I waited a week to speak with her, allowed enough time to establish a wordless communication, made sure she noticed me, our eyes initiating contact so when we finally did talk, there was an established familiarity. We went for pizza. Her name was Jill, a senior majoring in bio-mechanical design. I was completing my final two classes, interviewing for teaching positions, auditioning when a part came up, working my shift at the pool in the afternoons, rehearsing and performing at night. As our affair progressed, we shared whatever free moments we had together, our sex intense, Jill physical, liked to wrestle as if pinning down a rival.

In being together, I assumed to know, saw how hard Jill trained and studied, and convinced we were the same, I told her about the play I was in. 'Blast' was a three person high-wire act. The playwright—Sarah Kane—was like Pinter on acid, her social commentary anatomizing human nature, the way people camouflage their fears and insecurities by abusing one another. There were graphic elements to the play, but Jill insisted she was not easily shocked. That she was shocked when she came to see, as my character—*the soldier*—raped the other actor on stage, then plucked out his eyes and ate them, disappointed me. I tried convincing Jill that 'Blast' was an enlightened dance, incisive and condolent, and that my acting was like her diving, every move was choreographed for effect. She wasn't buying, said the play was perverse and sick, that diving was all precision and beauty, while my performance was ugly and violent and crude.

Angry now, I shot back that 'Blast' only appeared ugly and crude because she was too afraid—I might have used the word ignorant—to understand. We argued about this, Jill mocking as I confessed that Kane committed suicide in 1999 at the age of 28. I cursed and said the meanest thing I could think of, that people like Kane were rare birds, too extraordinary and beautiful for this world, like James Dean and Adolph Merckle, while Jill's diving was an indulgence, a foolish exercise which, even when performed perfectly, left no ripple and was immediately forgotten. I didn't believe this, of course, had always found Jill's diving amazing, but I couldn't say as much, couldn't convince her about 'Blast,' or anything else, our differences too extreme. We stopped seeing one another, Jill with her hands in the air swearing, "I don't even know you." I agreed, soon graduated and left the lifeguarding to someone else.

―――

Cam comes with me to the Bow. I'm not sure exactly when I decided to take him, though I think I knew all along. Whether Cam knew, I don't know, though when I drove from Falzo's and headed west, he didn't seem surprised. We finish my shift and I drop Cam at home, then head to my place to crash. Saturdays I don't set my alarm, try to sleep late, my body spent and in need of recharging, only my internal clock betrays me. Conditioned by the week, I stir early, wake around 11:00 a.m., doze off and on again until 2:00 then get up and shower.

Once I've dressed, I feed the cat, set my coffee to brew and check my computer. There's a link I've discovered that provides updates on the K2 climbers. Everyone is at the base camp still waiting for the weather to break before they make their way to the summit. The camp is beyond Jammu and Kashmir points, on the Pakistan side of the Karakoram Range. Different groups of climbers plan to take either the Abruzzi or the Cessen route up the mountain, converging at 26,000 feet, just below an enormous stretch of ice known as the Bottleneck. The groups will then cover the remaining 2,000 feet together, through the Overhang and on to the summit. Marco Confortola is one of the lead climbers, is shown in file footage looking confident and tan. I imagine myself playing Confortola in a film version of the climb, picture me with the flag ready to bury deep at the summit, announcing to the world, "I am Confortola!"

I click to the Tick, read about Turkish Prime Minister Recep Tayyip Erdoğan fining the Doğan Yayin media group 2.5 billion dollars for publishing commentaries critical of Erdoğan's government. Ted writes: "Somehow, I think Erdoğan may not grasp the concept of free press." That same day, flash floods swept through Istanbul, killing more than 50 people. The rains were the heaviest in Turkey in over 80 years, with bridges and cars, highways and homes lost in the deluge. "Coincidence?" Ted poses the question. Who knows? I remember some years ago I saw Alan Bates in 'Fortune's Fool,' and walked around in awe after, repeating his line: "This little world, this miniature state, teeming with countless human beings supported by it, all gossiping, whispering, intriguing." That's it, I think now too, the way things happen, inexplicable, that never fail to amaze us.

I take my coffee into the front room, have replaced the furniture Darcie removed with a coffee table and two wooden rockers. Even with the changes, there are places still in the apartment where I feel Darcie's presence; in the kitchen, near the tv, by the front window and on the bed. The effect is powerful. I'm aware of her scent, am convinced this is what triggers my memory, have scrubbed the walls and floor, vacuumed and washed the rugs, changed the sheets and blankets, and still she's here. Kyle thinks I should move, says new surroundings are important and therapeutic. I agree in theory, but wonder how I'd actually manage if I didn't have old ghosts to haunt me.

My television's a big brown box, bought second-hand after Darcie took the flat screen. The picture is fuzzy even with cable. In the bedroom I have a better set, but don't want to sit in bed any longer. I flip the channels, catch a bit of the Syracuse basketball game, then shut the tv off and open my 'Moonlight' notes. I have a list of actors I think are perfect for each of the seven parts, all grade-A talents, people I could never get but imagine just the same. In 1993, Ian Holm was the original Andy when 'Moonlight' opened at London's Almeida Theater. For my list, I have William H. Macy as Andy and Ken Stott as Ralph, Marcia Gay Harden as Maria and Kate Burton for Bel. Billy Crudup and Peter Sarsgaard are my brothers Jake and Fred, though both are a bit old for the parts. Maybe Sarsgaard could play Ralph and James Franco do Jake. All of this is nonsense, of course. I have no play to cast, no funds or prospects. I put the list away, tell myself I need to stop fucking around and get something done. "Come on, man," I say this to no one but the cat.

Last year, before my breakdown at the Galaxy, I pitched 'Moonlight' to Dave Karuim with the hope that he'd produce. Dave runs Karry On Productions, a casual friend and occasional drinking buddy, a Wharton grad, nice enough, resourceful, with bottom-line sensibilities and a sincere appreciation for theater. Six years ago Dave produced a musical version of David Lynch's 'Eraserhead.' Lynch was skeptical at first, convinced only after Dave explained his vision, described cultural trends, the public's appetite for music and mayhem. Staged at the Miller Theater, 'Eraserhead' did brisk business, moved to New York, and then out on tour, was underwritten at each stop by Karry On. Like almost all of Dave's shows since, 'Eraserhead' won awards, travelled well, made everyone involved a ton of money.

For 'Moonlight,' I was told to send Dave a cost analysis along with a copy of the script containing my ideas for staging and direction. I was optimistic, wrote up a detailed proposal. After 'The Birthday Party,' and following my month at Marimin, I phoned Dave again. By this time, 'Moonlight' had gone from a project of interest to an absolute necessity for me. Dave did not seem concerned about my fuck-up at the Galaxy, said this was show biz and no one cared about controversy for long. He was encouraging, if not promising, told me to sit tight and he'd reread what I'd sent. I waited three weeks, then phoned again. And again. I left messages on Dave's personal and business lines as recently as last week. For whatever reason, he has not returned my calls.

---

There's a story about Beckett's wife, Suzanne Deschevaux-Dumesnil, shopping 'Eleutheria' and 'Waiting for Godot,' around Paris in the 1940s. The plays were unlike anything most producers had seen, untraditional, hard to visualize, problematic in terms of turning a profit. Over and over, the scripts were rejected, until finally the producer Roger Blin agreed to stage 'Godot.' No visionary, Blin admitted afterward he chose 'Godot' only because it was easier to stage than 'Eleutheria,' and that he'd taken pity on Deschevaux-Dumesnil's persistence.

My persistence has netted no similar Blin for 'Moonlight. I've called friends, and friends of friends, contacted people inside the business and out, have cut the costs to a bare minimum, and still no one has signed on. Applying for grants is a waste of time, raising money while dragging the remains of my reputation around a pain in the ass. I'd have a better chance if I attached 'Moonlight' to G.O.D. as Ted's project has broader appeal, is eligible for academic, technical and political grants, fellowships, foundation and institutional support. On the internet, in chat rooms and blogs, MySpace and Facebook and Twitter, at conferences and postings on The Harry Tick, Ted discusses G.O.D. with political theorists, sociologists, computer programmers, the Discovery Institute, George Gilder and Jay W. Richards, historians and geneticists, theologians and private investors. All are intrigued, though few at first had money to invest. Then Mark Perril called and G.O.D. became suddenly flush.

  This was three years ago, late August, Ted had dragged me out for a run. I sat afterward, sweating in one of his plastic kitchenette chairs, my head halfway between my legs, huffing, my lungs on fire, in need of water and a cigarette. Ted in blue nylon shorts, an Aldwich Argonauts sweatshirt, gray socks and green Adidas cross-trainers, with knobby knees and bony shoulders, looked like a scarecrow pried from its post. The phone rang and Ted answered. Two nights later we were having drinks with Perril in his suite at the Grace Weston Hotel, Ted having brought me along for luck.

  In Aldwich, the Perrils shined, each in their turn. Great-grandpa Marshal founded our first daily newspaper, grandpa Mike expanding into radio, while momma Marsha acquired tv. At the time of her death, Marsha Perril owned six national newspapers, nineteen radio and five tv stations. As son, and now CEO of MVP, Inc., Mark Perril inherited everything. Impervious to naysayers, an astute surveyor of the landscape, an adherent of his mother's philosophy, assertive and farsighted, Mark began disposing of his assets within six months of assuming control. Citing the advent of a new age, Aquarius rising and the moon in a different house, he predicted the demise of newspapers and radio, sold off MVP's equity while values were still high, invested in fledgling cable companies, internet ventures and embryonic forms of electronic technology, news and entertainment, GEANT, GLORIAD and JANET, IPTO, HTTP and VoIP, Google and Orbitz and ITU-T, websites and servers, tech companies and their competition. A skeptical Board cautioned Perril. He ignored their concerns, demanded their support, jabbed a finger defiantly in the direction of their collective chests, then stood back and watched as each of his forecasts came true, tripled and re-tripled his fortunes again.

    We arrived at the Grace Weston at 8:00 p.m., were brought upstairs by a man in a blue MVP blazer and dark navy slacks. Perril greeted us, large as a draft horse, fleshy in the face and through the middle, his features at odds, handsome like Tom Wilkinson in 'Michael Clayton,' his jaw round, his forehead flat and thick hair graying, his teeth sharp and white as an ice blade grinder. We were offered drinks, chose beer. Perril drank bottled water, had on a dark suit, the tie loose, his socks yellow and shoes brown. After small talk, we spoke of G.O.D.

    From his chair in front of us, Perril provided a quick overview of his base knowledge, described what he'd read of G.O.D. on the Tick and elsewhere, the materials he'd gathered and researched. "I've a few questions," he said. When Perril mentioned Ray Kurzweil and Hans Moravec, Ted explained the difference between intrinsic/observer dependant thinking and observer-relative analysis, spoke of Dennett and Hofstadter, Moore's Law and the fundament of elegant consciousness, how computers had the potential to make 200 million billion calculations per second, relying on 800 million billion bits of stored information. "Unlike Searle and Denton," Ted said, "I believe computers can be more than an inorganic tool subordinate to human thought."

"G.O.D. as the future. Nothing artificial," Perril seemed sincere as he said this, lost me completely when he asked, "Then you support the historical exponential view rather than the intuitive linear view of technological progress?"

"Of course," Ted assumed the question was a given. He combed his hair away from his face and said, "We're not just plugging information into a machine, we're creating an advanced form of consciousness, a way of teaching and ultimately reprogramming human action."

"For example?" Perril settled deeper in his chair, wanted specifics.

"Take Pakistan," Ted moved his feet, brought his toes together, described the division between President Zardari's pro-western government and opposition leader Nawaz Sharif, said "G.O.D. can process the dispute and filter through 6,000 years of historical data, review the endgame from hundreds of similar conflicts in dozens of other countries to reach a logical solution. By comparing and contrasting social, economic and political concerns, cultural and national fallout," Ted said, "G.O.D. can provide a rational solution to any conflict."

"Maybe so," Perril loosened his tie further, sipped from his water, put the bottle on the lampstand beside his chair and said again, "Maybe." He appeared to be following a detailed line of thought, a checklist he intended to run through, thorough in his approach, the sort of man who would not have asked us here if he didn't have his game plan already laid out. He raised his shoulders, puffed his chest and said, "Assuming your G.O.D. is up to the task, and can rationally resolve some current rumpus by wading through history, how do you see getting everyone on the same page to support her findings?"

The question was the elephant in the room. As clever as Ted was, he'd avoided solving the puzzle, his intellect filled with faith, his application with blinders, he expected things to simply fall into place once the program was complete. Perril was more pragmatic, had identified the problem and said as much. I finished my beer. The room was well lighted by fixtures built into the ceiling. A wet bar stood on the far side of the suite. Perril got up and walked across the room, his large feet leaving impressions in the soft orange carpet. He found ice, filled a glass and made a drink, repeated his question without turning to face us. "Let's assume your G.O.D. does what you say and is capable of offering enlightenment to the unenlightened, what then? We're talking about political schisms, countries with people disenfranchised and those in charge not interested in rational debate."

Ted answered immediately this time, "There is interest. The market exists, resolution is the desired effect of all conflicts. G.O.D. gives governments a chance to retain power with limited violence."

"Sure, sure," Perril wanted Ted to know he followed the train of thought, "as long as those ruling recognize and adopt a rational approach."

"Exactly," Ted bobbed and tapped his knees.

"And yet, governments with a stranglehold on power don't have to act rationally, do they?" Perril came halfway back across the floor and said, "Listen to me. G.O.D. may be everything you suggest she is, she may be the sweetest apple in the bunch, but it makes no difference if everyone is eating plums and pears. Need exists only as it's created. You may see a market there, but a product must have demand. Governments are made up of people who want one thing: power. There is no altruism. There is no interest in reason or logic. In order to sell G.O.D. you must convince them that you hold the genie bottle, that you can keep their king in the castle." Perril told Ted, "All idealism aside, you can't just compose a list of countries with crises and think you can bring them G.O.D. Business doesn't work that way. You need contacts and connections. If you can't get Sharif on the phone, if you can't convince Zardari to take a meeting, what good is your G.O.D. to anyone? Without contacts, you're making cold calls and slipping your card under closed doors."

Ted understood, but said he couldn't think of that just yet. "I have to finish the program first. If G.O.D. doesn't do what I claim, it won't matter how many contacts I have."

Perril put his drink down on a side table and slapped the palm of his left hand as if striking the padding of a baseball mitt. He danced through his huge shoulders and hips, bent and mimicked fielding a ball from the orange carpet, scooped and pivoted, made a throwing motion toward Ted. "You're right," he kept his arm extended. "You have to focus on the task at hand. That's what you do. Let someone else worry about selling G.O.D. That's why there are pitchers and catchers." He set his feet again and turned his hips, made another throwing motion. This time, Ted reached down, picked up the ball, held it invisible, then flipped it back.

Perril laughed. "Tell you what," he made the catch, rotated his wrist. "You go ahead and do your thing. Give me a G.O.D. that I can sell, and I'll be your Joe Girard, your Billy Mays. Hell, I'll be Paul to your Jesus. I'll pitch G.O.D. for you, from A to Z. Albania to Zimbabwe. I'll make us both money. How's that for a pact?"

———

# 5

THE MOJO CAFÉ is three blocks from my apartment. Outside, the air has warmed little from last night, is too cold to be called crisp. I have my 'Moonlight' notes in my bookbag, head north, tug on my gloves, but for whatever reason don't completely zip my coat. I tell myself: I will zip my coat when I get to the corner. Tell myself: I will go to Mojo's and work on 'Moonlight.' Saturdays are a different dog from the rest of the week, open-ended, I have to concentrate, set goals to get from point to point and back again.

I reach the corner and zip my coat. Thoughts of Darcie fill my head. I think of Saturdays before, think of turning around and getting my truck, resetting my route.

I think of what I should and shouldn't do, think what I might do if I don't go to the Mojo and get some 'Moonlight' done. I repeat a few of the mantras from Marimin, repeat what Kyle said about action and deed. I'm getting better at resistance, I think, better at feeling better, I feel. I've not gone to Darcie's rehearsals or to see her perform in a show for a while, have spent weekends with Ted and other friends, gone to movies and plays, have eaten dinner with Andie and Jay.

Andie is Jay's wife, Adeline Sullivan-Greene, a New School grad, co-owner of Brown Binder Books, a smart stretch of Nordic spice, peppermint pale, her blonde hair thick and straight as Meryl Streep's in 'Manhattan.' Imbued with an acerbic sense of humor, ironic and dry, ambitious and bright, Andie puts Orhan Paumuk and Ian McEwan in the window of her store, sells Jim Harrison signed. No soft sentimentalist, no easy touch, she doesn't suffer fools, rides my ass routinely, talks of Darcie cold, discusses my future, refers to these last ten months as *the year that was*. I like Andie, like that she's with Jay, that she and Jay are good together. Where I hoot and howl at the moon, Jay and Andie are practical, approach love as a prolonged investment, do not rely on emotional threads that are tenuous and not made to last. After six years, Jay's attraction to Andie goes beyond the sweet scent of her skin and cosmic slope of her curves. I'm happy for them, have joked with Jay about his sex life, wonder if such good friends ever actually get it on. Jay assures me all is fine, says "Not everyone dances on stage, little brother." Obviously this is true, as last spring Jay and Andie had their beautiful bouncing, named for dad, my nephew Charlie Greene.

Inside, the Mojo has dark wood tables, cut round, the size of tire wheels. A dozen people or so sit with their laptops, with their lovers, sit in the mid-afternoon out of the cold. I order a turkey sandwich, drink more coffee, go outside twice for a smoke. The afternoon passes. I review my stage directions for 'Moonlight,' read the scene where Andy says to Bel: "How kind you are. I'd be lost without you. I'd flounder without you. I'd fall apart. Well I'm falling apart as it is—but if I didn't have you I'd stand no chance." I think about this, the chance I had and have, about Darcie then and now, about the duji I smoked and snorted and managed since to quit. I reread another line from the play: "I did your neck the other day... You had a spasm and I released it." I think for a time about eviction and release.

Cam calls around 5:00, has just gotten home from the hospital. I ask what his plans are now, what he's had to eat and will eat tonight. We arrange to meet tomorrow. I stay at MoJo's until 7:00, then walk back to my apartment, get my truck and drive downtown. Ted's invited me to a party where the Pups are playing, a late gig, a private affair. A movie with Jeremy Irons has wrapped, the producers want to give the cast and crew a proper send-off. I think I might go, have a few hours to get through first. Alone in my truck, I experience the absence of my old life more acutely. The feeling is common but not what I want. I think how pathetic this is, that what I feel most is what I don't want at all. I consider running over and checking on Cam, wonder if I should stop by Jay's, if now might be a good time to call Kyle and talk. I think maybe I'll go and catch a movie, or a play, think I'll go find Darcie, or have a drink first and then decide. I turn on my engine, turn on my heater which doesn't heat. I consider my physical needs, how I've put off sex to a point where I'm thinking—which is to say feeling—a little company right now wouldn't be a bad thing. I've not been with a woman since Darcie, am convinced to do so would be to concede too much, a surrendering of the ship I don't want to believe is sunk. Still, my celibacy is a desperation. I'm frustrated and impatient, and only figuratively getting fucked.

Ted has a friend he keeps wanting me to meet, a singer, he says. Sarah Winston. He thinks I'll like her, does not suggest more than this, only that making new friends is a good thing, and that it's not healthy the way I isolate myself so much; my solitude carried with me like a tramp's black suitcase. I've passed the places Sarah sings around town but have not gone in before, am typically only a little bit tempted. I check the time again, check where I'm heading, check the heater, which remains predictably unpredictable and refuses to warm. When it kicks over finally, the blast of hot air is too much, the sudden perspiration reminding me of withdrawal, the laying of wet moss on my skin, my body slowly made to cook.

I drive up North Haydenn where I park in back of Warrick's, walk around to the front, then head inside the club. Early still, there's no one on stage, the speakers mounted overhead offer a recorded loop of Coldplay. I sit at the bar, order a burger and beer. The bartender has one of those thick Tom Selleck mustaches that covers his upper lip like a horse brush. I ask about Sarah. The bartender tells me she's not singing tonight, says I should try Sevens. I eat, then drive over. Another bartender, this one taller, in a dark t-shirt, the club name embossed in a fancy font across his chest, says Sarah isn't scheduled tonight there either, sends me to the Mail Room.

The drive puts me back on Haydenn. All my running around is a game now, a way to kill time. If I was thinking, the reasonable thing to do would be to call ahead and see if Sarah's there, but finding her isn't so important, my focus on the moment, on having something to do. A few weeks ago, Andie tried fixing me up with a friend of hers. We were to meet at The Billy Club. I was told to look for a woman with dark hair, about five foot six, a sort of Phoebe Cates back in her 'Bodies, Rest & Motion' days. Andie said the woman—I don't recall her name—knew who I was from tv. Still, when she spotted me at the bar and walked over all eager and anticipative, and said, "Hello, Mick Greene," I answered as Andie had warned me not to. "I'm sorry, but you must have me confused with someone else."

I get to the Mail Room just after 9:00 p.m. The club's crowded, the tables fronting the stage filled, with more people standing back near the bar. On the walls are photographs framed, dozens of past performers hung in rows of two, Steve Earle and Bonnie Raitt, Dave Wilcox and Suzanne Vega, all signed. The ceiling's high, the acoustics with reflectors and diffusers to bounce and spread the sound. The wait staff wear blue shirts and black slacks. A woman on stage is singing 'What'll I Do?'—"When I'm alone/With only dreams/That won't come true/What'll I do?" She is, in a word, large. A colossal, full-figured and then some, her arms round, her hips wide, her body sculpted out of soft foam. She has on a white sweater dress, unbelted, the material fitted loose over her shoulders, her hips and thighs. Her hair is a burnt orange, cut short, slipped back around her ears. She moves like a houseboat at low tide, a weighty yet somehow smooth glide, her tree-stump legs beneath the lights enormous, the whole of her heft impossible to ignore.

I order a beer at the bar. Standing in front of the mike, Sarah sings: "What'll I do with just a photograph/To tell my troubles to?" Her smile is warm, her hands hold the mike stand as she sways gently, like one of those helium inflated blimps lifted above a parade. Her voice is full and rich, sultry like Adele channeling Sade. I sit at the bar while Sarah does two more songs, 'All of Me,' performed as a tease, and Robert Palmer's 'Can We Still Be Friends,' sung as a ballad. When her set's over, she moves from the stage to the first row of tables, sips a bottle of water while people come and talk with her. I wait a minute, then go and introduce myself, let her know that I'm a friend of Ted.

Sarah gives me her hand, her fingers inside of mine feel oddly light. She wears no makeup, has a natural look, a handsome face, high cheeks and round mouth, her eyes green. I compliment her performance and she thanks me for coming. We talk about Ted, establish the connection. Sarah sips more water. The sound of people talking around us, at the tables and bar, forces me to lean slightly in toward Sarah in order to be heard. I tell her how I went to Warrick's first, and then to Sevens and Sarah smiles, not sure what to make of this. I lean back again and the fullness of Sarah's figure becomes whole, her white dress like one of those Christo art works where material is used to cover an entire landscape. I check my watch, make as if I've somewhere to go, start to excuse myself and say, "I don't want to keep you," know Sarah has to get ready for her next set, when she surprises me. Rather than do as most people the first time we meet, and mention a performance of mine, a play or film she may have seen or been told about by Ted, instead of talking about my guest spots on 'NCIS' and 'Desperate Housewives,' she says, "I have a recording of *The Draftman Session*." The reference is to the one full album dad made, the master tape purchased and put out locally by Aldwich Music several years after dad had settled into working at Hurbert & Steine.

Sarah compares dad's playing to Earl Klugh, to Eivind Aarset and Michael Bocian, admits to being a music geek, a collector of musicology, of recordings old and new. She runs down the list of songs on dad's disk. I'm impressed, thank her on dad's behalf, answer obliquely when Sarah asks why dad stopped performing, say "It's a long story." She nods as if understanding, adds as a comfort, "It usually is."

Another couple comes up to talk with Sarah, and here I do say goodnight, turn and head back to my truck.

―――――

Aldwich in winter exchanges its outdoor concerts and festivals for indoor workshops and readings, plays-in-progress, lectures and panels and other creative projects, along with our ongoing productions, stagings and films. At the University, playwrights and composers, actors and directors come to teach, accept residencies for a term. This winter, Theresa Rebeck is workshopping her newest play, while last year Alan Bennett and Martin McDonagh each taught a class on theater. McDonagh was in the audience the night I collapsed at the Galaxy. At six foot four, with a nest of wild gray hair cut like a punk rocker and a face reminiscent of a whipped bowl of putty, McDonagh was also once a junkie. Having witnessed my crash and burn, he sent me a note while I was at Marimin, his message handwritten, its tone similar to the crazy cop, Tupolski, in his play, 'Pillowman.' Candid, if not unkind, McDonagh suggested: "The next time you decide to get stoned on stage, I propose you at least make sure the dose is lethal so your ruining the performance has a less pathetic and more dramatic effect."

The advice, as extended, was taken to heart. I think of this now, the need to get back to work, how there really is no point in doing anything half-assed. I head from the Mail Room and drive south, cut through the theater district, the marquees lit and flashing the names of shows, of actors and directors, each ruby letter glowing like part of some greater constellation. The belts on my engine squeal, the mix of hot and cold, of friction in need of grease. The wind outside blows old snow from rooftops. I have my hat pulled down, my coat zipped inside my truck. I think about Sarah, about initial impressions and what to make of her. A big girl to be sure, she seemed nice enough, had joked, "In the flesh," when I introduced myself, as if expecting me. It was cool that she'd heard of dad, cool how she knew her guitarists, cool the way she sang her own arrangements with a genuine appreciation for each song. I wonder if I should have stayed at the Mail Room, wonder what I'm going to do now, wonder if I left because I already know what I want to do, that maybe I've known since before I hit Warrick's and wound up across town.

    I drive down South Seventh, through the next phase of my Saturday, the hour when temptation and resistance twist together like hanger wire in the neck of the hook. I pull up and park. The Dive Inn sits between the Junere and Asbonne theaters. A one-time hostelry for the steel mill workers, in the years since, actors and musicians have replaced the laborers, come after shows and rehearsals to eat and drink. Before my misadventure at the Galaxy, Darcie and I were regulars at the Dive, though I've only stopped by a few times since. My performance in 'The Birthday Party' has made me something of a prodigal. There's an actors' code, I understand, the theater hallowed ground, above all else you do not fuck with the show. My indiscretion was a violation, my dragging personal shit on stage. I deserve the cold shoulder, do not complain, appreciate friends who remain sympathetic and cut me some slack.

    The front door of the Dive is painted blue. I stomp my boots, clear the snow, come inside and take a quick survey of the room, check to see if Darcie's here. I order a coke instead of whiskey, demonstrate my temperance. The Dive has lighter wood than Mojo's, the tables and booths longer, the floor worn with the grooves of heels. Salts and cabbage, beer and cigarette smoke—still permitted in sections—mix in the air with the voices and music. Although the Dive doesn't hire bands, there's enough talent nightly to leave a guitar, amp and mike in the back room and let whoever's in the mood play a song. This evening, Kodi Burnes is doing Marley's 'No Woman, No Cry,' the guitar dangling from an orange strap.

Aimee and Gwynn are sitting in a booth. They wave at me and I bring my coke. Both are older friends, mentors and materfamilias figures, Aimee teaches film at the University, an authority on the works of Huston and Cassavetes, Claude Mulot and Max Pecas. As an actress, Aimee's known for doing Stoppard and Albee, was once Martha in 'Who's Afraid of Virginia Wolfe?' played the drunken Earth Mother to my impressionable Nick. With thick black hair worn long in hippie braids, she has a sense of self that hasn't changed, a throwback style that remains constant against all trends that come and go around her. Gwynn is the university's associate director of theater, has appeared in the last dozen summer festivals as Shepard's Ella, Pinter's Ruth and LaBute's Carly, in Inge and Miller and Brecht. A few pounds heavier now in her middle-age, with blue eyes and silver hair mixed with yellow tints, Gwynn was my instructor for a year, performed with me in several one-acts and student-directed skits.

During my recent troubles, both Aimee and Gwynn were supportive, sent me jams and chocolates while I was at Marimin, phone often now to see if I'm ok. Aimee slides over and I sit down beside her. Gwynn asks and I tell them what's new, begin with my bouncing from club to club earlier, looking for Sarah. I fill them in about Cam, about our meeting at Parrot Lake, our skating and time at the Bow. Aimee touches my wrist. We talk of their own recent news, of works completed and in progress. I want to ask if they've seen Darcie, but decide against. Aimee asks about 'Moonlight.' Both she and Gwynn have done Pinter before, have read 'Moonlight.' I've always thought if I ever got the play staged that Aimee and Gwynn would be perfect for Maria and Bel. I repeat for them Bel's lines: "The first time Maria and I had lunch together—in a restaurant—I asked her to order for me. She wore gray. A gray dress. I said please order for me, please, I'll have whatever you decide, I'd much prefer that. And she took my hand and squeezed it and smiled and ordered for me."

"It's a great bit," Aimee has a hoarse laugh, like sand shaken inside a leather sack. Gwynn agrees, is eager to encourage me. They ask where things stand now and I exaggerate a bit, mention my ideas for cast and staging. I update them on Dave, how he's still interested and I'm just waiting for him to call me back.

Gwynn looks at Aimee and then at me. "You're still talking with Karuim?"

"Sure."

"About 'Moonlight?'"

"Why not?"

"Well then," Gwynn taps the tabletop. "Good for you, Mick."

"You're a bigger man than I," Aimee says.

---

Before leaving the Dive, I drink several quick shots of whiskey and know I shouldn't be driving. The humming in my ears is heavy, vibrates back against my teeth. Aimee and Gwynn want me to sit tight and offer to drive me home later, but I say I can't leave my truck, insist I'm fine. My heater refuses to click on, my fingers numb against the wheel. In my head, Sarah sings, "What'll I do?" I think of an answer, think I know.

I drive uptown, my head swimming, I remember the story of Vivian Merchant, Pinter's first wife and longtime muse, who drank herself to death shortly after their divorce. Love is this. Pinter's son, Daniel, blamed his father for Merchant's death, changed his last name to Brand, did not speak to his dad again. "There it is," Pinter was quoted as saying many years later. There, for sure. Despite the dark turn Pinter gives love in his plays, he remained unconditionally romantic in his personal life, his second marriage, to Lady Antonia Fraser, lasting over thirty years and was by all accounts a devoted union. Of his work, Pinter said, "A play is drama. I am incapable of writing a happy tale, but remain inspired to achieve a tranquil existence." I repeat this, *a tranquil...* It's a goal, no doubt, but how to pull it off? This I try to imagine.

Dave lives in Wellington Park, the same subdivision as Jay though further up the hill. Jay's house is contemporary modern, the architecture drawn from Le Corbusier and Mies van der Rohe, with large windows and a flat roof. I pass Jay's on my way up the hill, my truck tires skidding a bit on soft snow. Drunk, I still know to release the gas, avoid the brakes, turn into the skid until I regain control. I wait until I feel the road more securely beneath me before testing the gas. The effort is a reflex, I've always been good at driving, yet haven't mastered the same skill outside my truck, have a tendency to overcompensate, pump the brakes and lose control. Just after my release from Marimin, in an effort to soothe my transition, I had the folks at Paramour make me a special V.F.C. clip. The piece was of Darcie and me, our heads mounted on the shoulders of a couple making love. I watched the piece twice, was not nearly as aroused as I hoped, was too familiar with both our bodies to be fooled. The tape only depressed me, I erased the spot from my computer, rely now on the clips I have stored in my head.

Dave's driveway runs to the right of the house, wide in front of his garage. I park and get out, look toward the house, check for lights, think again about what Aimee and Gwynne told me. Only the front porch is lit, the house dark. I ring the bell and the dog barks. No one comes to the door. I walk around the outside, the dog following me from window to window, still barking. A fence keeps me from making it all the way around the house, forces me to turn and go back. I imagine Darcie inside with Dave, imagine them together, Darcie and Dave on the bed, in a fit of jackhammer love. I ring the bell again, make the dog crazy, sit on the front step, in the cold, and wait.

By the time they pull up, I think I might be frostbitten, am not as drunk as I was, my cheeks raw and fingers aching inside my gloves. I've been rehearsing what to say, how I want the scene to go. My plan is to tell Dave I was in the neighborhood, at Jay's, and stopped by to drop off my final notes on the 'Moonlight' script. I'll apologize for the late hour but say I was hoping to see where we go from here. I want to be George Clooney-cool and deliver my lines perfectly. I'll fake surprise at finding Darcie, wait for them to explain, will laugh and dismiss their relationship as no big deal, then ask Dave to write a check.

The dog barks again inside, having heard Dave's car. My legs are stiff, my nose running, my head combustive, I feel my pulse inside my ears, feel my chest beneath my jacket pounding. Dave wears a long overcoat, dark blue, with black muffs and matching scarf. My truck is parked so that he can pull into the right side of the garage if he wants. He stops short instead, gets out and surveys my truck. I move down from the house. Dave sees me now and slows his stride. Darcie comes around the car, her head covered by the knit cap I bought for her last Christmas, green with an orange rim and matching ear flaps. The car lights are on a timer, still lit. I continue across the drive, silent, tell myself to be calm, to keep my shit together, am thinking this while wishing I had just a little bundle to mellow me out, a hit of cheva to keep my heart from exploding.

Darcie watches and I watch her watching, note how beautiful she is and how much I still miss her. I want to grab her and shout "What the fuck?" but this doesn't seem a good idea. All my initial impulses are reckless, a product of my addiction, I try to employ a certain caution, my lapse tonight notwithstanding as I drank six shots of Glenlivet and drove to Dave's. At Marimin, after puking and shaking, I still insisted my addiction was not ground in a physical need, that I didn't crave the dope or require the hooch, but what drove me to the junk was Darcie. My doctors dismissed my theory as hooey, prescribed methadone, naltrexone and UROD to treat my symptoms, insisted I had things bass-ackwards, that my addictive impulses had to exist before I started to obsess about a lover. When I asked why it had to be this way, they said the proof was in the data, that my reaction was obviously chemical, the release of oxytocin and vasopressin exacerbating my condition, leaving me in need of treatment. Their reply did not address my question though, and staring at Darcie as she walks past me now, I wish my doctors were here so I could point and say, "See? See?"

I move my fingers like Riff in 'West Side Story,' hear in my head, "Boy, boy, crazy boy. Get cool, boy." A few feet from Dave, I'm sure that I will hit him, know that I want to and think I should, am convinced he's deceived me in some way. I want to show Darcie that I'm willing to hit Dave, for whatever this will accomplish. The challenge is something harder, I know, is more in the restraint. I manage to stop, put a cigarette in my mouth, fold my arms, think this is a good thing, a sign of control, that I won't go all Rambo. I try to ignore how ridiculous I must look, am disappointed just the same as Darcie walks right past me, pretends I'm not even there and heads to the house. Dave waits a second longer, then moves by me as well. I stay in the drive another minute. The chill is bitter, the pounding in my head a mamba march. I bend over, drop my cigarette. The car lights go out but the dog won't stop howling.

---

# 6

I WAKE SUNDAY, face down, still in my clothes, my neck sore from how I've fallen. My head throbs as if beaten with broomsticks, I roll over and the cat purrs, sits on my chest, wants to be fed. I move again and she jumps away. The light through my window comes uninvited. I blink, rub my eyes, wait until I can focus then look around. The bottle I bought on my way back from Dave's lays empty on the floor. There's a cigarette burn on my sheet, a brown hole I don't remember causing. I put my finger in the hole as if this will somehow remind me. It doesn't. The numbers on my clock are red. I blink twice more, read the time, count the hours lost between my leaving Dave's and waking.

What now? The pain in my head requires attention. I take the heel of my left hand and push hard against my brow, am hoping for relief but there's none to speak of. I squint again, hold my breath, move my legs slowly and kick off my shoes. The cigarette I was smoking when I fell asleep is cold and flat now, burnt down to the filter and crushed beneath me. I look at my jacket to see if there's a hole to match the one in the sheet, pat my chest to check if I've been burned. I think about Darcie, find my cell and hope that she's called, but she hasn't. I think about Dave, remember a passage in Pinter's play, 'Ashes to Ashes,' where the main character, Devlin, says to his wife, Rebecca, on the subject of her alleged infidelities: "When you have a wife you let thought, ideas and reflection take their course. Which means you never let the best man win. Fuck the best man, that's always been my motto. It's the man who ducks his head and moves on through no matter what wind or weather who gets there in the end. A man with guts and application. A man who doesn't give a shit. A man with a rigid sense of duty."

The speech is pure Pinter, a political rant with Devlin standing in for Pinter's view of government, the demand for control and imposing one's will filled with flaws, autocracy breeding insecurity and cruelty. Devlin's dogma is all about strategic survival, a tactic dangerous enough in politics, but when applied to affairs of the heart is as practical as fanning a flame with my dick. That said, I can't help thinking Devlin's right when he howls "Fuck." Fuck Dave, I think. Fuck him and the horse he road in on. I have no legitimate standing, it's true. Darcie's not my wife. I'm not being cheated on as we're technically not together, and still I hate what's happened, hate the way she took up with Dave, hate how I handled myself last night, the whimper when there should have been a bang.

I roll back over, cover my eyes with my right arm, my jacket cool and head heavy. I picture Darcie in Dave's drive, wearing the hat I gave her, wonder if her wearing the hat means something? I tell myself it does, that it shows our connection is still intact, makes me wish I'd said something last night, said "Nice hat," and waited for her reaction. Instead, I stood, arms folded, and watched her walk inside. I left a few minutes later. The strategy deprived me of any chance to reconcile the situation, but allowed me to survive the awkwardness of the moment. I drove to the all-night Rite-Aid on Lexington and bought a fresh fifth of Canada's finest in order to toast my cleverness.

―――――

    I reach for the radio next to the bed, test my head against the volume of other voices. Sports scores come on, a ticker tape of numbers I usually like to hear, but can't now quite decipher. I turn the dial, land on the all-news station where another voice offers world news as a form of entertainment. There's a film I remember by Sidney Gilliat, an old flick called 'The Constant Husband,' in which Rex Harrison wakes from amnesia only to find he's married to several women. Harrison's real-life wife, the actress Kay Kendall, plays one of his cinema-wives, the film another form of entertainment, presents romance as farce, a comedy of errors before true love wills out. In movies this is a given, the promise of happy endings a way to sell tickets, but real life is more of a muddle. Even before last night I knew this, how all of love confounds sometimes. I try for a minute to smooth out the curves, only the energy it takes to construct this deceit drains me, and weak, I lean my head off the edge of the bed until I nearly puke.

    I shut the radio off, lay back and groan before forcing myself to get up and check my other phone for messages. I open my computer, go to my emails where again there's nothing from Darcie. "Fuck it." I press the link for my K2 update, read about the climbers leaving base camp. A quote from Wilco van Rooijen, the leader of the Dutch team, describes the weather as, "Crisp and clear. A perfect day for climbing."

I take a look at the other headlines, see stories about Susan Boyle selling 2.7 million records in three weeks, about Charlie Sheen going after his wife with a knife, about the five Chinese oil workers kidnapped and murdered in the Sudan, and how in Mbabane, Swaziland, the SADC—the Southern African Development Community—refused to recognize the presidency of Madagascar's Andry Rajoelina following the country's latest coup. My head is a fog, I read as best I can, absorb bits and pieces then switch to the Tick. On Sundays, Ted profiles favorite causes, posts today about Potters for Peace and their effort to bring clean water to third world countries. "Overseas," Ted writes, "5,000 children a day die because of unsanitary water. Bacteria, E. coli, falciparum malaria, cryptosporidium, giardia, all are poisons that cause kids to literally shit themselves to death.

"Sick?" Ted writes. "Try this." He describes how 98 percent of the diseases in the water can be filtered away by using a $5 ceramic pot. The pot is composed of clay mixed with sawdust, or ground rice husks which, when fired in the kiln, creates pores so small the pots block off water-borne bacteria while letting clean water pass through. The results are undeniable, yet Potters for Peace can't get regular funding because investors want to figure a way to first make a profit. Nine hundred thousand kids have died in the last six months while governments and adventure capitalists haggle.

At the bottom of the article, Ted posts a sponsorship link, presents his own appeal for donations to Potters, asks his readers to take up the cause. This is Ted, active always, an exploder of windmills, he twists the bull's horns with noodle arms and wrings results out of the blood-dry turnip.

A disciple of Mises, his goal is to apply meaningful behavior to purposeful ends, his actions more than theory even after G.O.D. let him down.

What happened was this: Ted and Perril formalized their partnership. In exchange for a 40 percent interest in G.O.D., Perril paid Ted a lump sum, provided additional investment capital and a list of contacts as promised. Ted finished the program, added more Churchill and Lincoln, Sartre and Muhammad, Stalin and Milosevic, Omar Hassan al-Bashir, Nero and Nietzsche, entered material from Burleigh's 'Blood and Rage: A Cultural History of Terrorism,' Roberts' 'A Kind of Genius: Herb Sturz and Society's Toughest Problems,' Mayer's 'The Dark Side,' Laqueur's 'No End to War,' and Samantha Powers' 'A Problem from Hell: America and the Age of Genocide.' He ran tests using historical paradigms: How could Barbarossa have improved his relations with Italy? What of Charles V's effort to unite Europe? How might the revolution of 1848 in Paris have been more effective? The results were written into reports Perril used for marketing before presenting Ted with a list of potential clients.

They decided on Zimbabwe, flew to Harare where Perril had contacted the new Prime Minister, Morgan Tsvangirai, leader of the Movement for Democratic Change. Tsvangirai had recently won the country's popular election, but Zimbabwe's president, Robert Mugabe, refused to cede power, agreed at most to a shared government. The cooperation proved a fiction, what power Tsvangirai obtained ornamental. Mugabe still controlled the military, the courts and banks, moved methodically against the MFDC, had members arrested, tortured and killed. Robert Bennett, the deputy Agriculture Minister-designate and treasurer of the Movement for Democratic Change, was imprisoned on charges of terrorism, held against the findings of the court, all attempts to gain his release blocked by Justice Minister

Patrick Chinamasa and Attorney General Johannes Tomana, both Mugabe appointees.

Perril sold Tsvangirai on the idea of bringing G.O.D. to Zimbabwe and challenging Mugabe's imprisonment of Bennett. Ted plugged parallel situations into the program. What was the overarching effect of Mandela's imprisonment in South Africa? What of Sinduhije in Burundi? Gandhi and Bhutto? What of Bobby Sands in Ireland and Subandrio in Indonesia? All the data were weighed and recorded against the future interest of Zimbabwe. When G.O.D. found releasing Bennett served the country best, a detailed explanation was presented in a 29-page report. Mugabe said he would review the results, was not amused and mocked the process with the claim, "It is always the most desperate of men who turn to God when all other avenues have failed them."

Perril dismissed Mugabe as a crank, deposited the check Tsvangirai gave them, prepared a press release for all the major outlets, the wire services, blogs and journals, cable stations and online news sources. Ted returned to the States, waited to see what Mugabe would do, was relieved when Bennett was freed on bail, was still celebrating when additional news reached him. Shortly after Bennett's release, Morgan Tsvangirai was driving home with his wife, Susan, his bride of thirty-four years and mother of their six children, when a truck cut across the median and crashed broadside into their car. Susan was killed instantly, the Prime Minister badly hurt. The suspiciousness of the accident caused supporters to point fingers at Mugabe, but all demands for an investigation were rejected. Ted called me, shaken by the news, insisted G.O.D. was to blame. "None of this would have happened if Perril and I hadn't gone to Zimbabwe."

I tried telling him otherwise, reminded him how Mugabe had gone after Tsvangirai before, that there were at least a half dozen other assassination attempts, and assuming

Mugabe was responsible now, G.O.D. played no part. Ted wasn't buying, the timing too linked, his faith shaken, he said, "I should have seen it coming. There's always consequence, Mick. I didn't consider the fallout, was only looking at history and not the aftereffect. Brilliant, right? How could G.O.D. have missed something like that?"

―――――

My cell phone rings just as I'm switching on my coffee maker. The sudden sound causes me to jump, my nerves raw, I answer to find Cam on the other end, wanting to know if I'm coming. Hell. I apologize, say "My bad," check the time again, promise to be there in twenty minutes. The wind outside rattles my window. I go into the bathroom, rinse my face with cold water, brush the bitter taste from my tongue, test my head with a slow tipping forward. My clean clothes are scattered, I find what I have, pull on jeans and a sweater, take the stairs to the lobby, my legs unsteady and stomach worse.

My truck is parked against the curb. There's ice on my windshield despite the sun, I scrape enough away to give myself a porthole. The starter in my truck clicks twice before turning over. My heater teases, offers warmth and then retreats. I think of Cam waiting, think of Darcie and Dave, say "Fuck Dave," and "Fuck," again. The adrenaline rush clears my head, allows me to feel briefly better. I make a fresh list of what I need to do to get 'Moonlight' up and running. The catalog is long and quickly overwhelms me. I try to buoy myself by focusing on a scene from the play. Jake: "It's very important to keep your pecker up." Fred: "How far up?" Jake: "Well… for example… how high is a Chinaman?" The line's absurd, yet covers it all, elbows me to where I need to be going.

I pass Parrot Lake, the surface clear with no one skating. Kings of Leon is on the radio. 'Use Somebody.' My head hurts too much to sing along. When my cell rings this time, I have to dig it out of my bag. I don't recognize Sarah's voice at first, am not expecting her call, am surprised when she asks how I'm doing and if I'm feeling better than last night? I stop at the light on Welton, confused, I repeat the word, "Last?"

"When you called."

"I called?"

"Last night." Sarah laughs, "How drunk were you?"

A good question. The light changes and I proceed slowly, try to focus, my memory a liquid poured into some larger body of water, dispersed and hard to retrieve. I remember sitting in my truck, the engine off and the air turning to crystal. I have my whiskey, hear Sarah singing in my head, my need to talk with someone after finding Darcie, someone new and unfamiliar with my recent string of fuckups, must have led me to track her number down. I apologize for this, admit that I was smashed.

"You were smashed," Sarah says, the reason she's calling to check on me now. She's generous in this way, says I was upset but also funny.

"Still," I apologize again, turn off Welton, into Cam's neighborhood, am embarrassed, think how late it must have been when I phoned. Sarah tells me not to worry, that 2:00 a.m. isn't so late for a singer. "We've all been there," she has a way of saying this that is convincing. I picture myself last night, assess as best I can how I am now. *How are you, Mick?* I remember me this morning as I caught my reflection in the bathroom mirror, saw how shattered I looked, and then a second later, a shift of my shoulders, a determination to regroup, how different I became, or saw myself becoming. Pinter commented on this phenomenon, "When we look into a mirror we think the image that confronts us is accurate. But move a millimeter and the image changes. We are actually looking at a never-ending range of reflections." It's true, this never-ending range reflects who I am and once was, shifts from now to now to now and back again, each new look filled with history and potential.

Sarah has an appointment across town, says "If you're alright then." I answer yes, thank her again for calling, apologize once more for last night, let her know there won't be a repeat performance. "It's no bother," Sarah says I should keep in touch.

I promise, say "Everything's good." I'm icy cool, just like the weather.

———

Cam's waiting outside when I drive up, an hour late. I slide against the curb, unlock the door while he grabs his skates and climbs in beside me. The gloves I gave him are stuffed in his pockets, his knit cap tugged low and cut across his forehead, making his eyes look even larger. I've promised to take him to see his mom, the buses running irregularly on Sunday. Cam points north, asks if I know where I'm going. My sunglasses ride the bridge of my nose, I keep them on, my eyes red and head in need of an icy bucket. It's already after 2:00 p.m. Visiting hours at St. Mercy's today go until 5:00. We make the drive in fifteen minutes, park in the lot, ride up to the sixth floor and follow along a series of identical-looking hallways with alternating green and yellow stripes taped to the center; a color-coded mapping Cam understands and retraces daily.

Kate has a room in the center of the hall. Back when dad was sick, I used to listen as the doctors explained the consequence of his latest infarction, discussed possible procedures and treatments, some new drug or surgery that might be beneficial. Everything was at best educated guesswork, a trial-and-error, prophesies and hunches, like relationships, a throwing against the wall to see what sticks. I remain in the hall as Cam goes in to see his mom first. After a minute, he comes to get me. The curtain across Kate's window is open halfway, the floor cadmium yellow. Two other women share the room, are in beds on the opposite wall, watch as I walk past.

Beneath her sheet, Kate appears doll-sized, is covered up to her chest, her features worn, her arms hidden. Her cheeks are hollow, her lips dry, her skin pale and bones something less than birch sticks, and yet, despite her illness, there's a sense of stamina about her, a strength conveyed, a fortitude in her eyes, the way she stares at me, takes me in, establishes her authority.

I approach the bed, let Cam introduce us. Kate reaches and I touch her fingers which are thin and cool. With his mother now, Cam seems different, becomes a child again, his defenses lowered, he bounces on his toes, asks permission to get a drink of water, comes back and pulls on Kate's blanket. He has her eyes, large and brown, the same bantam nose and way of setting his mouth tight, as if forever keeping secrets.

Kate repeats my name, her voice like wool drawn across a spiny mesh, she forces herself not to whisper, has questions, is uneasy seeing me appear out of nowhere, all scuffed and patched together. A professor of rhetoric, tenured at the university, she looks at me as if I'm an argument about to happen. Her antennas go up, her mother hen protecting, whatever Cam has told her, she requires more information, wants to know my story, asks for details. I answer with an emphasis on the positive, tell her how I used to teach at Carter High, that I'm an actor and list some of my shows, describe the jobs I do for Jay, present myself as best I can and say nothing of my addiction.

Kate has Cam press the button that elevates the head of her bed. She lifts her shoulders, processes what I've said. On the nightstand beside her bed are two books and a laptop computer, some Kleenex and plastic cups now empty. She brings her left arm out, lays it atop the sheet, leans her head forward, asks me to write my name and phone number down on a slip of paper. While I'm doing this, she turns to Cam and says, "I spoke with Laura who checked with Erin. You haven't been staying with the Thompsons. Erin said you told her Laura was staying with you at our house."

"I did, but."

Kate cuts him off. "This is what we discussed, Cameron. You need to let Laura stay with you, or you need to stay at the Thompsons."

Cam in protest, insists he's fine, looks at me, hoping I'll help bail him out. I do what I can, shift the focus and say, "It's my fault. I should have coordinated things better. I think maybe once Cam and I met, things got confused."

Kate isn't buying, stares at me sterner now, asks what I mean, how my suddenly coming to spend time with Cam might in any way undermine his being looked after? For this I have no answer, realize as usual I've put my foot in it. Kate's the professor of rhetoric, while I'm clumsy with debate, am better with a script. She sends Cam off to get her a juice. I stand at the side of the bed, anticipate a further grilling, know I'm sunk when Kate reaches for her laptop, has me spell my last name, says "Is that Greene with three e's?"

Watching Kate open the computer, I think of all the online information there, my history easily accessed, my night at the Galaxy archived forever. I scramble to explain, but the effort isn't worth it, the tangled web and all. I describe what happened, confess my crash and burn, Marimin and the Bow and my current situation. I mention Cam, apologize for taking advantage, say I never meant to get involved and that if she wants me to leave, I wouldn't blame her.

Kate listens, stares at me for several seconds before closing her computer, cancelling the search. She looks toward the door, asks whether Cam knows. "And you're clean now?"

"Ten months."

"Testing?"

"I'm on probation."

"As Cam's mother," Kate says.

"I understand."

"What you've said."

"I don't blame you."

"I'm hardly persuaded."

"Of course."

"You need to do better."

"I'm trying."

"No," she touches her two index fingers together, left and right, making a connection. "I'm talking about your presentation."

"My?"

"Where is your argument? Are you trying to persuade me or just issuing a confession?" She says all facts are neutral, and that the key is in the way we communicate them. "Tell me why I should feel comfortable with you?" She sets her arms back down on the sheet, waits for me to answer.

Startled, I don't know where to begin. Kate wants advocacy, but what can I say? The invitation catches me off guard. I clear my throat, start over, pretend I'm in a play, appealing for endorsement, I improvise as best I can. "There was a time, briefly, before I met Cam, where I made some bad choices. These things are what they are, but that was ten months ago. It's history. It's over. My priorities are reconfigured. My relationship with Cam is important, is new, I know, but we both seem to benefit from it. The way we met, the way it just happened, these are things you can't question. I'm sure your friends are fine, and everyone means well, but Cam's comfortable with me. He doesn't want people he knows watching him while you're sick. There's too much of a reminder. I'm someone new, without context. He talks to me," I say. "We talk. He's a great kid," I tell her. "I understand your concerns, understand the responsibility. Whatever you want me to do, I'll do it."

Kate adjusts the pillows behind her back, returns her computer to the nightstand, looks at me for several more seconds, then says, "I want you to be who you say you are."

Fair enough. "I'm trying to make it hard not to be." This seems the right answer. Kate asks for references, asks for additional details. Cam comes in with juice, shakes the can, inserts the straw and leaves it on the stand by his mother. What sunlight there is falls through the window across the floor. Kate reaches for the pen and paper, writes down the numbers for Laura and Erin, wants me to check in with them, to keep everyone informed of where Cam and I are at all times. I have no problem, put the paper in my pocket. Kate gets out of bed, wants to show Cam she's getting stronger, the new meds working. Her body's a wisp wire. I think of Andy, laid out in 'Moonlight,' saying of death: "There must be a loophole. The only trouble is, I can't find it. If only I could find it I would crawl through it and meet myself coming back." I watch Kate stand, steady herself, picture the arc, the mortality of all things evident in every sight and sound and smell, the daily course that challenges our survival.

Kate has on a white hospital gown, open in the rear, she steps into thin pink slippers, pulls on a silk robe decorated on the back with the faded image of a dragon. Her illness has robbed her of vanity, leaves her not shy about letting us see her exposed. She walks the length of the hall. When we get to the end of the corridor, she touches the wall as if in victory.

Cam cheers. Kate reaches and takes his hand, raises it, looks toward me and sets her fingers tighter.

―――

Outside, birds circle in the cold, fly in and out of the parking structure. Ted calls while Cam and I are walking to my truck. I fill him in on all that's happened since yesterday, let him know about Sarah, Dave and Darcie. Ted listens, says of Darcie, "She haunts you, man. We need to call Bill Murray and get you ghost busted." He's glad I finally met Sarah, however weird my calling her last night. "Sarah's good people," Ted's a fan. Of the rest, he asks if I'm okay. He tells me to forget Dave and Darcie, says "You have to choose your partners better." The advice is self-deprecating, Ted waits for me to mention Perril. I give him a break, ask about his gig last night instead, tell him about Kate and St. Mercy, how Cam and I are off now to do some skating.

Cam walks in front of me, hands in pockets. I want to say something encouraging about Kate, how well she looks or some such thing I figure he needs to hear, but when I do say this, he doesn't answer, has gone suddenly quiet. Perhaps he understands what's happening better than me, the reality as I should know given dad, or maybe he just needs a minute to adjust to leaving his mom behind again. I don't press, turn on the radio once we reach the truck, let Cam search for songs.

We get to the lake at 5:30. Beneath gray clouds, we put on our skates. The ice is thick, the temperature in single digits, Cam moves in a large looping circle as I give chase. After a while I stop, take out a cigarette and smoke. The sun has set and the sky goes dark, the wind in a shoulder high swirl. I pull my hat down low, watch Cam skate in even faster loops. The moon shows him gathering speed, jumping over an imaginary line of barrels, his form already better than mine, the way he extends himself as smooth as string, bends and stretches, sets his back and lowers his center of gravity as he prepares to land. He goes around twice this way, estimates his distance, backpedals after each jump, hockey style, a trick learned from his brother.

I flick my cigarette onto the ice, skate some more, cut across the lake in rounded turns. Cam floats, wide at the perimeter, cuts back, makes mad dashes out in the center. At 6:30, we return to the truck, pull off our skates and step into our shoes. The heat from our skating fogs the windshield. I switch on the defrost which freezes the vapor to the glass, forces me to scrape the ice with my fingernails until the heater takes pity and blasts out warm. I hand Cam my phone, tell him to call Laura and Erin, the way his mom asked. When he's done, I have him call Kate, so everyone knows where we are. We grab a bite to eat at Burger Barn, then head to my apartment where the plan is for me to pack a few things before staying at Cam's tonight. Upstairs, I pack clean clothes, my 'Moonlight' notes and toothbrush. I fill the cat's bowl, check the messages on my machine, am in the bedroom when Cam comes down the hall and says, "Someone's here."

Between my two rockers, Darcie stands wearing the same hat and coat from last night, the orange flaps of her cap folded over her ears. The cat purrs and Darcie picks her up. I come halfway into the room, stop and stare, surprised and yet at the same time, in some weird way half-expecting. I want to do Brando or Bogart, to be Gable in 'Strange Cargo,' but am instead more like Matthew Broderick in 'Election,' more John Cusack in 'Say Anything.' Awkward in my effort, I have no clever line, settle for "Hey," and a benign, "How are you?"

Darcie drops the cat, slips off her hat and coat. I put my backpack by the chair. Cam remains to our left, near the kitchen. He looks at me, and then at Darcie as she sits in one of the rockers. I make introductions. Cam nods as if he understands. Darcie folds her legs beneath her, shifts into a near lotus position. I do not have the same flexibility, when I sit I place my feet flat. My cigarettes are on the coffee table between us. Darcie wiggles her fingers and I hand her the pack. She avoids my fingertips, teases me about last night, says "Where did you go? We were all set to invite you in, but you left."

"Too cold," I tell her. "I couldn't hang around."

Darcie flips the cigarettes back on the table. The cat goes to Cam. I fold my hands, want to ask Darcie what she's doing here, but there's no point, I know she'll tell me only when she's ready. With Darcie there's always a sense of anticipation. She signals for my lighter. Cam comes behind my rocker. The light from my bedroom sends shadows down the hall. The soles of Darcie's boots are hard rubber, the ridges raised like the surface of a tire. She keeps the treads tucked beneath her. I stretch my own legs out. Cam puts the tips of his shoes beneath the rear runners of my chair. I want to howl and talk of love, but having Cam here means I need to show restraint. Still, the urge with Darcie is constant, a reflex, the click-click-click in my head like a charge set to a timer. I lean forward, take a cigarette from my pack, ask about *l'affaire de coeur*, say "How's Dave?"

"He's pissed at you."

"Fuck him."

"I have."

"Shit."

Cam laughs.

"You should have told me," I say.

"Why?"

"Because."

"Because we're friends?"

"That's right."

"Ahh," Darcie looks at Cam, knows how much it troubles me to admit this, reducing what we were to someneutral and neutered state. She takes the line and cues it up. "As your friend, I thought it best not to tell you."

I don't want to argue, know I can't win, say simply, "As a courtesy then."

She considers this, flicks the lighter, moves the flame in a tight circle, goes: "But courtesy went down the drain donkey's years ago and hasn't been seen since." The line is from 'Moonlight.'

Darcie smiles when I correct her. "It's rationality. Rationality went down the drain."

She knows this, of course. I take the lighter, put my unlit cigarette in the ashtray, cross my legs. Darcie looks at Cam. I ask again about Dave, want to know, "How long have you been together? Were you with him while I was at Marimin?"

"No," Darcie pretends to be insulted. "I wouldn't do that. I'm a good girl, I am," she does Elisa Doolittle, winks at Cam.

I shift forward in my chair, say "I'm just trying to establish a chronology. For perspective. Were you with him when you kissed me?"

"When was that?"

"The last time I was at the Mecca."

"You mean when I bit your lip?"

I raise my fingers, touch my mouth. Darcie has me pass her the ashtray. Cam puts down the cat. The apartment feels warm, the air above my head heated. I watch Darcie draw smoke, lean back, the runners on her rocker rising. Cam moves closer to the hall. Darcie lets the chair edge forward slowly. The cat runs into the kitchen. I'm holding on by narrow threads, trying not to leap out of my chair. I picture Dave and Darcie after I left last night, imagine Darcie telling Dave that seeing me convinced her she made a mistake, that I'm where she belongs. The possibility provides just enough false hope that when Darcie brings her legs out, I think she might come sit on my lap.

Instead she points her cigarette toward me and says, "Last night was not a good idea." She's suddenly serious, her humor gone, her tone indicting. I ask if this is what she's come to tell me, and she says, "Yes." She sets her boots down. For her role in 'Killer Joe' she's cut her hair short and jagged, the color a mix of deep orange and brown, the style accenting her cheeks, her eyes and jaw. Her features are in a natural state of contrast, at once beautiful and bullying. She smiles through her teeth, insists "My being with Dave has nothing to do with you."

The claim is confusing. I reply mistakenly, "Of course it does."

Darcie touches the side of her head, tells me to "Listen. You can't be thinking about me. You can't come looking for me at one in the morning."

"I didn't actually come looking," I say, though this is a lie. I glance at Cam, try to decide where to go from here. The thing with Darcie is it's important to be smart, to give ground in order to make ground. I admit, "Last night was stupid. I shouldn't have come by. The thing is, I just heard about you and Dave and wanted to see for myself. It was a reaction is all. Over and done. I wasn't planning until I heard. I mean seriously," I tell her, "you shouldn't read too much into this. If you had told me before…"

"You would have done something else."

"I would have spoken with you then and that would have been the end of it." I need to convince her, want her to think, "The truth is, I'm pretty busy these days. I have some new work, some irons in the fire, beyond the Bow and Jay. I don't have time to stalk you."

Darcie puts her feet back beneath her. I can tell she's skeptical, my driving to Dave's last night working against me.

In order to prove my point, I resort to props, my story crudely constructed, I take out my wallet, remove a card I have tucked away. Cam comes and stands behind me, looks down and reads along. On the front of the card, printed in red ink is Deletron Electronics, the name Edward Coiyle and address below. On the back, in a fancy sort of calligraphy, the slogan: "If you're not wired, you're not plugged in." I hand the card to Darcie who turns it over and reads it twice. "What's this?"

"Backing," I say.
"For what?"
"'Moonlight.'"

Darcie groans. I tell her I'm serious this time, that I have everything figured out and Coiyle's going to help. Ed Coiyle owns Deletron, is an acquaintance, a casual fan, has seen me perform. When I crashed at the Galaxy, he phoned to wish me well. Last week, he called and said I should come see him, that he has a project in mind. That he has no interest in 'Moonlight' is a fact I don't make clear to Darcie. She puts her cigarette out, hands the card to Cam who turns it over, holds it up to the light as if inspecting a counterfeit bill. I realize mentioning Coiyle isn't enough to impress, that Darcie has never been an advocate of my trying to stage 'Moonlight,' and so I say, "Coiyle has other projects in mind. He has a plan." The lie is a tangle. Darcie reaches for her cap. "Good for you then, Mick," she says. "I'm glad you're busy and last night won't happen again."

I feel ridiculous now, even more than before. I want to start over, to call "Cut!" and reshoot everything. Instead, I go for broke, am thinking Darcie wouldn't have come tonight if she didn't want to see me, that she could have just called and complained about my showing up at Dave's, and why drive over after rehearsal, why come at all? I lean forward and say, "Tell me why you're really here."

"Honestly?"

"Yes."

She looks at Cam, then back at me and whispers, "I came to jump your bones but since you have company, we better not."

I don't know what to think until Darcie shakes her head and goes, "Jesus, Mickey, I told you why I'm here. I'm trying to help you. You're screwing up. Your getting drunk and driving to Dave's isn't cool. You want people to forget about the Galaxy, you have to stop reminding them you're crazy."

"Agreed," she has a point. "But you didn't have to come all the way across town to tell me."

"Quit over-thinking," Darcie says. "It doesn't suit you."

Cam's uncomfortable now, watches for my reaction. I rub my hands against my jeans and say, "All right then," do as Darcie tells me, am no longer thinking as I respond, "If we are friends, if you're really concerned and want to help, move back in with me."

"And why would I do that?"

"Because you miss me."

"Terribly."

"That's easily fixed."

"You and Humpty Dumpty," Darcie puts her legs down again, causes her chair to rock. I get up, take the card from Cam, stuff it in my bookbag with my 'Moonlight' notes. The green sweater Darcie's wearing, like the hat, is one I gave her. I wonder why she chose to wear it tonight, though when I ask, Darcie stretches the collar and says, "This wasn't from you, was it?"

Having her here, in the apartment again, after all these months, is hard to reconcile, the sense of belonging confused with the time she's already been gone. I go over to the chair, squat down in front of her, am completely exposed, have no restraint, repeat the only thing I can and say, "Come on now, tell me."

Darcie reaches and touches my cheek. I think for a moment everything's as it should be, the tenderness of her stroke and clear affection, the reason for all and why she's here. But before I can scoot closer and embrace her, she takes her hand and pushes me away, jabs the heel hard against my forehead, a rough communion. When I get up, my legs tremble. Darcie puts on her coat and hat, pets the cat which has leaped into her empty chair. "Break a leg," she says of Coiyle, waves at Cam goodnight.

I wait until she leaves, then go and get my backpack, pull on my jacket while Cam zips his coat. I turn out the light, lock the door and walk downstairs. The air outside blows cold, finds the heat on my forehead where Darcie hit me. I take two fingers and touch the spot gently.

———

# 7

ALL THINGS CONNECT, those six degrees of Kevin Bacon the same for everyone. Pick a stranger on the street and see how long it takes for them to reach you. Conversely, pick someone you think you know, and by degrees see how long before that presumption passes.

I spend the night at Cam's, stay up after he's asleep, the stars outside dimmed by clouds and distance. I turn on the tv, keep the volume low, listen to the latest update on K2. Outside Islamabad, the climbers are ascending, the forecast favorable, there's a chance they'll reach the summit by mid-week. I flip the channels, catch further news: the conflicts in Afghanistan, Iraq and Iran; George Clooney hitting the eight-month mark with his new girlfriend; three security sites attacked in Lahore, Pakistan; high ratings for HBO's 'Hung' and TNT's 'Californication'; armed men in Manila kidnapping a 78-year-old Irish priest; a woman disemboweled by her pet bear while cleaning its cage; a man in Maine, blind since birth, suddenly sees. The world is this and then some.

I phone Sarah after she gets home from singing, hope she doesn't mind. I tell her about Cam, about Kate and Deletron and Darcie. She lets me know about her gig, describes the work she does when not performing, the background vocals and voiceovers for commercials, documentaries and cartoons, foreign films and jingles. We compare notes on odd jobs, hers more lucrative than mine. I ask about her training, discover she was schooled in the classics, Handel and Mozart, Purcell's 'Dido and Aeneas,' Wagner's 'Tristan und Isolde.' In college, Sarah sang Octavian in 'Rosenkavalier,' then found Billie and Ella, Tracey Thorn and Bonnie Raitt, the Supremes, Tina Weymouth, McLachlan and Vaughn. I list my current favorite singers, Dallas Green and Imogen Heap, Beth Orton, David Grey and Alicia Keyes. Sarah tells me about an ex-lover now gone to Europe, conducting 'La Gioconda' on tour. I mention Ted, 'Moonlight' and Pinter. We go back and forth this way, comfortable with our chatter, for a little while we talk of G.O.D.

Monday, early, I drop Cam at school, come back around and head out to West Glenn where Jay has me replacing a sink and toilet. I stop at Turkin Supplies and pick up an American Standard. Back in my truck, I phone Coiyle, who seems glad to hear from me, calls me Mickey G. I mention 'Moonlight,' say I'm willing to discuss any project he has, but that I've an idea of my own. Eddie says, "Of course," though I'm not sure he's listening. He ends our conversation by passing me off to his secretary, has me make an appointment, says he looks forward to our working together and then adds, "I'd almost given up hope."

Most of the houses in West Glenn were built in the 1960s, with stack vent plumbing, copper pipes and four-inch flooring slats. Jay buys properties at foreclosure now, acquires low, the collapse of the market allowing him to stockpile, he hedges his bets against the market turning around. A sound strategy, the problem is his liquidity, his sales still weak, his cash flow reduced to a trickle. With taxes due, he's feeling the pinch, there are several houses he can barely afford to fix, an empty apartment building in East Warren he needs to unload.

I carry the toilet and sink through the garage, go down to the basement and turn off the water. After removing the original toilet, I check the flange, scrape off the old wax bowl ring, set the new bowl in place. I clean the ends of the pipes and connect the new pieces, use Johnny bolts to hold the toilet and make sure the tank is level. Once I align the rubber gasket that seals the tank to the bowl, I reconnect the water supply to the toilet's inlet, apply a silicone caulk around the base of the toilet and cross my fingers nothing leaks. I enjoy the work, ignore for the most part the metaphorical implication of my working with a shitter and how well suited I am for the job.

The new sink is easier to install. I connect the drain, the disposal and faucet, finish around 3:00 p.m. On my way to taking the old sink and toilet to the dump, I pick up Cam. We go to my place, where I shower and change into fresh clothes, then make us both tuna sandwiches. Cam has his skates, wants to see his mom and come with me to the Bow. I drive him to the hospital, have time to get him there and back if we hurry, but tell him the Bow's not going to happen, that he has school tomorrow and he can't stay out all night. Cam accepts my decision. I'm relieved, am trying to demonstrate responsibility, am out of practice, out of touch, out on Welton

Avenue, driving to St. Mercy's with the moon rising through the window in the back of my truck, trying hard not to think of last night, or the night before, or anything at all.

———

Sarah calls later, while I'm at the Bow, feeding the sharks. I'm glad to hear from her, glad to talk. She asks about Cam, about 'Moonlight,' about my day. We decide to meet for coffee Tuesday, before my shift at the Bow. "Bring Cam," she says, and gives me her address. I spend Tuesday afternoon painting a tri-level on the south side of Aldwich, pick Cam up after school. He sits beside me in my truck, works the heater and radio, the gloves I gave him in his lap. We're old pals now, comfortable together, settled into our routine, we visit Kate, then drive to Sarah's along the north side of town. Her apartment is on the first floor, a warehouse converted into condominiums, eight flats built large, Sarah got in early and put down cash.

I park in the lot around back, find Sarah's door and ring the bell. She is as I remember, a big girl, a broad boat built with a fleshy bow, her skin a deep rose-pale smooth, her face reminding me of a heavy Julianne Moore, her features rounded as if sculpted with tender thumbs in clay. She's wearing a tan top, untucked, the hem falling down over black pants. Her feet are bare, wide as roofing planks, the nails painted blue, a toe ring on each foot. I introduce Cam to Sarah as she lets us in, have told him that Sarah's a new friend, a singer and sweet lady, have also mentioned that she's queen-sized, so he won't be startled.

Inside, the floors are hardwood, bamboo, the space laid out as a loft, the walls a Madison brick, the furniture built to form; an enormous couch and chairs with outsized cushions and sturdy legs, the bed and bookshelves further back, a Camilla maple table near the kitchen to the right, a baby grand piano up front. Wafer cookies have been set out for us. "Low fat," Sarah shows high Botticelli cheeks when she smiles. Coffee is heating in the pot. The stereo plays a sort of pop-laced jazz, a Charlie Haden bass beat against something Elvis Costello might sing. We sit at the table, Cam with the cookies. Sarah asks about his skating, about Kate and brother Bob, all as I have told her. She has a way of putting everyone at ease, is genuine and so clearly comfortable in her skin that I can't find any affectations, staged mannerisms, social spasms or tics. Her large hands are folded around her coffee cup, the cup held lightly, as if a small bird was cradled within. I list for Cam the bands Sarah's worked with, the tv and radio spots she's voiced, how she did the Mermaid Mustard jingle, the Brentwood Builders tune, and Carnival Cruise Line ad. "Come sail away, on a holiday, with Carnival."

"That's you?" Cam's impressed, says, "Really?"

Sarah laughs. I sip my coffee. Cam licks the white filling from the center of his snack. We spend half an hour just like this, casual, moving from one subject to the next. Cam is comfortable, it's good to see him this way, his mind on things other than Kate. I experience a similar relief, a chance to lose myself. Sunday night, when I told Sarah about Darcie, described her coming by my apartment and how there were things I didn't understand, hoping she could explain to me, she admitted to not knowing Darcie at all, but that from experience, "There are people who, if you let them, will drive across town just to tell you they can't stay."

The music on the stereo clicks off and the apartment goes quiet. Sarah moves from the table, walks to the refrigerator and refills Cam's glass of juice. I notice her steps are light, nearly a glide, her zeppelin size no obstacle. I go to the stereo, look through the cds collected. On a separate shelf are a dozen discs of Sarah recorded during some of her live shows. I put on one with Sarah singing 'Nothing Compares to You.' Her voice is rich, both warm and fluid, seductive and commanding. I listen while Sarah comes over with Cam, stands beside me. I don't think of anything else until I realize this, how I'm not thinking about anything but the music. The arches of Sarah's feet are strong. When the song ends, everything is silent for a second and then the next tune starts.

———

I drop Cam at the lake, make him promise to call me in an hour, as soon as he gets home, then head to the Bow. The temperature tonight is too cold for snow, though there's a front coming, the weather changing. I walk the grounds, visit the fish, do some skating and jumping at the rink. The wind outside rattles the chains on the Corkscrew, pulls at the tarp covering the entrance to the Pirate's Cove. I put a Pop Tart on my heater, stand at the window inside my booth and stare at the wind. There's a scene I remember in 'Moonlight' where Andy and Bel are talking about his condition, and when Andy says, "I'm dying. Am I dying?" Bel answers dryly, knows him all too well. "If you were dying you'd be dead."

I shuffle my feet on the dirt floor, wait to acquire traction, consider calling Darcie then change my mind. The screen on my phone provides just enough light for me to read the Tick. I click over, find what Ted's posted on Jackie Selebi, the ex-chief of police in South Africa, who is being tried on 13 counts of corruption. "Imagine that," since Zimbabwe, Ted's writing has acquired an even more excoriating edge. All his dealings with Perril have stopped, the collapse of their partnership complete, the Tsvangirai *accident* proof that G.O.D. is flawed, Ted beats himself up, repeats over and over, "The end result is never the end result."

Perril is unsympathetic. "Caveat emptor," he barks.

Beware for sure. Last year Ted went online, posted essays on The Harry Tic, wrote editorials and commentaries on other blogs, visited chat rooms, discussed the danger of applying G.O.D.'s objective analysis in a subjective world. "Mea culpa," Ted apologized, rewrote his program, projected all possibilities forward, the consequence after consequence: what happened once the CIA assassinated Allende; after Charles I ignored the Magna Carta; Churchill promising blood, sweat and tears; Gandhi pushing peaceful resistance against the Brits in Kalarun; the damage done when Josephine broke Napoleon's heart.

Teed off, Perril took Ted aside, explained the principles of sales, how all products require momentum, the word-of-mouth validating the initial thrust. "We got Bennett out of jail, didn't we? We did more than promised. We are a for-profit institution, the purpose of our partnership is to make money. We are not a church. Perpetuate your ideologies on your own time. G.O.D. is here to be sold, like widgets and washing machines. It's not our responsibility to predict what will happen after we deliver the goods."

Ted disagreed, took legal action to dissolve the partnership. The court granted him exclusive rights to the name 'Government Objectivity Design,' but stopped short of precluding Perril from using the program. Perril hired a geek, came up with G.A.W.D.—Great Answers Wisely Delivered— a dog and pony show, a hollowed out version of what Ted created. Perril now pitches his program to all his political contacts, sells the *results* from G.A.W.D. to the highest bidder, provides rebel groups and political powers with whatever outcome they want, facilitates each faction's propaganda as long as they pay what is charged. "G.A.W.D. IS GOOD" Perril made bumper stickers and streamers for online websites.

I sit in my booth, huddled as close as I can to my

heater, the coils orange, give off only so much warmth. I think of Darcie again, in my apartment, think of Darcie with Dave and how crazy it is, their being together like fish eggs and frosting, it makes no sense. I try to dismiss what has happened, but the reality remains. In therapy, whenever I twist a particular truth, Kyle quotes his mentor, Albert Ellis: "All people are born with a talent for crooked thinking." Maybe so. Deception is instinctual, a camouflage provided, a source of survival, the way we fool ourselves in order to keep our heads above water. I wonder if this is what Ted is doing with G.O.D., if all his work to reconfigure the program is just a diversion, a way of fooling himself into believing he can still make things right. I scroll down on the Tick, read the second piece Ted's posted, a report on Kian Tajbakhsh, an Iranian-American scholar arrested in Iran on charges of plotting against the State. Ted writes: "Come on now, Ayatollah, since when is advocating democracy a plot?" I picture Tajbakhsh in his cell, consider the consequence of his act, and how maybe this is all we have. Maybe only consequence is real, the risks we take, the need to leap and see where we land.

I make the sound of a long whistle, a solid mass going over a cliff, then check the time, go outside my booth and stand in the chill of the wind. The chains and chimes through the hollow spaces make noises in the dark. The snow at the Bow is frozen hard, all white with ruts and slippery patches. I test my feet again, move them north and south, think of how I used to believe if I moved fast enough I could create distance, but I realize now that's crazy, that all I'm really creating is friction.

I think of Darcie once more, and of dad, how each is sustained through memory, though the process of transforming what *was* into history and dropping it into some permanent past is not as simple as I expected. I think of all things before, what clings regardless, consider the momentum needed to pull the weight of what *was* forward; Ted with Tsvangirai, me with Darcie, with the Galaxy, with the parts I lost by performing poorly, and with dad what I miss most acutely. The impressions made are like dog bites, the incisors sunk into fatty flesh, I can cover the mark with a medicated gel and hide it beneath a bandage, but the effect remains, on the surface and below, while I still flinch at the sound of distant barking.

---

Wednesday Cam calls while I'm in West Glenn, grouting and re-caulking the tub. Excited, he tells me Kate is getting discharged tomorrow, asks if I can take him to St. Mercy's and pick her up? I say sure, though when he asks next about the Bow, whether I'm working tonight and can he come with me, I tell him no, that he has school. "But I don't," he says. "We're getting mom, remember?"

I finish work, head back to my apartment where my dirty laundry sits in scattered piles. I gather everything up and take it down to the machine in the basement, load my clothes, add the soap, shut the lid and begin pushing buttons. Back upstairs, I feed the cat, go into the bedroom and get my guitar. My fingers are calloused but not in the way the instrument requires. I strum stiffly, play a bit of Radiohead and Death Cab for Cutie, then find my phone and call Kyle at his office. I get his machine, tell him about Cam and Kate and how I'd like to reschedule our Thursday session if possible. I end my message with a second request, want him to do me a favor.

In the basement again, I shift my load of laundry from the washer to the dryer. Just before 7:30, I retrieve everything, toss the clothes on my bed, then drive to Cam's. The forecast is for snow, I can feel it. While I drive, I think of the scene in 'Moonlight' where Andy says: "I bumped into Maria the other day, the day before I was stricken. She invited me back to her flat for a slice of plumduff. I said to her, if you have thighs prepare to bare them now." The scene makes me think of the last time I had sex with Darcie, the last time my cock stood and pointed me toward her muff plum dampening. I expand the image, retrieve Darcie in an erotic collage, create from memory a montage of moments, a highlight reel, Sports Center-worthy, those top ten plays which show us in perfect form.

Cam climbs into my truck, sets his skates on the floor between his feet. I say, "Hey," ask how he's doing and if he's hungry. We stop at Burger Barn before the Bow, order our food inside. Through the window, in the headlights of passing cars, a light snow falls. I watch the flakes shine. My cell rings and I talk with Sarah, then give the phone to Cam. Ten minutes later, we pull up at the Bow. Terence is at the curb as always, says "Fucking cold, man," has me sign his card.

Cam and I stand outside in the lot and wait for Sarah. We talk about Kate, our schedule for tomorrow. Cam has his knit cap pulled down, his face softly sketched, his eyes eager, his expression set against all doubt. He believes Kate's release means the moon and sun are once more in their proper orbit and there's no further need to worry. I'm beyond believing in anything unconditionally, but I hold out hope, say "She wouldn't be coming home if she wasn't 100 percent better."

Sarah arrives, her blue Jeep Commander almost as big as my truck, she gets out of the front seat like one of those cartoon characters, her body crammed through the narrow space, unfolding, popping out legs first, then arms and hips and shoulders. Her boots are black galoshes unbuckled, her ski jacket white, the hat on her head orange.

Cam goes over to Sarah, his skates held upside down by the blades, one in each hand. She says something to him about Kate, as he told her on the phone, then laughs and rubs his shoulder. I hang back, I don't know why, wait for Sarah to come toward me.

We take the path past the Corkscrew and Pirate's Cove, the fresh snow still falling, covers the ground, hides the ice. Cam runs to my booth, turns on the heater, sets the coils to high. When Sarah and I get there, we squeeze inside, try to find a way to make room, but the space is too tight. Sarah in the middle pins Cam against the wall, the blades on our skates a danger. I feel for the door and we tumble out again, head to the aquarium.

This time, as we walk, Cam circles behind, sets his stride inside my boot prints there in the snow. Sarah has on red mittens. I have my hands in my pockets, my skates tied and over my right shoulder. About the park, Sarah says, "Everything in winter looks different."

"It's bare bones."

"It's beautiful," she holds out her mitten and catches snowflakes falling.

The aquarium is three hundred yards north of my booth. I unlock the front door and the warm air hits us instantly. We remove our coats, leave them by the entrance, make our way down the first hall where the large fish are watching. The hallways are rounded like the hollow of a cave, produce perfect acoustics. Sarah sings 'Sweet Jane': "Anyone who's ever had a heart/Wouldn't turn around and break it./ And anyone who's ever played a part/Wouldn't turn around and hate it." Her voice is Joss Stone, is Adele, is what Megan Rochell wishes she could be, is full and soulful, wraps around the walls, floats overhead and fills the tanks.

Cam wants to feed the sharks. I go to the freezer and get the beef heart, let Cam climb the ladder and toss the chunks. The bull sharks come around all fin and muscle. Sarah moves near the front of the tank, while Cam slides down and stands beside her. More fish swim past. We watch for a while, move through the rest of the halls, check out the pacus, the barbs and groupers, the pike, stingrays and loaches. Sarah places her face against the glass and Cam does the same, waits for fish to draw near.

Back up front, we put on our jackets. Sarah tugs her cap over her ears, helps Cam find the glove that has fallen from his pocket. I watch them together, am a half stride behind as we leave the aquarium and walk to the rink. Sarah's black galoshes kick at the snow. She says something about the stingrays moving through the water like a magic carpet, and Cam lifts his arms and laughs. Inside the rink, he pulls off his shoes, laces up his skates and glides onto the ice. I go with Sarah to the bleachers, say "We can sit here and watch," but she wants me to skate. Cam circles around and asks if he can jump. Once I get on the ice, I do a lap then come back and tug three benches from the side, set them in place for Cam who makes the first leap, has me move the benches further apart. I take my own warm-up jump, my blades in a wobble though I manage not to fall.

Sarah cheers as Cam jumps again, clears eighteen feet while I crash this time, do a clown's hunched coast around the side, my hands on my back and my head hanging. Sarah goes "Ooh, ooh, ooh," makes sure I'm all right, then laughs. I come off the ice, pretend to be annoyed, say "If you think you can do better." I walk on my blades, go up the rubber mats set out on the floor to the storage cage where skates are rented. Sarah waits while I unlock the gate, find a large pair of hockey skates and bring them back down. She doesn't hesitate, kicks off her galoshes and stuffs her feet inside. Cam helps her tie the laces before we pull her onto the ice.

Sarah holds my sleeve and Cam's shoulder, her weight

testing the blades beneath. Her size is incongruous with the activity, and still she exhibits an unexpected grace, the same as when I saw her walk barefoot across her apartment and appear to be dancing. She bends her knees, sets her center of gravity, releases Cam and then me, moves off on her own, confident, her arms extended. When she slips, her legs go out in front of her, her back straight and arms still reaching. Despite her heft, there's a moment when she seems to float above the ice before falling. She laughs again, louder now, the sound bouncing off the bleachers as Cam and I come to help her up. The effort requires leverage. I lock my blades, roll my back, lean in close as Sarah rises.

---

Outside the rink, the snow is heavy now, not a blizzard but pretty near. Because the aquarium and rink are open during the day, I'm expected to shovel and salt the walks. The amount of snow falling will require me to work in shifts, removing layers at a time rather than in one complete turn. Sarah offers to help, but I tell her not to worry. She stays until 1:30 a.m., says she can drive Cam home and wait with him until I get there, but he wants to hang with me. We walk Sarah to her car, brush off the snow, say our goodnights as Sarah wishes us well with Kate in the morning. Back in my booth, we warm ourselves by the heater, eat a Pop Tart before manning the shovels and clearing the first several inches of snow from the paths.

Welton Avenue is one of the first streets plowed by the time we leave the Bow. I park at the curb in front of Cam's, set the alarm on my phone for 10:00 a.m., our plan to pick up Kate by 11:00. Bone tired, Cam goes upstairs. I lie on the couch beneath the borrowed blanket, doze for a few hours, wake with the first light through the window, roll once and try drifting off again, but my head's out in front, is already awake and waiting for me to howl.

I go into the kitchen for a glass of juice. Everything is clean, the sink and countertop, a half dozen bowls, glasses and plates washed and put in the rubber rack. I imagine Laura or Erin having come by to help, then decide the effort was probably Cam, his need to make things feel orderly and right. I find grapefruit juice in the fridge, the expiration date safe enough to sample. The house is comfortably warm, the snow outside having covered everything, the lawns and trees buried under, the rooftops and walkways similarly so. I sit at the kitchen table, the light overhead on low, a ceramic bowl in the center, the fruit gone soft, the bananas and pears brown. I dump the fruit in the trash, come back and sit again, flip through the newspapers and magazines Cam has brought in each day with the mail.

On the front page of yesterday's paper, above an article on the closing of Mustansiriya University in Iraq, and the murder of Natalya Estemirova in Russia, there's a piece on Rod Blagojevich, the hirsute ex-governor of Illinois who, while out on bail for charges of bribery, corruption, and abuse of power, has asked the court to let him appear on Donald Trump's 'The Celebrity Apprentice.' Seriously. You can't make this shit up. The whole fucking universe has gone troppo. I turn the page, find an update on the K2 climbers, read about their troubles; a Serb named Dren Mandic falling to his death from the Bottleneck; Jehan Baig, a Pakistani porter, also thrown from the mountain while attempting to recover Mandic's body.

Christ! From bad to worse, there's concern now that a large sheet of ice has come loose, snapping ropes and sweeping more climbers from the mountain. Reading, I can't believe, yet feel somehow that in following the climb, I've been waiting for exactly this to happen. I take my phone from my pocket, get the internet and search for updates online, find all the worst confirmed, a large ledge of ice has in fact broken free, knocking eleven climbers from the Bottleneck. The eleven dead, added to the others, is the most ever on K2 during a single ascent. The surviving climbers, stranded overnight in temperatures 40 degrees below zero, suffered irreversible frostbite, fingers and toes that will not recover, the oxygen tanks lost, the wind and snow creating a whiteout. "No one saw it coming," Wilco van Rooijen said after his rescue. "Everybody was fighting for himself and I still do not understand why everyone was leaving each other. People didn't know where to go, so a lot of people were lost on the wrong side of the mountain."

*The wrong side...* There it is. Everyone's instinct is for survival, but how we go about achieving this is not always reliable. If self-preservation is the key, why climb at all? Why engage the risk? I think about this, consider the things I do first to feel and then to stay alive, how all my wants and needs are at times confused, my performing on stage and falling in love. I think of my parents, of Pinter with Merchant, and me with Darcie. I think of holding on and letting go, of hope attained and hope abandoned, think of Cam upstairs waiting for us to get his mother.

I close the paper, fold it back, finish my juice and begin sorting through the mail Cam has tossed on the table. I organize what's there, put the bills in one pile, the get-well cards in a separate stack, the flyers and junk mail on the floor, the letters and packages moved to a separate corner. There's a note from the University, one from the Rhetorical Society of London, and another from the Department of Defense. I hold this last letter in my hands, consider all the possibilities of what it might be, from the perfunctory to something else, and wonder if I should open it. The seal appears pressed, like the pleat in a pair of military pants. I tear off the end, slide out the single sheet of paper, read the contents, which are delivered officiously and with dry detachment.

What details there are remain sketchy, the how and when and where ignored. I think of Pinter accusing the government of institutionalized disingenuousness, a manipulative form of communication, words twisted, language applied as distortion, what Kate and Cam need to know conveniently absent, the rationale for Bob's injuries shrouded in worn phrases parroting the defense of home and country. I check the time, barely 8:30 a.m., I'm not sure what hours the army keeps, but suspect someone will be there. I dial the number at the top of the letter, tell the woman who answers that I'm Lance Corporal Robert Mayhre's father. My claim requires proof, the woman asks for my full name and social security number. I pretend our connection's crashing and hang up.

The second time I call, a man picks up and I decide to play it straight. "Here's the thing," I explain about the letter, how Corporal Mayhre's mom is in the hospital and I'm watching her youngest son. "All I'm trying to do is find out where Bob is and how he's doing, so I can tell Kate something." The man on the phone asks for the ID number on the letter, has me hold on. The line goes quiet for a few minutes before he comes back and gives me another number to call.

---

I lie on the couch, try to sleep again, but can't. Every time I close my eyes, I see the climbers falling, see Bob in an equally adverse plummet. Ten minutes later, I find my boots and jacket, my gloves and hat, go outside and shovel Cam's walk and drive. Cam is up and dressing when I come in. I make coffee, check for eggs, settle for cereal and toast. After we eat, we head to St. Mercy's. I've put the letter in my backpack, say nothing to Cam. Kate is waiting for us in her room, her bag packed, her slippers replaced by brown boots with a soft felt lining. She's wearing dark slacks and a wool sweater that no longer seems to fit, the sleeves and shoulders dangling. A nurse comes in, pigeon-shaped, large chest and short legs, her gray hair combed flat as feathers. When I ask if there's anything I should know, I'm told, "It's all written out for you, sugar."

    The nurse wheels Kate downstairs. Cam stays inside with his mom while I get the truck, realize as I pull around to the pick-up area that I should have borrowed a car from Jay, my heater worthless as always, the front seat cold and cramped. I leave the truck running, wipe the seat as best I can and pray the heater will kick on eventually. Kate sits in the middle, is wearing a long blue coat now, her ears wrapped in a scarf, she thanks me for the ride, doesn't mention the truck, her shoulders set away from me, leaning toward Cam, her face pale, her fingers curled inside brown gloves. Cam is attentive, asks Kate twice if she's ok. The CML Kate has causes her white blood cells to get all crazy high, the body unable to fight infections. The new meds they have her on are working better than the Gleevec, she assures Cam of this, pledges to be back teaching by summer.

    I park in the drive, bring Kate's bag into the house while Cam stays with her up the walk. Someone has come and gone, left groceries on the kitchen table. The mail remains in the piles I made, absent the one letter. Cam takes Kate's coat. I put water on for tea. The window in the front room allows the house to fill with sunlight. There's an expectation of warmth but the day is frigid, the bright light all for show. Kate sits and Cam brings her an afghan. I wait for the water to boil, am thinking about Bob, about what I have to say and when I should say it. I decide now is not the time, that to say anything at this point would just be cruel.

I stick around long enough to make sure Kate's all right, check to see if there's anything else she needs, give her my cell number again, which Cam also has, promise to stop back later then head out to my truck.

---

Kyle calls as I'm driving across town. He got my message, lets me reschedule, doesn't ask for further explanation, makes no mention of Cam or Kate. I wait to see if he'll bring up the rest, think he may have forgotten, or is purposely ignoring the favor I asked. Unsure, I remind him. "About the Bow," I say, hoping he'll contact the court, act as my advocate and promote the idea of terminating my probation. "I'm ready to move on. Nearly 10 months is time enough for anyone. I'm clean," I insist my sentence has served its purpose. "I'm repentant, truly." I explain about Deletron, mention 'Moonlight,' and other work I'm certain I can get if I had my nights free again. "I'm looking for a little faith and time off for good behavior. Keeping me tethered to the post is killing me, man."

Kyle waits until I finish, says "And yet," then pauses in that way he has, not quite Pinter, less artistic, he breathes in, exhales slowly, not a sigh exactly. "Let me think," he suggests we talk next week.

Jay has me pulling carpet in South Aldwich, unveiling perfect strips of ash the original builder covered. I get across town before 1:00 p.m., the furnace turned just high enough to keep the pipes from freezing, I work with my gloves and jacket on, crawl around on my hands and knees, tug at the carpet and mat beneath. Clearing the floor means yanking out thousands of metal staples and nails with a screwdriver and pliers. The staples are thick and sharp, stab at my fingers, I start along the east side of the room and work my way toward the center, use a box cutter razor to slice the carpet into manageable bits. The mat below is a green silicone foam that disintegrates as I tear it away. I spend the afternoon on the floor, get maybe a third of the carpet, mat and staples up, roll the pieces I've pulled free and carry them into the garage.

Back in my truck, the dust from my gloves sticks to the wheel. I'm thinking about Bob again, call Ted and tell him about the letter, ask if I did the right thing, if maybe I shouldn't have messed with the mail, and whether I should tell Kate tonight. Ted says, "It's tough to know," but thinks in the end what I did was cool, that Cam and Kate deserve at least today to chill out, and with Bob not even back in the States, "What can they do? Tell them tomorrow." He has me spell Mayhre, says he'll make some calls of his own, talk with people he knows and see if he can find out more specifically what happened. I call Sarah next, catch her before she leaves to sing at Warrick's. When she answers, I say "Hey," no more than this, and still she hears something in my voice, is tuned into me now, enough to ask, "Mick, what's wrong?"

---

Home again, I make a tuna sandwich and fill my thermos. I'm tired as hell from too little sleep, but know if I try to nap I won't wake in time to get to Cam's and then the Bow. I look for the cat, assume she's hiding, as she does sometimes, a want not to be disturbed. I think maybe she's lonely. I've thought about getting her another cat, a tom to keep her company, but I haven't gotten around to it yet. One cat seems enough for me, and still, a second cat might make the first cat happy. All of this is conjecture. I don't know what to think really. Although I'm fond of the cat, she reminds me too much of Darcie. Having her here makes it so I can't forget, my memory engaged constantly, I wonder if maybe a second cat would also work for me, that if I get a second I won't think so much about the first, and how this would also be a good thing.

There's a scene in 'Moonlight' where Ralph and Andy talk of memory. Ralph: "Tell me. I often think of the past. Do you?" Andy: "The past? What past? I don't remember any past. What kind of past did you have in mind?" What I have in mind is not quite the past I'd like to remember, but then it's the only past I have and what can I do? I figure, as an incentive, if I focus more on the present and do a better job with myself, then in the future, when the now becomes history, I'll have cooler things to recall. This, too, in theory, seems worth a shot.

I put my cigarettes in my backpack, slide my 'Moonlight' notes and copy of the play in beside Michael Billington's biography on Pinter, and Kate's letter. Tomorrow, when I meet with Coiyle, I intend to ask again for help with the play. I rattle off a fresh list of who else I might still call, who hasn't said no already, wonder in my desperation if asking Perril would be too weird? I decide it would, then think about Feldman. Back when I was doing dope, Feldman got me duji, got me hash and coke. Feldman made serious money, was smart enough to invest his cash, bought a Coney on Forrest Street, and a share in a string of laundromats, but none of these deals excited him. "Movies, Mick," he used to say we should make one. I consider the partnership, consider the cash I need, tell myself money's money, that the arts have a long history of being propped up by shady jack, and what's the worst that can happen if Feldman and I make a deal?

I check the time, want to get to Cam's before my shift at the Bow. Three cars are parked in front of his house when I pull up. Friends of Kate have brought dinner, sit in the front room talking. Kate's hair is combed back, recently washed, she's wearing a different shirt and sweater, a few light strokes of makeup. I'm introduced to the others, say hello, chat politely while Cam grabs his skates. By 7:15 we're out on the lake. The ice is covered with a heavy powder we push through, the cold chasing after us as we cut wide circles, work our way in tighter loops toward the center. Cam's skating is more playful than usual, his happiness at having Kate home. We return to the house around 8:30, find Kate sitting in her chair, beneath the floor lamp, a William Keith book in her lap. The other women are gone, the rest of the house dark. Cam leaves his skates by the door, goes over and touches Kate on the shoulder, sets his hands softly, a need to feel her there.

---

Twenty minutes later I'm walking the grounds at the Bow. I visit the fish, shovel more snow, then spend time in my booth, sit with my legs stretched toward my heater, trying to get warm. The wind picks up. I read a chapter in the Billington biography on Pinter, am at the part where, in 1970, Pinter was looking for theater work that didn't involve his own plays, and decided to direct a stage version of Joyce's 'Exiles.' The production was a huge success. 'Exiles' is Joyce's polemic on the nature of freedom and the conflict between philosophical ideologies, human emotion and moral convention. The main character, Rowan, returns to his hometown with his common-law wife and baby, intent on living a totally free and untraditional life. Convinced a couple can maintain a relationship while allowing for open affairs, Rowan encourages his wife, Bertha, to consummate an act of adultery when she's propositioned by an old friend.

The idea unravels quickly however, as Rowan's unable to transform his intellectual ethics to real life, his advocacy ignoring the core of his own love for Bertha. He finds the affair he fostered "a deep wound of doubt which can never be healed."

No shit, Sherlock. What did he expect? Love and freedom are a tricky tightrope act. I put the book down just after midnight, walk to the gate and wait for Sarah as we arranged before on the phone. When I see the lights from her Jeep, I crush my cigarette. Sarah's face through the windshield is lit by the moon. She rolls her window down, holds out an enormous pair of white skates, the sight of which make me laugh. I grab my own skates from the truck, walk with Sarah back through the park and toward the rink. The blades on Sarah's skates are MK double star, she carries them with gloved hands beneath the edge. The wind cuts through the metal frames of the rides we pass. I turn up my collar while Sarah asks more about Kate, more about Bob, touches my arm. "The way things happen," she says.

It's true. We sit on the bench inside the rink and put on our skates. Sarah's largeness fills the space in front of me, her size reminding me of Camryn Manheim, not quite as tall maybe and slightly wider. Inside her white ski coat her body's round. She has on slacks, changed into after performing. Her feet stuffed down into the skates, she ties her own laces, pulls off her hat, shakes her head, her ginger hair bounces.

We hit the ice together. Sarah extends her hands, creates balance. I come around in front of her and skate backwards. The air inside the rink is crisp, the light from the bleachers settling soft on the ice. Sarah moves with knees bent slightly, skates away, comes back and steadies herself against my arm. I shift my blades back and forth, no longer searching for traction but willing to glide. We stay on the ice a little while longer, then go back to my booth where the frost outside my window grows thicker. There's no room to sit, and so we stand close, with Pop Tarts and whiskey. I think about these last few days, about all that's happened and what Sarah said before, how things come about and what can we do really but give each turn a good try? I'm glad Sarah's here, thank her for coming. She smiles and says, "De nada." I find my radio for music, sing a little, share what I have.

# 8

WHAT I KNOW assures me, everything else I'm not sure. In bed with Sarah, I think of more things I know for certain: the color of the sky, not blue but darker. I know Vera Farmiga slightly, know sunshine absent a filter burns, regardless of the distance, and that scientists at the Jet Propulsion Laboratory in Pasadena have discovered a second planet outside the Earth's solar system, one with life-sustaining possibilities, named HD 209458b. I know Gordie Howe not Wayne Gretzky is the Great One, that Kwame Kilpatrick got off easy and P. Leonardo Mascheroni didn't. I know 17 words in French and 29 in Spanish, know Nguyen Van Ly has grace and that Wen Jiabao is a danger, know a lake won't actually freeze at 32 degrees Fahrenheit, and impurities in the water will affect the temperature further.

I know the things I do are of my own choosing, and the phrase *everything happens for a reason* is misconstrued, that things happen without some overarching plan and only because we make them, the rhythms of our performance, for better or worse, the conscious placement of one foot in front of the other. I know that after my shift at the Bow, I followed Sarah in my truck, watched her headlights out in front of me, know we kissed before, there in my booth, shyly at first, curious and cautious. Sarah's face is large and sweet, my attraction to her sudden. Aroused, we kissed again, inside her apartment, crawled into bed where I explored the rules of engagement.

Sarah's mattress is king-size, set in a thick wood frame. We lay together, roll and pitch ourselves about, the legs creaking beneath us. Sarah's a wave rising. I swim on top, spread out, palm to palm and feet to feet, soar like a body surfing. I feel her warmth beneath, sail as she breathes, move and mount, kneel in front and enter deeply. Sarah's resonant, sings to me, soft and assured, her skin smooth, a copious Jell-O pudding I cover with my lips, my hands and tongue completely.

We lay now, side by side, Sarah on her back, her large breasts with nipples deeply brown. The lamp on the far side of the room is on, allows us to see everything. We talk for a time and then I get up and turn off the light. Together we sleep well. I've set my alarm, wake when I need to, shower with soap that smells like Sarah. The towel I use is a green terry-cloth, I hang it on the shower bar, then take it down and toss it in the hamper. Sarah's up and has made fresh coffee. She has a job this afternoon, recording the jingle for Chester Bay Cheeses ("Chester Bay, sweetly cheddar"). We sit at the table. I say something, then Sarah does, too. I check the time, kiss her again as I'm leaving, do not say "I'll call you," which seems wrong somehow. I'm not sure what will happen next, which is to say I can't be certain. At best, I know what I don't know and this is one of those moments.

———

  The traffic on Welton is light, moves easily in the late morning, no longer affected by the snow. As I drive, I think of things before, about Terra Klyne, a woman I once dated. Terra was an actress I met while working on Charlie Kaufman's 'Synecdoche, New York.' I had a small role as an actor playing an actor playing an actor inside a stage built as a stage in a theater that may or may not have contained all of New York. Terra was an extra. She had blonde hair. I hadn't been with a blonde for a while and asked her out for a drink. After a few weeks we pretended to be serious, went to dinner and movies, came as a couple to parties, had long exhaustive talks, left books and clothing at one another's apartment. For me, dating was a scratch applied to an itch. I wasn't looking for more, not with Terra, though I did like to date, wanted the companionship, conversation and sex. I enjoyed it all without giving it much thought, my being with Terra like eating a cold tuna sandwich when hungry, the meal was forgettable but helped pacify a need.

  In the middle of our fucking, I often thought of different things, the feel of the sheets, the sports scores and forecast for tomorrow's weather. I sometimes thought of nothing, in order to come quickly and sleep, and other times was so distracted by a bit of the day's news that I almost forgot what I was doing. With Darcie this didn't happen. With Darcie the sex was consumptive, invasive and uncompromisingly present. I used to assume the first time I slept with another woman that I would think of Darcie only, and realize as I'm driving east in the direction of Parrot Lake that with Sarah this didn't happen.

My appointment with Coiyle is at 1:00 p.m. I've told Jay I'll try to finish the floors later this afternoon, and can make up time Saturday if he needs me. The suggestion is not charitable, I'm short on cash and can use the extra hours. I leave Sarah's and drive to Kate's. It's a little after 11:00 and I want to talk with her while Cam is at school. Sarah's helped me rehearse what to say. She thinks I should jump right in, not take too long with preamble, that despite my training as an actor, my eyes are much too innocent and give me away.

Kate's made tea, offers me something to eat, leftovers from the food her friends brought. Dressed in a heavy sweater, black slacks and wool socks though the house is warm, her complexion's improved, is better than last night, the side effects from her new meds—a lethargy and underlying nausea, a slight swelling in her hands and feet—are supposed to pass; the doctors sort-of promise. Kate warms a plate of lasagna for me in the microwave. I take Sarah's advice, get to what I have to say as soon as I can. I mention Cam's relief at having Kate home, how worried he was, and still is, a natural reaction, to be concerned about his mom.

"And Bob, too," I use this as my way in, digress briefly with a story about my own brother, how Jay and I also used to skate on Parrot Lake. "It must be hard," I say, "having Bob gone." I pause here, not purposely but clumsily. Kate notices, her features jagged from the pounds she's lost, the bone pronounced beneath her cheeks and chin. By the time I reach into my bag and take out the letter, Kate's been staring at me for several seconds. She unfolds the paper slowly, glances up at me twice while reading. I'm sure no one has ever quite looked at me this way before. I give her a chance to finish, then say, "I made some calls. I wanted you to have all the information first." Over the next few minutes I explain the rest, what's left to understand, I go ahead and get it done with.

———

By 12:45 I'm parked in front of Deletron Electronics. I've called Erin Thompson and asked her to stay with Kate, want to make sure she isn't alone now that she knows. The letter and phone numbers I called yesterday have been left on the kitchen table. When Erin arrives, I take off. The exchange has left me drained, I'm worried about Kate, and Cam, how he'll take the news when Kate tells him. I sit in my truck outside of Deletron, wait for some small amount of composure to return, am glad Kate wasn't mad about my opening the letter, her focus beyond me now, beyond her own condition. The air in my truck turns frigid. I beat my hands together then go inside.

Coiyle runs Deletron out of a red brick building on the west end of the city. Privately held, Deletron produces state-of-the-art gadgets: webcams and mini-recorders, microphones and cameras, Vcom calibrators, AMOLED display rolls, loopback simulators and terminal blocks. I take the elevator to the third floor, above the manufacturing and R&D divisions, where Coiyle has his office. The carpeting in the hall is a bright blue-green, shaved close like AstroTurf, as smooth as a putting surface. Coiyle's secretary sits at one of those prefab cubicle stations, wears a tweed skirt and cotton legwarmers, asks if I want coffee.

A minute later Coiyle comes out of his office, pumps my hand, sings "Mickey G!" I reach down, have almost forgotten how short Coiyle is, barely five foot three, he has on mauve slacks and blue Nike sneakers, his face creased like a photograph crumpled and then smoothed over. His gray hair is permed, his glasses round and worn low on his nose, he circles me once completely, then asks, "So how have the dogs been treating you, old cat?" He laughs at this, motions me to follow him into his office.

Coiyle's desk is oak, the surface covered with papers, a laptop and cell phone, several pens and notebooks. A shoebox-size container sits in the center. He pushes everything but the box to the side, repeats "Seriously now, how are you doing?"

"I'm good."

"I heard about Darcie." He gives his eyebrows a rise and shoulders a shrug, says "All shows close eventually, right?" He leans forward, small behind his desk, has me talk about my recovery. I assure him I'm clean, promise to fax my Marimin graduation certificate. Coiyle finds this funny, bobs his head, his wiry afro shaking like Bozo. There's a speech he likes to give about the history of Deletron, how he built his business from dime-store transmitters to sophisticated circuitries, he places his fingers on the surface of his desk, moves them rhythmically, as if playing piano. "The key to progress is to be progressive," he gives me a wink, boasts of Deletron as visionary, then says, "Let me tell you why you're here."

He gets up, lifts the box that's been sitting in the center of the desk, holds it in front of him, lays it out in the palms of his hands, pulls it in, tucks it under his right arm, walks from behind his desk to the middle of the office, comes back, sets the box down on the bookshelf, opens the lid then closes it again, raises the box shoulder high and clutches it tightly. He scoots next behind his desk, cradles the box like an infant, steps around and sets the box in the center of the floor, drops to his knees, folds himself over and lays down beside it, before getting up again and asking me what I think.

I've no idea. "I don't know what you're doing."

"And yet you're curious?"

I admit.

"And watching?"

"Yes."

Coiyle lifts the box again, shifts it from his right shoulder to his left, stands in front of me, smiles and raises the box back over his head, holds the pose, then lowers his arms and places the box in my lap. "The key to any good show is creating interest."

Again I don't know what to say. Coiyle continues. "No matter what the show, people need to feel intrigued. From Shakespeare to slapstick, it's all the same. The trick is creating anticipation. The greater the riddle, the more intense the focus." He asks if I understand.

I think I do, in general terms, "But what are you talking about specifically?"

Coiyle leans back against his desk, turns his shoes out at the toe. His glasses slide halfway down his nose, he takes his finger and pushes them up, draws an analogy between theater and advertising, asks me to consider what I do each time I take the stage, how I'm trying to sell the audience my character. "The part you play is a commodity, you spend two hours delivering your pitch. It's more sophisticated than the actor hawking Ginsu knives or Kentucky Fried Chicken, but ultimately there's little difference. Everyone's peddling," Coiyle says. "Everyone's pawning what they have with the hope it will be bought."

"Maybe," I concede for the sake of argument, am trying hard to connect the dots, ask him, "What does all of this have to do with me?"

Coiyle answers by waving his arms apart, says "I want you to sell Deletron. I want you to put on a show."

"You mean you want me to make a commercial?"

"Not a commercial, a performance."

I still don't understand. Semantics aside, I'm disappointed. "This is the project you had in mind?"

"It's something bigger," he lifts the box again, asks if I'm up to the challenge.

"What challenge? I don't know what you're talking about."

He grins, tells me I should think of the box as the Abbott to my Costello, the Blanche to my Stanley, and Iago to my Othello, that I need to "Create the symbiosis and sell the show." He gives me the box again, goes and sits behind his desk, says "Your turn, Mickey."

I'm thinking now would be a good time to leave, even though I've nowhere else to go, no work beside Jay's and the Bow, and as I haven't brought up 'Moonlight' yet, I ask Coiyle, "Let me see if I got this straight. You want me to use the box as some sort of mystery prop in order to get people to watch, and by watching this will draw them to Deletron?"

"Bingo, Mickey."

"But how?"

Coiyle winks again, says "You watched didn't you?"

"Yes, but I didn't know what I was watching."

"You don't have to know, you just have to watch."

I'm lost. Coiyle nods his tiny head, repeats what he said before about intrigue, good advertising and theater. I put my hands on top of the box, which is constructed of a thick red cardboard, the Deletron logo printed on the lid and sides. I'm ready to decline his offer and say this isn't quite the gig I had in mind when Coiyle waves his hands, points toward the box and says, "Come on, come on. Give it a shot."

I get up, put the box on the desk, am about to leave when Coiyle mistakes my movement as part of my performance. "That's it," he says.

I stare down, have no idea what I'm doing, but decide for the hell of it to treat the whole charade as an exercise, the sort I've done a hundred times in workshops and on my own. Instead of racing around the office like

Coiyle, as I'm a better actor, I change the pace, create a different sort of performance, shift the focus from the box to me. I understand the box is essential, but feel I need to affect an interest beyond the prop, to introduce and incorporate my character into the equation as I move from the window to the wall, the bookshelf and desk and door. The box remains integral to the plot—whatever the plot may be—but I still have to win the audience over, use my physical gestures to suggest earlier drama, a sense of story beyond the moment, a history shown through my face, a reason why I'm here carrying around the box and hint of things to come.

Coiyle watches, holds the tips of his thumbs together and frames me as if through a lens. I move to the window, the box in my hands, stare out, then down, creating a connection between the box and the world. I come back into the center of the room, stop at the desk, the bookshelf, the chair. Each time I pause, I employ the box in a different way, am looking to add another layer of intrigue, go on until Coiyle claps and praises my performance. I have no idea what I've just done, but say, "I'm glad you're happy."

"It's perfect." He takes the box from me, puts it back on his desk, writes an address down on a card and hands it to me. "A day's work," he says. "What do you have to lose?" We spend ten minutes discussing the project in greater detail, agree on a date to shoot, then walk down the hall and say goodbye. I bring up 'Moonlight' and Coiyle promises, "We'll talk." He pumps my arm again before I step inside the elevator. As the doors close, I watch him staring in at me, waiting to see if I will ask. I decide not to disappoint, go ahead and call out, "So what's in the box?"

All the way down to the lobby, I hear Coiyle laughing.

———

I spend what's left of the afternoon in South Aldwich, tearing up carpet and mats, pulling out staples and tacks. My back is sore from crawling around, my fingers cut and dust again sticking to my clothes. I think about Sarah, about last night, think of calling her now, but remember she's working. I think maybe I should leave a message just the same and let her know how things went with Kate and with Coiyle. I think about our having sex last night, wonder what I think about this. I think of Sarah's size and how it does and doesn't matter. I think of Darcie, just because. Think of Darcie and Sarah at the same time, think of one and then the other. I think I like Sarah then wonder why I only think. I think what Ted will say about my sleeping with Sarah, think of Sarah with someone other than me, am curious to see how it makes me feel. I find it makes me feel like I don't want to think of this anymore.

I think about Cam and Kate and Bob, think of Coiyle hiring me for a performance, though we both know it's nothing more than a commercial. I think of all the complications that come from doing this sort of work, how three summers ago I was hired to do a spot for Zovirax, a herpes medication. In the ad, I'm sitting on the end of a dock, my feet in the water, on a beautiful day. There's a gorgeous woman beside me, and we're both smiling and leaning close together as I talk into the camera, my left hand on the woman's shoulder so everyone can see my wedding ring. I recite my lines, explain that because of Zovirax my herpes doesn't prevent the wife and me from fucking.

It's a ridiculous ad really, a serious distortion, trivializing the necessary caution herpes requires. I'm no prude, hardly that, but the spot is offered as an elixir to a desperate demographic. The pitch offers sexual transgressors a free pass, suggests it's ok to screw around as Zovirax offers impunity, the scabs and pus a manageable inconvenience. I did the spot willingly and cashed the check. A week later, I went to audition for a revival of James Goldman's 'The Lion in Winter,' hoping to land the part of Prince Richard, the calculating son immortalized by Anthony Hopkins on film: "You're so deceitful you can't ask for water when you're thirsty. We could tangle spiders in the webs you weave." Instead, the director took one look at me and said, "Hey, it's the herpes guy." He had me read for Geoffrey, the dim-witted son. I got the role, and performed perfectly as a fool, a side effect of Zovirax the commercial forgot to mention.

I take a break, smoke outside, switch my radio from music to the news, get a report on the tropical freeze in Florida, on Jay Leno's firing, and the resignation of Northern Ireland's first minister, Peter Robinson, over his involvement in the sanctioning of monies loaned to his wife's nineteen-year-old lover. Crazy shit. I catch another story about a pet bear killing its handler, this time in Russia, the bear wearing ice skates and a hockey helmet, and who the fuck had the brilliant idea to put skates on the bear? More shit? In the four years prior to America's financial collapse, CEOs at the top five investment institutions awarded themselves and their cronies $145 billion in bonuses, a sum larger than the GDP of Pakistan and Egypt combined.

The world is this, an accumulation endlessly flowing. I think again about the climbers on K2, imagine them on the mountain making their way through the ice and snow, concentrating on the next six inches they have to cover, progressing this way in order not to think about the danger. When the enormous shelf of ice broke free and shot down from the Bottleneck, I see the climbers looking up and saying the same as me. *"More shit."* I think of my removing the nails from the carpet, one by one until I'm done and can polish the wood beneath, think this is the best way to go until I finish or something stops me. I think of another scene in 'Moonlight,' where Ralph is talking to Andy's sons, Jake and Fred, about their father. "The man was a thinker," Ralph says. "Well, there's a place in this world for thinking, I certainly wouldn't argue with that. The trouble with so much thinking, though, or with that which calls itself thinking, is that it's like farting Annie Laurie down a keyhole. A waste of your time and mine. What do you think this thinking is pretending to do? Eh? It's pretending to make things clear, you see, it's pretending to clarify things. But what's it really doing? ...sending the mind into a spin, it's making you dizzy, it's making you so dizzy that by the end of the day you don't know whether you're on your arse or your elbow, you don't know whether you're coming or going."

I think it's true, the way too much thinking can be a danger, think dad thought too much about mom, am sure if he thought less he could have slipped the noose, maybe fallen in love again and taken better care of himself, been more determined to play his music. There's something to be said for knowing when to think and when not to, I think. What to push free of and what to consider. I cut more carpet, push everything toward the door, am thinking again about Darcie, and Sarah, the way things are and the way they happen. I think about Mises and dissatisfaction, about the human approach and human action, think of what I should do now and what I shouldn't, what I shouldn't think even if I feel I should, that feeling can confuse my thinking, and how in this way, too, I'm a lot like dad, that I don't know what to think about my heart, and think if I think too much I'm just going to get in trouble.

---

Around 5:30 p.m., I sweep the wood, collect the trash and toss everything outside. A fresh frost covers my windshield, I need to scrape before I can drive to Cam's. Halfway up Welton, I call Ted. The ringtone on his cell is Stanley Clarke's 'Life Suite, Pt. 1.' Ted answers and I tell him about Coiyle, about my talking to Kate. I mention K2, the thirteen dead and all the rest. "Slippery slopes," Ted knows, says in summary. I mention Sarah, tell him about last night, which Ted isn't expecting. I try to convince him it's all harmless, but Ted knows how I am in my affairs, his concern is for Sarah. "She's good people," he reminds me.

"I know. It's not like that," I say. "It's not just me being me because I haven't been me for a long time, remember?"

Ted considers this, says "Maybe not." He asks what I'm thinking then, and I tell him honestly, "I don't know, but I think my not knowing is a good thing." I'm not completely sure what I mean by this, but I like the sound of it, have thought it before, and say it again. I nearly say Sarah's a big girl and can handle whatever comes, but the phrase is worse than clumsy. I change the subject, talk sports and the weather.

The Eagles' 'Desperado' is on the radio as I pull up in front of Cam's. The front door is unlocked, I stick my head in and say hello. Kate's in her chair, her favored gray sweater worn with purple sweats, a pad in her lap, the phone nearby. Cam comes from the kitchen, slouched, eyes red and face pale. I've made a list of things to say about Bob, now that Kate's told him, but none seem quite right. I rely instead on what I know, point to Cam's skates there in the hall. We're quiet on the drive to the lake. Most of the snow has blown free, the ice bare and silver. I wait until we're skating, consider putting some soft spin on what's happened, but decide Cam doesn't need any sort of sweet Pollyanna bullshit, that downplaying Bob's condition is disingenuous. I go ahead and say, "The whole thing sucks. It's nasty bad, but you know what? It's real and there's nothing you can do but be there for him."

Cam considers this, skates away then comes back and tells me, "I want to see him."

"You will, soon." I repeat what I assume he knows, how Bob's in Germany, recuperating from surgery. When he's ready the army will fly him home, at least closer, to the VA Medical Center in Baltimore. Cam asks if I'll take him and I think he means to the VAMC, but he says, "No." He's staring at me now, standing on the edge of his blades. Earlier that morning, Kate had also said she wanted to fly to Bonn, had to be convinced otherwise, her health unreliable, the situation forcing her to sit tight. She made calls, got all the way through to Bob's floor at the hospital where she was updated on his condition, asked to speak with him, managed by persistence to reach him.

The chill on the ice cuts against our cheeks, the temperature already in single digits. Beneath the moon, our shadows shiver. Cam looks up at me again and says, "I can fly myself."

"You're twelve years old."

"So?"

"So man, come on. It's hard, I know, but just wait. As soon as they get him to Baltimore, I'll take you." I promise this, give Cam an estimate, swear it won't be long. The snow against the shoreline is frozen in white mounds. I look across to the far side, then back at Cam. We stop talking, skate further out, glide around until the circles we make become infinitely tighter and the space between us closes.

In my booth at the Bow, I sit with my legs propped against the wall, the chill off the metal chair stiffening my back further. The wind howls and the coils in my heater glow orange. Cam is with Kate. I call around 10:00 p.m., make sure they haven't conspired together and flown off to see Bob. Tired, I close my eyes but can't sleep. I get up, stretch, take out my notes and read through a bit of 'Moonlight.' After a while, I turn on my radio, get the latest sports scores and more news.

In Palm Beach, Florida, the *philanthropist* Jeffry Picower, accused of making more than $7 billion working with old friend Bernie Madoff on his Ponzi scheme, was found dead at the bottom of his swimming pool. Picower's body was taken to Good Samaritan Medical Center where the pathology report noted serious abnormalities with his heart.

In Ingushetia, Russia, the humanitarian activist Maksharip Aushev was gunned down inside his car while driving on the highway in neighboring Kabardino-Balkaria. As with the other 27 human rights activists assassinated this year, the Kremlin had no comment.

Brett Favre, the ageless gunslinger, continues to defy the odds and has the Vikings in the playoffs.

Jose Mujica, founder of the Tupamaro Guerrilla Movement, who spent 14 years in prison while Uruguay was under military rule, has won the vote for president. In succinct socio-populist fashion, Mujica declares that no salary or financial perks will be awarded to anyone in public office. Opposition politicians steadfastly disagree.

Maurice R. Greenberg, former head of American International Group, whose greed helped run A.I.G. into the ground, is now using taxpayer bailout money to start a new company with many of his former employees.

And in Dagestan, thousands of Muslims come each

day to view the *miracle baby*, Ali Yakubov, whose skin is said to display verses of the Koran, which appear and disappear on his legs and chest every few hours.

    I call Sarah and tell her this, the world as she is. "What I would like," I say. After my shift, I leave the park and head across town. The roads are plowed, scraped clear of snow, long patches of ice slick where the shovels and salt have created an unfavorable side effect. The door to Sarah's apartment is left open for me. I take off my clothes, slide down beneath the sheets in the dark. Sarah stirs, her body warm, large and soft and sheltering. We do not make love, don't talk or move once we settle close together. I sleep deeply and get up late.

---

    Saturday morning, Sarah's at her piano when I wake. I go into the bathroom to shower. When I come out, I sit on the couch and listen to her play. She is not a gifted pianist, her large hands stroking each key produce the simplest form of melody. Still, there is something about her playing that understands the root of a song. Her fingering is light, the effect pleasant. We spend the day together. I do not go and finish the floors, but work on my 'Moonlight' notes. At 3:00 Sarah and I run errands, stop by my place and feed the cat. We wind up at Cam's where I introduce Sarah to Kate.

    Sarah sings at the Mail Room Saturday night. We go back to her place afterward and make love. We're quiet afterward and I curl against her, my arm draped over her middle, as far as her size will allow. She takes her free hand and touches mine. Her largeness on the bed, in the space beside me, is familiar now. I set myself against her, am taller and place myself high, my chest against her shoulders, my knees into the softest curves. There's something comfortable about our silence. I think about 'Mountain Language,' one of Pinter's final plays, which takes place in an unnamed prison where the guards forbid the inmates to talk. In response, the prisoners develop a secret form of communication, find their way around the challenge of words. The silence between Sarah and me is similar, our lying there front to back in the dark, we connect in ways that do not even require us to whisper.

We stay together Sunday, much as the day before. Sarah works on her music while I sit at her kitchen table, run through my 'Moonlight' notes, review the list of people I plan to call, including Feldman. My pitch is scripted now, my appeal for cash leaving nothing to chance. We go to the movies in the afternoon, see Jeff Bridges in 'Crazy Heart.' Later, we meet Cam and Kate for dinner. I sleep at my place Sunday night, notice for the first time since Darcie a different sort of absence and how suddenly strange my bed feels.

I get up early Monday to finish the floors in South Aldwich, am thinking about the Bow tonight, how I don't want to go, am desperate to be done. I phone Danny, my case counselor at the court, get voicemail, leave a message, explain exactly as I did to Kyle what I'm thinking, appeal to Danny to cut me some slack. An ex-cop, shot six years ago breaking up a domestic dispute—the husband had a waffle iron, the wife a P3AT pistol—Dan called the incident "comic book stuff." In the middle of his intercession the gun went off and caught him in the hip, bullet fragments infecting the bone, leaving Dan with a permanent limp. A desk jockey now, expert at mixing pain pills and rum, he found time to earn a master's degree in social work, took a job with the court. I wonder if Kyle has written Dan the letter, wonder if he might call him directly, am unsure what chance I have at any of this, or how much it hurts to ask.

On my way south, I stop at Home Depot and rent a sander, strap it down in the bed of my truck. I spend an hour pulling up the remaining carpet, getting the wood ready to be sanded. The warm ash needs just a minor buff, I put on a fine belt, work with a mask and the windows open, the cold air chilling my hands. After, I use Murphy's Oil Soap to clean the wood, polyurethane to seal in the natural colors without any additional stains. I finish around 4:30, return the sander to Home Depot and head to Cam's.

All the downstairs lights are on as Cam lets me in, greets me eagerly, tugs at my arm, tells me before I can take off my coat, "They're moving Bob." Kate's in the kitchen, her coloring better tonight, she smiles as if she's also been waiting for me, asks if I've eaten then has me sit down. Cam follows me to the table, wants to know if I can still take them to Baltimore. "To the VAMC," Kate confirms. She puts chicken, cole slaw and chips on a plate, comes and sits with me. "It's winter break next week," she tells me Cam doesn't have school, says they can leave Saturday, can take the bus if I can't get away, but I've already promised Cam that I'd drive.

I call Sarah on my way to the Bow, tell her about Bob and my plan to head to Baltimore this weekend. Sarah's happy for Cam and Kate, asks about my probation, which doesn't allow me to travel. "It's cool," I tell her, though I haven't actually figured this part out. Sarah says it's important I get everything squared away, and if I do, I should take her car to Baltimore, my old truck a rough ride, Kate's car not much better, a 2004 Ford Focus with spent tires and worn shocks. I appreciate the offer, but don't want to leave Sarah stranded, am sure I can borrow something from Jay.

The flurries from earlier have stopped and the night is crisp and clear. I walk to my booth, turn on my heater, let the coils warm. Just after 10:30 p.m., I go to the rink and skate, then sit in the bleachers and smoke. I take out my phone and call Darcie, am not sure why I'm calling, have not phoned her once since the night she came to my apartment. When she answers, her voice is warm, though she tells me she's in a hurry, is driving and can't really chat. "I'm on my way home," she says this intentionally, as I'm expected to note, everything with Darcie by design. Last year she made a film called 'Snatching Eva.' The story had Darcie's character—Eva—kidnapped and brought in handcuffs to a dinner party. Her captors were hirelings, two stooges named Joey A and Joey B, working for an unnamed employer. The movie was shot in 35 mm, was shown at a half-dozen festivals before a straight-to-video release. This was too bad really. Although the script strains at being clever, indulging in elements of the absurd—like Alain Resnais and Alain Robbe-Grillet in 'Last Year at Marienbad'—what saves the film is how completely Darcie commands the screen.

 Even in handcuffs and dressed down in t-shirt and jeans, Darcie takes charge of the party, not with histrionics and cries for help, but by mingling and then seducing everyone she comes in contact with. The other characters interact with her as if Eva's shackles are a clever accessory. For Darcie, the character's hardly a stretch. She is by nature an enchantress, a charmer, a mesmerist and voodooist, persuasively diverting, she seduces all with hands behind her back. Whenever I sit and watch the film, I can never quite tell if it's Eva or Darcie on screen. "If you're in a hurry," I say, "I'll let you go." I pick up my skates, turn off the lights near the front door, am ready to hang up when instead I suddenly announce, "I've met someone. I'm seeing someone."

 The news does not trigger any reaction from Darcie. She doesn't ask questions, does not want to know who or how. The statement, in fact, seems to startle me more than her. In reply, without missing a beat, Darcie reclaims the upper hand and says, "Good for you, Mick. I'm glad to hear. Sorry," she tells me, "but I'm home now, I'm at Dave's and have to go."

———

I stand for a time, still inside, in the dark, unsure of what just happened. Through the glass of the front door, I can see the Tilt-A-Whirl and House of Mirrors. I put my skates down, go back toward the bleachers, use the light from my phone to find my way. Darcie's response, which is to say her ignoring my news, does not surprise me. Even though I failed to mention Sarah by name, I'm glad I said something, feel good about this, tell myself *I feel...*, and do not debate my intention.

Just after 11:00, I sit and think about calling Sarah, realize as I start to dial that she'll still be at Seven's singing. I decide to call Ted, then remember he's with the Pups. I go online, click to the Tick, read as best I can from the glow on the screen. Since last week, Ted has been following the events in Iran, all his posts now referencing the fallout from the election, Mahmoud Ahmadinejad and Ayatollah Ali Khamenei pinching the popular vote from the opposition candidate, Mir Hussein Moussavi. Demonstrators in Tehran have taken to the streets, chanting fraud and demanding justice. "100,000 people," Ted wrote, "in Iran!" The government, in response, in full crackdown mode, has arrested hundreds of *dissidents*, men and women, including former president Ali Akbar Hashemi Rafsanjani's daughter. The police and Revolutionary Guard attack the crowds with rifles and clubs, tear gas and water cannons.

There's a clip on YouTube, caught with a camera phone, showing 26-year-old Neda Agha-Soltan gunned down in the street. Since then, Ahmadinejad and Khamenei have censored the internet, suppressed all negative information, banned journalists from covering the marches. The demonstrations are declared illegal. "And yet they continue," Ted writes tonight about the *beauty*—he uses this word—of demonstrators risking their lives for democracy and political reform. "Leaps of faith," Ted extends his full support to the opposition movement. Excited, his writing exhorts everyone to recognize the significance of what's happening. "We are talking about a theocracy that has ruled every aspect of Iranian life for years being publically denounced and chided. The protests are life-affirming, the demonstrations Gandhiesque, the Velvet Revolution and the Gdansk shipyard in Poland all rolled together. It's 100,000 people getting behind Peter Finch in 'Network' and shouting 'I'm mad as hell and I'm not going to take it anymore!' The movement," Ted writes, "is essential. The protests must not fail."

I shut off my phone, go back outside and head to my booth. As I walk, I try to picture Tehran, imagine being swept up in something bigger than me. Before I can do this, I start thinking of Sarah, larger than life, too. I do not think of Darcie, which is to say I push her away when she comes into my head. There's a smell as I enter my booth, damp things, the mud floor hard and ceiling covered with layers of old and new snow. The metal of my chair remains cold, despite being six inches from my heater. I go back outside, stand with my hands bare and fish out a cigarette, think again of what Ted wrote about the beauty found in the leap of faith, and imagine how this applies to me. I wonder what Mises would say about the demonstrators in Iran risking their lives to resolve a collective dissatisfaction. Is this logical? Is there any rational justification for a human action that could result in death? How would Mises reconcile the extremes? Would he say what's happening in Tehran is a different sort of reasonable, inspired by the sweet raw awe, the thump-thump-thump that stirs and moves the soul? I wonder about passion and need, think of Sarah and Darcie again, about the leap of faith required there as well, think of my heart and where it takes me, and how am I suppose to act? I wonder about all of this, am curious to know about human action, and after Mises championed the necessity of reason, what did he think of love?

---

Around 2:00 a.m., I go back to the aquarium, am feeding the lemon shark when Danny calls through on my cell. I'm not expecting this, as late as it is and Danny never calling me before at the Bow, I assume it's about my message, think it must be, am nervous about what he'll say, surprised when Danny barks, "Where the hell are you, Greene?"

Here's a twist. I've no idea what he means, wonder if maybe I forgot an appointment, though it's too late at night for that. I'm guessing Dan's drunk, but don't want to ask, say instead, "Where do you think I am?"

Danny snaps, "You tell me."

"Birch Bow."

"Bullshit. I'm at the Bow now and your truck's not outside."

"You're here?" I'm lost, can't imagine why Danny would come by, another first, especially at 2:00 a.m. Dan doesn't answer my question, says instead, "If you're here, get your ass down to the gate."

I curse, worried about my truck, convinced someone stole it. I take my phone, talk to Danny as I go, try to get an explanation for what's going on. Fifty feet from the gate, I can see out into the lot. My truck is where I parked it but there's no sign of Danny or any other cars. "What the fuck?"

"You by the gate?"

"I'm standing right here. Where are you?"

"You have your shit?"

"What? No, all my stuff's in the booth."

"Well go and clear it out, we need the space." Danny gives me a minute to howl and dance in the snow, then tells me about the letter and phone call he got from Kyle, says "Getting the shrink involved was a nice touch." He grunts and goes, "You still have some hoops to jump through, Greene, but the Bow isn't one of them."

I go to my booth and pack up my heater, my 'Moonlight' bag, thermos and skates and head to my truck. I'm home before 3:00 a.m., set my alarm for 9, wake to the sound of sports scores and forecasts of the weather.

———

# 9

TUESDAY, BEFORE HITTING North Aldwich to do drywall in an old Colonial for Jay, I call Sarah, tell her about Danny and the Bow. I call Ted and Jay and Kate, too. My emancipation is a sign, I'm convinced, proof of good things to come. I stay in North Aldwich until 5:00 p.m., clean up and meet Sarah for a sandwich, then take Cam out to skate. The lake is rutted tonight by old snow frozen into the surface. I maneuver my blades as if expecting to fall. Cam finds his groove, cuts through spots where I still have trouble. We skate for an hour, then head back to the house where I sit and talk with Kate, discuss Bob and Baltimore. As I no longer have to be at the Bow, I leave around 10:00, head over to Sevens and catch Sarah's final set.

On stage, Sarah's face is a white sapphire moon, glowing beneath soft stage lights, her largeness its own constellation, her body still for me an unexpected sort of revelry. I wonder, briefly, not seriously but academically, if my being sprung from the Bow will in any way affect my feelings for Sarah. Will the refuge I took in her friendship be relegated now to a past life? Coming into the Mail Room and hearing Sarah sing Anna Elizabeth's 'What Happened to Real,' seeing her smile at me from the stage, I think I know the answer. We spend the night at her place, get up together and have breakfast before I go home and feed the cat, shower and drive to Kepermill Studios where Coiyle's waiting for me at the door.

He greets me as always, with a vigorous "Mickey G!" and hard pumping of my hand. I am told to put on a black dinner jacket, white shirt and no tie. Once I'm dressed, Coiyle has me get down on the floor and roll around. Apparently, my character's had a rough night. Coiyle's asked me not to shave or comb my hair. The photographer he's hired is Korean, stocky, in beige shorts and matching safari shirt. He wears his black hair long and straight, his accent heavily Brooklyn. We spend an hour taking still shots in front of a gray screen, by a window and near the door. The box I'm given is different from the other day, slightly larger and covered in felt, the lid clipped down, the Deletron logo no longer there. The photographer kicks off his shoes, talks to me while bouncing around the room, moves me like a mannequin, says "I'm going to move you like a mannequin." He settles me in poses that are completely contrived yet feel somehow right.

When we finish, I follow Coiyle a few miles east, drive to the Verimore Hotel where Marie Tegare, the director Coiyle's hired, is waiting for us. We go over the script, walk through the two main scenes. I'm filmed passing through the hotel lobby, going straight to the elevator, then again at the front desk, stopping at the bar, sitting on the sofa in the lobby, and in the red Queen Anne wing chair. The box is with me at all times. I pretend I'm at the hotel to see a lover, that I'm a courier with important documents to deliver, that I've stolen the box and am waiting to pass it on.

After the lobby, we go upstairs to room 437, where I walk to the window, carry the box back to the chair, move slowly around the room, to the dresser and closet, past the bath and around both sides of the bed. I concentrate on what I'm doing, try to give my performance a sense of intrigue and profundity, ignore how all of this is for a commercial and treat it as an important piece of film. By 6:00 p.m. we finish shooting. Coiyle seems pleased. He hands me a check for $1,500 and says he'll be in touch.

I change back into my jeans and sweater, let Coiyle know I'll be out of town for a few days starting Saturday and if he needs anything to call my cell. Once the film is edited, Coiyle plans to post clips on the internet. I don't see the point, have no idea how Deletron's supposed to benefit from any of this, the web already flush with thousands of more provocative posts. Coiyle has the box in his hands now, holds it high above his head, his frizzed hair rising as if drawn by static, he tells me "not to worry," says he knows how to draw fish to the hook. "Have faith here, Mick."

Words to live by. I tell him, "I'll do my best."

―――――

I drive from the Verimore Hotel to Cam's. Sarah's brought Chinese. Cam sits with me at the table while I eat, has a photo album he wants to show me, pictures of Bob in jeans, in a hockey uniform, in shorts standing beside a blue Impala. He turns the pages, points out pictures where he and Bob are together. I see them in a dozen different shots, in summer days and winter nights. Bob is as I imagine Cam will look in a few years, leanly muscled, a seriousness to him, his eyes wistful, a cautious reserve to his charms.

Cam and I go to the lake, skate laps, the stars overhead strung like holiday lights. Back at the house, Sarah and I stay a little while longer, then leave together, stand on the sidewalk where Sarah slips her arm inside mine. I thank her for bringing dinner, her kindness toward Cam and Kate appreciated. She reminds me of her offer to let us take her car to Baltimore, says she can drive my truck while we're gone. I'm skeptical, rattle off a list of my truck's deficiencies, the heater suspect, the hard seat and temperamental starter, worn tires and shocks. "It's not a ride I'd feel good leaving you with."

She holds out her hand, asks for my keys, says she can manage just fine and wants to show me. I kiss her then, softly, because I want to, take her keys in turn, have her follow me to my place where I ask her to stay with me tonight.

Upstairs, the cat watches while I bring Sarah into the bedroom, sit with her on the bed, there on the side where Darcie slept. I tell her this, say "This is the first time in a long while here." Sarah touches my cheek with the tip of her fingers. We undress quietly and get into bed. I look at her naked, the size of her legs and arms, soft as sweet bread. In the near dark, we make love slowly, lay afterward warm beside one another. I turn off the light. My bed is smaller than Sarah's, I have my left arm over her center, am stretched on my side, against her hip. She breathes softly and I adjust my own breathing to the rhythm of her heart. Listening then, I fool myself with memory, dismiss the shape of Sarah beside me, too large for Darcie though I tell myself she is, and then just as quickly know that she isn't, that Sarah is and Darcie was before but isn't now.

There's another part in 'Moonlight' where Ralph and Andy are arguing once more about memory. Ralph says,

"Walking down the Balls Pond Road, for example," and Andy insists he can't remember. "I never went anywhere near the Balls Pond Road. I was a civil servant. I had no past. I remember no past. Nothing ever happened." Bel and Maria join in, say of course things happened. "Lots of things... All sorts of things..." while Andy answers, "Well, I don't remember any of these things. I remember none of these things." I think of this in terms of me, the things I remember and those I should forget. I talk to Sarah about this, about 'Moonlight,' and how Pinter writes about memory. I talk more about the play and the way Pinter addresses relationships, his characters' treatment of love, both romantic and familial, how people engage, everything turned over and over, unsettled and misconstrued, how vulnerable we all are with and without the harsh hold love has.

Sarah has my pillow behind her head. She listens, then says, "There are things we can't ever know or understand completely about one another." She accepts as much, believes "Most relationships are formed on surface levels, though for love, what links us intimately are not the outward showings, but what lives in the gaps and pauses."

I like this, the suggestion very Pinteresque. I take my hand and touch Sarah's belly, kiss her softly, her neck and breasts. We lay in a tangle of limbs, my mouth to Sarah's ear. I forget about Darcie, say instead what I want now, ask Sarah to come with us to Baltimore, slide closer still and confess, "I don't know about any of this other than what I feel, and I feel you should come. I want you to and will miss you if you don't." I say her name, say "Sarah," and ask her again.

———

By Saturday, I've finished two new projects for Jay, have my laundry done and my duffle packed, put my 'Moonlight' notes in my bag, my books and cigarettes and lighter. Sarah's made calls, shifted her schedule around. Our plan now is to stay through the week, I've asked Ted to take care of the cat. Sarah brings her jeep to my place the night before. We set the alarm for 8:00 a.m., wake on time, shower and dress and head to Cam's.

All the lawns in the neighborhood are buried still beneath crisp styrofoam squares of white snow. The sun is bright but distant, melts nothing. Cam's waiting for us near the street, waves as we come around the corner. I leave the car running, keep it warm while Sarah goes inside for Kate. The first two hours I drive with Cam beside me, Sarah and Kate in back. When we stop for gas, Sarah takes over. Kate now sits up front reading. Sarah searches for music on the radio, the stations fading in and out the further we get from Aldwich. Cam has a PSP he plays, while I've brought the morning paper, check for updates on Iran: Alireza Hosseini-Beheshti, an aide to Mir Hussein Moussavi, has been arrested on charges of treason, Moussavi, Mehdi Karroubi, and former president Mohammad Khatami threatened with the same. "Their behavior shows they won't stop opposing the system," Hadi Moghaddassi, a spokesman for Parliament, states with no apparent irony. Earlier, Hossein Rassam, an employee of the British Embassy in Tehran, was jailed for *fomenting violence* during the demonstrations. A political analyst, Rassam did nothing more than transmit the events of the protests to his superiors in Britain. Crazy shit. I imagine what Ted will write on the Tick.

The trees outside my window are bone winter bare. I look at Sarah in profile. There's a passage in 'Moonlight' where Bridget says: "I am walking slowly in a dense jungle. But I'm not suffocating. I can breathe. That is because I can see the sky through the leaves." Here the sky lays low, drops the horizon onto the road, gives the impression we know where we're going. Sarah follows I-95, takes us almost into Baltimore before we stop and stretch our legs again. I drive the rest of the way, get off at exit 395, head to Martin Luther King, Jr. Boulevard, then toward Paca Street, turn onto Fayette and the hospital.

The VA Medical Center is three enormous buildings linked. A sign near the front says the hospital's parking garage doesn't reserve space for visitors. I don't understand this. To park now we have to go back to Paca, or South Howard, where the walk's too far for Kate, the temperature forbidding. I pull up to the door, suggest everyone get out and I'll go park. Kate carries her meds in a brown leather purse, leans close to Sarah after she climbs out of the car. Sarah whispers something, takes Kate's hand. I drive back to Paca with Cam who suddenly wants to come with me. We find a public lot, park and walk against the wind. I pull my hat down tighter, Cam stays to my right, away from the curb, his eagerness to see Bob tempered now, the uncertainty of what to expect. I ask if he's ok. Rather than answer, he pretends not to hear.

We're issued visitor passes at the main desk, take the elevator to the fourth floor and wind around. The VAMC is cavernous, each hallway a wide stretch of green-beige tiles. Soldiers able to leave their rooms sit in the halls, rolled out in wheelchairs, others lean on crutches, play cards in designated areas, hold queens and deuces in bad hands. Sarah's waiting for us outside of Bob's room. She smiles purposely, hoping to reassure and soothe before ushering us inside. The room is something of a mini-ward with three beds on each wall. Bob's bed is to the left, the furthest back. Kate's sitting in a chair beside Bob who has his mattress raised, his blond hair shaved, his cheeks and jaw-line sharp. Unlike the photographs I saw the other night, his face is darker, his innocence more exposed, a raw sort of witness, he looks a bit like the actor Rupert Friend in 'Lullaby for Pi.' There are marks on his right arm from recent IVs, morphine and dilaudid, fentanyl and possibly the synthetic G.E., I would guess. Despite the drugs, his gaze is clear, his eyes alert, much as the first time I saw Kate at St. Mercy's, and yet somehow different still.

Cam comes up to the bed and gives his brother a hug. I stop a few feet short, Sarah beside me. Kate has removed her coat, her hands clasped and thin shoulders slipped slightly forward, she appears spent, emotionally exhausted by the reunion, she's nonetheless determined to smile. I imagine the scene while Cam and I were walking up from Paca Street, Kate attempting to comfort, keeping herself composed, the maternal tug to make things right and the reality that she can't, all tearing at her now. She watches Cam, looks at Bob, sees Cam watching Bob, and Bob looking at all of us in turn. I introduce myself, ask Bob how he's doing, a reflex, the question best left alone.

Bob has a white sheet pulled up to his waist, his chest covered by one of those scratch-cotton hospital gowns. The sheet lays flat at the end of the bed. Bob's voice is slightly hoarse, though not unclear. "You're the actor," he says of me.

"I'm the one."

Cam begins to rock a bit, back and forth. The moment's inevitable. Bob understands, rolls down the sheet, a confusion at first between what should be there and isn't. Cam and I stare, as Kate and Sarah did before, the presentation performed without ceremony. What's left of Bob's legs is wrapped in thick gauze, the stumps carved just below the knee, the whole of each calf gone, the feet a memory. There's an unanticipated smell, a mix of medicines and something else. I struggle for a moment to process the sight, the picture wrong, my brain trying to reconnect what's missing, to readjust the focus and reset the dial. Cam steps back, stops and comes close again, his fear giving way to something else altogether, the fraternal tie in its purest form. He touches Bob's shoulder, and lower, down in the space where his fingers trace the absence as if inspecting the effect of a trick gone terribly wrong.

---

Kate's reserved two rooms at the Green Lantern Lodge. Cam and I leave the VAMC first, walk back to get the car, on the elevator going down Cam howls, a seismic release. I let him cry. When he stops, we walk outside, the wind in our faces. We drive back, pick up Sarah and Kate, who talks about tomorrow, about buying Bob clothes, a robe and sweater. "A blue, blue sweater," she says.

The carpeting inside the Green Lantern Lodge is dark, not green but a well-crushed purple. The hotel pool is frozen over. We eat in the restaurant downstairs. After dinner, I take Cam to the game room and we play air hockey. He's better now, is able to laugh, shows a competitive edge as we slide the plastic puck around. Kate's asleep when we get back upstairs. Sarah's reading. Cam has asked to bunk with me. We watch tv until he, too, grows tired and falls asleep. I catch the end of a movie—Vincent Gallo's 'Buffalo 66'—then switch to the news, get an update on the demonstrations in Iran. More than a thousand protesters have been arrested now, journalists still barred from reporting, information comes from a network of underground sources, stories leaked about *dissidents* being murdered in prison, charges trumped up in order for the government to begin parading the protesters through the courts. The first of the demonstrators have already been charged with *Moharebeth*, waging war against God, the punishment death. It is, I think, the sort of insanity you can't make up, a situation quickly getting out of hand. I flick the channels, let different images fill my head until I finally drift off.

---

Sunday morning, Sarah and I drop Kate and Cam at the hospital, then take a drive through the city. We buy the Baltimore Chronicle, find a cafe where we sit drinking coffee and reading the paper. The cafe is small, with brick walls and wooden tables. I check the sports scores, look at the Arts and Leisure section where there's a notice for a production of 'Guys and Dolls' at the Baltimore Playhouse, with Eric Cramer cast as Nathan Detroit. Eric was Goldberg to my Stanley in 'The Birthday Party.' I'm glad for him, tell Sarah this. She rubs my hand across the table. Before leaving Aldwich, Sarah bought a copy of 'Moonlight,' has read it through as another sweet surprise, smiles now when I say, "Anyway, leave him aside, if you don't mind, for a few minutes." I touch her palm with my thumb, find her fingers soft and warm and wide.

We go back to the hotel and make love. I take my time and kiss Sarah all over the smooth broad surface of her skin, my head between her shoulders. Sarah turns, her breasts full and heavy. I lay on them and fill my hands, place myself again on top of her, my stomach flat against her plump round belly. Her soft red hair covers my face. I think of things as they are, the possibilities only recently supposable, the reason for the Galaxy and all the rest. I leave myself outstretched on top of Sarah, my world moved by her breathing, I close my eyes, feel her below, open my eyes again and recite another line from 'Moonlight,' a claim by Andy of how we get from there to here: "That's destiny speaking, sweetheart," I whisper into her neck.

---

Monday morning, I sit in the lounge with Kate, a few doors down from Bob. Cam and Sarah have gone for a walk, Bob is in physical therapy, working on his stamina, on weights and gymnastic bars, is in the pool with his stumps in waterproof sleeves. The chairs in the lounge are a worn lime plastic, the window covered by venetian blinds. Kate is bundled in her coat, though the temperature inside the VAMC is warm. She has a notebook in which she records the progress of Bob's recovery, talks to doctors and nurses, discusses his therapy, the timeline for his transfer to a facility closer to home. As soon as Bob's wounds have healed, he'll be fitted for prosthetics. Kate's researched the latest technology, has made a list of what's state-of-the-art, has learned about magneto-rheological technology, Segway HT and the Arise. She lets the hospital administrators know Bob is to receive nothing but the best, which she will pay for herself if need be. She keeps a separate file on the specific problems of amputees, infections and vertigo, the need for proper exercise.

For three days now, I've maintained my own sort of record, monitored as best I can Kate's condition, am trying to safeguard her health, am not quite sure what to look for other than signs of her overdoing, an unusual fatigue. I ask how she's feeling and she stares at me as if she doesn't quite understand the question. Mostly we talk about Bob. Kate has stories to tell, the process cathartic, a need to look back, a sense of responsibility for allowing Bob to enlist. I'm curious about this, from what I know it seems unlikely Kate would have encouraged Bob to go. I suspect his decision is something more personal, a point made without actual consideration for the war. I picture him enlisting right after high school, impatient and over-compensating for his own dead dad, rudderless, he jumped into the kettle and got burned.

Kate says I'm wrong, that Bob was at Columbia when he enlisted, was finishing his second year. I'm surprised, would not have expected Bob to leave college for Iraq. I ask for more details, want to know what inspired him. Kate's writing in her notebook, her head down when I ask, her hand stops moving, she pauses a few seconds before looking up. Rather than answer me directly, she says, "Do you like poetry, Mick?"

"Well enough," I've no idea why she's asked.

"Have you ever read Charles Hamilton Sorley, Wilfred Edward Salter Owen or Alan Seeger?" Kate mentions three poets I've never heard of. I tell her this, ask "Why?"

She describes how each was an active pacifist in the early 1900s, artistically and personally opposed to World War I. "Each also enlisted. Seeger was the most famous, having written the anti-war poem, 'Rendezvous.' He was killed in 1916, at Belloy-en-Santerre during the Battle of the Somme. Why do you suppose they enlisted?" She puts the question back to me.

I tell her, "I don't know. I suppose they had their reasons. What does this have to do with Bob?"

Kate has the collar of her coat turned high. The sun from the window reaches us through the slats. She gives me another minute to think, then starts to explain.

---

Tuesday and Wednesday, Sarah and I again take Kate and Cam to the hospital early, spend time on our own in the city, come back to the hotel and make love before visiting Bob. Today the nurse is changing Bob's dressing as we arrive. We wait in the hall. Kate's in the room, wanting to learn all she can. Cam is with us, also interested, he pulls me back inside where we peek around the curtain.

Bob's stumps are a red raw gob stitched across in a jagged seam. The nurse wears latex gloves, slips a fresh folded sheet beneath what remains, removes the gauze carefully, cuts and unwraps, the old salves and medicines washed away and a new gel applied. I look down at my shoes, think of all the legless guys I've seen in movies, Gary Sinise, Ronald Reagan, Tom Cruise and Woody Harrelson, John Voight confined to his chair in 'Coming Home,' the torso stump thrashing in 'Johnny Got His Gun.' Each are storyboard attempts to approximate the experience, representative though in no way comparable to the real deal. When the nurse finishes, Bob keeps his head on his pillow, eyes on the ceiling, his hands across his chest. Later, as Cam's with Sarah and Kate's on her phone making calls, I wrap Bob in a blanket, find his gloves and hat and coat, and wheel him outside.

We pass through the glass doors, park ourselves on the walkway, to the left of the main entrance. The air's cold but the wind is calm, the snow pushed into large mounds at the outer edge of the parking lot. I light a cigarette, stand facing the sun. Bob adjusts the blanket that covers his half legs. The cap Kate has bought for him is two shades of blue with a Baltimore Raven logo on the front, the rim tugged over his ears, his forehead covered almost to his eyes. His coat is military, a rough khaki, the same shade as his blanket, his black gloves also army issue.

I offer Bob a smoke, but he says no. After five days, this is our first time alone. I assume Bob has questions about his mom and Cam, things we've not been able to talk about before. I start telling him as if he's already asked, describe Kate's condition, discuss the new meds she's on and how they're working. About Cam, I say, "He's a good kid. He's dealing with everything the best he can. He's resilient, you know?" I mention our time on Parrot Lake, the reference causing Bob to look at me intently. He runs a gloved finger down what remains of his thighs. I've been waiting, admittedly expectantly, for Bob to flash signs of anger and resentment toward the damage to his legs, but throughout these last five days I've seen only calm. In his room, when the pain from his wounds causes his fingers to curl and he breaks into a sweat, he doesn't curse or complain, but sets his jaw a little tighter. His composure seems itself a sort of release, an acceptance I don't understand, even after Kate spoke with me. I've told Sarah I think maybe Bob's still in shock from the loss of his legs, but she senses it's more than this, that the calm Bob exhibits is part of a conscious commitment.

Maybe so. Who knows?

Cars come and go in the lot. Soldiers in uniform pass in and out. Bob tips his head back, breathes the cold air. I finish my cigarette, crush it in the snow. The sun at its highest point reflects off the roof of the VAMC. The wheels of Bob's chair are locked in place, his blanket tucked under his stumps. A black car pulls against the curb and a man in full uniform gets out of the back seat looking much like George C. Scott in 'Patton.' His jacket is covered with rows of tiny colored medals, each a merit badge awarded for some unnamed service. We are fifteen feet away, enough time for Patton to spot us and salute. I have no reason to respond, while Bob in his chair raises his hand, though only to his mouth, taps his lips with his index finger. The gesture is a puzzle. General Patton pauses suddenly between us, looks at Bob, down at the blanket, and up again.

Bob stares off, exactly as he was before, toward the far side of the lot and into the street. He's not so much avoiding the General as demonstrating his indifference. If the General wants to say anything to Bob, he will have to get his attention first. He considers this, is now two feet from the side of Bob's chair, asks "What's your name, soldier?" The reply comes not with all the usual protocol of *Lance Corporal Robert Mayhre, sir*, but a more informal and deliberate, "Bob."

The General appears flummoxed, then angry, he gives thought to making a scene, is discouraged by an aide coming up on his right shoulder. The aide puts a hand on the General's back, whispers something before the two walk off, the glass doors parting as they approach the VAMC. The whole incident takes less than ten seconds. Bob again looks back toward the far side of the lot. I'm laughing now, startled, my curiosity piqued, I think of what Kate said and want to know more. When I ask, as supportive as I can, I do so in a way that invites Bob to start anywhere he wants. "What's going on, my man?"

Bob shifts his head, lets me see his eyes. I haven't brought my gloves, and the chill on my fingers, even deep inside my pockets, is intense. I think for a second Bob's going to do as Kate and answer evasively about some such theoretical thing I can't understand, talk of poets and personal epiphanies. Instead, he waits until I point at his legs, then touch my lips as he did earlier, and say, "I don't blame you for being pissed, the war cost you a lot."

"It cost me, but I'm not pissed." He says this sincerely, expects me to believe. When I remind him again of his dissing the General, Bob shakes his head and tells me, "I felt that way before. What happened hasn't changed a thing."

I don't get this. "What do you mean?" I look back at his legs, try to understand, ask if he didn't endorse the war, why enlist? To all of this Bob tips his head the other way, stares off and resumes watching winter birds land on distant wires. I wait until the chill takes hold completely then wheel him back inside.

———

Coiyle calls on Thursday. Cam and I have gone across town to the Sportsplex where we rent skates and stretch our legs out on the ice. The exercise is good for us, a healthy diversion. As we're leaving the rink, Coiyle gets me on my cell, sings "Mickey G.," asks how I'm doing, has me remind him, "Where are you exactly?"

I say Baltimore and he asks if I've been to the Marina. "If you like seafood, try Captain James Landing, or Mama's on the Half Shell," his voice comes at me in high squeaks and whistles. He wants to know when I'll be back in Aldwich, asks me to swing by his office when I get in, so we can talk.

I assume he has some reshoots for me, but Coiyle says no, that the first clip is already edited, cut and posted online. "Haven't you seen?" He lists YouTube and Myspace, MTV and Facebook, Amazon Unbox, Watch Now, Jaman and GreenCine. "People are watching. You did good, Mick." He presents statistics, the increase in hits on the Deletron site since yesterday morning, the sales figures up. Coiyle's theory is that television commercials are passé, hot clips online viewed more than the top tv shows, with production costs at a fraction and viewers already on their computers, the impulse purchase requires just a click. He simulates the sound with his tongue, says "We're in the pink here, Mick. People are watching and want to see more."

I tell Coiyle I'll be back in a few days and come see him then. At the hospital, Cam gets Kate's laptop and we run a search, call up the clip on YouTube. The video's done in soft shades of color, the lighting muted as I carry the box under my left arm toward the Verimore Hotel. When I get inside the lobby, I go to the front desk for my key, then carry the box to the bar, order a drink and light a cigarette. The camera lingers on me. There's no music, no sounds other than what the microphone picks up naturally. At the end of the clip, the camera follows me as I go upstairs and pace around my room, the box still with me, I walk side to side, back and forth. There's a knock at the door and I turn around. The words Deletron Electronics appear briefly at the bottom of the screen, right before the film ends, leaving everyone to wonder what they just saw and what will happen next.

Cam has the laptop on Bob's bed. He clicks over to MySpace and we watch again. I'm still not sure what it's all about, but the others seem to like it. Kate says there's something irrepressible in my performance and Bob agrees. Sarah leans over and kisses my cheek. I'm not convinced, am about to say it's all a gimmick, my walking around with the box like watching a balloon float off, or the flames of a fire dance, but my cell starts to ring and friends are calling, a few at first and then more as we get back to the hotel. They've seen the clip, are each amused and curious, envious and impressed. They kid me in a way that's refreshing, say "Shit Mick. Nice jacket. What the hell? What gives with the box?" and "Who knew you were still acting?"

———

# 10

WHAT TO MAKE of this? Or anything? Who knows? The Yankees win the Series and the Penguins steal the Cup. Susan Sarandon leaves Tim Robbins and beds Jonathan Bricklin, 32 years her junior. Bernie Madoff, now in prison, won't shut up, mocks the S.E.C. for the six complaints they had on file against him since 1994 and failed to pursue. In Afghanistan, the brother of President Hamid Karzai, Ahmed Wali Karzai, a known frontman for the country's opium trade, has recently been outed as a paid hireling of the C.I.A. In Iran, more *dissidents* are arrested, the car of opposition leader Mehdi Karroubi shot at by pro-government supporters, the Kurdish activist, Fasih Yasamani, executed at Khoy prison, the protests in Tehran now spreading to other cities. At the funeral of the senior cleric Hussein-Ali Montazeri, an outspoken critic of the government, thousands gathered in Oum, are assaulted by the police and Revolutionary Guard, dozens arrested, the Ayatollah Ali Khamenei again declaring all gatherings illegal, calling the demonstrators "followers of the path of Satan." Ted writes on the Tick, "Seriously now, how fucked is that?"

We leave Baltimore Sunday, just before noon. Barring any setback, Bob will be transferred to the New Princeton Rehabilitation Center in Aldwich within the next ten days. Our mood as we drive remains optimistic, the prognosis good. We reassure one another how well Bob is doing, the observation set against the magnitude of his injuries, we say things can only get better, pronounce with confidence a host of half-truths, dismiss the alternatives, the what-ifs and could-be-stills.

Sarah and I drop Cam and Kate at home, then drive to her place where I carry the bags inside, dump our dirty clothes into the washer while Sarah checks her mail and messages. In a few days she's scheduled to sing background vocals on the new Pearl Divers cd. She's looking forward to this, studied the lyrics in Baltimore, sang for me in the late mornings, she returns calls now, confirms her schedule, lets everyone know she's back.

Once our clothes finish their cycle and are tossed in the dryer, we head to my place where there are 27 new messages on my machine. This coupled with the calls made to my cell confirm Coiyle's claim that the Deletron clip is getting noticed. Sarah finds a pad and pen, writes down the names and numbers of people looking to get in touch with me. She composes two lists, those that are friends offering congratulations, and people with projects they want to pitch.

I stand in the kitchen, listen to each call, shrug at the

end, unimpressed, I tell Sarah, "I'm sure most of these guys have half-finished scripts they think I can get greenlighted for them. That's how the game goes. It's like when some guy hears you sing and hands you his card, tells you he's a record producer when what he really is is a dude with a tape deck in his mom's garage." I refer to Coiyle's clip as a novelty, a commercial with a twist. "Things will cool off soon enough."

Sarah agrees, is smarter than me, says things will cool and that's why I need to contact these guys now. "It only takes one good connection. How much can it hurt to find out if there's one in the bunch?"

I don't know. "Maybe." I read through the list, admit some of the callers have done their homework, mention my performance in 'The Glass Menagerie,' in 'Closer' and 'Pillow Man,' and 'Cat on a Hot Tin Roof,' though no one brings up 'The Birthday Party.' There's a message from Billy, my old agent, who hasn't called since dumping me after the Galaxy. Bill says he saw the clip, was alerted by others impressed enough to ask about Mickey Greene. "I have work," he wants to get together, for old time's sake, tells me to give him a ring. I look at Sarah, weigh the whole of everything, remind myself to delete the call.

The next-to-last message is from Dave. I'm surprised but tell Sarah it's nothing, that it's just Dave being Dave, how I'm sure he doesn't have a part for me, doesn't want to work with me, isn't rethinking getting involved with 'Moonlight.' "He just wants Karry On to seem part of the buzz."

"But that's a good thing," Sarah saves Dave's message, thinks I should talk with him, to hear him out, she says, "Unless you don't want to."

The statement resonates. The elephant in the room is Darcie. *Unless you don't want...* I'm careful not to say the wrong thing, am thinking there's no risk in talking with Dave, business and bedfellows pretty much standard in our industry,

I can't see that I've anything to lose, and still it feels strange. Sarah's brought night clothes, changes into a pair of old sweatpants without strings, a large white t-shirt with the face of Charlie Chaplin faded to gray. I pull off my pants and get into bed, curl close and talk now, not about Darcie, who we haven't spoken of really since those first few days when I was drunk and quick to confide everything. I don't want to talk about her now, though my not wanting to talk of her, or about Dave, is something I don't want Sarah to connect to larger concerns. I try to reassure her, go ahead and say, "I'll call him, no problem," and leave it at that.

The window in my bedroom is covered by a flannel drape. There are no streetlights shining outside and the room is dark. I roll over and kiss Sarah's stomach, the large fleshy expanse and soft center beneath her shirt. We talk of Baltimore. I'm glad Sarah came, appreciate how generous she was with Cam and Kate and Bob, pleased we had the chance to spend the week together, to get to know one another outside of Aldwich and find we're compatible in all the odd moments of the day.

Sarah rubs my head, slides her hand onto my back. I feel her fingers, her wrist against my spine. We stay this way as Sarah asks about 'Moonlight,' wonders what would happen if I was offered a part in something new, some play or film that excited me, would I still want to do Pinter?

I tell her, "Yes," answer without hesitation, insist one has nothing to do with the other, my ambitions separate. "Not doing 'Moonlight' isn't a consideration."

Sarah sits up, reaches and turns on the lamp beside my bed. The light has one of those soft white bulbs good for reading, but against the dark its sudden brightness hurts my eyes. I cover my head, squint through my fingers, find Sarah framed there in front of me, her face wide and beautiful, her shoulders big and full as she pushes her hair from her face.

Her hands are plump doughy mittens, she finds my cheek, touches me, shifts on the bed and settles against me, her size adjusting, a way she has of moving with ease. She tells me about 'Moonlight,' "I have some money. Enough to get you started. If you need, I have."

———

Sarah sleeps in a deep sweet stillness. In the dark now, I lean closer, stare at her face. Earlier, after her offer, as I didn't reply and left it laying there on the bed like some odd sock I wasn't quite sure what to do with, I kissed her instead, made love without giving her an answer. I know I should have said something, but couldn't decide what. Sarah's gesture is selfless and sincere, is what people do when they're in a relationship. I repeat this six times in my head, think as Sarah sleeps, consider our status, our being together, how her wanting to help me is genuine, is natural, the leap taken from serious heights.

I get up and go into the front room, find my phone in my backpack. Once, several years ago, I dated a woman named Lucy Sobel, an antiquarian I met while doing an indie film, 'Caveat Crimes.' I played a crooked antiques dealer who comes up with a plan to have copies made of his more expensive pieces in order to sell off the originals. Lucy was hired to help provide legitimate-looking items for the film. We dated exclusively for two months. I was fond of her, though not in love, I found her pretty and funny and adventurous in bed. One night, Lucy came to my apartment with a pair of pants and shirt she bought me, a gift she said, something she thought I'd like. The gesture threw me. Two days later I stopped seeing her. When I told her it was because she couldn't just give me a pair of pants and shirt, she thought this a poor excuse and left with the clothes in a plastic sack.

I go into the kitchen, stand by the window and have a smoke. Yesterday, while still in Baltimore, I read an article in the morning paper about Michael Arnold, the business manager for the British composer Peter Maxwell Davies. After 30 years of working together, Arnold was caught stealing $800,000 from Davies' accounts. As Ted would say: How fucked is that? Thirty years is serious betrayal. How do people do the shit they do? There's no easy answer. Nothing is ever clear, in the end we're all capable of odd acts. I consider this, what Arnold did, and Sarah, too, the iniquity of Arnold's crime and the crazy risk Sarah's taking offering me a chunk of her savings. I ask myself what I should do, and what am I doing? On which side of the fence do I fall, and how far am I willing to go for 'Moonlight?' And Sarah? I think again of Sarah sleeping, think of where I am and what gesture I should make to get things started. I go ahead and call Feldman.

---

Monday Jay has me working in East Warren. I do drywall patches inside the building my brother needs to sell. The place is six floors of empty, all detritus and dust, the apartments deserted, the lights, doorknobs and heating grates torn out and pawned by old tenants. Most of the windows are either broken or pried loose, pulled from their frames, any bit of wiring or fixtures that could be taken and sold long gone. A bad investment, Jay admits. The neighborhood turned and the market sank, Jay's anxious to dump the place and cut his losses. "If not by spring, I'll have you torch her for me," he jokes about the blessedness of insurance. "'Save the Tiger.'"

"It's the American way."

Ted comes to see me this afternoon. I'm on the second floor, cutting drywall sheets and covering the holes as Ted hollers up from the lobby. He takes the stairs, finds the apartment, has on sweatshirts, at least three, a Los Angeles Lakers purple and gold pulled over additional layers. I work in thin cotton gloves, can maintain my grip this way, the chill coming through the busted windows notwithstanding. The drywall sheet I'm about to cut is ten feet wide, larger than most drywall, which comes in four-foot boards, but Jay buys in bulk, gets the longer sheets at a discount. While in Baltimore, I spoke with Ted twice. He asks me now about Bob, asks about Sarah, jokes with me about the Deletron clip, sings like Eric Burdon from War: "I dreamed I was in a Hollywood movie, and I was the star of that movie."

"Funny," I trim a hole, cut the sides to make a square, then match the opening with a piece from the drywall. Once the cut patch fits, I apply the tape and compound mix, say about Bob, "He's a good guy, I think, kind of hard to get a handle on, like Zorba, you know, like Kanji or some monk, all fierce and innocent at the same time." I tell Ted what Bob said about his decision to enlist and how the loss of his legs changed nothing. "At first I thought he couldn't deal with supporting the war after getting blown to shit, but I don't think that's what he's doing." I repeat what Kate said about the pacifist poets, and how I saw Bob mock the General in front of the VAMC.

Ted has on heavy gloves. He folds his arms, his fingers sticking out from under, he offers a bit of Mises-speak and says about Bob, "Occasionally people are less concerned with the consequence of their actions than the decision to act. If the reason a person acts is well-founded, the consequence, however self-damaging, does not negate the meaningfulness of the deed." All of this is delivered as if rehearsed. I wipe my gloves on the front of my jacket, say, "What the hell, man? Where did that come from?"

The white dust from the drywall flakes off while I cut another six-inch square in the wall, reshape the crude hole made by a fist or the end of a baseball bat. Ted goes to the window and sits on the sill. The only light in the room slips through that portion of window I've not taped over with newspaper to keep out the cold. With my ripsaw, I cut the drywall sheet in one clean stroke, careful not to press too hard and splinter the board. Once the patch is set inside the hole, I apply the paste. Ted has on brown Nauticas, water stained, the leather creased across his ankles. He stands, shifting back on his heels, rocking slightly, the way he does when playing with the Pups, or when there's something on his mind, a quiver, almost indiscernible at first, a building up through the shoulders, moving into the arms and hips as he concentrates against the backbeat of select rhythms. Offstage, he catches himself, reaches beneath his hood and runs a glove through his hair. I ask, "What's up?" and he tells me.

"More than 3,000 protesters have been arrested," he says of the situation in Iran. "Those we know of," he describes the kangaroo court established to try the *dissidents*, the murders committed in jail, the chief of police, Ismail Ahmadi Moghaddam saying "The era of mercy is over." Any use of email, cell phones and the internet in support of the protests is treated now as treason. "It's all chips in," Ted says.

I slide the uncut half of the drywall sheet into a more stable position between the sawhorses and leave it there, stare at Ted and ask him to repeat what he just told me.

"I'm going."

"The hell. How?"

"Getting in isn't so hard."

"But the whole country's shut down. You can't do any reporting, can't post on the Tick. If they catch you you're dead."

"They won't catch me."

"Fuck."

Ted ignores this, says "It's important to get a first-hand account out. The press is censored, everything we see comes third-hand, from reporters like Robert Worth in Beirut, Nazila Fathi in Toronto, Alan Cowell and Brian Stelter in London and the United Arab Emirates. It's all a rehashing. I want to get inside."

"And do what?"

"I told you," Ted says.

"And G.O.D.?"

"There's interest."

"Bullshit. Come on, man," I'm struggling to find the best argument, turn to Mises and say, "How is what you're doing logical?"

"Just because something's dangerous doesn't make it illogical."

"Sure it does. That's exactly what it makes it. Look at Bob. The man lost his fucking legs because of some crazy impulse. Now you want to risk getting killed?" I repeat, "Where's the logic?"

Ted smiles in that way he does when whatever I'm saying is futile. He adjusts his hood, covers his hair and half his forehead, insists "I am being rational here. I've given this a lot of thought." He says going to Iran has a purpose, that there's a discernible value, a claim I jump on and ask again, "What exactly?" I put my ripsaw down on the drywall, ask for details, want to know who's helping get him in and where does he intend to stay? Rather than tell me, Ted says, "Everything's set."

"Just like that?"

"No, I was working on it while you were gone."

"Great," I finish with the wall, put my tools away, close up the mixed compound and tape, and head downstairs. The air outside is crisp and free of dust. Ted tugs at the sleeves of his sweatshirts as we walk to the curb, the snow beneath our boots stiff and crunching. The temperature is again starting to fall, is maybe fifteen degrees. No one else is on the street, this side of East Warren slow in its redevelopment, several blocks in bad repair, the houses wood framed, beaten about the edges, the gentrification of the neighborhood having fallen off, developers hedging their bets, a twenty-minute drive from downtown Aldwich, all the buildings have a brittle, startled look.

Ted's car is an old Saturn, dark blue. In the back seat are newspapers, pens and books, crumpled bags from Wendy's and Burger Barn, a blown out amp, and the neck from a Fender bass. Ted unlocks the driver's side door, does not open it, turns and stares back at me across the roof. He runs through a further list of recent shit: The Iranian government closing three pro-reform newspapers—Arman (Goal), Farhang Ashti (Culture of Reconciliation) and Tahlil-e-Rooz (Analysis of the Day)—the universities under siege, Mir Hussein Moussavi and Mohammad Khatami threatened now with more than arrest, writers and filmmakers being rounded up and disappearing.

I'm on the sidewalk, my truck parked nearby, my keys still in my pocket. I kick at the ice, am looking for something else to say, decide to tell Ted about Feldman, let him know that Feldman's offered to loan me money for 'Moonlight,' cash I can pair with Sarah's if I take hers, and hopefully attract other investors. "I'm doing what I need to," I throw this back at him, childishly perhaps, but the closest I can come to drawing parallels between his decision and mine. Ted goes quiet, gauges what to say about my getting in bed with Feldman, knows if he challenges my choices I'll simply point out that my involvement with Feldman may be suspect, but it's less immediately threatening than his. He decides against debate, takes two steps back and opens his car door, says in summary, "It's never anything but a gamble, Mickey."

Here I agree. I want to talk about this, to speak of

consequence, the things we do and don't do, how everything's a roll of the dice, it's true, but it's important to have sound calculations, otherwise you wind up high on stage, falling from your chair at the Galaxy, miles off course. There are times, sure, when the stakes are bigger and the bets we place are at odds with logic, but always then the end must justify the risk. That's all I know, or believe I've learned. I understand too, there's risk in not taking risks, but going to Iran is crazy, the odds stacked and chance for success minor. Instead of saying this though, I keep quiet, realize finally, even if I don't want Ted to go, that I can't actually tell him what is and isn't worth it.

I take a cigarette from my pocket, am about to light it when the flame blows out in the breeze. I raise my free hand to cover my lighter, protect the flame as best I can while the wind tries to get between my fingers.

———

Tuesday morning, I leave Sarah's in time to drive Ted to the airport. He's flying first to London, has G.O.D. on a disk, promises to keep in touch. I spend the week in East Warren, doing what I can to repair Jay's building and get it up to code. The wiring is fucked and Jay will need an electrician, the few connections I'm able to play with hardly worth the trouble. I fix the windows, the walls and doors and floors within the budget Jay set for me. Each night, on my way home, I stop and visit Kate and Cam, then go and meet some of the people who called after the Deletron clip went online. All have projects, though only a few are funded, and of those, there's even fewer worth discussing.

I agree to these meetings because Sarah's encouraged me. Back at my apartment, I have a stack of scripts to wade through, including two treatments Billy sent over. Sarah has a discerning eye. Out of the pile, one script shows promise, a film about an actuary who falls for a performance artist. Sarah likes the quirkiness of it, the integrity and gentle intensity of the main characters, the story both stark and sweetly subversive. She asks if I know the writer/director, Noel Ferne. I do know Noel, though only by reputation.

On Thursday I work a half day for Jay, then drive downtown to meet with Coiyle, Billy and Dave. Again, I've agreed to speak with Bill and Dave because Sarah thinks I should. I leave East Warren just after 1:00, meet Coiyle at Furderlane's. Yesterday the second Deletron clip appeared online. In this one I'm upstairs at the Verimore, standing by the window in my room, the box cradled in my arms. I pace around, move from the window to the dresser, the dresser to the bed, the bed to the door which I open now and let a women with blond hair and a black dress inside. The clip follows our initial exchange and interplay with the box, and then fades out. The public response is nuts, is completely inexplicable and even better than before. People are actually anxious to see what's going to happen, are already demanding a third clip. They've started blogging and texting about my performance, writing notices about me, personal pieces, references to my time with Darcie, to my stage and film work, all of my earlier achievements, and of course my addiction and recent collapse. Sales of Deletron products continue to hit high water marks. Last night, Sarah checked Amazon, found three Deletron products in the top ten for electronic sales: a webcam, an MP3 player, and a transformer that allows video games to be broadcast on tv.

Coiyle's waiting for me at the bar, comes and pumps my arm. He is, as always, animated, bounces between the stools, talks at me rapidly, tells me of plans to extend the clip's placement online, to pushing the blogs, the media both web and print, a strategy for launching the clips on cable tv, to paying for commercial time on HBO and even the networks. "We're only getting started, Mick." He asks if I read the contract he sent over on Monday, wants me to sign a service agreement, making me the face of Deletron, an exclusivity arrangement, locking me in for at least a year. Sarah and I have read the deal, have questions about the specifics of what the gig entails, a need, too, for Coiyle to define exclusivity. I let him know I have some other projects coming in. "Some film offers, maybe, and 'Moonlight.'"

"Sure, sure," Coiyle says he understands. "As long as you don't pitch the competition, we can work around whatever else comes up." In his left hand is a long cylinder tube. He holds the tube high, lowers it again just as quickly and pops the top. Inside is a poster of me in the black suit jacket, standing by a window in a pose the photographer set. Coiyle takes the poster out, unrolls it and says, "We're going to splash you around a bit. You'll be paid, of course, for the stills we use. It's all in the contract," he turns the poster around, shows it to the bar.

---

I leave Coiyle and meet Billy two blocks over at Keller's. The sky's distended, hangs down like a gray piñata. I lengthen my stride, my hands deep in my pockets, I'm in a good mood. The deal with Coiyle is an unexpected windfall, the money solid, the contract generous and the downside small. Still, when I tried talking to Coiyle about 'Moonlight,' he put me off again, said, "All things in time there, Mickey."

Billy sits at a side table, looks as I remember, like John C. Reilly with his sad sack mug, eyes dark yet eager to please, his grin ingratiating, complexion red, a drinker's russet, his suit a rumpled charcoal, a green tie worn loose, his hair brown and slightly thinning, when he turns his head I notice his sideburns have grayed. He gets up and we shake hands. "You look good, Mick," he makes no mention of the 10 months he went without contacting me, aims instead for détente. "You remember that time," he says, and when he finishes, he reaches across the table for my wrist, becomes suddenly fraternal, asks how I'm doing really.

I say, "I'm fine," and Billy jiggles his head like one of those bobble dolls they give away at the ballpark. "I've kept tabs," he says, "whether or not you think. Maybe I should have called, but I warned you, didn't I? I tried to help, you know that. I said if you crossed lines that would be that." It was true, less sycophant than sound advisor, Billy was fair with me until the end, diligent enough when getting me work, an advocate of tough love, he provided me with several doses, became frustrated in the weeks leading up to the Galaxy, had counseled and cajoled me, then hit me with termination and no love for almost a year.

He's drinking club soda, in deference to my recovery. To fuck with him, I order Dewar's. Billy debates, then tries to joke, says "Doctor's orders?" and has the waitress bring him a beer. "I saw the clips," he gets down to business. "Both the first and second. I've taken more calls about you since yesterday." He says, "There's some interest. The camera still loves you," he wants to know if I read the treatments he sent over. I tell him I did and that neither was any good. Billy waits to see if I'm serious. I drink my whiskey when it comes, dismiss the scripts as weak. "Why send me your D-list shit if you're trying to impress? D-list I can get on my own."

Billy insists, "What I sent you is top notch, handpicked. Either script would be perfect. These projects are as good as anything you've ever done."

"Yeah, well, maybe that's the problem." I put my drink down and say, "I'd like to do better."

Bill lifts his beer, lets me know, "You want to swim with the big fish, you first need to get back in the water."

Fair enough. "But don't I get to choose where I swim?" I tell him then about the Ferne script, how I've found something I like. Billy asks questions, says "Ferne's good," wants to know who made the contact, whether Ferne wants me and if I've read for the part yet. "Tell me about the script," he promises he can close the deal, if that's what I want. There's a client agreement he's brought with him, just in case I liked any of his treatments. He pushes it across the table, says again, "If you want, Mick, I can help."

I light a cigarette, blow smoke toward the bar, ask Bill if he remembers 'Moonlight.'

"With Nick Cage?"

"No man, that's 'Moonstruck.' I mean the play. The one I was working on before."

"Ok. That one, sure. Why?"

"I still want to do it," I tell him.

"Is someone looking to produce?"

"No, I mean I want to do it. I want to put it on. And I want you to help."

"With what?"

"I just told you."

"You want me to pitch a play no one's looking to stage?"

"I'm looking," I tap the table. "I want you to get me backing."

"From who?"

"I don't know. That's your job."

"Assuming you're a client." He's negotiating now, tells me to sign the agreement. "Let's nail down the Ferne film first. You land that through me and I'll see what I can do for your moon shot."

---

The Waverly Grill is seven blocks from Keller's. I get my truck, drive across the numbered streets, my heater in its usual disjunction makes a cat's hiss then stops completely. The traffic is heavier now, there's no place to park in front so I head around back, check the lot to see if Dave's car is here yet. On the radio, the college station plays Gato Barbieri's 'Last Tango in Paris.' I begin running movie reels through my head, digital clips of Darcie and Dave naked as blue fish, flapping and flailing, dorsal and ventral fins slapping and slipping in and out. The image is upsetting, makes me wonder what I'm doing here. I change the station, get an old Hootie and the Blowfish song, let the tune calm me.

Dave's sitting in the rear of the Grill, checking messages on his cell when I walk in. He looks up, pauses before smiling, doesn't stand, but extends his hand across the table. His fingers are small, I'm not sure I've ever noticed this before but am happy to do so now. My own hands are long, nicked and raw. Dave has a sunlamp tan, keeps himself brown all winter. He drinks red wine. He is, I think, a red wine drinker. "Dinner's on me," he points to the menu. It's just after 5:00 p.m. and I'm not really hungry, but go ahead and look for something expensive to eat.

We warm up with small talk. Dave's eager to show he's comfortable with me, mentions actors we both know working in and around Aldwich. Because he can, he describes Darcie's rehearsals for 'Killer Joe,' the new yoga exercises she's doing, and her latest workshops at the Mecca. No reference is made to my appearing in his driveway. "For what it's worth," Dave says, and offers a chronology, takes me through the history of their affair, as Darcie refused to do before in my apartment. He insists, "We didn't hook up until late summer," six months after 'The Birthday Party.' I've no way of knowing if this is true, am determined not to care, and go so far as to say, as Darcie did, "This has nothing to do with me."

Our waitress comes and we order our meal. Dave talks about the clips, says, "They're clever bits. You're very good, Mick. You always were, in the right part." He asks how it feels to have people notice me again, wants to know about Coiyle, about working again, and what sort of projects I'm considering now. I tell him, "I have a few things," and Dave says, "I'm sure you do." He reaches down beside his chair, hands me a large yellow envelope, lets me know, "Here's what I have."

I take the package and place it beside my own chair without opening it. Dave smiles, puts his hands on either side of his drink, says, "If you're uncomfortable with me, Mick, we can stop. I just thought you were smart enough not to burn bridges. Business is business, right? Whatever happens outside the ring is irrelevant."

"The holy trinity of clichés."

Dave ignores this, says, "It's the internet. Everything's changed. The immediacy of the buzz comes like that," he snaps his fingers. "Once it hits, there's no turning back. Decisions have to be made quickly. I could ignore you, sure, but why should I do that? I'm an open-minded guy. If there's a part to be played and money to be made," he smiles again, shows ridiculously perfect teeth. "You're a hot flash, Mick. I'll give you that. Coiyle did a nice job exposing you. There's some personal baggage sure, but all that does is make you more compelling. People are curious, those who knew you before and those just getting to know you now, they all want to see what you do next."

"And you want to help me?"

"I told you, I'm here to help myself." He drinks his wine, looks at me seriously and says again, "If you don't want the work, we don't have to do this. If you're not up to it, I'm not going to waste my time. This is business, not charity. This isn't me throwing you a bone." He wants me to understand his motivation is purely mercenary. I believe him, though I still don't pick up the envelope, am thinking I should negotiate first, the way I did with Billy, that if Dave really wants to cash in on me, we should work a trade. "About 'Moonlight.'" I tell him in exchange for backing the play, I'll read what he brought.

Amused, Dave slides his drink to the side, stares across the table, his eyes a dark hazel, he tells me to "Forget the play. No one wants to do it."

"I do. And you did."

"I agreed to take a look, that's all." He runs through a long list of reasons for turning me down, numbers crunched, a cost analysis, projected sales, statistics from similar shows, lesser-known works by O'Neill, Ayckbourn and Albee not making their investments back. His assessment is objective, has nothing to do with Darcie, he swears, or my incident at the Galaxy. "If I thought for a minute the play might make money," he says, "it wouldn't matter if you OD'd naked in the middle of Letterman. The fact is you're dealing with a difficult script at a time when high art is a tough sell."

I try again, but Dave's dead set, plays the angles, cuts me off, forces me to move in the direction he wants. "Forget 'Moonlight,'" he says. "Just read what I brought."

The waitress serves our food. Dave's ordered steak, runs his knife through the center, inspects the cut. He asks again what I plan to do next. I'm defensive now, say that I have plenty of opportunities, a stack of scripts to choose from, tons of other offers, and folks interested enough in working with me to take on 'Moonlight.' Dave concedes it's possible, but repeats he doesn't think it wise. He wants to know specifically what I've read to date, who else has contacted me and what scripts I'm still considering. I tell him about Noel.

Dave puts his fork down. "Ferne's solid," he says. "His first film was great. He's a smart guy. A good director. And writer. So he contacted you? You like his script?"

"It's the best I've read."

"Excellent." Dave takes his steak knife and points toward the side of my chair, says he's glad to hear, tells me again to read what he brought. "Let me know what you think."

———

# 11

WHAT BRINGS US together and tears us apart? Who knows? And still shit happens. Last week, scientists at the Addis Ababa University, working with professors from the Eritrea Institute of Technology and the National Yemen Seismological Observation Center, determined that a 35-mile long rift in the Ethiopian desert will eventually become an ocean, connecting the Red and Arabian seas. The crack, which is barely 20 feet wide now, first opened after the Dabbahu volcano popped its lid in 2005. The resulting rift is said to involve the African and Arabian plates located hundreds of miles below the Afar Desert. The plates are moving apart at a rate of half an inch a year for the last 30 million years.

In a million more years, scientists speculate the new rift will fill with waters from the Gulf of Aden and join the two seas between Yemen and Somalia.

All things in time, I think. What eventually will become the widest gulf begins with the smallest fissure.

———

The distance from the Waverly Grill to Cam's house is approximately eight miles. I drive east through traffic. On the seat of my truck is the envelope Dave gave me. Inside is the Noel Ferne script. Dave laughed, a sorry coincidence, he called it karma, explained how Karry On was producing the film, though he swore he didn't speak with Noel before phoning me, said this was proof everyone thought I was right for the part.

I was still trying to wrap my head around this first surprise, when Dave added, "There's one more thing."

The name of the film is 'Juli in Chains,' and as of last week Ferne had cast Darcie as Juli. "Dead serious," Dave removed all doubt, said putting Darcie and me together was good for business, that bloggers had already discovered our history and posted comments, that we work well together, are familiar with one another and would bring an invaluable sort of intimacy to the film.

I told Dave, "Right. What the fuck? I don't get it. For months you've been avoiding me, keeping your relationship secret and not returning my calls. Why are you pressing to put Darcie and me together now?" It made no sense. Did he think, with my probation over, that Darcie and I would find some project to do together, and that he didn't want us staging our reunion without him? Better to bring us in on a film he was producing, in an environment he could control, than let things happen on their own. If this was where his head was at, "You're crazy." Forcing the issue when there's no longer an issue to force. "I'm over that," I told him this. "I don't see the point." I'm with Sarah now. "Darcie can play Juli without me. The script is good and doesn't need a gimmick. There are plenty of other actors you can hire."

Dave's response was to repeat what he said before about his intentions being mercenary, that he was only interested in producing the best film possible, and making money, and if casting me was the surest plan for both, then Goddamn it, cast me he would. He said this a bit too loud, as if arguing with himself, the words escaping. He tried staring me down, but the face he made dissolved into mimicry, or maybe it was irony, or vulnerability, a hint of each, I couldn't quite tell. Possibly, too, he was thinking of Darcie and the look revealed his own sense of love. Maybe this was what I didn't get at first, emotions that exposed Dave's feelings for Darcie I had never stopped to consider before; his own fears and things he needed to know for certain. He set his jaw against the whole of it all and said, "Humor me, Mick."

---

I drive down Welton Avenue, turn in and park on the street, visit with Kate, get news on Bob before heading to the lake with Cam. We do laps, stack loose branches to leap over. Cam clears each jump easy, while I crash hard at eighteen feet, lay for several seconds sprawled on my back. There's a moment when Cam seems to think I'm seriously hurt, a dark certainty that everyone close to him suffers in this way. I notice his face and get up as fast as I can, let him see I'm fine. As proof, I stand on the edge of my blades and dance. Cam laughs, resumes skating, goes and leaps the branches where I just fell.

I drop him back at home around 9:00 p.m., then drive south to the Next Note, where Sarah's recording with the Pearl Divers. Along the way, I check my phone to see if Ted has called. He hasn't. On the Tick this morning, he posted his first piece, did not give his location, but the photographs made clear he's in Tehran. Those protesting against Ahmadinejad are shown being attacked by the Revolutionary Guards, men and women dragged off. Ted refers to the Guard as "The worst kind of enemy, soulless and savage." He quotes Rasool Nafisi: "The Iranian government is no longer a theocracy, but a regular military security force with a façade of a Shiite clerical system." To date, more than 600 detainees have died. I want to talk with Ted and make sure he's ok, but he's asked me to wait until he calls. I phone Bob instead, dial through to Baltimore and ask how he's doing.

Downtown, I turn west, find Palmer Street and the Next Note. From outside, the studio looks like an old garage, the wood walls white and roof sloped sharply, with green shingles covered almost entirely by snow. The driveway's gravel, with a dozen or more cars parked across at various angles. I find a spot to leave my truck, wait until the red recording light above the front door shuts off then head inside. However tumbledown the outer shell, everything in the studio is state-of-the-art, including a Pro Tools HD3 system and Digidesign C/24 control mixing board. The main room has a piano and guitars, a drum set partitioned behind a carpeted wall, and separate recording stations for vocals. I find Sarah standing near one of the soundproofed booths, a pair of headphones on the back of her neck, a green knit cap half covering her hair.

She's talking with two guys, her head in a metronomic nod. I go over and Sarah smiles, takes my hand, squeezes, introduces me to Terny Riksen and A.G., the engineer. Terny's the lead singer for Pearl Divers, a skinny stick, pasty pale, he has a sort of Scott Weiland I-haven't-eaten-in-days look, wears cowboy boots and a gray herringbone vest, sips from a large coffee in a white styrofoam cup. Shorter than Sarah, together they look like an oddly formed numerical design, the number 10 with Sarah round, her white top loosely fit, her slacks black and shoes matching. Terny gives me a fist to hit, says "Hey man," then "Hey, aren't you the guy in that thing?"

There's bottled water and fruit on a table, a couch on the left side of the room, a few other people hanging out. Sarah asks about my meetings. I put my arm around her waist, extend it as far as I can, bring her close beside me. A.G. goes back to his engineering booth, signals for Sarah to enter one of the soundproof stations. I move to the side. The music for the next song has already been recorded, the guitar, piano, drums and bass along with Terny's vocals. A.G. runs everything through the main speakers. I hear the melody and rhythms, the contrapuntal lines slipped in between the chords, the guitar picking triplets out of the air. Terny sings with a throaty sort of cat scratch, the appeal of his voice a combination of phrasing and brio.

Sarah's voice, in contrast, is a special instrument. While the piano and guitar extend the harmony, Sarah surrounds Terny's lead, makes the arc of the lyrics fuller, the richness of her singing giving the song its grace. She lifts the melody from its center, heightens the rhythms and colors the beat. When the music ends, Terny goes and slaps high fives with everyone. Sarah comes out of the booth and the others hoot and whistle until she covers her face. A.G. in the engineering room clicks on the intercom and calls Terny and Sarah over. I give thumbs up before going outside for a smoke.

The moon's higher now, almost directly above, the temperature outside in single digits. I pull my gloves on after getting my cigarette lit, the smoke mixing immediately with the steam from my breath. The snow in the driveway is crusted over, I take the heel of my boot and scrape away the surface, think about Dave again, about Dave and Darcie, about Noel and the film, what I should do and what to tell Sarah. I picture Dave after he said, "Humor me, Mick," how I nearly felt sorry for him, though this passed and I grew angry again, was sure Dave was playing me for a fool, that he was casting me in order to finish me off once and for all, would hire and fire me, ruin me for sure.

I remember how I suddenly wanted to hit him, the urgency of my desire surprising, I thought seriously that I would, that I was supposed to and shouldn't worry what came of it, that some things were worth the risk. I think now of what might have happened if I had hit Dave, how this would have solved everything and I wouldn't have had to worry about whether or not I should work with Darcie. In the end, I didn't hit him, of course, though standing here now, out in the cold, I think how strange it was to have considered this, how before rehab I never wanted to punch someone, never once when I was high, never even when I was drunk, but after Marimin and Darcie, some odd filtrate seems to have replaced my passive tendencies. It's as if, in being reprogrammed to monitor my self-destructive side, I've become more aggressive in defending my ground.

The red light blinks on above the door of the studio. I wait a minute, take out another cigarette, stay in the drive and think about what to do, about decisions made and not made and what might come of them yet. I think about the article I read the other day on the rift that had opened in the Ethiopian desert, how shit happens beneath the surface and then erupts. The cars parked in the drive have their windows frosted over, I can no longer see my reflection in the glass. I think again of Sarah, look at the frost, how the cold air chills what's warm and turns to ice, the rime that's made another perfect example of how irrepressible nature is, what forms and forges regardless.

———

After Sarah finishes recording, we go back to her place, strip down and get in the shower. Sarah has a freestanding unit, the base pan installed then framed by fiberglass sheets and plaster. The drain's connected to the sewer line, the shower itself large with white tiles and a clear plexiglass door. In the water, Sarah washes my back, my arms and legs. I turn and do the same for her, enjoy her largeness, let my hands explore her arms and breasts, her belly soaped, her skin smooth and perfect. I move behind and wash her hair, have told her now about Dave, about Darcie and Noel and all the rest.

Sarah slides against me, the water off her shoulders splashing. I wait for her reaction. Despite what I told Dave, I'm still thinking about the film, how good the script is and that I like the part. I think that I can work with Darcie, though whether or not this is bullshit, I really don't know. I'm not G.O.D., I know this much, know how programming me with an overload of information just makes me dizzy. Sarah listens to me talk about the film, helps to process all I'm saying. When I finish, she offers her own opinion about the script, reminds me how impressed we both were by Ferne and the story, says the timing's right for my career, the chance to work on a potentially great film, and that nothing's really so complicated unless we make it.

Who knows? It's hard to predict. There's a scene in 'Moonlight,' where Maria's talking with Fred and Jake about their father: "He was always ahead of the game. He knew where the ball was going before it was kicked. Osmosis. I think that's the word. He's still as osmotic as anyone I've ever come across." The line, each time, makes me wish I was osmotic, wish I knew what was going to happen so I could make the right decisions. I don't let on this way to Sarah, don't mention Darcie at all, in fact, or very little, say simply that I'm no longer so sure this is the project I want to turn to right now. A vague complaint. Sarah smiles in a way different from Dave, is not trying to trick or convince me, is giving me my options freely. She holds my fingers wet against her and says, "About all this. About you and Darcie, I can see it."

---

I spend the next two afternoons working for Jay in North Aldwich, replacing ceiling boards and insulating the attic. The weather's clear, slightly warmer, the ice on Parrot Lake still thick. Each morning I get up and check the Tick, hope to find a new posting from Ted. Not hearing from him directly, I continue to worry, use his posts as a way to fit him into an ongoing timeframe. I read other links and newspapers, acquire a certain knowledge about Iran, can recognize names and historical references now. Today, the tone of Ted's writing is anxious, his frustration exposed. "In Tehran, being suspected of free thought is reason for arrest. More than 1000 *dissidents* have now been detained, neutered and bumped off." Ted publishes the names of the dead, including Amir Javadi-Langaroodi, Ashkan Sohrabi, and Mohsen Ruholamini, the son of a moderate politician, beaten to death in jail. A memorial ceremony to honor those killed during the demonstrations is planned for Thursday at the Grand Mosala in central Tehran. Both Moussavi and Mehdi Karroubi are scheduled to attend. Ted writes, "It should be a hell of a party."

Saturday night, Sarah and I have dinner with Noel and Dave at Panson's on the south side. I hold Sarah's hand, introduce everyone, adjust the chairs so Sarah can fit beside me. We drink tea. Noel's wearing a short sleeve shirt, as if he's forgotten the weather. He has thin arms, shoulders sunk and flat, his chin sharp and unshaved, his brown hair long, a pair of horn-rimmed glasses set high on his nose. Dave has on a lamb's wool sweater, dyed dark. He's polite with me, friendly with Sarah, says he's glad to have me on board, then makes no further comment about it.

We talk about 'Juli,' exchange notes. Noel describes how he wants my character to dress and speak and move, encourages me to offer ideas of my own. I appreciate this, am glad to be talking shop again, which I haven't been able to do for some time. Over salad, Dave lays out our schedule for rehearsals and filming, tells me about the permits he's pulled, the crew he's lined up, those dates that are now set in stone. He's brought a contract with several pages of conditions I'm to meet, drug tests and punctuality provisions, the obligatory hoops my history forces me to jump through.

A man starts playing piano in the bar, the music quick and breezy. I touch Sarah's leg beneath the table, am happy, excited to be getting back to work and not thinking about anything more than this when I feel fingers on my shoulder, cool from the chill outside, a voice I recognize, an apology for being late, a free hand extended toward Sarah, followed by, "Hi. I'm Darcie."

———

Sunday, I wake at Sarah's, the bed a river of sheet and comforter I swim across. Sarah's already up and at her piano. I watch her for a minute, lie on my side and take in the whole of her halfway across the room. The sun's above the window, I roll and stare, check the time. In an hour, I need to leave for Noel's. Rehearsals are set around Darcie's schedule for

'Killer Joe.' I'm nervous and excited, eager to work, afraid my chops have atrophied over the last year, am sure Darcie will come ready to roll, will set the bar above my head and have me scramble just to reach it. I want to focus on doing my part, on this and nothing else. At dinner, Darcie didn't once mention working with me. I wonder now about the conversation she and Dave had before casting me in the part, what her feelings were, if she was opposed or in favor. Driving home after dinner, I waited for Sarah to offer her assessment of Darcie, finally asked, "So?"

Sarah's answer, following another slight pause, a clearing of her throat, a want to be precise, a definitive response, though who can rely on just words? I listened for what came in between, concentrated on Sarah's delivery, the truth in her inflexion, a verbal shrug, a neutral impression, Sarah said, "She seems nice."

---

I find my script for 'Juli,' bring it to the kitchen table where I sit with Sarah and run through lines. The part of Juli requires absolute disinhibition, a lack of reserve that comes from a troubled place. Sarah understands, is a talent in her own field, but as a singer and not an actress she's overly compassionate, tries to dance around the dark edges of Juli's personality, plays her as an ingénue rather than enigmatic. Later, at Noel's, Darcie and I do the same scenes again, have our own first rehearsal. As Juli, Darcie morphs into the role, her interpretation transcendent, she acts with a knowledge of her character that delivers dimensions light years beyond performance. A mystery constantly, she's still said nothing about my being hired for the film, has offered no opinion, no hint of caring one way or the other.

Noel gives direction, is hands-on, his vision fully formed though he's open to dialogue. Dave sits off to the side, takes everything in. When we finish, we review our work, jot notes in the margin of our scripts, discuss what to try next time. Darcie doesn't engage me in any way other than what's relevant to the film. Only as she's leaving does she joke and tell me to go home and work on my character, that I should pretend I'm falling in love with her "just a little bit."

———

# 12

BOB IS IN transfer, is brought down from Baltimore in a green army van. I'm in East Aldwich, putting new light fixtures in an old colonial. Sarah's doing voiceovers for a Pedro Almodóvar film, the American dubbing, she reads lines in translation for three separate parts. Kate has asked if I can pick Cam up from school so she can be at the New Princeton Rehabilitation Center when Bob arrives. I say yes, of course. Since Baltimore, Kate's been feeling better, her body responding to the new medications, she's put on weight, has more stamina, plans to resume teaching soon, a new class on the Poetics of Rhetoric, with Cicero, Aristotle, Ogden and Whately. All of this is good, and still there are limitations, Kate's CML barely in remission, she exhausts herself researching programs beneficial to Bob's recovery, making calls and preparing the house for his return. I tell her she needs to pace herself, while she insists she's fine. I've given up trying to argue, have promised to build a ramp in front of the house for Bob's wheelchair, make a note to get the wood.

Just after 3:00 p.m., Cam and I take the expressway to the New Princeton exit. The NPRC is on the north side, some twelve minutes away from Cam's school. We park in the gated lot, take the elevator to the third floor, where Bob's sitting on the side of a bed in one of the wards. Kate's there, talking with a woman in uniform who's explaining the process for getting Bob from the NPRC to home. Soldiers with families, those whose wounds have sufficiently healed, are able to treat the NPRC as a way station, a place they pass through, returning as outpatients for treatment and therapy. For those whose injuries require additional attention, who arrive like meat packaged and shipped, armless and legless, earless and eyeless, addicted to Vicodin, OxyContin, Fentanyl, Ultram and worse, those with post-trauma complications and nowhere else to go, the NPRC winds up a more permanent location.

The ward's crowded. There's a smell to the place like an old gym. Kate has kept her jacket on, seems chilled inside her coat. When I get close enough, she does something she's never done before, slips her arm inside of mine and holds on. Bob's bed is in the center. Cam drops down while Bob and I shake hands, chat familiarly now. The ends of Bob's pants are clipped and rolled under his stumps. Beneath his bed, beside his duffle, is a pair of black boots, army issue, the laces tied together, left as some sort of ignominious display. The woman in uniform is attractive enough, blond beneath her cap, the cut of her skirt tailored tight to her hips, her legs in nylons. She hands Kate two envelopes with forms, refers to Bob as Lance-

Corporal Mayhre. When she leaves, there is a stirring on the beds. We stay at the NPRC for a couple of hours, make sure Bob is settled, let him know that all of this is temporary and he'll be home soon. The word *temporary* gets his attention. He sets his hands on his half legs, looks off across the room.

---

Darcie and I rehearse. Together we're cool, have established a rhythm, a way of working together without any problems. Whatever was before, isn't now, I tell myself. We're pros and find a way to achieve a new level of intimacy without being intimate. Everything we do is part of a cooperative centered on improving the film. I'm committed and spend extra time discussing the script with Noel.

To play Juli, Darcie has asked me to help her with guitar. I agree, for the sake of the film, though I know she can already play well enough, has owned an old Martin D-18V since college. We work together before and after rehearsals. Darcie performs as I expect, her phrasing and chord progressions fluid, her singing bluesy, a sort of Zooey Deschanel meets Bonnie Raitt, resonant and well suited for the part. I offer to have Sarah give her some pointers for her voice and she agrees, but somehow this never comes off.

---

Ted on the Tick, for the first time, admits he's in Tehran. He's taunting, I think, as if he's been waiting for the right moment, a sense that others already know and are looking for him now. He chides Khamenei, chews out Ahmadinejad, mentions the meeting he had with Mir Hussein Moussavi and Mohammad Khatami and their discussion of G.O.D.

Coiyle calls and wants to shoot new scenes for Deletron at the Verimore Hotel. I tell him no problem, set my schedule with Noel and Jay, arrange to meet Coiyle and crew Saturday afternoon. Marsha, the actress I worked with before, is there. She's very beautiful, with long yellow hair, thick as a witch's broom, cut at her shoulders and worn straight. She has on a black evening dress, fitted across her breasts, the hem falling to her knees. Like my jacket, the woman's dress is creased to show she's been out and about for some time.

We start upstairs again, in the room. The woman picks up the box, moves as I did before, goes to the dresser, to the window, to the bed and chair, where she sits with the box in her lap. When I take the box from her, she follows me. We ride the elevator down to the lobby, head to the bar where a man is waiting for us. Older, with a rhinophymic nose and white hair, as ugly as the woman is handsome, his features are like spoiled fruit, round and pocked, his forehead too large, his eyes severe and silent. We sit in a booth, the box placed in the center of the table.

I smoke a cigarette. The man drinks. The woman drinks as well. The man stares at the box. There's something both calming and intimidating about him. No one talks, though we seem to be arbitrating a deal. When the man smiles, I see his teeth are gray. He reaches down on the seat beside him and produces a rose. The woman with me takes it, holds the stem above the thorns. As we leave, the woman slips her arm inside the man's. It's unclear who has the box.

———

The shoot runs several hours. Just after 4:00 p.m. Sarah and Cam come to watch. We finish with the scene in the bar, after which Coiyle takes me aside and pays $3,000 for the day's work. He hands me a second check for $10,000, the terms of the contract, initial payment on his locking me up for the year. The amount is more money than I've had at one time since dad died. I'm thinking maybe with the checks added to what Sarah offered and Feldman's pledged, I can actually stage 'Moonlight.' The thought is premature, of course, the money not enough to rent a venue and start auditions, but I think what I want to do is rent a venue and start auditions. I take the checks and hand them to Sarah. "I'm no good with this," I ask her to put them in some kind of account.

In bed that night, Sarah and I listen to a rough cut of the Pearl Divers' cd. On each tune, Sarah's singing impresses. I encourage her to record her own songs, suggest her agent throw a broader net and land her better jobs. She talks to me of 'Moonlight.' We are together in this way, comfortable and comforting, conscious of each other outside ourselves, the fulfillment and extension. I think of when I loved before and how it's different now. Sarah's happy for my work, my arrangement with Coiyle and filming with Noel. She believes in the power of positive momentum, is convinced absolutely all good things come because we make them. About 'Moonlight,' she says that I should go ahead and jump, that sometimes things have to be set in motion before the other pieces can fall into place.

On nights we sleep at Sarah's, I sometimes bring the cat, let her wander around the loft, look for secret corners to hide in, or be with us out in the open space. A cautious creature, she spends time beneath the couch, under the piano and behind the bookshelf. Eventually she comes to the bed, curls herself at our feet. Unlike with Darcie, when Sarah and I make love, the cat rides the waves, does not jump down and flee.

Tonight I sleep with my hand on Sarah's hip, dream of her body as an entire landscape and me the size of a beetle, making my way along in hiking gear. When I wake in the morning, rather than tell Sarah about my dream, I ask if she remembers the scene in 'Moonlight' where Andy and Bel are talking about their relationship, and Andy says: "How I loved you. I'll never forget the earliest and loveliest days of our marriage. You offered your body to me. Here you are, you said one day, here's my body. Oh thanks very much, I said, that's very decent of you, what do you want me to do with it? Do what you will, you said. This is going to need a bit of thought, I said. I tell you what, hold on to it for a couple of minutes, will you? Hold on to it while I call a copper."

The scene affects me in a dozen different ways. Sarah and I stay in bed, discuss what Pinter meant. Sarah talks of 'Moonlight' again, asks if I've given any more thought to what she said before. I kiss her, set my hands on the round of her belly, which has become like catnip for me. We go that afternoon and meet with the owners of the Grand Palm Theater. The GPT is a small venue, but perfect for our needs. I've decided Sarah's right, that waiting no longer makes sense. I want to take the money I have, what Sarah gave me and what I can borrow from Feldman, and see how far we can get. A leap of faith to be sure, but what isn't? We negotiate a six-week run, sign a contract and put down the cash required in advance. With the Summer Festival, we have to commit now or risk not getting any place before next winter. The cost of the theater drains nearly all of my funds. I'm excited and nervous. We're scheduled for July and don't even have a cast.

---

Kate returns to New Princeton daily, is driving now, spends time with Bob, meets with doctors, discusses therapies, the plan for getting Bob up and about on new legs.

On Wednesday, the final paperwork goes through and Kate drives Bob home, where Cam and I are waiting. As best we can, the house has been made over in order for Bob to get around. The ramp I promised to build is finished, the front porch expanded, the shelves inside the kitchen lowered, spaces cleared, the carpet on the first level pulled up and the den downstairs converted into a sleeping room. Despite all this, miscalculations occur, the maneuverability of Bob's wheelchair, his capacity for reaching and rounding corners, the counters too high and bathroom too small. Even the simplest tasks require a period of adjustment, trial and error, modifications made on the fly.

Throughout, Bob is uncomplaining. In blue sweats, the bottoms tucked in where his stumps end, he says no more than "Ahh," doesn't shout or flail his arms against the sides of his wheelchair, just nods his head in silent assessment and reevaluation. His composure is constant. I stop by after rehearsal and visit Bob in the den. The bed Kate had me bring down is a rollaway, turned so that its left side runs against the wall. A second mattress, better than the thin standard mat that came with the bed, is placed on top. Kate's in the front room. Cam upstairs. Bob sits on the bed, his back against the wall, a few books and a notepad beside him, a laptop Kate bought for him near his pillow. The tv's on but the sound is off. Bob looks up, closes the book he's reading.

I sit in the leather recliner, keep the footrest down so as not to stretch my legs out. Bob pulls his right stump up, reaches inside the opening of his sweatpants and massages the ends. His hair has grown, his features softer. The light in the den is white, the window draped, gives the room a self-contained glow. I ask about his therapy, the temporary prosthetics they have him up and standing on. He describes the process of relearning balance as "strange," the need to put all his focus on just trying not to fall.

The den is wood paneled. Bob's wheelchair is parked near the door. I tell him about Sarah, about 'Moonlight' and 'Juli in Chains.' For a while, we talk about Ted. There are bookshelves built into the wall behind me, each shelf lined with texts. The tv is tuned to the news, the sound still muted, the remote beside Bob. On the screen, a man in a dark suit stands with a shot of the Capital Building behind him. Cam comes down and says, "Hey," starts talking sports, Sidney Crosby, Slava Kozlov and Joe Corvo, until Kate calls him back to finish his homework. The image on the tv changes, is now Kitty Pilgrim chatting with Christiane Amanpour. A film clip appears, footage from Baghdad, a line note at the bottom of the screen, a street scene in the aftermath, the roadside upended, filled with smoke and ash. Bob watches, adjusts his half-legs again, pulls on his sweats, tilts his head back and rests against the wall.

There is, for just a second, a flash of recognition that cuts through Bob's composure, his eyes reluctantly, reflectively, observing. He goes no further than this, keeps himself in check, looks at the tv until the picture changes finally to a commercial for Windex. I don't expect him to say anything, as he never talks about his tour, am surprised when he mentions Baghdad, Basrah and Kirkuk, Najaf and Mamoon.

A second commercial shows a yellow Hummer. I wait for Bob to continue, but he stops here. The list of cities causes me to picture the clip again. I think about all the shit Bob must have seen in Iraq, try as always to get him talking about his enlistment, say "Things must have been fucked while you were there."

Bob doesn't argue this, says only, "Things are as they are."

"And you went?"

"I went."

"Why?"

"Because things are as they are."

"Of course," I'm trying to follow. As unclear as Bob's answers are, it's the most he's said on the subject since Baltimore, and hoping it's just a matter of asking the right question, I say, "I'm sure you had a reason for going."

"I did."

"Care to share?"

Bob holds up two fingers, not quite a peace sign, more like rabbit ears folded slightly over at the tip, and says, "I went when I found the idea of not enlisting impossible."

"But what does that mean?" I still don't get it.

With his other hand, Bob passes me the book he was reading when I came in, a biography on Antoine de Saint-Exupery. He asks, "Have you read him?"

"Other than 'The Little Prince?'" I answer, "No."

He has me turn to a yellow-tabbed page in the book and read what he's highlighted, a quote made by Saint-Exupery on his impressions of war: "War is not an adventure. It is a disease. It is like typhus. War is organized murder and torture against our brothers."

I like the quote, am reminded of Pinter, who said America's invasion of Iraq was "business as usual," that Bush and Blair were "fanatical thinkers," both "ignorant and dangerous in their absolutism. Mass murderers," the invasion "a bandit act..., blatant state terrorism, demonstrating absolute contempt for the concept of international law... War is the destruction of human beings which—unless they're Americans—the United States refers to as collateral damage." This is what comes to mind. I wonder why Bob's shown me the quote from Saint-Exupery, ask if he agrees with the sentiment, and when he says yes, I go "But you enlisted."

"Right." Bob sets his hands beside his hips, raises himself off the mattress, arches his back and then his shoulders. On the bed, his half legs barely reach the edge, the absence of what should be there conspicuous. He tells me that, like the pacifist poets Kate mentioned, Saint-Exupery was fundamentally and philosophically opposed to war, and yet he enlisted in World War II as a pilot. "He was already 42," Bob says. "They almost didn't take him, but he was a good flyer. The Germans shot him down while he was gathering information for the Allies." Bob places his hands back in his lap, his eyes so quiet he seems almost on the verge of prayer. I take a cigarette from my pocket, am no closer to understanding anything. "So Saint-Exupery died fighting a war he didn't believe in?"

Bob corrects me again. "Saint-Exupery enlisted because it didn't matter whether or not he believed. The war was real."

I still don't get it, think of what Bob said before about things being as they are, think of what Pinter said about reality, how in art there are no hard distinctions between what's real and what is unreal, that for an artist the endgame involves exploring reality through the imagination to arrive at *truth*, while as a citizen the approach is different, the need to stand up and demand the truth from government. I look at Bob without his legs and know that this is real, that this is something true and irrefutable, and yet how to explain it? I go ahead and ask once more, "So what does all this have to do with you? What do you mean when you say not enlisting was impossible?"

Bob places his hands on the cover of the book I've returned to him, and tosses the question back at me. "What was Saint-Exupery doing joining the war if he opposed it?"

I still have no idea. Whatever Bob wants me to know, I'm lost. I tell him this, hold my unlit cigarette out, move my fingers slowly, repeat what he said before as a way of possibly finding a clue. "Saint-Exupery enlisted because the war was real."

"Because the consequences were real."

"And what about the consequence of dying? And you losing your legs?"

Just as he said at the VAMC, Bob insists, "That doesn't matter."

"But how? How does it not matter?"

He shifts his hips, his legs like two sticks broken. I consider what Ted would say, how there are things we know and don't know, the decision at hand and the risk taken, how once a course of action is chosen, what happens does not alter the correctness of the original decision. I still don't agree, did not with Ted and can't with Bob. I tell Bob this, mention the pacifist poets all ending up maimed or dead, and Saint-Exupery too, how none of it makes sense. "I'm not sure what you're saying." I ask him to explain, want to hear specifically now, "What happened to your legs and what went wrong exactly?"

Here again Bob's answer confounds, he lays the book across his lap and says, "Everything and nothing."

I get up from the chair, go and open the window shade, the dusk outside a soft silverfish. Bob reaches for his laptop, has me come and take it from him. On the computer screen is the last posting from the Tick. I check the main page, find the same post as yesterday, the coverage of the demonstration at the Beheshte Zahra cemetery, people in peaceful assembly attacked by the Guards. Abdullah Araghi, leader of the Revolutionary Guards in Tehran, has now threatened to "Cut out each infidel's heart and feed it to the *tinan*. We are not joking, we will confront those who want to fight against the clerical establishment." The statement is followed by a quote from former president Mohammad Khatami: "Araghi is a fool. He is also a danger. The Guard do not support the clerics but have used the sham election as a coup. Araghi would like to be king."

There as witness, forced into hiding, Ted still manages to give a personal account, describes the smells and color of the air. "A whitish mist, hot as blue sand heated."

Bob asks how Ted is doing, and I answer, "He's underground. I don't know where exactly."

I put the computer back on the bed. Bob rubs his thighs, uses his arms to shift around. He knows Ted and I are close, that I tried talking him out of going to Iran, asserted Mises in my argument. "At some point a person must be reasonable."

"But what is that?" Bob asks me now to explain. Before I can, he says, "The problem with reason is that it's hard to define. What is logic? Does reasonableness exist individually or is it universal?"

I answer the best I can. "I think each situation has its own core logic, and each individual applies reason differently."

"But how is that possible? Don't situations exist independent of the individual? Your friend is responding to the situation in Iran, not the other way around." Bob says, "That being true, as the situation in Iran is constant, how can the inconsistent responses of individuals all be reasonable?"

"Because," I try again, "the situation isn't constant. Or at least it's not perceived that way. Everyone sees things differently."

"Then you think reason is arbitrary? That the Guard in Iran are just as reasonable as the demonstrators?"

"I didn't say that." Bob has me spinning. If he is setting me up, I'm ill-prepared. He asks, "Aren't the choices we make supposed to be based on a fundamental right and wrong?"

"Yes, but again you're assuming reason and logic are ethical decisions and everyone shares the same view."

"But the individual's view doesn't matter, does it, if reasonableness exists outside of us?"

I don't know. I understand only in fragments, suspect Bob has been incubating his argument for some time. The last of the day's light has disappeared outside the window, the moon yet to offer any real glow, leaves the snow on the lawns and the flat tar stretch of street in a blackwash transition. I put my unlit cigarette down on the window ledge. Bob massages the muscle in his left shoulder, reaches toward his wheelchair, which is parked at the foot of his bed. He pulls it closer, sets the brake and raises up on his arms, lifts himself over the side as fluid as a gymnast working the parallel bars. His stubs stick straight out, he settles down inside the wheelchair, undoes the brake, rolls backward, adjusts so he is facing me. "The individual matters only through the acts we choose to do," he modifies his initial claim slightly, then says "It's the choices we make personally that create the grand scheme. But in the grand scheme, the individual vanishes."

I hold up my hands, am lost, try to review. "Are you saying because the situation in Iran exists independent of any one individual, what happens to Ted in the grand scheme is insignificant compared to the importance of reporting the truth?"

"Yes," Bob answers. "Pretty much that." He tells me I should picture the world as a series of rings, one set inside the other, with the innermost ring establishing the axis around which everything else spins. "To have a constructive effect on the world, we must understand our relationship to the axis." He uses Saint-Exupery as an example, how he flew missions for the Allies even though he opposed the war. "Saint-Exupery understood the war was real and hoped his involvement might reduce in some way the extent of the dying." He mentions Ted again, says "Your friend understands. He knows to live in the world means addressing what's real."

"Sure, sure," I give Bob this, then say, "But everything's

real, large and small and in between. Why does our response have to be extreme in order to be validated?"

Again, Bob says, "Who's to say what's extreme?" He resorts again to rhetoric, is his mother's son. "Each decision is up to the individual. Truth is the one constant. To complain about something and then do nothing to influence it is hypocritical."

"I don't know," I stand near the recliner, try to reconcile reasonableness and constructive action, to which Bob replies, "But all constructive actions, regardless of how extreme, are reasonable." Although he's several years younger than me, I feel as if I'm chasing after Bob for some elusive bit of knowledge. I sit down in the chair, retrace my steps, ask as I have a dozen times before, more hopeful now, "What about you? All Saint-Exupery and Ted aside, what were you trying to do? Why enlist if you're against the war? What did you think you could pull off? What happened to your legs man, and how does it all fit together?"

Bob gives a quick start and stop to the wheels of his chair, rolls and brakes, the momentum lifting the front end of his chair off the ground. He does not look away as he did before outside the VAMC, but stares at me instead, begins to talk, so suddenly it takes me a second to realize what he's saying. "We were in Basrah, assigned to road blocks, doing searches off Exit 12 along Highway 80, which runs down from Kuwait. There were four of us that morning, our Sergeant and three LCPLs. The flow of traffic over Exit 12 into the city was constant. I was halfway through my first tour, was six months overseas. I had enlisted because the war was savage and I thought I could make it less so," he glances down at his legs, then up at me, almost shyly now, as if his claim needs support, or at least my understanding. He quotes statistics, the number of Iraqi civilians killed since the United States invaded Iraq—650,000—the number of suicide bombings—

over 600 each year—the number of Iraqis displaced by the war—more than 5 million.

"We developed a system for inspecting the cars. Most of what we did was by the book, though everything required intuition. One car we stopped that morning was an old Chrysler LeBaron with four people inside, a man and woman up front and two kids in back. Things seemed normal. We searched the trunk, did a sweep of the outside, were about to let the car pass when the woman looked at me strangely." Bob describes the woman's face as panic swallowed. "Her head was covered by a scarf, her mouth forming words I couldn't understand, her eyes opened wide as if screaming. The car windows were closed, despite the heat and lack of air. I tapped the glass and the woman pointed back at her kids, then showed me the doors and windows were locked and she couldn't get out. I saw the man behind the wheel beginning to fumble with something, heard my Sergeant shout and kick the door. The woman started pulling on the handle, the kids squirming, sensing."

Bob says, "I was a few feet from the right side of the car. The others were on the left, their rifles pointed at the driver. Everything was happening too fast, and too slow. We were all sure then. I thought here was my opportunity, the reason I was there, that all I had to do was smash the glass and get the kids out before the car blew up. Things made sense in that moment."

He describes his Sergeant "still shouting, and then the others started shooting. The driver had his hands further off the wheel and beneath the seat, and suddenly the car's jumping, and then we're all running for cover, me out in front, but the bomb never went off. We waited a minute, then went back to look. The man and woman up front were dead, the kids in back going crazy. Beneath the front seat was a shoebox filled with a dozen paperback books banned by the government, copies of 'Traffic and Laughter,' '1984,' 'Brave New World,' 'The Gulf between Us,' and "The Satanic Verses.'" Bob stares at me again, his fingers settled on the end of his stumps. "Two days later, I'm out on patrol when an IED went off beneath us. I was thinking of how I turned and ran, how I left the kids in the car, and would have done so even if there was a bomb. I was thinking this when everything around us became a bright white light. It's perfect really, in its own way, don't you think? What happened to me twice, I mean, how I had my legs cut out from under."

I don't comment, don't pretend to know, which is to say I do know but can't tell him. I want to say he did nothing wrong but am sure Bob will argue. We sit for several minutes after this, quietly, until Cam comes in and wants to know if it's too late to skate.

---

I get up early and work for Jay in East Warren, am fixing more of the floors now, and the ceiling in his building. Kate has taken Bob out to the NPRC for his therapy. Tonight I have rehearsal, a scene in 'Juli' I'm trying to nail down. I get confused at times, reading lines with Darcie, looking to deliver them as I would for purposes of the film, but bringing too much of me to the part, and then consciously drawing back again against the spirit of the film. It isn't that I don't know what I'm doing, that I forget I'm in character and Darcie is too, but that when I get on a roll, and am reciting my lines, my mind wants to ad lib, to jump ahead—or backwards—and lets me know this is the way I might have done things if Darcie and I were still together. It's nothing I take seriously, which is to say I'm serious about my acting and nothing else. I'm more than happy with Sarah and attribute the occasional mix-up to a phantom pain, the sort of sensation Bob says he sometimes still feels in his arch and calves that have gone missing.

———

Ted has not posted now for three days. I'm worried enough to try and call. He doesn't answer. I text and again get nothing.

———

The latest Deletron clip has appeared online, continues to attract attention. When I go and hear Sarah sing, people recognize me, come over to talk, want to know about the box, ask for clues, offer guesses, have thoughts about the woman and the old man. Coiyle calls to say Marshall Herskovitz and Edward Zwick, creators of 'thirtysomething' and 'quarterlife,' have contacted him about turning our clips into a regular show. Bloggers still write about me, add additional stories about my addiction and recovery. Suddenly there's serious interest in my Stanley, pictures are discovered of my collapse, shots snapped on cell phones that night at the Galaxy and posted online. Coiyle creates topspin, posts better pictures taken at different times, gives everyone something new to look at, tells me, "It's all good, Mick. You're a man reclaimed. For that there's no such thing as bad press."

My email folder is constantly full, the MySpace and Facebook pages Coiyle created and linked to Deletron jammed with comments and messages and a thousand new friends. Coiyle has his secretary Twitter for me, tells the world what I'm supposedly doing. Sales of Deletron merchandise breaks more records, Coiyle books me for appearances at trade shows and conventions. He's excited about my plans to make 'Juli in Chains,' promises to give me a decision soon about investing in 'Moonlight.' Billy sends me scripts, arranges auditions for other films and plays. I'm making calls of my own, trying to land actors and rehearsal time to get 'Moonlight' started.

At 3:00 p.m. I pick up Cam from school, stop for a pizza slice then grab his skates from home. "There's something I want to show you," I say. This afternoon a junior hockey team is practicing at the Birch Bow rink. Cam and I sit and watch while the kids on the ice do a skating drill, slide around orange cones with their sticks and a puck. The coach stands holding his own stick, wearing hockey gloves and an ancient pair of black Ace leather skates. His shaved head steams in the cold, his hard jaw set beneath a ropey gray moustache, his large ears are red, he keeps a whistle between his teeth, even when talking. I tell Cam to put on his skates while I go and explain to the coach how we're new in town and that my kid wants to play hockey. I sign the waiver, promise next time to come with helmet and stick and gloves.

The coach motions Cam over, points to the duffel, has him get a helmet and stick, then turns to me and says, "You sure he's fifteen?"

Cam in line watches the others make wide loops at each cone, the angle of their skating safe though inefficient. Even the best kids keep their heads down, focus on the puck, lift their eyes to see each cone, then look down again at the ice, up and down so that their rhythm is a bobble. Some of the kids miss a cone, others lose the puck. Those who make it through without a miss celebrate with high fives. The helmet Cam wears fits loosely, the stick he finds is almost right. He has on the large gloves I gave him which are nearly hockey-size. Standing in line, he takes the puck left for him by the kid who just finished chugging through the cones. There are twelve cones in total. Cam starts, by the time he's four cones through all the chattering on the rink has stopped and everyone's watching.

———

We continue rehearsing 'Juli in Chains' around Darcie's schedule for 'Killer Joe.' Noel wants to begin filming in a few days. He and Dave have already nailed down locations, worked through the logistics with the crew. I see Cam and Kate and Bob before or after hockey practice, around my rehearsals and the hours I still work for Jay. Most nights I sleep at Sarah's. The Pearl Diver's new cd has been mixed and pressed and set for early summer release. A tour is planned, with Sarah invited to sing at a handful of shows. Again I say she should ask to do more than backup, that the band should let her solo or even open, but Sarah doesn't want to make demands, is happy they're pleased with her singing. "It's their gig," she's content to wait and see what happens.

During rehearsals, I'm better now at staying in character. My concentration is improved, my ability to deal with Darcie as Juli, however complicated it is to play the part of a guy in love. I tell myself I'm up to the challenge, have learned to maintain my discipline and distance, what emotions I don't need I push away with my right hand, grab back what the film requires with my left. My chops return, my job to perform off Darcie, to react as she acts. I have no problem with this, am happy to keep to the script, to do the scenes the way they're written.

———

On the Tick, Ted's posts remain sporadic. A bad sign. He texts me finally, for the first time. "Entrenched," he writes. "Getting in was easy." The implication of his message makes me nervous. I text back, want to know what's going on, when he's coming home and how he's doing really? Ten minutes later, Ted replies, "Not now. Can't."

I don't know if he means he can't come home now, or can't text. I write back but get no further response. I check the comments left by readers on the Tick, see if there's anything I've missed, some particular note encrypted and meant for me that Ted would expect me to recognize. I find nothing, reread the most recent posts where Ted describes the demonstrations as "ongoing but bloodied." On Thursday, two more leading reformers, Saeed Shariati and Shayesteh Amiri, were jailed. Word of the arrests is leaked, the Ayatollah Ali Khamenei denouncing the arrogance of the free press with brimstone: "The dissemination of information will not be tolerated."

Ted quotes the poet Gil Scott-Heron, "The revolution will not be televised." He quotes The Who's 'Revolution,' reprints comments by the *dissident* cleric Ayatollah Hussein-Ali Montazeri, who mocked Khamenei and Araghi's call to violence with: "How did this happen? People murdered for mounting a peaceful protest here in Tehran? Who could have seen it coming?" Hussein Moussavi is also quoted: "These things are blackening our country, blackening all our hearts. If we remain silent, it will destroy us all and take us to hell." As a token, Khamenei and Ahmadinejad decide to release 100 corpses from jail, along with a handful of arrested protesters. Attached to the gesture, Ahmadinejad has asked the head of the judiciary to treat the liberated prisoners with *Islamic mercy*. "Jesus man," Ted can't resist writing, "let's hope not."

---

Before Cam's next practice, we go to Periman Sports and buy hockey gloves, pads and helmet and stick. After practice, Cam still wants to skate. We pick up Sarah, head to the lake where Cam spanks pucks against a log. Sarah glides with me some thirty feet from shore. She has her floppy blue hat pulled down over her ears, her white coat zipped high, is more comfortable on her skates now, shows me the maneuvers she can manage on her own.

The wind hints of something warm, a trace of spring coming in the weeks ahead. Cam skates further out on the ice, circles and races around with his stick in front, the puck set in the curve. He keeps his helmet on, a white plastic cap I thought he'd balk at wearing but he doesn't seem to mind. The blade of his stick shifts left and right as he maneuvers between imaginary defenders, pulls back and releases a shot.

Sarah cheers. Cam comes and offers her the end of his stick which she takes, lets him tow her out to the center of the lake. Despite her size, Cam's still able to generate enough momentum to move them across the ice.

I watch Sarah laugh and throw her head back while Cam increases his speed, cuts a wide loop until Sarah lets go, bends over and sails along. The snow on the ice is a light white dust that scatters and floats in powdered swirls. Far enough away from me, Sarah's shape seems almost small. I wave my hands, want her closer. Sarah circles around, starts toward me again. Halfway to shore, she nearly slips and falls, only to gather herself. The ice between us is coarse and silver. I skate to where she is, hold out my hands, steady myself as she slides in, set my blades down hard and lock my knees. I do not move, am a fixture waiting as Sarah reaches. I let her grab me, am relieved when she does, give her balance and mooring, don't want to do anything now to upset her.

---

# 13

FILMING FOR 'JULI' starts on Friday. We do interior scenes, work in the mornings and afternoons, shoot around Darcie's schedule for 'Killer Joe.' I've discussed with Jay the need to redo my schedule. He's cool with this, is glad I've got the gig. I promise to squeeze in as much work as he needs, but Jay tells me not to worry, the market's still down, half the houses and buildings he owns impossible to move. I think maybe, with things improving for me, it's time for Jay to take me off his payroll altogether. "I can do what you need for free," I insist I owe him this much for keeping me afloat when I was going under. Jay appreciates, tells me not to worry, says "You I can afford, little brother."

Today I manage to finish some work for Jay out in West Glenn. He has me laying kitchen tile in a 1960s Tudor. The old tiles are green and glued to the floor. Yesterday I cut the sheets of linoleum into strips using a hard razor, then took a screwdriver and pried the sections free. Half the tiles broke, leaving pieces stuck to the wood. I poured Krud Kutter, a high-end solvent, over the remains, dissolved the adhesive, scraped and tossed everything into a metal trash can. Once the old tiles were cleared, I smoothed down the floor. Today I carry the boxes of new tiles from the garage. Jay's bought 3b Italian ceramic, blue and gray with rust-orange flecks. I use a carpenter's square to measure and mark the middle of the floor, dry-fit a row of tiles, leave equal spacing for the grout joints. The floor is dry enough to spread the grout without my needing to waterproof the wood. I place plastic spacers between the tiles to maintain the grout lines, use my trowel's notched edge to wipe the adhesive from the surface of the tiles before it dries.

After the first rows are set, I check my work with a leveler, mallet-tap each tile down until the kitchen's covered. Twice I stop and smoke, go online and see if Ted's posted anything on the Tick. He hasn't. I think about my conversation with Bob and the story he told me, think about Ted, and Sarah, about Sarah and me and the work I'm doing to get my legs back under. I think if I could do anything now, besides 'Moonlight,' and making Sarah happy, and Cam, that I'd find a way to get Ted home safely. I think this is what I should do, in the grand scheme as Bob said, but I don't know how. I can't call anyone, can't trade information or ask for favors. If I was making a movie, I'd play the part of the friend who flies to Tehran to save his buddy, but in real life that sort of theater dies after the second act. Inside the house, my radio is tuned to WRVR, gives me old songs, Stephen Bishop, 'On and On' played with just guitar and the perfect phrasing. I go back in, work some more, forget for a time what I was thinking.

---

Kate and I have arranged a schedule for getting Cam to and from hockey. Each day, if I'm not filming, Kate drops Cam off and I pick him up. I catch the end of practice, watch Cam fly around the ice, completing drills, working the puck during the scrimmage, using his speed to get his teammates involved. Afterward, I take him home, visit with Bob for awhile. If Sarah's free she joins us for dinner. If she's singing, and Noel doesn't need me, or I don't have other appointments, I go and hear her perform.

Auditions for 'Moonlight' have started. I've narrowed the list of actors down to a manageable number, am contacting only those I like and have a chance to land. I've met with Aimee and Gwynn and offered them the roles of Maria and Bel. After renting the Grand Palm Theater, the money I've left to spend on casting is almost gone. I'm honest enough with the actors I speak with, confess my limitations, make pledges rather than promises. Of the seven parts I have to cast, three actors reject my initial offer, refuse to work without the money nailed down, while the others say, "What the hell?" accept the risk, are willing to see what happens.

I call Feldman, tell him what I need. We discuss the quid pro quo before he writes the check. He's all business now, wants to know exactly what sort of return I'm promising on his investment.

---

Tonight we're filming 'Juli' outside. The snow Noel's been waiting for has finally come, he rushes everyone downtown and sets the scene as we rehearsed. I'm at Sarah's when Noel calls, get downtown and change my clothes. Darcie's already there, dressed as Juli in a brown wool sweater, green and white sundress, red winter cap and canvas sneakers, the ends of her fingers stick out of gloves with the tips cut off, her socks orange, rolled just above her ankles. The snow is heavy, the final storm of winter. Juli plays guitar, sings oblivious to the weather. People hurry past, the sleet and snow too much for them to stop and listen. Eventually only Roy remains.

The scene's important as it marks the first time my character has to admit Juli's quirkiness is something more than amusing, her eccentricities beyond artistic expression. Noel has written a revelatory script, the kind of love story that succeeds by avoiding emotionalism. The film does not add twists and turns to stir the plot, but remains honest, each character revealed in layers, fleshed out in multiple dimensions. Darcie's ability to play Juli both dark and light is essential, her complexities and accessibility, her mix of innocence and extravagance all both studied and innate. My job as Roy is to see things with the audience, to provide observation and reaction without a filter.

Standing there in the snow, I listen to Juli perform. The camera is aimed at my face, catches my happiness, followed by confusion, sadness and concern as the weather worsens and Juli remains impervious. I convey Roy's disorientation, how engaged he is originally, then anxious and nearly defeated. The camera stays on me, slides slowly back, records the scene as I take off my coat and put it around Juli's shoulders.

We finish shooting just after 11:00 p.m., change out of our wet costumes into drier clothes. Noel leaves to review the night's rushes, the crew packs up and drives home. Darcie and I go for coffee. We've not done this since the start of filming, have a habit of separating quickly at the end of each day's shoot, but tonight the weather has us in need of something warm. Darcie suggests and I see no reason not to.

The lighting in the diner is florescent. I take my cigarettes out, set the box beside my cup. Our waitress has pink hair, pale skin and black eye liner, an emo face in an off-white uniform, her features careworn yet attractive, convey both boredom and exhaustion. She sits at the counter, smoking. There are three other customers inside. Almost midnight, we're a block away from where we finished shooting. Darcie has on a blue sweatshirt, dark jeans. I slip off my jacket, toss it down on the seat beside me. Darcie asks if the jacket's new.

I assume she's joking. It's the same black coat I've had for years, but she insists she doesn't remember. "Seriously?" I don't know what to make of this, what it means that she's forgotten, if she really has. Ultimately, I think, memory reveals what is and isn't important to us. A year before Darcie and I met, I was working on a film version of John Hawkes' 'Death, Sleep and the Traveler.' I had a minor role, shared two scenes with an actress named Zoey Nazek. Zoey had long legs and red licorice lips. We began an affair that lasted several weeks. When filming ended, I left on a short tour where I played the Assistant in David Hare's 'The Bay of Nice.' Zoey went to do another independent film. We swore to keep our romance going, to hook up again in a matter of weeks and resume where we left off. Almost immediately though, on my own, my memory of our days together faded. I tried to remind myself of earlier feelings but they were impossible to retrieve. By the time I got back to Aldwich, I didn't feel a need to call and waited to see if Zoey would get in touch with me. She didn't. When we ran into one another, several months later, we laughed at the way the initial heat so quickly cooled when left unattended.

I think of Zoey now in terms of Darcie, how some old flames smolder and cling to the recesses like an old coat, while others simply fade. Darcie drinks her coffee black, takes a cigarette from my pack. I slide her my lighter. She asks about Sarah. I do not ask about Dave. We talk about the night's shoot, about Noel and the work to come, discuss Deletron, and 'Killer Joe' which is set to open next week. Darcie asks about Ted and I tell her. She flicks my lighter, smokes as I do. Sitting across from one another in our booth, I don't think this is strange, am sure my not thinking about this is a good thing. "Do you remember," I say, and mention a time before.

I don't mean to, but think suddenly how much I used to love her. That I haven't thought this way for some time is also a good thing, I think. I'm sure I'm only thinking of this because we're sitting here having coffee late at night the way we used to, and as I'm thinking of this, I'm convinced what I'm thinking is really only a memory and nothing more. I think about this, about memory and how addiction is also merely the mind remembering some earlier pleasure and wanting to experience it again. When I was in therapy, I once asked Kyle if he ever thought addiction could be viewed as a kind of love, and is it even possible to love without being addicted? Kyle clicked his pen, said addiction is the opposite of love, that a person can't love fully and contently if there is no freedom.

I look at Darcie, picture Juli, say "You look like Juli."

Darcie shifts her shoulders, shows her eyes beneath the light. "Do I?" She signals our waitress for a reheat on her coffee. I stare at the blue and gray lines in the surface of our table. We talk about Cam and Kate and then again about Sarah. I tell Darcie about the Pearl Divers, am boastful, take pride in Sarah's achievements. Darcie listens, is watching me as I talk, stops me and says, "It's cute."

"What is?"

"The way you talk about her. The two of you, I can see it."

I appreciate the comment, recall how Sarah had said the same, only in a different context, when talking about Darcie and me doing 'Juli.' Darcie holds the heat of her cigarette out, says "Screw the bloggers, right?"

I'm surprised she has mentioned this, the recent rash of comments, posts and pictures of me and Sarah online, unkind references to our dating, questions about what I'm doing with such a big girl and phrases far worse. I've seen these posts, have tried for the most part to ignore them, tell Darcie, "It doesn't matter," that this sort of shit is predictable and will pass just as quickly as it came.

"No doubt," Darcie moves her hand back. The cigarettes we smoke are cheap, Red Star, a bad habit, the taste heavy on my tongue, I can afford better now but somehow think I'll be more inclined to quit if I force myself to smoke a lesser brand. My logic is off, as usual; I've just gotten used to second-rate.

Darcie says about the bloggers, "Perception stings, but washes clean."

"It will, and does, yes," I agree. "Like shit."

"Like shit, right."

"It does no good to react. You know how this stuff goes."

"I do," Darcie better than most. When I went face down at the Galaxy, she got caught in the backlash of bad publicity that connected her to me. I set my elbows, hold my hands like a tennis player about to receive a serve. Darcie has a gift for delivery, the way she puts all her weight behind each word. She blows smoke, says "I like Sarah, though I only met her once." I can tell when more is coming, watch the light in Darcie's eyes. "I think it's perfect," she says, "the way you found someone so unlike me this time." She smiles, her comment baring catty claws.

I drink my coffee, consider again the right response, am not sure what there is, but then it comes to me and I offer up the one thing that hits the mark, "She makes me happy."

Darcie sits straight, touches the damp tips of her hair, smiles differently. Her coffee steams. She reaches over the arm of her chair, takes the ash from her cigarette and flicks it down at my shoe. "Happy's good." She shrugs, a concession, still fucking with me, she resists extending full agreement, says "Happy's the stardust in the bottom of the fish bowl, Mickey." Before we leave, she comments again about my coat.

---

I return to Sarah's late and crawl into bed. The chill from shooting outdoors has settled deep in my bones, the coffee I drank at the diner more stimulant than warm elixir, I curl myself against Sarah's side. In her sleep she shudders, then wakes and asks, "How did it go?"

I run through the entire night's shoot, my arm over Sarah's belly, my leg tucked between her thighs. I squirm, roll about, put my hands beneath my ass and feel my own cold. Usually coming in at night I'm hyper, unable to sleep right away. Sarah lets me work off my excess energy. Tonight I'm more than this, jumpy and restless. "Sorry," I say, my apology unclear, I tell her about Darcie and the diner, how we went to shake off the chill. I do not talk about the blog posts, have not spoken to her yet about these and am not sure she has found them. I talk more instead about the movie, about the scene we shot and how I hope we got what Noel was looking for, how love is a puzzle, what stays and goes, surprises and endures, everything we think we know but really don't.

Sarah lies beside me, her body in baby blue pajamas, made to rise and fall like a large buoyant ferry while I continue to toss about. The snow outside reflects the moon, sends a glow through the curtain, softening the dark. I close my eyes, open them again, stare at the ceiling which is streaked with cotton webs of light. My head is filled with snapshots. I tell Sarah what I remember about the first night she came to the Bow, how she was wearing a knit cap and a white ski jacket. "I remember your skating," I say.

Sarah touches my hand, says she remembers, too, describes my leaps across the ice, the gloves I had on and the jacket I was wearing. I kiss her shoulder, hold her tight. She pats my arm, tells me to "sleep, baby. Sleep."

———

# 14

TED COMES HOME the following Thursday. I'm on the south side of Aldwich, painting a ceiling for Jay, when he calls. I jump from the ladder and hurry across town. Ted's sitting on the couch in his apartment as I come in. Unshaved, his bass turned on, his face covered by a red-black beard, his skin is tan, his arms and chest even thinner than before, he's playing a bluesy riff. I get him up, give him a hug, feel him light as driftwood. For the last several days all the postings on the Tick have stopped, the final piece I read covering the 150 *dissidents* set to be tried together, students and store clerks arrested during the demonstrations, accused of crimes against the State and God. *Moharebeth*! Confessions were coerced

## The Consequence of Skating

and broadcast on Iranian tv. Ted wrote: "Stalin Lives. The Ayatollah's kangaroo court is hopping now."

He sits back on the couch. I drop into the chair across from him. The apartment's cool, there are crackers and sardines on the coffee table. Ted pushes his hair behind his ears, picks a string on his bass. I'm deliriously relieved he's home, have a thousand questions, decide to start with the most immediate and work my way from there. "How'd you get out?"

"Luck," Ted admits as much, says "Certain people didn't appreciate my reporting." The Guard came looking and he was forced to flee, was driven by friends to Kuwait, packed inside the spare tire bin of a Ford Escort, flown to the United Arab Emirates, to London and then Aldwich. The trip took 47 hours. "Home again, home again," he's exhausted, his constitution usually wired like the motor in a fan, greased for perpetual motion, is now set to pause. He folds himself forward, plays Bogdon Vasquaf while cradling his bass, says "I want to go back."

I ignore this, tell Ted about Sarah, about Cam and Kate and Bob, about Deletron and 'Juli' and working with Darcie. Ted plays his bass softly as I talk, finds the music soothing, finishes with Jethro Tull/J.S. Bach's 'Bouree,' then puts the bass down, turns his amp off. I ask for more news about his trip, for things he's yet to write about, wonder how his meeting with Moussavi went and what's up with G.O.D.

Ted tugs at the end of his beard, reaches to wrap his fingers around the frets of his bass. He's quiet for a moment, for more than this, is thinking how to tell me, I can see him working through his options, and deciding at last to skip over the gloss, he says in summary, with absolute finality this time, "G.O.D. is dead."

Darcie opens in 'Killer Joe.' Sarah and I buy tickets. Darcie is a revelation, impresses as always. Seeing her on stage again, the way she morphs from one part to the next, from Juli to Sharla back to Darcie, is dizzying. The play itself is a wild ride, savage and poetic and hilariously ugly. Letts is a wizard, is clearly insane. Reviewers call Darcie "untamable" and "razor sharp," her Sharla "performed with the gravity of a hailstorm." Dave throws a party to celebrate. Sarah and I go but don't stay long. As we leave, Darcie comes and kisses my cheek, calls me Roy and laughs.

After the party, Sarah and I go to Bruno's on the Hill where we dance a slow shimmy, Sarah with her arms raised high, her big body moving gracefully while I sway in front of her. I have a few drinks, nothing too much, no more than I can handle. Back at my place, I tell Sarah I love her. This is unplanned but as I want to say. I hold her clumsily, my arms searching for a way to reach around. In the middle of the front room, between my two rockers, I lean so that my face is directly in front of hers and say this, how I love, there in my apartment, among the ghosts.

---

Tuesday I film a scene for Noel, an interior shoot of Roy's apartment. Alone with just the camera, I move about in much the way I did for the Deletron clips, draw from the earlier experience, understand how each motion must reveal something about Roy without being obvious; the way he makes his coffee, brushes his teeth, pulls on his shirt and socks, all offering insight.

We wrap 'Juli' on schedule, six days after Darcie opens in 'Killer Joe.' Noel takes everything we've shot and starts editing the film. I've seen only occasional rushes, brief bits from disconnected scenes, I wait for Noel to call and tell me if I'm any good.

———

I'm busy now with 'Moonlight.' Each part in the play is cast, contracts signed and rehearsals started. In my free time, I still have to scramble for cash. Feldman calls to see how things are going and I tell him, "No worries, man." I phone friends again, and friends of friends, go after Coiyle who's promised his support but has yet to scratch a check. Billy shakes his head when I tell him that he needs to get involved. I remind him that I held up my end with 'Juli,' and I expect him to do the same. He complains that 'Moonlight' is a tough sell, wants me to concentrate on the new scripts he sent over, the stack that now covers Sarah's kitchen table. I grow impatient and snap, "I'll read what you have when you get 'Moonlight' a real goddamn producer."

Rehearsals run each night at the Performance Mecca. The time put into the play is paying off, our walkthroughs coming together, I rely on the notes I've made to help with my direction. After rehearsal, the cast and I sit and talk. Ted's set up a website where people can learn about 'Moonlight,' pre-order tickets and make donations. The site looks great but no one knows it's there. To draw attention, I've spoken with newspapers, bloggers and radio stations about giving us some advance coverage. A few bloggers and talk jocks agree to mention 'Moonlight,' if I'll do an interview and give them a story no one else has heard. I let them ask whatever they like, answer as best I can. When they bring up Sarah, I tell them, "Yes, we're together." If they press for more and comment on the oddness of our pairing, I laugh and call them assholes, give them a little flavor, make them feel foolish, something for their audience. "Love man, who can explain?"

I see Darcie around town, run into her here and there. The blog posts about my dating Sarah continue. The success of the Deletron clips, and now with talk of 'Juli,' and 'Moonlight,' and possible future projects, makes my name an easy one to kick about online. Sarah has seen the posts by now, is ignoring it at first, though sensitive, questioning, she wants to know what I think. I tell her, "I don't think," and this is for the most part true. I sit next to her, rub her shoulders, kiss her softly. We're on the couch and there is hardly room, the danger of falling over, the crash and thunder. I go ahead just the same, slide Sarah down, find the center of her, move myself on top and within, want to enter, to have her feel and let me, too, the movements I perform like a wet dog shaking, an attempt to shed what otherwise tries to get under my skin.

---

Cam has a hockey game on Saturday, goes with his team by bus. Sarah and I drive down to Everton City with Bob and Kate. Bob has his first set of new legs to use out of rehab, wears them with a sleeve over his stumps, a silicon socket shaped like a plunger cushioning the fit. The legs are graphite, silver, with no outer casing to provide an anatomical look. Bob in long pants steps and braces himself with crutches, is almost walking, tests and regains his stride in something of a lift and wobble.

We sit in the stands and watch, Kate with her coat drawn tight. On the ice, Cam's skills are obvious. He takes the first face-off and flies from the center circle, doesn't bother with fancy moves to free himself up, goes straight ahead, his balance and speed superior, he bounces off shoulders and hips without losing stride. The puck on his stick finds the opening above the goalie's right shoulder, makes the score a quick 1-0.

We cheer wildly. Bob beats his crutches while Sarah sings and I whistle and Kate claps her hands. On his second shift, Cam catches the puck from the wing, again goes down the center, takes a hard check from one defenseman and then another. He falls, flips the puck off to a teammate who glides right and sends the puck back to Cam who's raced around the back of the net. The other team takes notice, implements a strategy designed to keep Cam off the play. They send defensemen at him as soon as he gets on the ice. Cam is checked and hit, knocked into the boards, tripped and spun around. After each attack he gets up, skates on, doesn't retaliate or complain to the refs.

By the end of the second period, the score is tied 3-3 and Cam has all of his team's goals. Early in the third period, he gets the puck behind his own blue line, races the length of the ice, lays the puck off nicely to a teammate who finishes the play with a low slapshot that scoots through the goalie's legs. Just before the goal Cam is hit hard by two defensemen who converge and crush him. The refs don't see the action off the puck, miss the elbows thrown and high sticks that knock Cam to the ice. I shout, wait for Cam's reaction, expect him to get up swinging, but he gathers himself and skates back to the bench, his teammates and opposing players watching.

The game is lost on two late goals by the other side. Cam on a last second breakaway is tripped but not given a penalty shot. We go down and wait outside the locker room, catch Cam before he gets back on the team bus. Everyone praises his play. He accepts their consolation. I hang back, let the others have their turn, then grab his duffel, walk with him out to the bus. I want to tell his teammates how it's their job to protect their best player, that Gretzky had his Semenko and Bobby Clark his Dave Schultz, but I leave that to their coach and say instead, "It's good what you did, keeping your head and all."

We're halfway through the parking lot, Cam's knit hat pulled down over his ears, a bruise on his right cheek. He shuffles in his stride as if every muscle's sore. When he stops and takes his duffle back, he looks at me and I realize what I said was wrong, that he wants me to understand this, how he did fight back, that he's been fighting for months now and keeping his head's just part of it. I reach for him and pull him close. Cam lets me do this, doesn't say a word at first, then slides free. I wait as he gets on the bus, watch him sit with his team, see how they surround him. I stay out in the lot until the bus pulls away, then follow him home.

---

Billy arranges three auditions for me in L.A., each project a studio-backed film. I tell him thanks, but I can't go, that I have 'Moonlight.'

"Two days," he insists the meetings in L.A. are already set and I can't afford not to go. "We're talking 48 hours." Jay and Ted agree. Bill promises to make some calls for 'Moonlight.' I talk with Sarah, ask her to come with me, have her phone her agent and see what he can line up on short notice. I give the 'Moonlight' cast a brief break, fly out to L.A. and do the auditions. All the parts I read for are supporting, the kind of roles I need right now, I admit. I do ok, read the scenes with and without other actors. The producers seem to like me, are familiar with my work. Noel's put in a good word. I answer when they ask about 'The Birthday Party.' The grilling goes lightly, and surprisingly, as twice a producer takes me aside, wants to know my thoughts on Marimin and whether I'd recommend it.

Friday night Sarah sings at a showcase her agent was able to get her into. Held on the back lawn of an estate owned by Herb Alpert, more than a hundred people attend, talent scouts and record executives, producers and club owners looking for new acts. When it's Sarah's turn to perform, she stands beside a piano, on a wooden stage. A white canopy is stretched high with strings of pale lights. For some reason there's an ice sculpture of a chicken hawk in the center of the lawn. Sarah's size is a novelty, creates an odd first impression. She does three songs, Adele's 'Cold Shoulder,' Anita Baker's 'Caught Up in the Rapture,' and Joss Stone's 'Tell Me What We're Gonna Do Now.' People walking the grounds hear Sarah through speakers, are drawn to the stage, stand awed, not expecting. They cheer after each song, demand an encore. She gives them Aretha.

We stay in L.A. overnight, reserve a room at the Wilshire Grand. It's late when we come in. Sarah goes into the bathroom, while I check my phone for messages. We're both tired from the day. I turn on the tv, flick through the channels. Sarah is humming, I can hear her on the other side of the door. I find the end of an old British film—'It Always Rains on Sunday'—on the classic network. The movie stars Googie Withers and John McCallum, with McCallum playing an escaped con hiding out at the flat of his ex-lover, Withers. I watch the final scene, am a fan of both actors, note that Withers looks a bit like Darcie. In real life, McCallum and Withers married a year after the film was released, in 1948, and remained married for over sixty years. I look for signs of this in their acting, hints of their love in the early throes and how it endured.

The night before Sarah and I left for L.A., I was coming into the Mecca for rehearsal just as Darcie was leaving. We stood in the hallway where she told me reps for Joe Montello were attending her performance in 'Killer Joe' this weekend, that she was being considered for a part in the Broadway revival of the Terrence McNally play 'Lips Together, Teeth Apart.' I was happy for her, said "Break a leg." Darcie wished the same for my auditions. I asked how she'd heard, and she smiled as if I'd said something funny.

I'm sitting on the end of the bed as Sarah comes out of the bathroom and presents herself naked to me. I'm pleased, of course, and assume my face registers as much, but maybe it's because I've been watching McCallum and Withers, and thinking of Darcie, that the scale of things in my head is smaller. Seeing Sarah suddenly there, her breasts large and beautiful above the soft wide swell of her belly, her hips sturdy and set as separate sentries on either side of her trimmed patch of pubic hair, her thighs round and solid, her feet broad, reliable planks, I may have, for just the briefest second, exposed in my expression a different reaction.

Sarah notices and reacts to my response, a quick uncertainty, a want to turn away, only to force her smile back in place, her eyes given a chance to recover. During our travels, Sarah has managed everything with assurance, an awareness of her size and surroundings, comfortable in her skin, she's adapted to the limitations of space in airplanes, in taxis and restaurants and passing through crowds. I do not think of her in any way but as she is, have no wish to even try. I remember what I told Darcie at the diner, how Sarah makes me happy, and this is true. What awkwardness there is at times does not create any real problems between us, is at most an insignificant disparity. Not that I'm naïve, or in denial, or in weaker moments I haven't paused to consider the whole of everything, but then this is only natural, to see what is and move forward.

I get up, click off the tv, go and kiss Sarah. The taste in my mouth of her mouth is a mix of mint and warm wine breathed through me. I kneel and kiss her further, gently there where there is all of her to lose myself in and taste differently. Her hands on my head, she waits until I stand again, looks at me and wants to know, "What were you thinking?"

I say, "Nothing," tell her about the movie, how I was caught up and not expecting, is all. We crawl into bed, get down beneath the sheets, make love slowly then curl together for sleep. We've mastered the art of lying together, Sarah's large shape and my long frame. I wrap myself around her, my chin against her shoulder. The mattress in our room is firm and resistant to how I want to sleep. I'm too tired to care. The air around us has a different smell, or so I imagine. We remain curled in a coordinated spoon, my body slipped into Sarah's fleshy folds. I drift off and begin to dream.

The dream I have is another one of those peculiar episodes I can't quite explain. This time Sarah and I are on a beach. We're both naked though no one bothers to notice. Sarah's carrying a tiny version of Darcie in her hands, like an insect caught. Several times I ask Sarah to put Darcie down, but each time she does, Darcie leaps back up again. On the nightstand, beside the bed, my cell phone rings just as in my dream I'm reaching for Sarah's hands, looking to take Darcie from her and resolve the situation myself. I answer my phone groggily, hear Darcie in my head say "Fuck, Mick. Fuck."

There's a second before I'm completely awake, when I confuse everything, what's real and not, the sound of Darcie's voice in and outside the dream, where she is, and isn't, the distance and time, what is here and there and in between. I try to look around but the darkness is chronic. I sit up, struggle to get my bearings, am puzzled, and something more. A feeling. I go, "Baby, what is it?"

―――

Another example of how bad I am without a script and constantly in need of clear direction. I once did Inge's 'Picnic,' was cast as Hal, the drifter and would-be lover of

Madge, and worked with a director who had a unique vision for the play. He told me to do Hal less straight-on cool, as was the traditional interpretation performed by the great Ralph Meeker at the Music Box Theater in 1953, and later by William Holden on film. I was instructed instead to be more over the top, a party clown. The idea was strange. I was confused, convinced the play would implode if Hal was portrayed this way. Early rehearsals were a disaster, the high rim shots of my character clashing against the earnest performance of the other actors. After a week I was a tight knot twisted, when the director told me to now start reining in Hal. Bit by bit I layered the clown with various degrees of vulnerability, intelligence, anger and fears, everything I was not permitted to explore before. The result was a more nuanced and complicated character, the residue of my initial effort adding greater depth to Hal and the play in total.

Which brings me to this: How am I ever supposed to know what to do exactly without sufficient direction? If I had played Hal safely from the start, I would not have reached the same end, would not have been as successful. But how would I have known if I wasn't told? What if I was content with a lesser show, comfortable and without ever realizing there was more to achieve? What if I just went on as I thought was good enough, when really it wasn't, if all along there was meant to be more to my performance?

―――

I take my phone into the bathroom where the light above the mirror gives my skin a yellow glow. Darcie's talking still, I do what I can to calm her down, try and be clear on what's happened. She tells me Montello's people came to watch 'Killer Joe' tonight, and she's convinced she gave her worst performance ever. "Fuck me, Mick," she says.

I stare at my face in the mirror, wonder once we hang up if I didn't just dream the whole thing. I check the last number on my cell to be sure, rinse my face, take a pee, close the lid to the toilet and sit down. There's a newspaper on the floor, a copy of the LA Times bought earlier. I pick up a section, scan the headlines, stop at the obituaries where there are two entries. The first is a long piece on the gangster Lefty Rosenthal, who used to run sports betting parlors in Vegas. The obit goes into great detail about Lefty's illicit dealings, the car bombing he survived in 1982, his friendships with Frank Sinatra and Minnesota Fats, the 200 pairs of pants he owned and the number of times—37—he invoked the Fifth when testifying before a Congressional subcommittee on organized crime. In 1995, Martin Scorsese turned Lefty's story into the film 'Casino,' his character played by De Niro. There's a huge photo of Lefty at the top of the page, his blond hair greased back, his mouth in a smirk, adjusting the knot of his tie.

Printed below is a much smaller piece on Father Peter Jacobs, a recipient of the D'Oro Award, champion of the poor and addicted in New York City for 53 years. Known to take confessions in bars and back alleys, Father Peter had opened a restaurant—the Palatine—in order to employ otherwise unemployable members of his parish. At his funeral, his largesse was lauded by everyone from Walter Cronkite to Yoko Ono and Derek Jeter, and still the photo included in the obit is smaller than a postage stamp, a sixth the size of Lefty's.

I read the two pieces, consider their placement on the page, their juxtaposition and how weird the world, the way things find themselves aligned at times, the incongruity and near cosmic associations we fall into. I think of Darcie that night at Panson's, the way she made a point of sitting next to Sarah, purposely accentuating their physical disproportion. I make a mental note of other differences, the main one, what matters most, the measure of their effect on me, how Sarah soothes like soft cotton while Darcie's dark candy, a treat to be sure but in excess prone to run right through me.

I come back to bed, tell Sarah what happened, how Darcie was upset about 'Killer Joe' and just wanted to talk. I expect her to ask why she called me and not someone else? Where's Dave, and did I really answer the phone and say baby? In the dark, Sarah doesn't ask any questions however, says only, "Poor thing." She shifts on the mattress and goes back to sleep. I lay for a while, thinking first one way and then the other about who she meant exactly.

———

# 15

WE FLY HOME the next morning. On the plane I'm restless, in need of exercise, I can't quite get comfortable. I hold Sarah's hand, shift toward the window, review my 'Moonlight' notes and sections of the script. Rehearsal resumes tomorrow. I have some new ideas, some plans I hope will make the staging better. The airport in Aldwich is moderately sized. We land on time, get our bags and walk to Sarah's jeep, drive through rush hour, heading east into the city. It feels good to be home, I tell myself, 'There's no place like...' Sarah gets Shakira on the radio. I want to stay in tonight, let Sarah know, "I want to stay." Once inside her apartment though, I can't get settled, pace about, turn on the tv, then the laptop, search for news and check the Tick.

The Nobel Peace Prize winner Shirin Ebadi has had her medal seized by the Iranian government, is accused of being a *dissident* undeserving of the award. Ted writes: "What Ahmadinejad knows about peace could fit nicely beneath the heel of Ebadi's softest slipper." Soon after we get in, Ted calls and asks about our trip. I let him know how great Sarah did, and he whistles, tells me editors from the New Press are interested in his doing a book on Iran. "We're meeting tonight for drinks."

"Very cool," we make a date to hook up tomorrow.

I have my shoes on still, am thinking maybe what I want to do is run over to Cam's, bring the jersey I got him in L.A., Rob Blake's #4, that I'm just hyped up from travelling and maybe staying in isn't a good idea. I think I can run over to my place, too, check my messages, grab the cat and come back. I ask Sarah, see what she wants to do, if she wants to stay in or go get a drink maybe. She considers, then says that I should go and do what I want. "You go, baby," she says.

My truck is in Sarah's lot. The engine needs a few minutes to warm, my heater completely fucked. I note the time, calculate what remains of the evening, tell myself I won't stay out late. I think about Darcie, and then about Ted, think what he told me when he first got back from Iran, how G.O.D. is dead and the mistakes he made this second time have convinced him. About his meeting with Moussavi, Ted said, "He was very gracious and appreciative of my posts." Ted showed him G.O.D., pitched the salient points on how the program worked, the correctness of objective cognition and how they could plug anything in they wanted and G.O.D. would resolve it for them, and project the consequences.

Moussavi sighed. The court had just added 25 new *dissidents* to those on trial, 165 *dissidents* in total already before the court. Guilty verdicts were returning death sentences.

A Jewish teenager, Yaghoghil Shaolian, and 24-year-old Clotilde Reiss, a French academic, were among those indicted, the aggregate of *dissidents* awaiting trial now totaled over 1,500. Moussavi wondered what G.O.D. could do for them. "I'm sure your G.O.D. is good," Moussavi said this before explaining why the program was worthless, how it was of no help to predict the consequence of attempting to implement reform, that the demonstrators didn't need G.O.D. to forecast the government's reaction. "What is needed," Moussavi said, "is a purposeful plan to diminish and then remove Khamenei and Ahmadinejad from power. Without this your G.O.D. is an exercise, is academic, a parlor trick whispered in the universities and churches."

Sitting on his couch, his bass picked at softly, Ted had conceded the point, how naïve he was to think if he could just find what was empirically right that all else would fall into place. "But the world doesn't work that way, does it, Mick? All we can do, the best I can do, is report the truth and help get the word out. After that, it isn't up to me, or even G.O.D., is it?" He spoke of history then, of Babylon and Nineveh, Mesopotamia and Egypt, the Sumerians and Assyrians, the city of Ur, how the Babylonians built oddly shaped buildings called ziggurats in order to be nearer the heavens. "What else is there?" He rolled his shoulders, leaned forward, said as solace, "We do what we do. We're all descendants of Babylon. We set our sights and aim for the stars."

---

I check the time again, decide to drive to Cam's and bring him the jersey. I stay only a short while, visit with Kate and Bob, wait while Cam pulls on the jersey, shows himself off. Kate is still feeling better, the new meds helping. Bob, too, in the course of his own recovery, his walking improved, his crutches used mostly out of habit, his hitch and step nearly stable. All is good to see, a process I'm reminded, a pattern of setback and recovery. I leave just before 8:00, get in my truck and turn north, off of Welton, away from Sarah's. A light drizzle has started, too warm to freeze, the water beads and rolls off the hood of my truck.

Downtown, the light on North Seventh turns red, the traffic running in front of me alters the direction of the rain, sends a wet wind across my windshield. Sitting there, I picture Sarah as she sang out at Herb Alpert's, recall the ice sculpture of the chicken hawk and the people surrounding the stage. I think of Darcie again, what she said on the phone and how her calling had set off a buzzer deeply implanted, like some subconscious suggestion triggered, like Lawrence Harvey in 'The Manchurian Candidate,' the ringing of the phone accessing a nerve. I think of what I'm doing now, what I want to say to Darcie, have come out to say and knew this, that I wanted to speak with her tonight, even as Sarah and I were flying back to Aldwich. I tell myself I want Darcie to know she shouldn't have called me, that she can't be phoning me in the middle of the night. This is why I've come out now, to make things clear. I think of nothing else for a block or two, then think of Mises, for confirmation, and how I am acting now to cure a particular dissatisfaction.

―――――

Off Seventh, I remember speaking with Bob before I went to L.A., and asking if there was a girl he had in his head when he was in Basrah, someone he knew who kept him going, and how his answer surprised me. I expected him to tell me about a coed he met at Columbia, a girl he dated and slept with who complicated his decision to enlist and dreamed of when away. Instead, he said, "The girl I had in mind wasn't real."

I remember this now, how I almost asked if he made her up, only to stop and realize what he was saying.

———

A mile up, I turn east onto Pembler Blvd., then over to Third Street and downtown. The rain is harder now. On Third, I duck into a Mobil station, fill up my truck and get a coffee. The attendant inside the station is Lebanese, sits behind a glass so thick his features are distorted. I go back outside, hang out for a while in my truck. The steam from my coffee mists the windshield, a fog settles then slowly clears, leaves the glass wet.

There's a scene in 'Moonlight' where Pinter addresses self-deception. Jake: "Chinese laundry?" Bel: "Your father is very ill." Jake: "Chinese laundry?" Bel: "Your father is very ill." I wait until my coffee's gone, until all I have and haven't thought about falls away and I've only the here and now to deal with. I drive through the theater district, my heater click-click-clicking, blows hot then cold. I reach and turn it off, picture Darcie finishing her night's performance in 'Killer Joe,' taking curtain calls at the front of the stage. Just after 10:00 p.m., people leaving the theaters from other shows begin to fill the streets. The rain slows, the lot in the back of the Dive is almost full. I play the parking game, tell myself if I can't find a spot I'll just go back to Sarah's, that I'm not all that keen on being here anyway. I pull out of the lot and circle the block once, past the Chinese Laundry. When I come back, I squeeze into a place between a Nissan and a Ford Fusion.

Inside, I stand at the bar, order a drink, talk with some people I know. I move to a table when one's available, sit facing the door. A man next to me is reciting lines from 'Buried Child.' ("You're not going outside are you?" "No." "I don't want to wake up and find you not here." "I'll be here.") I check my watch, debate a second drink, decide if Darcie doesn't show before I finish I'll leave. This seems fair. I accept the terms, stir my ice, drink real slow.

When Darcie comes in, she finds me right away. She has on one of those white underarmor shirts that runners wear to keep warm, her hair in bangs cut jagged for the play. She doesn't seem surprised to see me, says "Hey baby," laughs and shakes the rain from her shoulders.

A bit of stage make-up remains on her cheek, left over from the night's performance, an occupational hazard, light patches that don't come clean with the first wash. I touch the place on my own cheek, show her where she's still painted. Darcie takes the heel of her hand and rubs. I pass my cigarettes across the table. She reaches for the one I'm smoking, but I don't let her. I ask about Montello's people and Darcie says, "They called." She rolls her head back, doesn't bother to tell me, knows I know and waves me off when I say, "Congratulations."

"They want me to read in New York, is all," Darcie takes my lighter, is used to getting what she wants, like a princess warrior, a hunter-gather. Our waiter comes and Darcie orders chicken fingers and a beer. She asks about my auditions. I answer in detail, use this time to settle in, to tell her about each producer and the films involved. As I talk, I prepare myself for what I came to say, my delivery and approach, all of which is predictably clumsy. Halfway through a story about one of the producers I met with, I wind up blurting out, "About L.A. About your calling," I want to be precise, as best I can, knowing communication is a hard stone to pass. I think of what Flaubert said, that "Language is a cracked kettle on which we beat out tunes for bears to dance, while all the time we long to move the stars to pity." What I want here isn't poetry but clarity, a way to convince myself and

Darcie, "It's no longer ok for you to phone me so late." I do my best to sound serious, remind her that I'm with Sarah now.

"How is Sarah?" Darcie asks.

I ignore the question, say "Your calling in the middle of the night isn't cool. You and I can talk, we can work together, we can have coffee, but you can't phone me at two in the morning."

"So you have a curfew now," she's fucking with me, purposely. I try to show that I'm annoyed, ask if she forgot about the time difference out west. Darcie shrugs and says, "I didn't forget."

"Perfect," I'm starting to think I shouldn't be here, that coming to the Dive was a mistake, the hours of buildup just that, a siren's call from which I should have known to steer my ship. With Darcie, much of our time together was spent jousting like this, the danger of losing my head if I didn't weave and bob just right. Loving her took its toll, demanded its pound of flesh, required a year for me to recover. I glance down at the table, at the fresh ice in my drink, and the chapped lines across my hands. I remind myself how making it through filming 'Juli' was a great accomplishment, a watershed achieved in no small part because of Sarah. I'm happy and don't care about anything else. "What about Dave?" I put the question to her.

Darcie seems indifferent and answers, "What about him?"

"Why call me at two in the morning when Dave's there?"

"You act," she says. "Dave doesn't. You get what it's like."

"But Dave doesn't have to get it," I tell her. "He only has to get you."

Darcie looks at me strangely, as if there's something in my face she just remembered. She smiles, pulls her lips in against her teeth. I want to kiss her, am disappointed, insist the urge is nothing, a reflex, like hunger and sadness, I can control the effect and say inside my head, 'I will not kiss her.' The waiter brings Darcie's chicken. I sip my drink, crush out my cigarette, sit back in my chair. Music plays in the rear of the bar, an old bit by Buffalo Springfield. Darcie bites her first piece of chicken in half, releases steam, waits for me to talk, is patient this way. I think of the Bow and the night Sarah, Cam and I fed the fish, how the sharks inside the larger tanks took their time, knowing the chunks of chum tossed in were trapped and there was no need to rush the kill. Darcie has the same deliberateness about her now, seems in no hurry to move things along. She drinks her beer, still high from her night's performance, an adrenaline rush, she has a glow. I remember all the many late nights we used to find creative ways to wind down, am thinking of this now, don't want to think of this, but there it is just the same.

Darcie senses something, teases me, asks again about Sarah, wants to know, "How's the sex?"

"Come on." I say, "You need to quit."

"Why? We're friends, right?" She offers to tell me about her and Dave. I claim I'm not interested, that her affair is none of my business. Darcie puts salt on the chicken, eats it with the sauce, tells me anyway, "On a scale of one to ten, on a good night," she shows me the tip of her tongue.

I take another sip of my drink.

"If you don't want to tell me," Darcie says, "I can only guess it's no good. Maybe you should get a lover."

"What? I never said."

"If this relationship's important to you, don't let the sex mess it up." She's off on one of her riffs now, breaks another piece of chicken and puts it in the sauce. "Why deny yourself?" She holds the chicken out, extends an offering. I reach but she moves her hand away.

Agitated, I start again, say "Here's the thing," yet I've no idea what the thing is anymore. "The only reason I'm here is to make sure we have an understanding." I try this, don't even know what I mean, but ask Darcie just the same, "Do you get what I'm saying?" The question is its own Chinese laundry. Two summers ago, I performed the part of Richard in Pinter's play, 'The Lover.' Richard was a cuckold, completely aware of his wife's affairs and still by circumstance resigned. His wife's name was Sarah, the play written with a sort of caustic civility. Of the days Sarah spent having sex with her lovers, Richard asked if she thought of him at all. Sarah: "How could I forget you?" Richard: "Quite easily I should think." Sarah: "But I'm in your house." Richard: "With another." Sarah: "But it's you I love." Richard: "I beg your pardon?" Sarah: "But it's you I love."

I tell Darcie, "I love Sarah."

Darcie says, "That's nice."

"It is nice."

"If you want nice, it's nice."

"What else would I want?"

"Are you seriously asking?"

I don't answer. Darcie continues to eat, tells me now, "I'm thinking I should take a lover." The comment comes at me deadpan, as a matter of fact. I don't know if Darcie's joking, am unsure how I'm supposed to reply. I remind her of Dave, say "Don't you already have one?"

She doesn't answer, finishes her chicken, takes the cigarette she was smoking before her food came and relights it. "I need a place," she says.

"For what?"

"For me and my lover."

"But you don't have a lover, do you?"

"How can I have a lover if we don't have a place to go?"

I'm careful here, unsure what's happening, the

warning whistles ringing. I check my reply for flaws, ask again about Dave.

"I don't think Dave wants me bringing a lover to his place, Mick." She laughs, then says, "I'm not with Dave anymore."

"What? Since when?"

"Does it matter?"

This news, too, catches me unprepared. I don't know what to say at first, settle for, "I'm sorry."

"Are you? That's sweet. You're sweet, Mick."

"I'm not sweet," I say this a bit too fast, am not even sure why. I tell Darcie, "I don't care about Dave."

"Why should you?" Darcie draws smoke, exhales slowly, has a way of looking at once predatory and coquettish. When she says again, "Maybe I can use your place, now that I need somewhere to stay," I tell her to stop.

"But aren't we friends?"

"You have other friends. You have money."

Darcie pretends to pout. "You're at Sarah's all the time now."

"That's not the point."

"What is the point?"

"There is no point," I say. "That's the point."

Darcie counters. "I told you, I just need a place."

"That's not my problem," I lean back, try to maintain my position, which is a wobbly perch. "I'm going to go," I say. "It's getting late."

"It's not late," Darcie says. "It's always early." Here is more Darcie-speak, the methodology applied to her strategy, how she's able to say everything and nothing, as Pinter would appreciate, the creativity which mocks the vagary of language. I remember another play I did, Tom Stoppard's 'Rock 'N 'Roll' at the Clive Theater. I was Jan, a grad student returning home to Czechoslovakia in 1968. In one scene, my Jan discusses rock music with a character named Ferdinand. Bands are listed along with their influence on us, but the other actor started messing up the sequence, throwing me off, mentioning the Velvet Underground when he should have referenced the Beach Boys, said Cream when the script called for the Mothers of Invention. Later he mixed up his lines on destiny and defeatism, leaving me to scramble through the whole act just to keep us on track. This is how I feel now, that the lines Darcie's feeding me are loose threads I need to gather up and string together.

"It's just for a few days," Darcie starts in again about my apartment, says "Think about it."

"I have." My answer, I realize, should be more emphatic, but is falling off. Darcie's relentless, despite my resistance, like brush wire on limestone, she's wearing me down. Knowing her as I do, much better than Dave, for all the good it does, I try to think three steps ahead, but my effort feels falsely plotted. I answer less convincingly than before, "I don't think it's a good idea."

"And why is that?"

"It would only confuse the cat."

"Maybe," she says. "Unless."

I tell myself I don't understand, tell Darcie, "I didn't come to the Dive for any of this. I didn't come to see you." When she laughs, I feel embarrassed, say, "Go find your lover first, then you can sleep at his place." It's terrible, I know, the duplicity, the way we break down, use our words to mean something else completely.

Darcie smiles, says what she says as I used to imagine she might say again someday. She lifts another piece of chicken from her plate, breaks it in half, puts it in my hand the moment I start reaching.

# 16

AT SARAH'S, I stand in the dark, pull off my pants, my jacket and shoes, walk over quietly and get into bed. It's late and I try slipping down slowly. Sarah stirs just the same, reacts to the chill from my skin and shift of the blanket. The red numbers on the clock on Sarah's side of the bed show 2:00 a.m. I apologize for waking her. She checks the time, asks if I'm ok, wants to know where I've been.

I tell I went to Cam's, and then to the Dive for a drink and wound up talking to Darcie. "I wanted to talk with her," I let Sarah know, am confiding not confessing, am feeling good about how things turned out, the way I managed the situation effectively and correctly, my actions constructed toward a proper end and how I did the right thing. "I didn't like Darcie calling us so late in L.A.," I say *calling us,* "and wanted to set her straight. I told her this," I say.

Sarah's silent for several seconds, then goes, "I see." Perhaps it's the timing, and our laying there in the dark, but I can't recall Sarah ever using the phrase *I see* quite like this. I try to deflect all insinuation, answer as if there's only one way to react to what I just said. "Good. Right. I mean we're friends and all, but I thought it was important for Darcie to know there are boundaries, times to call and times not to."

Sarah stays completely still beside me. Large in the space, she also seems in that moment to have disappeared. I can sense only the dip in the mattress, the indentation made and the distance between us. Sarah processes the information then repeats, "You wanted to speak with Darcie?"

"That's right."

"But you didn't call her first?"

"No, I didn't call."

"You just went to the Dive to see her? Were you planning this when you left here?"

I'm not used to Sarah sounding this way, tentative and inquiring. She says again, "If you just wanted to talk with her about not phoning us so late, why not call her and let her know? Why drive to the Dive and hope she comes by?"

Another good question, another flaw revealed. I stutter in search of my words, admit "I don't know. I guess I wasn't sure I really wanted to talk with her, that I was thinking I should but didn't want to make the commitment, does that make sense? I didn't want to deal with it. I mean her calling us so late was inappropriate and all, but we are friends, and had just made a film together, and she was upset about 'Killer Joe,' and do we really care that she called?"

Sarah has settled into the rhythms of my chatter now,

is listening to me, hearing what I am and am not saying, picking out the words she wants to address.

"If you didn't care, why go?" The pressing is proving my undoing. I don't want to think, don't think I can answer, say simply, "I was trying to do the right thing."

"I don't care," Sarah says finally about Darcie. "But it bothered you?"

"Me?" Here is the rub and how to explain. I start with, "Yes, it bothered me, but only because I didn't want you to think, I mean, I thought it might upset you, but if it didn't then good. It's over and done." I'm relieved, but know that's not the end and that I have to tell her the rest. I start once more, retreat then say, "About Dave, Darcie left him."

From here, the story becomes a runaway train, I avoid only the part where Darcie spoke of taking a lover, explain how Darcie asked to stay at my place for a while. "Because she knows I'm here with you. I said no." Again this is the truth, but then I circle back, describe Darcie's persistence, the tight spot she's in and how she wore me down. "It's no big deal. It's nothing really," I try to be convincing, yawn nervously here in the dark, touch Sarah's leg which seems to stiffen. I remove my hand, go "It's like you said," and insert the words that Sarah offered in a different context, misapplied and misinterpreted now. "Why should we care?"

———

In the morning, Sarah makes eggs. We are cordial, composed and cool. I sit at the kitchen table, click through links on Sarah's laptop while she cooks. On the Tick, Ted has posted about the executions in Iran. Arash Rahmanipour, Mohammad Ali Reza Zamani, Hamed Rohani Nejad, Davood Faricheh Mirardebili and Nasser Abdolhosseini all indicted as *dissidents* and sentenced to death for their role in *fomenting reform.* As part of his newest project, worked on since returning from Tehran, Ted plans to identify every one of the 3,000 *dissidents* arrested, to create an interactive website where each prisoner will have their story posted and people can read about them, sign letters of protest, provide aid and take up their cause. Ted's focus now is on the dissemination of information, a renewed conviction, a want to collect the facts and spread the word. Knowledge is power, Ted sees this, as dad said years ago, information is key, all movements requiring, there's a reason despots try shutting down the free press. By delivering the news, Ted says, people can rally one another, the effort purposeful and practical and better than G.O.D.

I read to Sarah, tell her about Ted, try to discuss different things that don't have to do with last night. We spend the day avoiding confrontation, do not talk about Darcie, don't go by my place to feed the cat. I meet Ted around noon at the MoJo Café where we run through all the latest turns. Afterward, I conduct an early rehearsal for 'Moonlight,' then come back and pick up Sarah for dinner. We eat with Cam and Kate and Bob. Twice my cell phone rings, but I have it on vibrate and don't return the calls. Sarah and I are fine. We come home early, get into bed and sleep.

———

Monday, I drive to South Aldwich, do more patchwork for Jay. The rain last night has left the streets slick with puddles. I accelerate through the low points in the road, where the water lays in wait and causes my truck to hydroplane. I float for several feet, am in those moments both driving and not totally in control. Billy calls around noon with good news from L.A. I phone Sarah but she's in studio. The day is overcast, the sun teases now and then, but mostly it's gray.

I leave work early, head to Sarah's, want to see her before I go to rehearsal, but she doesn't come back in time. I drive to the Mecca, where all my actors arrive by 6:00 p.m. except for Barry Garrin, who plays Andy. I call his cell, get voice mail, wind up doing Andy myself from memory: "Where are the boys? Have you found them?" We run our lines through several scenes. I lose myself in our effort, feel good about this and don't think of anything else.

There's a passage in 'Moonlight' where Andy says of Ralph: "He was reliable enough when he was sitting down but you never knew where you were with him when he was standing up." I stand following rehearsal, think I should sit but can't quite settle into a chair. We discuss the notes I made, talk about the cadence of each performance, what is and isn't taking shape. Around 9:00 p.m., on my way outside, I call Barry again. He answers this time, has his explanation ready now, his excuse prepared when I ask him what happened tonight. In the end, he expects me to understand, makes it sound as if I should have seen it coming.

Everyone has left the lot by the time I get to my truck. The heater hisses hot air, seems suddenly determined to make up for the entire winter. Here is what I get, I think, for trying to do the right thing. I drive across town to Wellington Park, the rain falling again, harder than yesterday, the last time I was at Dave's the temperature was twenty degrees colder. I pull into the drive, park as close to the house as I can, then run through the rain to the door and ring the bell.

"What the fuck?" I'm pissed as hell and want Dave to know. The story Barry told me is shit, the way some people handle disappointment, always looking for someone else to blame. There's a narrow window to the left of the door where I can see inside. I ring the bell again, spot Dave walking toward me from the far end of the hall. Instead of undoing the lock and letting me in, he comes to the window, stands there staring at me, is wearing not his usual slacks and sweater, but an old green flannel shirt, red sweats and black slippers. He looks beaten down, a bone-deep sort of weary. The roof extends out over most of the porch, though the wind blows rain in against my neck and back. I knock on the glass, tell Dave to let me in, say "Come on, Dave man."

It's important to be cool here, to not rant at Dave so that he turns away and I wind up with nothing. I need to be smart, to lay things out in an orderly fashion, make sure Dave understands whatever he's heard is bull, but I don't know where to begin. I decide to work my way out from the center, to go with what Barry told me and correct details. "I didn't sleep with Darcie, man," I say. "Whoever told you that is lying. I was trying to do the right thing, to make sure Darcie and I understood each other, that's when she said the two of you had split."

Dave in the window remains silent, does no more than raise one eyebrow, then says softly, so that I have to put my ear to the glass and wait for him to repeat. "When was this?" he asks.

"When? What? With Darcie? Saturday night, man."

Dave says, "Darcie didn't break up with me until Sunday."

"What?" Shit. Fuck. "I didn't know, man." I see what I'm up against now, decide there's no point in soft-pedaling why I'm here. "Whatever, Dave," I say. "I'm sorry, but you can't go fucking with my actors. You can't be offering them better gigs if they bail on 'Moonlight' just because someone filled your head with crap. I have a contract with these people, Dave. I gave Darcie a place to sleep is all. She said you guys broke up and she needed a place to crash. I didn't sleep with her. I spent the night at Sarah's. Shit man, you can check."

Dave folds his arms, leans his forehead against the glass. I stand beneath the overhang, the rain's runoff cold,

I go ahead and tap the window, say again, "Come on, man." Water soaks through my pants as I repeat everything, go step by step this time, from my arriving at the Dive, to taking Darcie to my place, to heading to Sarah's. I say, "If people saw us leave together and told you, well that's all it was. They don't know. You saw how I was with 'Juli.' I was totally cool, Dave. I was completely professional. You're the one who wanted us to work together. You're the one who needed to see. Why are you fucking with me now?"

Rather than answer, Dave remains in front of the glass, watching me, his face with hangdog damage. I slap the brick, say "This is stupid. Let me in, man."

Dave doesn't move. I wipe water from my neck, try a different approach, my objective still to save 'Moonlight,' I appeal to our shared sensibility, how helpless we both are where Darcie's concerned. "Listen man," I say, "I am sorry. Believe me, I know how you feel. I thought about you. I did, but shit. You know what I mean? You know how it is, the effect Darcie has. She asked me for a place to sleep, that's all. She said you two had split and maybe I shouldn't have gotten involved. Maybe I should have weighed things from all sides and not helped her out. Hindsight, you know? Your being pissed is understandable, but messing with 'Moonlight' is stupid. I didn't do anything to you, man. Seriously Dave, what more do you want me to say?"

We're just inches apart, both leaning into the glass. Dave's expression remains pinched. I wonder if he knows about Darcie calling me in L.A., think of how she joked about getting a new lover, and how she tried to hold my hand as we left the Dive, messing with me, laughing as I drew away. I'm curious about what Dave does know exactly, who's spreading rumors and, "Who told you anything, man?"

Dave lifts his chin here, takes me in and then steps off, stands a few feet from the window, his arms unfolding, hanging limp, his shoulders giving in to the start of a tremble. In answer to my question, he mouths one word, says this, repeats again and again, louder and louder still, until I turn and walk off.

———

The drive back across town takes fifteen minutes. The rain has reached the underside of my collar and beneath the cuff of my jeans, invading my socks. I pat my arms and pants down with a rag from inside my truck. It's after 10:00 p.m. when I park near the Kepper Theater, talk my way in, am able to wait for Darcie while she finishes her show. Her dressing room is small, the walls a lime green, the paint faded to where gray cement is visible beneath. I sit in the room's one chair, leave a message on Sarah's cell, tell her things are running late and I doubt I'll get a chance to hear her sing tonight. I realize I haven't eaten since lunch, am lightheaded, my stomach growls. Darcie comes from her curtain call, finds me in her room, is again not surprised to see me, says "Hey mister," and squeezes my shoulder as she walks by.

I stay in my chair, have a cigarette going, though I'm not supposed to smoke backstage. The noise outside in the hall is of other actors moving past. I've rehearsed what I want to say while driving over, am determined to keep my focus, don't want to bark premature as I did with Dave, am looking to keep to the course I set the other night, as I told Darcie then, confided to Sarah and convinced myself was true.

In costume, in the glow of her performance, Darcie appears electric, an animal wet and wild. She takes a towel from a hook behind the door and wipes her face, says "Tonight was good, thanks for asking. A good crowd." She tosses the towel toward me and starts to undress, is deliberate and not at all shy. The jeans from her performance are peeled away, her shirt pulled off, her bra beneath removed with her back to me. She turns around, walks toward me, slips the robe from behind the chair.

I don't react, though Darcie wants me to. The thing with Darcie, another thing I know, have known, is that it's important not to empower her, to show any shock or surprise, or worst of all any form of weakness. I wait until she's standing back in front of me before asking how my apartment's working out. Darcie says, "It felt good to sleep in my old bed."

"Technically," I tell her, "It's my bed. It was then and is now."

"Well, thank you for inviting me into your bed."

I drop my cigarette, crush it beneath my heel, think of that time at the Mecca when I kissed Darcie and she bit my lip. Someone in the hallway whistles. I use the sound to clear my head, figure enough preliminary chatter has passed, and say, "I just came from Dave's." I explain about Barry, about 'Moonlight' and what Dave has done, what he thinks happened, and why. "What did you say to him about the other night?"

"I told him I was with you."

"You mean that you were at my place?"

"No," Darcie slips her robe on, stands in front of the chair, does not bother to fasten the belt, the two halves parted so that her breasts are barely covered. She is, quite literally, half the size of Sarah, is a different sort of sexy, the kind that affects me instinctively. I move my hand, motion for her to close up. Darcie ties her belt while I ask, "Why did you tell Dave anything?"

"He wanted to know."

"He said you didn't break up with him until Sunday."

"Did he?" She holds a finger to her chin as if she's trying to remember. I lean back in my chair, want to know, "Why did you say you were with me?"

"Because I was with you."

"But you weren't. You were at my place, that's all."

Darcie goes to the counter in front of the mirror, picks up her soap and says, "Was I?"

I don't understand. "What are you talking about?"

"My mistake," Darcie rolls her wrists. "I guess I was thinking about tonight."

I play this off as best I can, do my Gary Cooper, am cool like Richard Edson in 'Lulu on the Bridge.' "That's not going to happen," I say.

Darcie comes and takes the towel from my lap, puts it over her shoulders, behind her neck, like a fighter. She goes and stands across the room, the clothes she's removed left at my feet. I picture Sarah, see her on stage, wonder what she's singing, how she looks and what she's thinking right now. I think of Darcie, realize I don't know anything, ask why she's doing this?

"Doing what?"

"Fucking with me. Why now?"

Darcie moves closer, close enough for me to pull her onto my lap if I wanted. She knows this, marks the space she needs to fill. "Now is good," she says.

I put my hands beneath my thighs as if I don't trust them. Darcie lingers, then steps back, starts toward the door, says she's going down the hall to shower and tells me to "wait."

There's a line in 'Moonlight' where Andy says: "The truth is I'm basically innocent. I know little of women. But I've heard dread tales." I tell myself this is the problem, that it really isn't my fault as I don't know what I'm doing. This, of course, is another lie. The energy it takes for self-deception abandons me now and I use the time Darcie is gone to recover. She comes back ten minutes later, her hair half dry. Seeing me still in the chair, she towels naked in front of me, dresses in the fresh clothes she wore to the theater, has me re-lace the string in her left boot. We leave around 11:00, go across the street to King Chow's, where Darcie dips her egg rolls in an plum sauce. She has vegetables and rice and a fortune cookie. Her lucky numbers are 16, 27 and 48. She shows me the slip of paper, points to where it says, "You will do well with change." My own fortune is not as easy to decipher, speaks of shallow waters being the first to boil and to freeze.

At my apartment, Darcie takes off her scarf, drops her coat in the chair, walks through my front room and down the hall. I follow, sit on the end of the bed and untie my shoes. Darcie slides into my lap. I notice right away how light she is. She pushes her cold hand up under my shirt. I shiver. Darcie stands and undresses again. I look at the smallness of her body, the shapes and curves, how she fits me differently than Sarah, her size leaving me to reach for nonexistent boundaries and edges. Darcie shoves me back, slides up onto my chest, sits as Sarah can't.

I roll her off, hold her down, harder than intended, I'm not sure why. With arms spread, Darcie doesn't struggle against my grip, doesn't have to, laughs, knows I'll give way whenever she wants.

---

It's late again as I get back to Sarah's. I assume she'll be sleeping, but approaching the door I hear music, realize she's waiting up for me. I stay outside, listen to her playing piano while I think about what to do. The night air is cold, the light in the lot shallow. Sarah's musicianship is unfussy as always, her large hands delicate across the keys. Noel has asked her to compose a tune for 'Juli,' and she's excited by this, has worked hard, her piece restrained and not showy, a melodic six-note progression that gets in your head and stays there.

When I come in, Sarah stops playing. I take off my coat, go and kiss her cheek, tell her about tonight, how rehearsal went and the way everyone stayed to talk. I explain about Dave, his reaction to Darcie's crashing at my place, how he's ambushed 'Moonlight,' and that I had to go to his house and negotiate a cease fire. My performance is sketchy, is of a guy who just got home and is talking to his lover about his long night. I concentrate on this as Sarah sits and listens. She's in her sleeping sweats, her orange top and blue bottoms faded. Her expression is subdued, is one I purposely don't try to interpret.

I want to kiss her for real but am afraid. I think about this, who I've kissed and want to kiss tomorrow. I think of what Darcie said about happiness, how I confused contentment for something else, and when I tried to argue and said she was misconstruing what I was after, she shook me off and swore, "Me, baby? Never." I remember what else Darcie said, how I had to know we'd get back together, that our time apart was necessary but, "Now is good." She announced this as if there was nothing more to it, as if she had a date marked on her calendar and the last year was simply part of my probation.

Sure, that. All necessary. What didn't I know? Not this, I swear. How could I when Darcie kept insisting we were over? But ask me what I wanted, eight and six and four months ago, ask me why I went to the Dive on Saturday instead of just ignoring Darcie's call, and I have a harder time with denial. Even as I told Dave and Sarah, told Darcie and Ted how I went to do the right thing, the energy required to prop up this false front wears me down. What does Mises say, I wonder, about human action that's inspired by deceit? Does he find truth irrelevant as long as one achieves the targeted end? What would Albert Ellis say? Would both he and Mises tell me to forget the bullshit as action is all that matters and it's impossible to deny what we want once we set out to obtain it, or would they ask me why I was in denial in the first place? What was it I didn't want to admit, and what did this say about what I was doing?

I leave my boots on. Sarah notices but doesn't mention. What I love about Sarah, truly, is the ease with which everything's achieved. With her, I don't experience the complication of being together, the press and pull and needle pushed further until my skin crawls hot. There is instead the satisfaction found not as the stardust in the bottom of the fish bowl, but something natural and genuine and as I miss already.

I go and sit across the room. From her bench, Sarah is in front of me now, which is to say that I'm behind her. The fullness of her shoulders and hips are in view, offer a weight I don't think I can move anymore though I want to try. I think about this as I start talking. Sarah stays at her piano, listens to me without interruption. I wish I could keep quiet, want to say nothing, to make light of what happened, like Bel did with Andy. ("You've had me." "Oh you. Oh yes. I can still have you.") Instead, my words are all high sparks, flint and friction. Sarah doesn't turn and look at me, not right away, waits until I finish, then shifts around on the bench, finds me sunk in the cushions of her couch.

---

# 17

DARCIE IS SLEEPING when I get back to my apartment. I do not wake her, stand at the foot of my bed, there in the dark. The cat prowls, comes and rubs against my leg before disappearing to safe corners. The air inside is filled with multiple scents, Darcie old and new, along with Sarah, everywhere now. I bend over, look for Darcie's clothes on the floor. The sight of them makes me suddenly lonely. I look toward the window, think again of 'Moonlight,' how Andy asked Bel: "What's happening?" and she replied: "Are you dying?" to which Andy could only answer: "I don't know. I don't know how it feels. How does it feel?"

I feel foolish, find myself picturing Sarah, thinking of

how she looked not an hour ago when I told her. I walk back to the front room, turn on my computer, click to the news. Tiger Woods has been caught in a scandal, his mistresses are now being profiled in alphabetical order, the number having reached double digits. There is an obituary for Patriarch Pavle, head of the Serbian Orthodox Church, and a piece about the solar prominences occurring on the sun, bursts of gas that ignite, setting the surface of the sun ablaze, fire on fire, with flames shooting off into space at a speed in excess of 2 million miles per hour. I imagine the heat of this sort of flame, try to wrap my head around the idea of something hotter than the sun.

I turn off my laptop and crawl into bed. Darcie doesn't stir. In the morning, she acts as if finding me beside her is completely as she expected. She goes into the front room to do yoga on a makeshift mat, doesn't ask what happened with Sarah as I come out to the kitchen a few minutes later. Even as I tell her, she doesn't seem interested. I feed the cat, fix my coffee, set down two cups, listen to the water running in the bathroom as Darcie goes off to shower. I check again to see how I feel, picture Sarah in the shower, am thinking this when Darcie comes out, wrapped in a towel, her size childlike when compared to the image in my head.

Darcie has a workshop to run in an hour. She mentions her auditioning soon for 'Lips Together, Feet Apart,' says that I should come to New York with her. I have 'Moonlight' in rehearsal, need to replace Barry and can't get away, but tell her, "Maybe." Darcie shrugs, moves around the apartment, collecting the things she needs to take to the Mecca. I watch her set her coffee down, only to search for it a few seconds later, asking "Where's my coffee?" This is exactly what she used to do when we were first together. I watch her closer, look for signs of other things that have and haven't changed.

Last night, before I returned to Sarah's, I performed in bed with heavy hips and hands, my chest pitched and mouth open, devouring all that Darcie offered. Convinced I had to commit completely in order not to think, I made myself wild, managed almost in the middle of my thrashing to forget Sarah; our time together removed like one of those cardboard advertisements in the center of a magazine, torn out and discarded so the interrupted pages could slide back together. Once Darcie and I finished, as I showered and dressed to leave, my thoughts went back to Sarah, is where they are now and what does this say about me, other than what I already know?

I take Darcie her coffee. She sips and hands me back the cup. After she's gone, I find my jeans, think about the day ahead, and tonight, when Darcie is here with me again. I'm glad she's here. I say this, just to hear me say it. I think about the times I told Sarah that I loved her, think of my confessing what happened with Darcie and why I did this. My explanation involves three entirely incongruent reasons, blurs together my handling of desire, need and fear. This is what I think, for what it's worth. I think Darcie's here to stay, that things are as she said, good for now, though where things go from here, I've no idea. I think I will just wait and see what happens, though I know this sort of plan is no plan at all. I need to show more conviction, and yet here's the problem, my convictions of late have been wanting and I've little faith in what I choose to do anymore.

---

I head out to West Aldwich, where I spend most of the day painting the first floor of an old Colonial. Jay has me using a yellow paint. The color's light and helps expand the airiness of the room. I work the walls with a professional Nap

9-inch polyester/knit roller, cover the space smoothly and with the sort of efficiency that leaves no trace of my ever having been there. I have my phone and my radio, am listening to classic rock, 97.1, when Lou Reed's 'Sweet Jane' comes on. I stop painting and let the song play through.

By 4:15 I finish work, pack my truck and drive to Cam's before rehearsal. Kate is reading at the kitchen table while Bob and Cam are in the den. I sit with Kate and talk about Sarah. Kate keeps an afghan around her shoulders though the house is warm. After several good weeks, she's begun having trouble with her new meds, has started feeling sluggish again, her joints and skin sore to the touch. She sits beneath the glow of her favorite lamp and warms herself like a chick in an incubator. The doctors plan to change her from Hydrea to Sprycel, are considering Tasigna. The drugs—much as the Gleevec, which failed earlier—are designed to block the protein made by the BCR-ABL cancer gene, allowing the white cell count to drop. I reheat her tea in the microwave, ask how she's feeling.

The book Kate's reading is a treatise on rhetoric by Anthony Weston. Additional books are stacked to her left, beside a pile of papers. I can tell by the way she looks at me that she already knows, that Sarah has called or come by and they've talked. I want to do the same, to give Kate my story, but as I begin my narrative unravels. I wonder what Sarah told her, ask "How's she doing?" say "I'm sorry," admit "I think I made a mistake," only this sort of noncommittal backtracking does nothing to improve my standing.

Beneath the light, Kate has a yellow cast to her skin, though her voice is firm and her eyes forever clear. "There's no such thing as a mistake," she says, waits to see if I understand. I don't really, but tell her I do. "What were you thinking?" she asks, does not want excuse but the truth. The question covers such a wide range of possibilities that

I don't even try anymore, put my hands in my lap and shrug my shoulders.

———

At rehearsal tonight, I don't tell the others about Dave, explain simply that the issue with Barry is being resolved, and the plan for now is to go forward until I can replace him. I do not ask if anyone else has been contacted by Dave, though I need to know, am hoping maybe he's done with me, am afraid to bring the subject up and assume someone will tell me if Dave calls. I promise to have Barry replaced in the next day or two, and for tonight again I do the part of Andy.

I call Ted on my way home from the Mecca, tell him about Darcie and what I did. Ted goes, "Shit." The response sums up the situation neatly. Having warned me, Ted's not pleased, doesn't ask about me until later, wants to know "How's Sarah?" On the Tick that morning, I read what Ted wrote about the number of *dissidents* arrested in Iran swelling now to 3,400. Ted quoted Ahmadinejad: "We have laws. People who violate the public rights will be dealt with severely. It's a law based on democratic principle." Of course it is. Everything is democratic as long as we get what we want. When I confessed to Sarah about Darcie, I suggested our sleeping together wasn't planned and just sort of happened. The idea was so absurd that Sarah groaned and asked if I really thought saying this was better?

There's a story, I remember, of Pinter going to Turkey with Arthur Miller in 1985. The two were representing International PEN and the Helsinki Watch, traveling to protest the torture of writers held in Turkish prisons. A dinner was given in Ankara to honor Miller. Over cocktails Pinter confronted the Turkish Ambassador, accused him of supporting crimes against humanity, and when the Ambassador denied the charge, Pinter challenged him to experience "the reality of electric currents on your genitals." The reaction was swift. Pinter was asked to leave the dinner. Miller left with him. Of the experience, Pinter said: "Being thrown out of the U.S. Embassy in Ankara with Arthur Miller—a voluntary exile—was one of the proudest moments of my life."

I think of this now in terms of my own self-deceit, how the Turkish Ambassador could not have actually believed his denial when he swore no writers were being tortured in his prisons, and how I had not really believed I'd gone to the Dive just to tell Darcie not to call me. Assuming I knew why I went, did this also mean I knew what I wanted? Was there a causal connection, or was I just acting on impulse again? This is what I don't know. What I think I know now is that I went when I didn't really want to and how do I explain this? I remember what Kyle said about love and addiction being two separate things because love requires freedom and addiction affords none. I think when I told Sarah I loved her that I was free to do so, and when I went to the Dive to see Darcie that I had no choice. I think of Mises again, and wonder is it ever possible to act against what we really want? Where is the logic in that? The question, once more, supplies its own answer.

I pull up in front of my apartment, park my truck, think back to the solar prominences, the sun set on fire, the heat upon heat, what burns and burns and burns again, the flame ablaze, leaving nothing to chance.

---

In the hall outside my apartment, Sarah's left my clothes in two boxes. I unlock the door, push my clothes in with my foot. Darcie comes home around 11:30, after her evening's performance, sees my stuff and jokes about the status of my luggage. I tell her about Sarah and she wishes Dave would do the same. Tomorrow Darcie plans to go and get the rest of her shit. The question of her staying with me, of our staying together, has not been specifically discussed, is now a matter of presumption. I sit in my rocker, ask about 'Killer Joe.' Darcie answers in detail, goes into the kitchen when I start to talk about 'Moonlight.' I tell her the trouble I'm having replacing Barry, and how I'm worried Dave's scaring everyone off. Darcie comes out with a bag of chips, sits across from me, undoes her boots and says, "Maybe what's happening is a good thing."

I don't want to argue, am willing to listen, would rather believe Darcie has something in mind I hadn't thought of, has still my best interest at heart. I take out a cigarette, decide not to smoke, put the cigarette back, ask Darcie to explain what she's thinking. She has on orange socks, I see this as she kicks off her boots. I think of Sarah's feet, her sturdy platforms compared to the thinness of Darcie's hooves. "You've been off the grid for a while," Darcie signals for the cigarette I tucked away. "You have some momentum now, you should be getting jobs, doing a movie or a play, not directing Pinter."

"I could do worse," I say this for no reason, know how Darcie will respond.

"You could do better," she asks if I've heard from L.A. I lie and say no. Darcie puts the chip bag down, looks for a lighter, wants me to see how 'Moonlight' is keeping me from getting real work. I don't answer. Darcie groans in that way she does when I don't buy what she's selling. She disappears into the bathroom, does two quick lines of coke just out of view, in deference to my addiction. When she comes out, we go into the bedroom, put on the tv. Darcie flicks past the news to find a movie, stops at Toni Collette in 'Muriel's Wedding.' ABBA sings and Darcie clicks the remote again, finds Letterman chatting with Michael Imperioli. We watch for a while and then Darcie changes to something else, wants me to stay up for a movie with Guy Pearce. I have work to do for Jay tomorrow, can use the money and need some sleep, but when I say this to Darcie she complains about my being a handyman, tells me I have to start prioritizing my time.

"Actually, I like the work." I say about the jobs I do for Jay, "it's physically fulfilling and I'm good with my hands." On this we agree. Darcie slides closer, offers me opportunities to practice my trade.

———

I get up early, call Bob, tell him I don't feel much like working alone today, ask if he wants to come out to West Aldwich and help me finish painting. I dress and drive to Cam's. Everyone's in the kitchen. Bob by the fridge has switched from crutches to canes, moves with his head tipped forward, his balance better. Kate has her bathrobe pulled over flannel pajamas, her coloring gone from yellow to a pasty gray. Cam's quiet, sits eating cereal. No one mentions Sarah, though I know what they're thinking. I drink coffee. Bob and I drop Cam at school then head across town.

Jay's put a post-it sticker on the dining room wall, for this room he wants blue and green. I spread a tarp over the floor, bring the paint in from the garage, give Bob the first can to open and stir. We work with my radio turned to the morning sports, get the scores before changing to tunes. The roller Bob uses is on a three-foot pole, he leans in and slides the paint up and down. I dip my brush, work the seams. Around 11:00, I take a break, start making calls to more actors I hope will replace Barry in 'Moonlight.' I give everyone my best pitch, try to undo Dave's voodoo hex. In the middle of my calls, Jim

Baine phones. Jim is our Jake. "Was Jake," he says.

'Instant Karma' John Lennon sings on my radio, fills the front room and beyond. I go outside to the porch for a smoke. The rain's stopped and the air has a heaviness to it. Bob comes out, using one cane, stands with both hands in front of him, like Charlie Chaplin in 'The Little Tramp.' It's warm for April. Bob shuffles in a half circle, positions himself and drops down on the porch bench, which is really a large swing suspended by four silver chains. He puts his heels together, his fake legs turned, his cane in between, his blue Nikes with paint stains on them. He asks about the calls I made. I explain about Dave, present the whole tangle. Bob touches his cane to the top of his right shoe. The grass on the lawn is a flat pea green. I flick my cigarette, watch the ash end smolder in the wet sod.

Water drips from the gutter overhead. Bob adjusts his left knee, his fake legs in loose blue jeans, he keeps his cane between. The whiskers on his cheeks add shades to the contours of his face. I think of Sarah buying a copy of 'Moonlight,' think of the money she put into the play and how I plan to pay her back, promise to do so no matter what. I tell myself this as if it makes everything else all right. I look at Bob without his legs, think of Sarah again, consider the different levels of injury one can inflict.

"Everything will be ok," I tell Bob this, light a fresh cigarette. He waits for me to say more. When I don't, he shifts forward, the swing beneath causing his body to sway. He asks about Darcie, wants to be sure, "You're happy then?"

"It's complicated," I answer this way. Smoke passes between my fingers. Bob's cane is a hard brown stick, unadorned, the rubber tip black, there to keep him from slipping. I turn and stare into the house. There's a knot in my neck from painting, an ache in my shoulders. I rest against the railing on the porch, tell Bob, "Honestly man, I don't know."

I compare what's happened to me these last several months to the act of swimming across a lake, the way the surface of the water parts the moment we pass through, then smoothes over after we're gone. "It looks as if we've never been there, as if nothing's changed, but everything has. With each stroke there's distance covered and not one thing is as it was when we first left shore."

Bob moves the heels of his blue Nikes apart, touches his false knees, rolls his head slightly forward in that way he has of making everything seem understood. I look at his legs again, realize how stupid I am to have said what I did. "Who knows better, right?" I repeat the rest of what I told Kate, how maybe I made a mistake.

Bob replies the same as his mom, "There's no such thing."

"An error in judgment then. I'd like a mulligan, after the fact." I try this, but here, too, Bob says, "The only thing after the fact is more *now*." He's like Ted, is cutting me no slack, a friend challenging me, forcing me to be accountable, which I need, I know, and still it's hard. I try to rationalize, think of what Ted said about anything worthwhile requiring risk, and yet risk doesn't distinguish between good choices and bad. I say this, then repeat, "I want to try and start over."

Bob braces himself against his cane, stands carefully on his new legs, has to shift through his hips to get his motion started. His steps are retrained, he moves toward the house, his walk an assemblage of past and present motions. "Ok," he responds to what I just said, tells me to "Go ahead then."

I flick my second cigarette over the rail into the garden dirt. Bob is two steps ahead of me as we leave the porch. I walk inside, try to catch up.

We finish painting by 3:00 then head back to the city and pick up Cam from school. Agitated, I want to skate, am hoping a little huffing and puffing will do me good. The rink at the Bow is almost empty when we arrive, just a few kids taking lessons, going through their spins. Bob sits and watches, says "Next time" when we offer to get him out on the ice. Cam has his hockey skates, does laps, circles around the outer edge. I follow as best I can, the slow and settle into my own pace.

After an hour, we leave the Bow and grab something to eat. Cam asks about Sarah, is anxious to talk about her now, wants to know when he can see her again. I say she's a friend and can visit any time. Cam's hoping for more, asks if we can see her tonight. I tell him no, that I have rehearsal. He stares off as if he doesn't quite believe me, seems worried that my ending things with Sarah means I'm ready to demolish other relationships, is afraid everything is vulnerable still. He asks if he can come to rehearsal with me. I say, "Sure man," am happy to have him. Bob calls Kate, checks to see how she's feeling and if there's anything she needs before we head to the Mecca.

Darcie's already left for 'Killer Joe' when we pull up. We toss our empty Burger Barn bags in the trash and walk inside. There are posters on the walls, blown up photographs of past performances around town. In the hallway leading back to the stage where we rehearse, additional posters are hung of classic shows performed outside of Aldwich. In 1946, Marlon Brando appeared on Broadway in an Elia Kazan production of 'Truckline Café.' Brando was twenty-one, an unknown, cast in the minor role of a G.I. whose wife cheated on him while he was overseas. The play was poorly written and bombed after only thirteen performances.

Brando, however, was incredible. At the end of the play, he stood on stage alone and confessed to drowning his wife in the sea. His delivery, an early incarnation of Brando-speak, was electric, the reviews anointing, the audience awestruck, the future of acting forever changed.

Who saw it coming? I think of this now, remember what I said to Bob before, how I'd like to start over and see what happens, but I still don't know what this involves. I'm less like Brando, I think, and more like the audience watching, hopeful but unsure what I'm about to see, clueless and then surprised how things appear sometimes out of nowhere, like sandstorms and hummingbirds, the fins of fish through the tide, and the riddle of dreams.

Aimee and Gwynn are in the auditorium. Lauren Piele and Dean Garrett, as Bridget and Ralph, arrive a few minutes later. We're still missing Andy and Jake, and now Nathan Einess, cast as Fred, is late. The attrition is epidemic, Dave's handiwork ongoing. I bring everyone up to the stage, rally them the best I can, promise to fill the other roles as soon as possible, say that I'll continue reading Andy myself tonight. We're a collection of loose ends. I'm jumpy, no longer know exactly what to do. The others offer support. I thank them for this, for agreeing to stay on. Taking the stage, I say, "I am Andy," and find my mark. The others follow. As for Jake and Fred, the brothers then, I hand scripts to Bob and Cam, ask them to join us. "Typecasting," I say. "Let's see what you got."

---

# 18

DARCIE COMES HOME after 'Killer Joe,' gets ready to take the red eye to New York for her audition. She dances around the apartment, from room to room, gathering what she needs. I'm not going with her. We're three days removed from Jim Baine quitting 'Moonlight,' and Darcie doesn't really need me, will be back tomorrow night.

I sit in my rocker, my laptop on the coffee table, the tv running. Earlier, I checked my email, spoke with Coiyle and Ted after rehearsal, reviewed the latest news online. Disgraced ex-congressman Tom DeLay is set to appear on 'Dancing with the Stars.' David Letterman is blackmailed by a man threatening to expose his extramarital affairs. The news is filled with this sort of nonsense, and still every bit of it is real. On the Tick, Ted lists more names of executed *dissidents*, while Iran's chief prosecutor Gholam Hossein Mohseni-Ejehi insists: "So far we have shown restraint. If these demonstrations continue, we will be forced to resort to harsher measures." Harsh, indeed. To strengthen its core, the Iranian government is also planning to establish 6,000 Basij militia centers in elementary schools across the country. Ted mocks the effort, quotes Crosby, Stills, Nash and Young: "Teach your children well."

Darcie is wired, races past. She has rented a dvd, an interview with Tracy Letts. I watch while Darcie packs. Letts sits at the end of a square table, the lighting overhead dim, atmospheric, intentionally dramatic, as if at any moment something notable will be said. Physically, Letts is similar to Pinter in his mid-forties, narrow framed with sharp, carriage-worn features, his thinning hair combed in a flop. The interviewer sits at the opposite end of the table, asks questions that Letts responds to with a combination of informative appeal and self-effacing avoidance. In front of the camera he exudes confidence mixed with a certain shyness and sense of coyness, as if he preferred leaving all examination of his work to the stage.

In the kitchen, Darcie cuts coke on a flat glass plate, no longer bothers to keep her shit away from me. The interview ends and Darcie wants to run lines with me now, scenes from McNally's 'Lips Together, Teeth Apart,' as we've done a dozen times already. Sensing diminishing returns, I talk to her of other things instead. I'm restless in a way that has me nearly calm, am feeling like one of those Mexican cliff divers who takes deep breaths from the lip of a ledge before jumping off. For the last three nights, I have worked with Bob and Cam on 'Moonlight.' The idea of casting them is crazy and desperate, yet has opened my eyes to a host of new possibilities, a different way of interpreting the play. On fake legs, Bob gives visual reference to Jake's inner trauma, while casting Cam in a role written for someone more than twice his age lends innocence to Fred's cosmic gravity. To hear him say: "Listen son, I've come a long way down here to attend a series of highly confidential meetings in which my participation is seen to be a central factor," accents Pinter's humor, turns 'Moonlight' into a perfectly serious farce.

Darcie's not impressed, remains convinced my idea is nuts, asks why I bother with actors at all? "Why not use puppets?" she says. I assure her that I have a plan, that 'Juli in Chains' is finished, and after 'Moonlight' I'll be in more demand than ever. Directing a Pinter play will prove how serious I am long-term. This is what I tell her, though it's all so exhausting, having to defend myself this way. Now that we've lost Lauren Piele, our Bridget, to Dave, Darcie says I need to accept the reality of the situation and throw in the towel.

I tell her instead that I've made further adjustments. When Kate came down to watch rehearsal yesterday, rather than ask her to read Bridget, I had her do Andy. Who better suited, given her illness, to embody the part and explore the issue of mortality? I decided to flip-flop the genders, switched Dean from Ralph, moved Gwynn over from Bel. "I think I can pull it off," I say, but Darcie's only sure this proves I've lost my mind, tells me, "Straight up, you're insane. A gender-bender, Mick? This after you've already cast a kid and a gimp?"

I defend my idea, defend Cam and Bob who are coming along, each a work-in-progress, quick to their parts, more comfortable after three days of study. I want to phone Sarah and let her know what's happened, need her to encourage me, to hear what she thinks, but have not quite found the nerve to make the call. I talk instead about Ted, tell Darcie what's going on in Iran, how the demonstrators' fortitude blows me away.

Darcie dances some more, says "What?"

I tell her about the forty mothers gathering in Leleh Park to mourn their sons and daughters murdered during the demonstrations, all arrested by the Guard, explain how the Iranian musician Mohammad Reza Shajarian, in protest against Ahmadinejad, has insisted the state radio and television stations stop broadcasting his work. The act is tantamount to suicide. Ted on the Tick appeals to the United States to extend asylum to Shajarian before it's too late. He requests the same for Narges Kalhor, daughter of Ahmadinejad's cultural advisor, Mehdi Kalhor, after Narges screened her documentary 'Rake,' which exposes human rights violations in Iran. "Think about it all," I say.

Darcie gathers clothes and toiletries from the bathroom, repeats the word herself, goes "Speaking of balls." Half-dressed, she continues dashing through the apartment, comes over and rubs my neck, wants to have sex before she goes to New York. "A good luck fuck." She checks the time, insists I "hurry up."

I don't so much move as am taken by Darcie who lays me back, tugs off my pants and works my member to her liking. Having Darcie as a lover again requires a certain mental adjustment, I need to focus in order to feel her there, have to concentrate not to think of Sarah. I think of Sarah and get hard. In transition, Darcie has me as she wants, works me to an engorging state, leaves me briefly in order to hurry back to the kitchen where she rubs coke on her pussy, a bit of junk absorbed through the membranes of her clit. She shudders, comes back and shimmies down.

I think about this, Darcie's needs and all, what she loves and doesn't. She pounds me good, bounces and slaps and claws my chest. I remember the lines in 'Moonlight' where Bel argues with Andy about her sexual conquests, and that she doesn't *have* people, though Andy swears differently. Darcie moves her hips. I remain on my back, let her dance, concentrate on what there is to remember. The haziness is constant now, like the phantom pains Bob described when he first lost his legs, again everything I hope to find when I reach for Darcie is no longer there, though memory hints and teases and tries to convince me. I think of Sarah, close my eyes and reach wide. The past is a mist, as Andy said. "Once... I remember this...once...a woman walked toward me across a darkening room."

Darcie howls as she finishes. "Fuck," she groans. Just like that.

---

I drive her to the airport. The roads are without much traffic at this time of night. My tires are worn, skid a bit. Darcie checks her ticket. I pretend everything's cool, that I'm Paul Newman in 'Cool Hand Luke.' I tell myself that I'm beyond the moment, though when I think of this, I realize how impossible that is. "I think," I say, and the way I sound gets Darcie's attention. When I tell her, "You did great in 'Juli,'" and that I'm glad we had a chance to work together, Darcie stares at me, looks through the space between us. It's clear she understands, is smart this way, says "Whatever, Mick." A second later she laughs.

After this we're quiet. I focus on the road in front of me. Darcie reaches for the radio, then changes her mind. I drive up the exit to the airport, follow the ramp toward the area designated for departure. We pull over to the curb and Darcie gets out. I lift her one bag and leave it on the sidewalk. We don't embrace though I say "Good luck," then watch her disappear inside the terminal. The lights in front of the airport are bright. I slide into my truck and head back into the city, take the highway east.

---

"No," Sarah says when I ask if I woke her. "No" again, when I ask if I can come by. The moon runs out in front of my truck. I hold my phone with three fingers, decide against small talk, tell Sarah straight out, "The reason I'm calling." I'm shameless now, from top to bottom, try to explain Darcie as a panic and poor judgment and, failing at this, focus on what Bob called *the now*. I tell Sarah that I love her, that I need her to know, no matter what. The *what* is important, of course, a huge matter, *what* Sarah does in turn, *what* happens now the point to everything. I once auditioned for the role of Brick in Tennessee William's 'Cat on a Hot Tin Roof.' I'd always wanted to play Brick, was the perfect age, had the right look, was convinced I could convey his internal conflict, all his confusion and such, the marital and paternal shit. But then I didn't get the part. Instead, I was asked to play the role of Cooper 'Gooper' Pollitt, Brick's sycophantic older brother.

Cooper was adversative to Brick, could not have been further removed from who I imagined myself to be. For several days I beat myself up, wondered what I did wrong at my audition for the director to look at me that way. Was this how people saw me? Was I nothing like I thought I was? I wound up doing Cooper unbound, created a character severely fucked, awkward and jealous and calculating. I performed as Iago absent the cleverness, all of my Gooper there on the surface, a man-child, a tempest to Brick's more deeply textured brooding and exactly as the director hoped I'd perform. I think of this now, driving in my truck, trying to convince Sarah to see me, how everything is an audition, and no matter how much I want something, the eventual decision comes down to others, what they think and expect of me in turn.

I ask again if I can stop by, but Sarah changes the subject, has something different to talk about now. I try to get a read on her voice, follow each word as if chasing pale light through a tunnel. When she finishes, I insist on coming over anyway. I leave the highway and head across town.

Sarah's jeep is in the lot. I park alongside, knock on her door, do not bang or lean heavy on the bell until she answers, but tap twice and hope that will be enough. The door is locked and Sarah lets me in after a minute. Unlike Darcie, whose body confused me while we were back together, I haven't forgotten Sarah's size. Her largeness is as I remember, wide and welcoming, though her hair is darker, dyed to make a change. I like the look, the color in contrast to the pearl of her skin. I tell her this, want to kiss her, but she moves away.

Boxes are stacked inside the apartment, labeled and set to the left of the door. I follow Sarah toward the piano, the offers she's received from L.A., as she told me on the phone, include the chance to record. Club dates are promised, additional jobs for commercials and voiceovers. There's opportunity in the City of Angels, West Coast bands want Sarah in the studio, her agent with a list. All of this is good news for her but not so much for me. When I reach for her this time, I catch her hand. "Let me go with you," I'm serious, say again of Darcie, "that's over," that it could not have ended any way but this and does she understand?

Sarah says she does. She says she forgives me, and for a moment I think things are all right. I hold her hand tighter, describe the offer I got from one of the producers in L.A., how I turned him down but am ready to go now, to leave Aldwich and move with her if she'll let me. Sarah slides her hand free, walks behind the kitchen table. I hurry after her, position myself on the opposite side, lean halfway toward her, as far as I can, my hands in front and neck extended as I try to convince her that "we can get past this. Why can't we just let it go?"

The moon through the window frames us. Sarah is as beautiful as she has ever looked to me, is divine, I swear. She says my name, says it softly, says clearly, "Mick, I already have."

---

The point of everything is what? Incident and recovery. Action and consequence, want and need. I drive from Sarah's to the all-night Meijer's where I buy two five-gallon plastic containers, red with a black funnel cap. On the radio, the news offers updates on Madoff in prison, on Tiger in rehab in Mississippi, on the demonstrations in Iran. I fill the containers at the Pump 'N Pay, the gas slopping heavy when carried to my truck. My heater rattles all the way to East Warren. I ignore the sound, do not play the radio anymore, am thinking about Cam last night as I drove him home from rehearsal, while Bob went with Kate. I wanted to talk about 'Moonlight' and the specifics of Cam's part, but got off track.

"The thing about Fred and Jake," I started, "is they have all these emotions. Their history with their dad, this confusion they don't know what to do with and so they deny it, conspire together, create their own world to avoid dealing with the real one. People do that sometimes, you know?"

Cam looked at me. There's a line in 'Moonlight' Cam recites as Fred—"I bet she taught you a thing or two"—and each time he said it during rehearsal, he gave me a similar look from stage. We passed Parrot Lake. One of Sarah's jingles played on the radio and Cam turned it up. I started talking then about the way things happened sometimes beyond our control, things we wish afterward we dealt with differently, before they became permanent. Through all of this, Cam stayed quiet. He glanced out the side window, the glass fogging as he breathed on it, he wrote something there with his fingertip. In his driveway, as he opened the door to get out, the letters he wrote disappeared. I waited until he was gone, then leaned over and blew on the space to see if what was there might return. For a second, it did.

The front door of Jay's building is padlocked. I leave the gas containers on the steps, go back to my truck, get a hammer and break the bolt. Inside the hollow of the building, I check to make sure all the rooms are empty, walk to the roof, then back down, find rags in the basement, look for a good place to start. The basement walls are cement, the ceiling reinforced, resistant to an easy burn. I bring the gas upstairs again, decide to split the difference and cook things from the middle. The apartment I pick has a musty smell, the empty space square and dark.

I think this is a good idea, that all things burn out from the middle, the flame only seeming to cook hottest at the end. I think of Sarah inside her apartment now, think of her six months from now, settled in L.A., in a place near the ocean, a bungalow built of white wood and slate, with a small garden where she'll grow Dutchman's Pipe and tomatoes. I imagine the vocals she did for the Pearl Divers giving the group its first real hit, while her other song, the one she wrote for 'Juli in Chains,' doing even better. I'm sure of this, wish for it, wish her well.

The walls inside the apartment are fairly smooth, the repairs I made a few weeks ago taking hold. I put my flashlight on the floor, move my palms along the surface of the wall, try to feel the places where my work came together and the slightest trace of a scar remains. My fingers slide softly, just as they used to when exploring Sarah's belly and back. I take my time, study the plane, search for the connecting point, find a seam where I filled the holes and sanded it level. In the shadows, much of the damage is hidden, but my fingertips are sensitive and locate the original scuff. I reach for my hammer, anticipate the force I'll need to split the seal and break what's mended.

The window in the apartment has a view of the street. There are no lights outside, the moon directly above the building offers a distant glow. I think about Jay, about Bob and Ted and Kate, and what they'll ask me when they hear what's happened. I think about Mises, about logic and reason, love and loss, about human action and inaction and what falls between. The basement rags are stuffed in my pockets, the colors white and red and green. I continue to run my hand against the wall, am excited and ready to do this, want to do this for Jay, am not thinking about anything else. I tell myself—*I am not thinking*—and how great it will feel, after everything else I've fucked up, to perform something selfless and beneficial. All the buzz I've gained from the Deletron clips seems silly now, my work on 'Juli' and with 'Moonlight,' the parts I'm being offered and may yet get, don't matter without Sarah. What I want instead is to perform a charity as close to love as I can get, something lasting and significant where I can step back afterward and say, "There, I did that. I did what I set out to do and it actually caught fire."

I lay the rags by the gas containers, approach the wall again, tap for studs to catch the flame, feel for cavernous points to work the rags down deeply. I try not to think anymore about Sarah, concentrate instead on the task at hand, on helping Jay get out from under. I hope his insurance pays off well, ignore how easy it will be for me to get caught, that Meijer's and the Pump 'N Pay probably have security cameras, my purchase of the containers and gas easily traced. The cops are bound to check, but what can they prove? Anyone breaking in could just as easily have set the blaze. I decide it does no good to worry, that I can only control so much.

My hammer has a rubber grip, keeps my hand set. I line up my stroke, the first blow cracking the seam, the hole no bigger than the hammer's head, round and gaping, like a mouth surprised. I think of Cam's surprise when I told him about Sarah, think of him in my truck, how he wrote Sarah's name several times on the glass. I picture Cam and Kate and Bob next winter, the cycle of seasons and Cam wanting to skate. He'll be taller then, past my shoulder, his legs more powerful. I'll join him on the lake, my old blades in need of sharpening, I won't be quite as crisp as last year, sore in the back and knees from the old jumps I took that sent me crashing, the bumps and bashes as a consequence of skating.

I think of 'Moonlight,' the reviews and returns on the play, how the audience and critics will be so surprised by what we've done they'll support our effort. Our ticket sales will be solid if not brisk, nearly enough for me to pay back Feldman and Sarah, the rest of the money I'll make up from my savings and what new work I take on. I take my hammer and strike the wall again, shatter the place where everything comes together. Stepping back, I look at what I've done, the new fissure in the wall opening like a vein. I think of Sarah again, can't help myself, imagine her coming to see us all in 'Moonlight,' flying in from California. With no other actors available, given all the final changes, I will have played the part of Bridget, the gender switch and different age consistent with our production.

Sarah will have kept in touch with Kate and Cam, will come to Aldwich again next winter to visit and check on Kate's condition. I'll invite Sarah to stay at my place but she'll say no. She'll have her hair orange again, will have acquired a tan, will look beautiful, large and brilliant. I won't have been with anyone for a very long time, will be waiting still, though I won't tell her this. Sarah's coming for a visit will make me happy, though having her here if Kate's no longer in remission won't be what I want. Ted will say I shouldn't think of things that way. He'll fold his hands, warn me against driving myself crazy, say that certain things have no rhyme or reason, and I should just be glad Sarah's here at all.

Maybe, I don't know. I hit the wall again, run my foot through the dust on the floor that my hammering creates. Maybe this is all there is, I think, blowing things up and starting over. Maybe after 'Moonlight' I'll find something new to do, will work with Ted on his projects, will visit Iran and lose myself among those who understand the significance of being invested. Maybe I'll be allowed to teach again, will like that, I think, and consider all the stories I can tell my students. I strike the wall harder still, think how sometimes our choices seem crazy while we're waiting for something else to happen. The truth is, no matter what, all things heal in one form or another. Everything mends and comes apart again. Like it or not, this much I know for certain, for whatever good it does.

I take the rags and soak them in the gas, pour more gas into the hole, around the room and into the hall. I think some more about next winter, how Sarah and Cam, Bob and Kate and I will go to dinner. Afterward, Sarah will leave with them, while I stand out in the parking lot of the restaurant. I'll remember a line from 'Moonlight,' how Bridget at the very end recalls her parents telling her: "We've been invited to a party. You've been invited too. But you have to come by yourself, alone. You won't have to dress up. You just have to wait until the moon is down." I've always found the lines perfect, so cruel and sad and completely honest.

I have my lighter out, the smell of gas mixing with the musky scent already in the building. When I flick the flame, everything for a moment is brighter. I put my lighter away and go downstairs, climb into my truck, start the engine, turn off my heater. I stare up at the sky, the moon overhead and the stars as well, all silent and glowing. I want the moon and stars to stay as they are forever and never come down. I want the chance to reach them. After 'Juli' comes out, I hope I'll get a few new offers, some strong roles in films and plays. Following the Summer Festival, auditions are planned for a national tour of Conor McPherson's 'The Seafarer.' This is a play I've always wanted to do. Maybe I'll land the role of Ivan, or Nicky, or even Mr. Lockhart. The tour could pass through L.A. and Sarah and I might see one another. I would like that and hope I can make it happen. This is what I'm thinking as I turn on my lights, adjust the radio, head home to feed the cat.

---

# ACKNOWLEDGEMENTS

This book was written during a very difficult time. To all of you who showed support, I appreciate more than you will ever know. To those who ran to the hills, well, I doubt you will be reading this anyway so my saying fuck you will probably be wasted. To my first family, Mary, Anna and Zach, onward! With love. To my Dzanc Books and Black Lawrence Press family, thanks for all. To everyone else, I'll see you in the funny papers.